STORMFIRE

STORMFIRE

A *FOUR KINGDOMS: ORIGINS* NOVEL

JASMINE YOUNG

www.jasmineyoungauthor.com
jasmine@jasmineyoungauthor.com

"'YOU CANNOT OVERCOME THIS STORM.'"
AND HE SAID: 'I AM THE STORM.'"

—*THE LEGEND OF THE FOUR,* AUTHOR UNKNOWN
BOOK ONE, LINES 1312-1313

Skyrros
Ocean
Mt. Mynati
Korinthia
The C
Central Plain
Aeropolis
Capital
Koiphi Islets

LUNAR PEAKS

KINGDOM
OF
AIR

MT. ALAIRUS

◈ TOWNFOLD
VILLAGE

COLOSSEUM

KRETE FORESTS

S

N

◈ ARCUREA

W   E

JAYPES

PART ONE

FALL

CHAPTER ONE

A royal army of five hundred soldiers had arrived at Mount Alairus, and by the end of the day, one family would burn.

Jaime Pappas ran between Ptolemy's Library and Town Hall. Once, these were great buildings of marble colonnades and ivory. Now they crumbled from neglect.

His bare heels skidded against the unpaved streets, splashed across puddles in his haste. A water jug balanced against his thick wool himation, the outer garment on his shoulders. Not even the beggars with their empty bowls lingered under the archways.

Fear set every vein in his body ablaze.

His mother had warned him to avoid the heart of town, especially Champion's Square. The soldiers were like a swarm of blowflies there. He'd never seen a royal soldier in his life, not *here*, in the frigid alps of the northeast.

Today, they blockaded every intersection and postern gate. Human monsters carrying seventy pounds of steel. The sound of their jangling cuirasses and greaves whirred his heartbeats into a hum.

Looming over them was a bronze bull statue, liver spotted with patina. His last memory of a bull was the young one the Lord of Mount Alairus sacrificed to their god, knife plunging into its chest, its dying squeals overpowering the autumn gusts.

He shivered, but kept shuffling toward Champion's Square. Jaime was disobeying his mother because of the pyre.

Periander Kreed, the blacksmith's adopted son, whispered they were building one in the square.

Jaime slowed as the uneven path leveled into the village's center. He was careful to drop his eyes.

Peri also said the people who ogled the pyre's foundation learned the hard way.

"What art thou looking at?" the Archpriestess would say. "If thee hast time to bethink and behold, then the Holy Lord of Fire wot that thee hast time for labor."

He couldn't understand her temple jargon, but Peri explained those unfortunate fools were forced to gather and chop kingpine wood from the mountain. No food or rest until the pyre was completely built.

Gods.

And now it was ready.

Jaime hid behind a wagon of barley, raising his chin ever so slightly.

The scaffold was twice his height. A massive stake punctured the middle. The top of the wooden beam displayed the New Jaypes Emblem in crimson paint: an albino dragon. That was the King's holy sigil.

Clouds blanketed the skies—they had for as long as Jaime could remember—but judging by the faded light that seeped through, nightfall would be here soon.

Why haven't they announced who they'll burn yet?

Behind the stake, high up on a fortification wall, a pair of milky white eyes stared down at him.

The Archpriestess, Damasia.

She had ridden here at the head of the army. Her head was shaved, her lips the color of dried blood. The New Jaypes Emblem carved the flesh between her dark brows.

His throat constricted. His asthma was returning.

The longer he looked, the more it looked like white mist was rising out of the air behind her, its tendrils curling over her shoulders to grab him.

Just the trick of the light. Look away!

He spun around—and the vertical handles of the jar slipped through his fingers.

Broken shards sprawled before him like clay eggshells, little rills of well water weeping into the dirt.

Jaime choked out a cry.

You can't plough. You can barely barter. Can't you at least carry water?

When he looked up again, the Archpriestess's unblinking eyes were still fixed on him.

The white mist surrounding her was gone.

Jaime forgot the broken jar and sprinted home. For some reason, he was convinced he would turn to stone if he glanced behind him.

The soldiers cursed Townfold Village for being a "gods' forsaken tundra" and even "Lord Jaypes's pisshole," but the bare simplicity of the unplanned streets and mud-brick houses soothed Jaime's sweating body.

Decades ago, Mount Alairus was known for its silver mines. The network of villages that now made Townfold grew fat with wealth. But then, before Jaime's first birthday, the King depleted the quarries to fund his armies. The Townfolders, once wealthy merchants, were forced to migrate to the lowland cities or grow barley on the mountain's frozen escarpments.

Most chose the former option.

Fortunately for Jaime, his late foster father owned a farmstead east of Townfold's collapsing palisade. Jaime sprinted across a wooden bridge and out of the village. Gulped down the beauty in the silver strata of the dark skies, chilly-cold at this altitude. These peaks had a primitive salt-and-pepper look most of the year. Mount Alairus was like an unrefined hunk of marble.

He desperately needed it to stay that way. It was what he knew. The only thing he knew. And perhaps it was the last place in Jaypes Kingdom untouched by the King's hand.

Their country house appeared over the dark horizon. He snatched the breather out of his pocket. Sucked deeply. The ephedra herb in the tube soothed his burning throat.

His asthma receded.

Jaime's bare feet slapped against the inner courtyard, its northside shadowed by a colonnaded porch. Their house, like all houses here, faced the south to maximize warmth. The familiar heat from the brazier and the earthy smell of charcoal evened out the shivers on his skin.

"Mamá!" he wheezed. "I'm back, but I lost the jar. Where are you?"

No answer.

He skipped up the stairs to the second floor. Stopped inside his bedroom.

A cut of wool hung over the door leading into the second bedroom—a room that had stayed empty for as long as he could remember.

Two shapes stood behind the gaps of the curtain.

His mother's tight black ringlets faced him. A husky man with oiled, clean-cut hair held her arms, but the curtain blocked Jaime from seeing his face. The overpowering scent of perfume—iris extract, with a pinch of marjoram—watered his eyes. They were talking in secretive whispers. He heard his name and a short curse.

He is downstairs. His mother. *We must tell him—*

No, no, we cannot tell him.

Jaime stepped inside.

Hida Pappas, his mother, abruptly blew out the stonemist incense on their altar. Blocked it with the small frame of her body. The stranger whipped around, diving for his shortspear on the bed.

Jaime's mouth fell.

Gods.

"*Hilaris?*" he exclaimed.

His older brother was here.

Gods, gods.

This used to be Hilaris's bedroom, back when he lived on the farmstead. Now he was the ward and heir of Gaiyus Sartorios, the Lord of Mount Alairus.

His mother explained everything to Jaime that night, seven years ago, when he came home to find his brother's supper bowl untouched on the table.

"Hilaris tried to steal Lord Gaiyus's silver drinking cup, but the Free Guard caught him—Holy Lord, my shame! They brought him before Gaiyus, but your brother prattled off why he did it, some nonsense about the economics of trade and profit. Lord Gaiyus was so impressed by him, he took your brother to his villa to live as his ward."

His seven-year-old self pressed his lips together. "But Hilaris is coming home tomorrow, right?"

She paused.

"No, Jaime."

After that day, Gaiyus Sartorios didn't give a second glance at him. Or his mother.

Well.

Actually, Lord Gaiyus gifted Hida a fertile plot of land just below the akropolis, where his villa was. It would have yielded them two, three times their current income.

As if that could make up for stealing Hilaris.

But his mother had the good sense—and recklessness—to tell the old man, "Keep it." All the other farmers had long since moved into the town proper for protection after Gaiyus became lord. Hida, however, said, "It falls on me to steward my husband's farmstead. Jaime and I are Hektor Pappas's last surviving family. I hope you will understand."

Lord Gaiyus's silver orating tongue went stiff that day. Jaime loved his mother all the more for it.

Now, tonight, in the dim firelight, sweat trickled down Hilaris's temple.

"Jamian," he breathed, calling him by his full name.

Who is he? This doesn't look like the Hilaris I remember.

Jaime stayed put on the beaten earth floor. The smoke from the dying incense curled into the air between them.

"What are you doing here?" Jaime croaked.

"I brought you something from Lord Gaiyus's library." Hilaris's upper arms bulged as he lifted a heavy tome off the strongbox. "*The Legend of the Four.* Not many survive in our Kingdom. This is old, and worth a man's fortune."

Jaime went rigid. Any fool would know he couldn't read.

They used to be close, but the gap between them grew so obvious now—his brother with his spotless politician's chiton, and Jaime with his loins and wooly exomis, the inner tunic that drooped over one shoulder.

Jaime spoke through his teeth. "You come home after pretending we aren't your family for seven years, and . . . and then you bring me a *book?*"

"Jaime, we must discuss—" Hida began, but Hilaris interrupted.

"It's not like that, Jamian. I know you can't—" He struck the wall with his fist. "I didn't come here to insult you. In my world, giving a man a great work means you highly esteem him. I was going to share it with you. It's a spellbinding epic."

In my world? Seriously? In my *world?*

Hilaris stumbled over his tongue. "Let me tell you my favorite part, at least. Did you know banestorms were real three thousand years ago? They're mega-storms the size of a continent. Back in the ancient days, some were even big enough to annihilate the entire race of mankind. A young warrior named Jaypes Ascaerii decided he would find a way to quell it."

"Hilaris," their mother urged. "We have little time—"

"And when Jaypes told his chieftain he was leaving, the chief laughed at him. 'You cannot overcome this storm,' he said. And you know how Jaypes Ascaerii replied?"

The muscles in Jaime's calves trembled.

His brother continued, "Book one, line 1313: 'I am the storm.' A month later, he returned to the mortal world as the God of Air. There's always hope, Jamian, no matter how dark the days become."

The storm in him broke. Jaime hurled himself at Hilaris.

"You just can't help yourself, can you?" he screamed. "Even here, you have to be a big orating ass! Hilaris Sartorios, that's who you are! Is there a line in your book for that?"

Hida cried his name and stepped between them, but Jaime's hands formed claws. He raked them against the white folds of Hilaris's chiton.

"Why don't you take your flowery epics and stuff them in Gaiyus's chamber pot, my lord!"

But his brother was stronger, bigger. In one pivot, he slammed Jaime against the chipped wall.

"*Jamian.*" Hilaris's hooded eyes were wet. "I'm here because we need to leave. The pyre outside—" His voice cracked. "It's for us."

"You're fifteen!" Jaime screamed back. "The Royal Decree doesn't apply to you!"

"I'm fourteen."

"Get off me! And get *out*—"

Hilaris looked at him seriously. "Why would I lie about that?"

The room started to ripple and blur. Jaime's heart felt like it was plummeting at the rate of an eagle's dive.

"The Royal..." He swallowed, his throat dry. "The Royal Decree applies to you? To *us?*"

Jaypes was the only Kingdom where your age could mean your life or death. If you were a boy born in the same year as the missing prince—2982 Empyreal Time—the King's soldiers ran their spears through your belly. This year, any survivors would have been fourteen. If you were fourteen this year, and the Capital found out you lied about your birth date to the annual census, you were burned at the stake for high treason.

"If," Jaime croaked, "if you burn...we burn with you."

Hilaris peered up at an invisible stain on the ceiling.

"Yes."

That was the rule: if a boy charged as guilty burned, he watched his entire family burn with him.

"But—*I'm* fourteen." Jaime rolled the breather around his pocket feverishly. "What if—if they're after me?"

"They're not after you."

Hilaris gripped his right wrist. The oil lamp illuminated a humiliating brand under his wrist: a circle intercepted with an *X*. The universal symbol for the handicapped.

"Your asthma," his brother said. "You're exempt. The King doesn't bother with cripples."

Jaime yanked his arm away. "I'm not a *cripple*," he spat.

"The only other boys of age are Periander Kreed and Cassie the orphan." Hilaris raised his voice over his. "Cassie is a mute. And your friend, the Kreed boy—he gets sick what, six times a day?"

"Leave Peri out of this."

"Grow up, Jaime. Am I right?"

Peri and Cassie had handicap symbols burned onto their wrists, same as him. Hilaris *was* right. Like Jaime, they were exempt from the Decree.

All the other boys of age across Jaypes Kingdom were executed a long time ago—which meant if the Archpriestess rode here all the way from the Capital, *someone* had been lying about their age for fourteen years.

"Lord Gaiyus is clearing an escape route for us." Hilaris sidestepped Hida, his hand squeezing hers, and placed the tome back into the strongbox. "We're going north, into the mountains."

"*You* are," Jaime cried. "Not us. We're not responsible for *your* mess!"

"Pack your things. Both of you. Quickly."

Jaime sucked again on his breather. It didn't help the paper dryness of his lungs or his watering eyes.

"*Gods*. This is impossible."

But it *was* possible that Hilaris was also born in 2982—because they weren't blood brothers. Jaime was adopted. That wasn't unusual in these villages. Thousands of Jaypan men had died in the Storm of Flames, the war following the King's invasion. Hilaris's blood father, Hektor Pappas, lost his life in it. The widows left behind adopted orphaned children like Cassie, the mute boy. Or Peri, whom the blacksmith fostered. Or Jaime.

Still, Hilaris's confession didn't make any sense. Hilaris and Jaime looked worlds apart, the former with his drum-deep voice and sculpted shoulders and intense pewter eyes. Also, Hilaris was a whole two heads taller than their mother.

His brother could pass for *sixteen,* not fourteen.

"You lied to the census." Jaime marched to Hilaris and kicked the strongbox aside. "You lied to the King? What were you *thinking?*"

"It was the only way to keep your brother with us," Hida said. "I was ready to take that risk."

"You too, Mamá?" Jaime pounded his fists at the air. "You're involved in this too?"

Hilaris grabbed him by scruff. "Keep it down, I said, or you'll draw the soldiers to us!"

"Shove off!" Jaime elbowed him. Hilaris let go. He threw his hot gaze past him to Hida. "This is ridiculous. How did they suddenly find out Hilaris's age if he was lying the whole time?"

"I don't know," she whispered.

Hilaris strutted to the door. "It—it doesn't matter right now, Jamian. We can talk later. Do you have everything you need?"

His breathing quailed.

It would be so easy to hate his brother. But Hilaris was right. Jaime didn't have time to hate right now. That would come later, when they were safe in the wilderness, and he could slam Hilaris's stupid tome in his own face.

A long breath.

Jaime closed his eyes.

"How long will we be in the mountains for?"

"I'm not sure. Commander Julias will take us as far as the Sky Pass. After that—I'm thinking we can go further north. The airpriests will give us refuge in the High Temple. That will keep us away from the lowland city-states and the royal patrols."

"Yeah, and it'll also keep us without food to last us a week. Or

water, unless your lord father is planning to deliver us jars by cart."
Jaime suddenly remembered. He switched his gaze to his mother in
guilt. "I brought drinking water from the well, but I dropped the jar
on the way back. I saw the Arch—"

"Jaime Oilythumbs," his brother interrupted.

He rolled his eyes, but it was a familiar jab from their childhood.
The tension in his chest eased a little. He decided not to mention
the white mist that had leached out of the Archpriestess.

Probably just his imagination.

"The barrows," Jaime said. "There's a vessel in your papá's grave
with coins. Right?"

"You're going to steal Papá's death offerings?" The smile
vanished from Hilaris's face. "Aren't you decent?"

Hida's gray eyes misted. "Jaime, there must be another way."

Stealing death offerings was a giant offense to their god, Lord
Jaypes. But Jaime stopped believing in the gods a long time ago.

Death offerings usually took the form of coins. If they were going
to play mountain shepherds out in the wild, they would have a
better chance of survival if they could at least barter for food with
money.

Jaime stuffed his hands back into his pockets.

"There *is* no other way. Don't you ever leave the high halls of
your villa? If we go into those mountains without supplies"—Jaime
nodded at the door—"you might as well just let them burn you."

"We can't take that risk." Hilaris relit the incense. Its myrrh-like
odor choked Jaime's nostrils. "The Archpriestess has soldiers
watching every patio to make sure we aren't kneeling in prayer to
Lord Jaypes. And you want to try to get past her barricade?"

"You're unbelievable."

Hida Pappas left Hilaris's side of the room and took Jaime's
hands. Her fingertips were rough as barley husks, but so warm.

Somehow, even on this frigid mountain, always warm.

"My son," she whispered, "let the winds lead you."

It was an old saying from another time, another life, when she lived the glorious days of Old Jaypes. Their country house used to be filled with her songs, memories of Jaypan adages and hymns and folk stories of heroes embarking on odysseys. In recent years, as the storm clouds outside grew darker, she stopped talking about Old Jaypes altogether.

Let the winds lead you.

Thickly, he recited back, "I shall find my feet."

The storm swirling in his insides quelled. In its place, hundreds of tiny hearts pumped all over his body—in his temples, in his lungs, in his ears.

For her. I'll work with Hilaris for her.

Jaime kissed her pallid cheekbone.

"I'll be quick, Mamá."

He walked past Hilaris and stopped in the doorway. After a pause, he glanced at his brother.

"Come on, Lord Hilaris."

At this angle, the lamps limned his brother like he was alight. A single tear glistened down his speckled cheek.

They faced each other, two shades of light under the same flame. It dawned on Jaime that it didn't matter if Hilaris knew how to read, and orate, and fight with a spear.

This *was* his big brother. His brother was back.

Jaime let go of his breather and forced his hand out of his pocket.

After a pause, Hilaris took it. Squeezed tightly. The last time they shook like that was another lifetime ago, in the shadows of a stick fort they built together inside the ruins of Town Hall.

"Okay, Jaime." His brother smiled. "Let's go."

CHAPTER TWO

Another surprise hid inside their stable, where Sokrates, their old donkey, snored.

Hilaris led the courser out by the reins. It was a magnificent gelding with a dappled coat as dark as Hilaris's hair.

Jaime's mouth dropped. "You have a horse?"

Horses were walking regalia of wealth and power. Most officers of the Free Guard didn't even own them.

But of course Hilaris would. What *didn't* his brother have?

Jaime had never ridden one before. His head didn't even reach the courser's shoulder—Hilaris had to haul him up into the saddle. With one kick, his brother sent them flying across the daisy fields. Beneath the shadows of dusk, every sway of the knee-high foliage looked like brandishing spears.

The barrows were east of the double gate leading up to the akropolis, and overlooking a sheer cliff, which would force them dangerously close to the barracks. Like the rest of Townfold, the curtain walls here were patchy at best. As they drew near the town prison, sickness rose up in Jaime's throat.

Orange blossoms glowed across the stadium grounds. Once, they hosted great chariot races. He'd heard the rumors, but he'd been careful to avoid this side of town.

Now he saw the truth with his own eyes: a pile of human ears spilled over the sand. Countless pairs. Fresh blood seeped over severed skin.

"Sweet gods." Hilaris slowed to a halt.

Jaime's breathing grew rapid.

No, no, no—

Before the King's invasion, torture didn't even exist in his Kingdom. But visiting merchants whispered gruesome stories of the things the Western Kingdoms did to their enemies. The King himself hailed from that bloody side of the world.

Murderer. King of Genocide.

This was done under his orders.

But why?

Crimson banners fluttered by a notice board the soldiers nailed up. Jaime squeezed his brother's waist for balance. "What does it say?"

"I'll tell you later, when we—"

"*What* does it say?"

Hilaris paused. "It's punishment for heresy. They were caught worshipping Lord Jaypes—"

"Gods." Jaime coughed down his nausea. "Gods. I hope Mamá put away her incense. I *told* her to stop lighting it."

"I don't know that she ever will."

Hilaris spurred his courser forward again. Thunder rumbled in the distance. Jaime ground his teeth.

"What did Lord Gaiyus teach you about the King? Why does he hate us so much?"

"Jaime, they were worshipping the God of Air. The King is a Fire Sage. They were foolish—"

"A Fire Sage..."

"Yes, Sages can control one of the four elements: air, water, fire, earth. They're known for their currents, streams of elemental energy that can crush an entire army."

Jaime glowered. "I know what a Sage is. Just because I can't read doesn't mean I'm stupid."

"The King is a rogue Sage from Kaippon," Hilaris continued. "The Kingdom of Fire. We're Jaypes. The Kingdom of Air—"

"I *know,* okay?"

"Which makes it illegal for him to rule over us—only an Air Sage can rule the Air Kingdom. A Fire Sage can only rule the Fire Kingdom, and so on. It's a holy law the gods declared three thousand years ago."

That he didn't know. But he wouldn't admit it.

"To your first question," Hilaris orated on, "that's why the King hates us. We remind him he's sacrilegious carrion, and he cuts out our tongues. Or ears, I suppose now."

"He'll cut out yours if you don't learn how to stop talking."

"The word you're looking for is 'pontificating.' Although I'm only trying to educate you."

"Seriously, how many books did Lord Gaiyus stuff into your head?"

Hilaris laughed. Jaime grinned weakly.

What a mess.

The Alairans never bothered to hide their worship—at least, not until today. Before today, the mountainfolk would burn whole firepits of incense in their ancestors' temples, carve prayers on laurel trees, watch bulls get slaughtered in festivals hosted at the old pantheon below the akropolis. It wasn't that they were defiant. They just didn't know any better. A royal army hadn't stepped foot in these fringes for twelve years, and everyone—Jaime included—forgot the King even existed.

Hida used to pester Jaime to pray in the pantheon, but he always refused.

"If Lord Jaypes is real," he challenged, "how come he let a foreign king conquer us?"

How come he lets the King mutilate us, Mamá?

As they rode, Jaime's fear crept up his neck. The torches were blinding against the stormy sky. Daylight was officially over. They had maybe five minutes left before The Burning was called.

It would take at least ten to get to the barrows and back.

From here, the barrows appeared: a dirt path winded up the base of the mountain. They nearly were free from the gorge when a voice rang out behind them.

"Is that Jaime? And Hilaris?"

Fear burst in Jaime's chest. His brother stiffened.

They pulled to a halt.

A young Jaypan waved at them outside the barracks, where a dozen little kids gathered around a brazier. A spear twice Jaime's height leaned casually by the seething coals—the kind of spear soldiers used to skewer boys of age.

"Nides," his brother said quietly.

Nides Doupolous had volunteered to join the King's royal armies a handful of years ago. That man alone had seen more worldly things than all the elders combined. Most kids thought he was a hero.

The elders called him a filthy traitor behind his back.

Nides cupped his mouth. "My two favorite Pappases in the world! And one of them Lord Gaiyus's favorite, from what I hear! How is that sulky old man?"

The hairs on Jaime's arms stood straight up.

Does Nides know Hilaris is the one they're looking for?

Hilaris returned a stilted smile.

Nides's cuirass jangled as he waved a hand. "I was just telling the kids my best war story yet. Come, join us!"

Jaime glanced in the direction of Champion's Square, obscured by hundreds of thatched houses.

A live burning hadn't happened on Mount Alairus since Jaime lived—and here Nides was telling one of his war stories?

Was this a joke?

He has to know the truth. He came marching here with the Archpriestess. Maybe he also knows we're trying to run.

But resisting Nides would be even worse than refusing to stay. If they said no to him, he would demand to know why. Or he would show offense. And then not even a banestorm could stop Nides from calling the soldiers on them.

"Let's stay for his story," Jaime whispered. "We don't have a choice."

Hilaris's lip pursed, but he reined his courser around. The tendons in Jaime's shoulders knotted together. They were riding in the opposite direction of the mountain path, away from the barrows. Time was flickering out. Any moment now, the soldiers would seize Hilaris and chain Jaime and his mother to the pyre.

"Good man." Nides smiled as Jaime dismounted and joined the back of the crowd. "So I was just telling everyone about the time my battalion marched with the King's vanguard."

Drory, the six-year-old with the cowlicks, crossed his arms. "Story, story, just tell it already!"

"And I saw the King raise fire."

Gasps.

Jaime raised a skeptical brow. "*You* saw the King draw a fire current?"

"I was there the day he burned Thessalona City to the ground."

The excited whispers of the other children fell mute.

"Impossible." Hilaris spoke with practiced calm. "No one can burn down a City-State, not even a Sage."

Nides just laughed.

"No, no, I *heard* about it," Drory whispered. "My daddy said it was a rebel, uh, stronghold."

"The King is what the epics say he is," Nides said. His beady eyes fixed on Hilaris. "It only took one current. Before he raised it, a man could feel it in the air. A deep, bone-chill cold stirred in our hearts. It felt as if the whole earth was moving, coming alive with energy enough to make the skies collapse. We swore it would be the end of the world that night. And then…"

"And then?" Drory gasped.

The light of the coals tossed Nides's face into angular shadows. A chill ran down Jaime's spine.

"Then a sheet of fire rose from his body. Four gods, it was massive—a tunnel of great light split the clouds open, hundreds of times higher than the city gates. The men believed he had opened a doorway between our world and the gods'. The King rode a league away from the rest of the army, but even at a distance, the scorching heat cooked us inside our corselets. And when he released it…"

The crowd went dead silent. Nausea liquified Jaime's insides.

"Thessalona bled inside flames. One thousand feet in height, and half a mile wide—*puff!*" The children gasped. "Gone. One hundred thousand lives dead. You could even hear the screams of rebels and their families."

That's why the elders said Sages can't be defeated. Holy skies. Forget the royal army. How does Hilaris think we can escape the King?

"Cool," Drory whispered.

Nides laughed. Just as he was opening his mouth, a snowy horse and a shortspear tore through the firelight. The children screamed. Hilaris yanked Jaime out of the way.

"Have you no decency?"

Julias Markus, Commander of the Alairan Free Guard, towered over them.

Jaime went still.

He was just over five and a half feet, but he marched as if the Kingdom's stormwinds billowed at his heels. The earthy smell of myrrh clung to his flesh. The few reckless Alairans who still dared burn incense did it with their windows sealed shut. But Jaime heard from village murmurs that the commander had positioned his incense holder on an open windowsill. Kept a stick burning the entire time the army marched the streets.

Nides greased on a smile. "Please explain, Commander. Why is telling tales indecent?"

"Making merry on the eve of a burning is, boy!" Julias snapped. "And what tales are these, that you teach our children to revere fire? Where are your loyalties?"

The children were quickly dispersing. Hilaris tried to leave with them, but Jaime grabbed his chiton and nodded at the soldiers watching the scene from the barracks.

Nides glanced at the spear pointed at his chest, then back up at the commander. "I'm stunned by your bluntness, old pappos. Are you saying you oppose the King?"

"Watch yourself."

Nides reached for his sword hilt. "Is that how you address a commissioned soldier of the royal army? *You*, a foreman of peasant militia—"

The older man backhanded him.

Jaime's jaw dropped.

Nides fell onto his elbows, one hand holding his bleeding lip in shock. "I'll tell the Archpriestess!" he squealed.

"Pray, tell her."

The soldiers were rushing over in a wave now. Blazing in the light of the brazier, Commander Julias glanced back at Jaime.

The lump in his throat grew. Julias Markus wore his dark hair parted in half, cut to his shoulders, with a short beard that stopped at his larynx. Jaime couldn't for the life of him grow a beard, but he tried multiple times to grow out his hair the same way. Discreetly, he even tried to braid a few strands—Julias's braids made him look kingly, gritty—until Peri laughed at Jaime for looking ridiculous. In his fantasies, Commander Julias would adopt Jaime the way Lord Gaiyus did his brother.

He's staring at me, not Hilaris.

For some reason, he knew this was important.

"Jaime," the commander murmured, "get your mother to the Sky Pass. Quickly."

He nodded, thrill sparking through his body. Suddenly, it felt like wings were attached to his heels. He waved at his older brother to follow. While the soldiers surrounded the commander, they remounted and dashed away in the direction of the barrows.

A lonely switchback led them into the northeastern wild. Kingpines towered above them, smelling of mint. Jaime breathed them in deeply. Some of his adrenaline eased. Out here, the snowcapped peaks in the distance looked like the silver thrones of kings.

The sky flashed.

"Storm's coming," Hilaris said.

Jaime glanced back at him, queasy. "A storm's always coming."

They ascended higher, sailing over curtains of golden broom. Wild rams pranced out of their way. He peered over the mountainside, its scruffy surface aslant from this angle. To the west of Townfold Village, the Estos River vanished into a waterfall just beyond the main gate.

It seemed like an eternity had passed before they reached the escarpment overlooking the barracks. Countless barrows speckled the hard soil, stretching all the way up the basaltic shelves and into the marbled skies.

"Over here!"

Hilaris knelt before a gravestone. He read the etching aloud:

Hektor Pappas, 2936-2983 E.T.

His brother's face fell somber. Although he'd never met Hektor, Jaime squeezed Hilaris's wrist for comfort.

Hida said she found Jaime at the foothills, unfurled in a brush of lettuce weed. Hektor had died in the war just one month earlier. Despite barely being able to feed herself, she took Jaime in as her own.

Since that day, whenever he asked who his blood father might be, Hida skirted the question.

Jaime was certain it was Commander Julias.

So many things pointed to it—how the commander always overpaid for Hida's shabby textiles. All the times he snuck her food, money, and supplies with his payments. The way his stone-gray eyes would land on Jaime's, and stay there, every time they passed each other. And the resemblance. They bore the same square face, long nose, thick bed of wavy hair, even the same egg-shaped hairline.

"You remind me of someone I used to know," Julias told him years ago.

"Who?" Jaime whispered.

But the commander wouldn't say. Aside from tonight, it was the only time they ever exchanged words.

"Move out of the way; I'll do it," Jaime told his brother.

Although the coffin would be several feet under the earth, death offerings were placed inside the headstones. Jaime lifted the top open. Hilaris hesitated, then helped him.

His fingers scratched something hard. Jaime hauled it up and pried the lidded vase open.

Two pouches sagged with coin.

Hilaris was religious and refused to touch it, so Jaime wrapped them up in his himation. He was about to close the three-legged vase when Hilaris gripped his arm and pointed at its bottom.

Dappled stormlight passed over another object, round as a coin, and the size of his closed fist. It was nearly invisible in the dark.

A stone medallion.

A flurry of cracked strokes formed a symbol onto its face. It resembled a mammoth ram with L-shaped horns, a hoary beard, and a mane thicker than a lion's.

"Gods," Hilaris breathed. "I've seen that before in Lord Gaiyus's library. That creature's an elhorn. They're extinct now, and . . . and this. It's the Air Emblem."

The holy sigil of Lord Jaypes.

The elders said banners used to fly with it when Lairdos Ascaerii, the last Air Sage, was King. They even said the presence of the Air Emblem was power. It carried the dread aura of the God of Air himself.

Just looking at it gave him goosebumps. Like Air worship, displaying that Emblem was banned.

"Jamie, don't touch it—"

But it was too late.

The second his fingers brushed the Emblem, a shock wave of air blasted skyward.

CHAPTER THREE

It slammed him and Hilaris flat onto their backs. A monster-sized current, taller than Mount Alairus's highest peak, surged out of the medallion. Clouds galloped across all corners of the Kingdom. The escarpment trembled. Jaime shut his eyes as the supernatural storm covered his body—and the entire mountain—in shadow.

Hilaris shouted something, but the winds buried his voice. Jaime closed his eyes. *Whispers.* From hundreds of ancient airstreams. They rushed around his earlobes, gathering towards some urgent point in the north.

Jaime's mouth flapped open.

The world's going to explode—

And Jaypes Kingdom fell silent.

Below him, Townfold Village burst into streams of panic and uproar. Soldiers, chickens, and goats scrambled over the streets. Kingpines lay on their noses. Gaping crevasses split the network of villages. Ironically, the pyre was the only thing left entirely intact.

Hilaris flipped himself upright.

"What have you done?" he bellowed. "You offended Lord Jaypes! I told you it was sacrilege to break into Father's grave—"

Jaime screamed back, "If I didn't, we'd starve—"

"You raised an *air current!*"

Terror scourged his chest. Even though the mountain temperatures had dropped, sweat drenched his exomis.

I'm not a Sage. That's impossible!

If he was born royalty, then discovering his ability to wield his god's element would've called for Kingdom-wide celebrations. Most members of the royal Houses showed their Sage powers at puberty.

But the worst thing that could happen was if you discovered your Sage-powers and you *weren't* of the royal family. If two Sages from two different Houses breathed in one Kingdom, that meant war. Only Sages could be Kings. And only one Sage House could rule the throne.

In the Four Kingdoms, to have a Sage outside the royal family was rare; it had only happened a handful of times in the last three thousand years.

But still.

It *could* happen.

And if King Usheon found out Jaime raised a current—

"I'm *not* a Sage," Jaime said shakily. "This is just a stupid old artifact. That blast never happened—"

"Are you mad?" Hilaris yelled. "You're going to pretend it didn't happen?"

"It *never* happened! Okay? Hold these." Jaime shoved the coin pouches at Hilaris and looped the medallion around his sweating neck.

"You can't take that!" his brother cried.

"I'm not leaving it here! If they find it in your papá's grave, it'll only bring us more trouble than you already have!"

Hilaris clamped down on his shoulder. "Look, Jamie. Look at what you've done."

Black clouds spilled over Townfold Village like poison. Thunder snarled across the entire sky, and high winds streamed around the mountain, howling like wolves.

"You've started a banestorm."

"You read too many fantasy books," Jaime snapped back. "Banestorms aren't real."

As they rode back down the mountain, Jaime vaguely felt something watching him. He peeked over his shoulder.

Aeneas, the old goat shepherd. And his seven-year-old son, Evander. They'd seen everything from the other side of the barrows.

Jaime suppressed a shudder.

He decided not to tell Hilaris about it.

Halfway down the escarpment, a lone silhouette gazed out towards the Estos River. At first, he thought it was a person—no. *Not a person.* It resembled a headstone. This one was larger than the others. A fillet, carved with a garland of windflowers, crowned its top.

An airmarker.

Some of the elders said that back before the skies grew sick with storms, Old Jaypes used to have a mapped network of air streams. This stone was supposed to be an ancient marker for Northwind, the largest air current in Jaypes.

Jaime wondered what would happen if he pressed the uncanny medallion against its stone. Would air currents shoot out of his nose? Would he start flying over the mountaintop?

Don't be ridiculous. You're not an Air Sage!

The second they reached the bottom of the foothill, Hilaris pulled to a halt. Jaime's head crashed against Hilaris's back.

A throng of horses waited outside their farmstead. One of them was caparisoned in Kaipponese silks—a high officer was here. Behind them, human cages perched on the backs of two wagons.

"*Mamá!*" Hilaris screamed.

He dismounted and charged forward, but Jaime yanked him back by the arm.

"No!" he blurted. A hurricane of fear whirled inside him. "They'll see you; they'll catch you!"

Hilaris clawed him. "Let go, you fool!"

His brother tore through the foliage of wildflowers towards their country house.

A scream burst up Jaime's throat. He flung the coin pouches at the ground.

Instinct forced him to dismount and run after Hilaris—he couldn't leave his family behind. He wouldn't run away.

A dozen soldiers stood in the inner courtyard, blockading all doors and exits with their shields and spears. One of them dragged his mother out of the living room by the hair. Another skipped down the steps with a bagful of stonemist incense. Hilaris stared at them, staggering in a circle.

Jaime's knees sagged.

You're too late.

CHAPTER FOUR

A stout shape stepped through the colonnade.

His face was shaped like a clay pan, jowls sagging from decades of ample dining. And he had plenty of rump.

Even without any introductions, Jaime knew who this was—Chief Strategos Reizo Kita, righthand official to the King himself.

He's real. He's here, *in our farmstead—*

"Clan of Pappas," Reizo trumpeted. Heavy accent weighed down his Moderna, modern common tongue. "In the name of His Holiness the King, you are under arrest for treason and purgatory!"

"Perjury, sir," a Jaypan officer coughed.

Kaipponese—natives of the Fire Kingdom, where the King was from—didn't exist on this mountain.

Sickness spilled into Jaime's fear.

They looked different with their black, teardrop-shaped eyes. They even had their own language, though Jaime knew none of it. Many of their native customs were strange to him. Like how they bowed a lot and got offended if you didn't bow back. Or how they preferred rice to bread.

Worst of all, if a Jaypan struck a Kaipponese, it was lawful for the authorities to take your offending hand. If they were feeling nice. If they weren't, it was also lawful for the Kaipponese to hack you apart on the spot.

So when Hilaris pivoted to attack, Jaime screamed.

"No!"

His brother yanked a shortsword out of the scabbard of the nearest soldier, slashing at the Strategos. But Reizo backed away in one swift step. The soldiers lowered their spears between the wall of their shields.

The familiar hurricane was filling Jaime's chest, expanding, shaking the walls of his lungs from pressure. He didn't dare suck on his breather. Not in front of these soldiers.

Don't kill Hilaris. Please, please don't kill him—

The soldiers overpowered his brother in three strokes. A hilt collided against Hilaris's temple. Blood burst through his flesh. One stamped him down, face to the floor, with a dirty lace-up boot. The others fitted chains over his wrists and ankles.

Hida turned away, tears glistening on her cheeks. This was the end of their household.

How did everything go so wrong in just twenty-four hours?

Strategos Reizo turned to Jaime. Those coal eyes fixed on him. His heart thundered.

"Your turn to say something?"

"No, sir," he choked.

"Good, good." Reizo Kita bowed politely at Hida. "You have a good son. May Lord Kaippon rebirth him as a warrior in the next life."

Hida spat at his feet. A Jaypan soldier struck her jaw. In one second, his fear drained into rage.

"Don't touch her—" Jaime bellowed.

But someone twisted him around, slipped fetters around his skinny wrists.

"Go on, stinking grub."

The soldier holding him shoved him forward.

Inspired by his mother's courage, Jaime flipped around and sank his teeth into the man's exposed arm. The soldier thrust him away, lip bared. Jaime crashed through the door.

"Strategos! That one is ours."

The shout came just as Jaime collapsed onto the threshold, beaten earth skinning his elbows.

A squat shadow marched out from behind the second wagon. Julias Markus held up a signed warrant. His jawbone was bleeding from a recent wound. A dozen of his Free Guard backed him.

"The Archpriestess agreed to turn him over to Lord Gaiyus," the commander said. "Our lord wishes to interrogate the boy on the matter of his brother's treason."

Commander Julias bowed low.

The hostility eased from Strategos Reizo's shoulders. He bowed back—a short, annoyed dip—and gave a nod.

Fury scorched his gut.

Lord Gaiyus.

How could the Lord of Mount Alairus say he would help them escape to the Sky Pass, only to dispatch the Free Guard against his ward's family?

He doesn't care about us; he never did.

Jaime struggled to break free of his chains—if only he could throw a punch at the commander's face—but the Free Guard held onto him tight. The commander grabbed a fist full of his hair, slammed him against the cage's bars.

"Enough!"

Jaime closed his eyes.

"I trusted you," he whispered. "Papá."

The last word seemed to catch the commander. His bearded jaw clenched and unclenched. Then his eyes briefly dropped.

Admit it. Please. I'm tired of the lies.

Julias moved closer so the bulk of his body blocked their faces from the soldiers.

"Quiet, boy." He peered into another direction. Jaime followed his gaze—and sucked in a ragged breath.

A unit of horsemen were galloping up the switchback where he woke the medallion with a storm. They held torches, maces, and hunting nets. Jaime hoped his shaking fingers weren't visible.

"Play the part," the commander murmured. "Gaiyus Sartorios is trying to save your life."

⁓ৎপিঞ্চ⁓

They blindfolded him before they reached Townfold's walls. Jaime concentrated on his breath. Hida always told him that if he ever lost his breather, counting to four—breathing in—and releasing on another four, would help.

Breathe deeply.

Jaime breathed as deep as he could. The sound of Free Guards' boots echoed somewhere underground.

"Let him go," came Julias's low voice.

The blindfold came off. They loosened his chains. Jaime rubbed at the chafed flesh on his wrists.

A square of firelight awaited ahead of him. Julias paused, and moved to Jaime's ear.

"Do not be afraid. You will learn the truth about your papá tonight."

His chest thudded.

What does that mean? Aren't you him?

The other Jaypans stared at him solemnly. Jaime marched into the blinding light.

Oil lamps lit a chamber of limestone, small and unremarkable in size. Yet his eyes watered from the myrrh-like reek of stonemist incense. A silver tapestry hung behind the half dozen men inside. The same symbol as the stone medallion.

The Air Emblem.

All six wore the white togas of politicians, but the tallest one— the only man with his back facing Jaime—had a purple sash draped over his shoulder. His eyes widened. Purple was expensive dye, said to come from the sea snails of the western Koiphi islets.

The cloying smell of roses—perfume as expensive as purple dye—itched his nose.

Jaime sank to his knees.

"Lord Gaiyus," he said.

His brother's warden turned around. Gaiyus Sartorios's hair was gilded with silver. His arched, calculating brows made him look indefinitely resentful. Jaime never personally meet him before, and when the lord's gaze fell on him, it was like being cornered by a wolf.

How does Hilaris call this man Papá?

The Lord of Mount Alairus crossed the chamber and rested his gold-ringed hand on Jaime's chin.

"Please, rise, Jamian."

Breathe.

Jaime raised his head.

"The Archpriestess believes we brought you to my villa to question your knowledge of Hida Pappas's perjury."

"You have to protect her, and Hilaris—"

"Shh," Gaiyus said gently. "We have little time. The Archpriestess is out hunting in the mountains. The burning has been delayed, but only until dawn. We are here to discuss what she is looking for, and why."

Hunting in the mountains. Jaime shivered.

"What do you mean?"

Lord Gaiyus's eyes shifted. As soon as Jaime followed them, panic swelled in his chest.

A shaggy man crouched in the corner, staff wobbling between his fingers. Aeneas—the goat shepherd.

"Aeneas told us what happened at the barrows. He claims you raised the banestorm that now hangs over us."

Banestorm.

Jaime winced.

Surely that was too strong a word? What nonsense did Hilaris orate about at the farmstead—banestorms existed only in legend, didn't they? Mega storms that once tore the continents to pieces and gulped down entire islands of tribesmen. No banestorms had existed since the formation of the Four Kingdoms three thousand years ago. Or maybe even at all.

"It's not a banestorm—"

"My son," the shepherd croaked. "Evander—he's still out there, my lord. He stayed behind to look for Leonidas—our missing goat. If they find him—"

Gaiyus raised his hand for peace. "We will look for Evander." His wolf-gray eyes switched to Jaime. "Present the Sacred Relic for us, please."

"The what?"

Lord Gaiyus smiled tightly.

He peeked at Commander Julias, who stood by the doorway with a hand on his hilt. The commander nodded at him. Hesitating, Jaime pulled the medallion out from under his himation.

Firelight washed over its ancient symbol.

Sharp inhales from the other men.

Gaiyus took it, his lips thinning into a line as his neatly trimmed fingers caressed its edges.

"The Air Emblem."

Immediately, the other politicians narrowed their eyes at Jaime. It was like he'd committed thievery—or murder.

"I found it in Hektor Pappas's grave," Jaime hollered. "I didn't mean to break into his death offerings. It was the only way I could supply my family once we made it past the Sky Pass—"

"The King is already looking for you."

He froze. "What?"

"The entire Kingdom saw that monstrous current rise in the sky. Only our god—or a Sage—could have awoken such a thing."

"It was an accident. I'm not a—"

"No, Jaime. I suspect Hida must have seen the Relic around your neck the day she found you. It was a fatal error in her judgment to not seek me for counsel."

"Did she know what it was?"

"No," Commander Julias cut in. "She could not have."

Gaiyus folded his ringed hands together. "The Archpriestess and Reizo Kita, the Chief Strategos, hold much power in this Kingdom. If they intend to keep it that way, they will find the boy who awakened the Relic. Or the King will burn them. They believe, mistakenly, he is out in the mountains."

"My son—" Aeneas howled.

"It will only be a matter of time before they find out that boy is right here in my township."

Jaime shoved his hand into his pockets, rolling his breather around his fingers. "But...why are they searching for *me*?"

"You know why."

"*Why?*"

Julias exchanged looks with Lord Gaiyus, and the latter nodded. The commander of the Free Guard marched into the light.

"Because of the Relic, Jaime. There are a few things you must understand. Do you know why the King established the Royal Decree?"

"He's looking for a boy born in 2982."

"Are you familiar with the Sacred Codex?"

"Kind of. It was written by the Four Kingdoms' first Sages. I think it's a bunch of international laws?"

"It is the creed of the Holy Church of Sages, or the Sagian Church as we call it today. The Church was indeed founded by the first Sages. As House Ascaerii is head of the Jaypan church, the High King of Larfour is head of the Sagian Church—*the* Church that governs all Sage rule in the Four Kingdoms; yes, our very way of life. Our current King of Jaypes, Usheon Ottega, has profaned the Church and our god."

"Because he's a Fire Sage," Jaime said. "We're the Kingdom of Air."

The other men ducked their heads uncomfortably—this was the kind of treason you didn't talk about unless you wanted your tongue cut out. Julias looked straight at him and nodded.

"The King before Usheon was Lairdos Ascaerii, an Air Sage descended from the sacred bloodline of our god. A month before Usheon's invasion, Lairdos stepped off the cliffs of the Capital."

Jaime widened his eyes. "Stepped off?"

"An unfortunate suicide no one understands," Gaiyus interrupted. "For our purposes now, these details are irrelevant."

Julias gave a respectful nod. "Usheon, a former daimyo— Kaipponese feudal lord, that is—was a rare individual who discovered Sage-powers and was not of the royal house.

"Now the Kaipponese Emperor, Viro of the Tazuga Clan, is feared by many. Usheon was no fool to challenge the Emperor for the Fire Throne. His eyes fell on the neighboring Kingdom of Jaypes. We were feeble and weak without a King, and under the pretense of trying to protect us, he invaded, forced our Queen's hand, and declared himself King. With the West preoccupied with war, no one cared to stop him."

"No one could," a crabapple-faced politician said.

Jaime picked at his breather. "What about the Queen? She wasn't a Sage?"

A sigh escaped Lord Gaiyus's throat. "Our beloved Queen Sarendi was, unfortunately, of ordinary blood. A year after her marriage to Usheon, she bore him a son."

"Then came the Royal Decree," Julias said.

"Alas"—Gaiyus turned to the fire—"Usheon's desecration of the holy creed Julias spoke of earlier could not go unchecked for long. A day after his son's birth, seven airpriests from the High Temple carried a message from our god himself. They divined a prophecy: to punish the King for blaspheming the Church, Lord Jaypes aligned the stars in such a way that, on the fifteenth year of Usheon's reign, his own beloved son would overthrow him."

Jaime's brows creased.

But the gods aren't real. If Lord Jaypes hasn't been around for this long, how can they take a prophecy seriously?

Instead, he said, "The gods can make things like that happen?"

"It was unusual, certainly, having airpriests receive such a powerful divination. But yes—no one can question the holy judgment of Lord Jaypes. Usheon was outraged, of course. He ordered the execution of the priests and his own son."

Jaime fought down a shiver.

"Ah, yes, even his son." Lord Gaiyus's voice grew quiet. "His lust for power is remarkable."

A cold silence drifted through the chamber. Gaiyus handed the medallion back to Julias, who looped it gently over Jaime's neck. Their lord paced across the stone chamber, the whiff of roses trailing behind him.

"Did Hilaris ever tell you who I..." Gaiyus glanced at Julias and the other politicians. "Who we are?"

Jaime shook his head.

"At one time, we led Lairdos's Old Senate. I was Head Senator, second only to the King. My friends here—Eukles, Herodotus, Alexion—had the foresight to escape the capital the night before the invasion. Julias Markus was the Queen's brother."

His jaw dropped open.

The Queen's brother?

"After Aeropolis Capital fell, the King forced me to watch as his fire burned the rest of my Senators. He exiled me to Jaypes's cold fringes, to humiliate me. In that time, we built the Air Alliance, the final resistance against the despot who sits upon the throne. That unholy fiend who rules us murdered our beloved Queen and wise court friends, denied us the sacred burial of our dead. His lies have poisoned the Jaypan armies and turned our own priests against us. He has commanded the genocide of thousands of Jaypan children.

"But in this final season before his fifteenth year, everything has changed. A storm is rising, Jaime. Because of you, the gods are now on our side."

The old man's voice was low, but Jaime felt spine-chilling thrill creeping under it.

Something between a laugh and croak scratched his throat. "I don't understand…"

"Alas, but you do," said Gaiyus Sartorios, voice blooming like a woken storm. "Before the King could slay his son, the Queen escaped with the boy. His men found her, but never the child. Even after the King tortured her under the palace, she refused to reveal his location." He clasped his hands together again. "The King sent his soldiers to Mount Alairus because he thinks your brother is the missing boy. This year, our prince would be fourteen."

"Stop—"

"The Sacred Relic"—Lord Gaiyus's eyes fell on the medallion—

"responds to Sages. If one holds it, regardless of what his natural element is, that Sage has the ability to wield Air."

Jaime shut his eyes.

"It responded to you because you are a Sage. That is the only explanation for the banestorm outside—"

"It's not a banestorm. And I'm a Pappas—just a farmer. You're wrong."

Hida knew about the medallion. Did Hilaris know?

She never said anything about it. Instead, she hid it away in Hektor's grave. So many lies. What else—?

Commander Julias caught Jaime before he fell. He couldn't feel his lungs. If he talked anymore, he was afraid the world would swirl into darkness.

"Are you saying…"

Jaime forced the words out.

"Are you saying the King is my *father?*"

CHAPTER FIVE

"Do you know what this means?" Lord Gaiyus said.

The light of the flames suddenly were too bright, too sickly.

"The King is a Fire Sage. This medallion gives you the power of Air." Lord Gaiyus's voice lilted. "You must call a duel against your father—a battle to the death—or more people die. People like Hektor Pappas. People like your mother and brother, who are scheduled to burn at dawn."

"The King is *not* my father," he screamed, "and I'm not calling anything!"

Jaime fled the chamber.

The Free Guards at the entrance hesitated, unsure whether to lower their spears.

Politician Crabapple yelled, "Stop that boy! He has the Relic—"

One of the guards grabbed Jaime. He wrenched himself free.

"Don't touch me!"

A sudden gale of wind knocked the guards to their knees.

The chamber gasped. It had to be a coincidence—a loose stormwind somehow finding its way under the bowels of the mountain. Everyone kept their distance. No one dared move.

Gaiyus studied him, eye twitching, and finally said, "Let him go."

No one dared move—except for Commander Julias. "Arm yourself, at least," he hissed, pressing a knife to Jaime's chest.

He took it and yanked himself free.

His bare feet pattered out of the pantheon, directly below the isolated akropolis where Lord Gaiyus ruled from. *So that's where we were.* Townfold's network of villages was built on the mountain's slope, and for a second, his entire home sprawled below him in full view. Every faraway tier crawling with the King's soldiers.

Not my fault—none of this is my fault—

Jaime streamed in the direction of the sky, the slope of the rocky fields burning his thighs. Away from the familiar districts of flat-roofed, mud-brick houses. Away from Champion's Square, where the pyre waited for him. The climb stole his breath.

He wanted to disappear into Mount Alairus's great cloud-tipped peak. From down here, it looked mighty, an altar for gods and Jaypan warrior-heroes, a paradise where not even the King could conquer.

The kingpines thickened. His thighs burned long before he reached a quarter of the way up the mountain. Jaime slipped the knife between his teeth, felt around the bark of a pine, and scaled upward.

Rain flattened his bristly bed of hair. Stormy gusts nipped at the brand mark on his wrist.

They're wrong. Commander Julias is my father. He has to be.

He pressed his head to the bark, shutting his eyes.

Hours passed.

Rain battered the forest.

How had things become such hell? On Mount Alairus? Where the worst thing that ever happened was the occasional eloping and streaking?

They've lost their minds. I can't even plow with my asthma, and they want me to fight the King's fire currents with air?

Jaime cupped his face into his hands.

What had Hektor Pappas had been like? He saw a bigger man in his head, imagined the oval shape of his face, the stark kindness that was said to light his pewter eyes. The same eyes Hilaris had. In those visions, Hektor would teach him how to wield a spear, and catch golden eagles, and win pretty girls with long dark ringlets. For as long as he could remember, he envied all of the Townfold boys who had papás that survived the war.

But you do have a papá. Only your papá is different. Your papá killed thousands of boys, just in case any were you.

He gripped the medallion tighter. In the stormlight, the Air Emblem almost seemed to glow.

What god divines a son to kill his father? I don't get why men like the commander worship you. I think you're a coward. If you're real, answer me.

Nothing.

The storm outside pounded the mountain harder. The skies grew darker. He couldn't stay in this tree forever.

If the burning wasn't happening till dawn, he still had a few hours to break his mother and brother out.

I'm not killing the King. I don't know if Gaiyus will rat me out for trying to run. But the commander won't. Maybe he'll even come with us.

Jaime had sensed something budding between Julias and his mother the past few years. The way they would murmur with each other in the dark. Touch each other goodbye outside their farmstead when they thought Jaime wasn't looking. Sometimes, Hida would slip him a package of honey cakes between a bundle of textiles he bought from her.

Julias Markus would help him.

When he reached town, Jaime's feet stopped dead. Sickness creeped up into the back of his throat.

A small body hung upside down over the wooden doorway that framed Townfold's eastern entrance. Flayed. Peeled down to the wide, bulging eyeballs. Dark droplets *drip, drip, dripped* into the grass.

Evander.

The shepherd's boy.

Jaime pressed a hand over his mouth and fled through a collapsing arbor. Acid scorched his throat. Jaime retched, his eyes welling.

No. Evander's not—I'm not the King's son. They have it all wrong.

Distant laughter made his head jerk up. It sounded like it was coming from a side alley.

Who could be laughing right now?

He wiped his mouth and followed the noise.

On the irregular slopes of the street, five boys danced around a skinny shape. One of the boys gripped the skinny boy's head and shoved it into a pail, holding him down despite his flailing arms.

"Still can't talk?" The biggest boy—Rimas Vulcus, the pallbearer's son—laughed. "Maybe we can change that."

Jaime recognized that shape—big shoulders, awkward, long limbs, head proportionately small against the rest of the body. He also bore the symbol of an x-ed out circle on his wrist. It was Cassie, the mute boy.

Rage blistered in his chest.

Townfold is going to flames, and you're attacking a crippled kid?

"Let him go!" Jaime bellowed.

The other boys whirled around, their bare feet crunching in the brush.

"What are you doing?" Jaime said. "Don't you know what day it is?"

Rimas's yellow teeth showed through his grin. "Your burning day, Stormy Lungs?"

Suddenly, Jaime remembered the knife under his himation.

The boy holding Cassie pulled him back up. The latter gasped, collapsing into a bush of fennel and coughing up water.

Rimas pointed at Jaime. "Go on, let him have his turn!"

Red blinded his vision. The knife ended up in his hand, unsheathed, just as they were a footstep away.

The boys exclaimed and skidded to a halt. Rimas's eyes shot open. They backed away slowly.

Jaime advanced.

His bloodshot eyes locked on Rimas. The other boys fled. Jaime pounced, knocked Rimas into the dirt.

This boy had called him names his entire life. But Rimas Vulcus and his friends picked on Cassie even more, beating him up in puddle-filled alleys and under rickety bridges when they thought no one was looking.

That wouldn't happen anymore.

"No!" Rimas threw up his hands. "It was just a game, I swear! I swear—by all four gods!"

Someone gripped Jaime's wrist as it came down.

Rimas sobbed and dashed into a grove of hemlock trees. Jaime screamed. Sprung at his attacker, but in turn the silhouette grabbed his left wrist.

"Jaime!"

The commander's beard nearly scraped his face. His heavy myrrh smell stung Jaime's eyes.

"What in the high hells are you doing?"

"They were going to drown Cassie—"

Julias's eyes shifted to the knife raised in Jaime's hand. Jaime had never raised a ladle on anyone before. But now, endless waves of heat pulsed out of his chest.

Maybe I am a monster like the King.

Cassie's breaths grew heavy. Jaime caught his eyes only for a split second before Cassie fled behind the rickety houses, head sticking out like it was trying to escape his body.

Julias's stark gaze returned to him.

"Listen to me, Jaime. My men are freeing your mother was we speak. We have to get both of you to Achuros."

"Who?"

"He is an airpriest in the south, the only one I trust with your life—"

"What's an airpriest?"

The commander sighed down his urgency. "Ancient scribes. Keepers of the High Temple. Each Kingdom has one. Only about a hundred still survive in Jaypes. They read Lord Jaypes's omens and train Air Sages, the way Achuros will train you to duel the King with Air—"

"No, I'm *not* fighting the King!"

"*Jaime.*" The commander clasped his shoulders. "We have little time before—"

A low horn sliced through the pregnant storm clouds.

That was the same horn they blew when the Archpriestess announced one family would stand on the pyre. Which meant this horn signaled it was time for a burning.

Mamá—

Jaime wrested free. The knife vanished into the ankle-high grass. The commander called him, but he stormed in the direction of Champion's Square.

Lightning flashed over the black skies.

45

The slope of Townfold Village loomed upward, displaying the dozens of New Jaypes banners pinned to familiar landmarks. His chest cracked. So many places he never thought twice about. The smithy, south of the square, where he shared countless bowls of gruel with Peri Kreed's family. Ptolemy's Library several blocks ahead— he and Hilaris used to chase each other under its tattered awnings when they were kids. Charis Poupolos's toy shop in the east. The day Lord Gaiyus rode off with Jaime's brother, Charis saw everything and handed Jaime a miniature horse on wheels.

"Keep it." The old toymaker winked.

I was supposed to grow into a man here, maybe even find a pretty girl and marry her.

Jaime's view of the slope broke when a soldier marched past him. He pressed himself behind a water jug, desperation blurring his eyes.

Things are never going to be the same again. It's only going to get worse and worse and worse...

He was terrified of defying the soldiers, but he was even more terrified of what would happen to him and his family if they stayed. And what would happen to the Alairans? Twelve years ago, the King stripped the mountain of its wealth, leaving empty husks of quarries behind. What would he do to it this time?

As Jaime rounded the altar with the bull statue, he crashed into a shield.

"Jaime!" a voice cried.

Hida pushed through the crowd of Free Guards and pressed him tightly against her. Jaime held on to her. As the sky broke, heavy rains seeped through his himation, breathed cold into his skin.

"Did you know?" he whispered.

For the first time in years, he drank in the way her hair nestled against her nape. The way her fingertips were calloused from years of weaving and threshing barley. The smell of the brazier's charcoal on her skin. This woman had plucked him out of the wilderness, clothed and fed him when she could barely afford to feed herself.

She *was* Townfold Village, and Mount Alairus, and everything in Jaypes Kingdom that existed.

"My son, not now—"

"It *has* to be now, Mamá! Did you know I was the King's son?"

The town guards watched them, ankle boots pawing the ground.

"I had an inkling." Her voice was steady, but tears cut down her cheeks. "Everything I've done was to protect you and Hilaris. Lord Jaypes forgive me. I have failed both of you."

He gripped her hands tightly. "No, you didn't. Lord Jaypes did this, not you."

"We cannot blame—"

"Now let's go get Hilaris."

"The Archpriestess has him, Jaime," said Damias, one of the younger guards. "Rumors are floating about that you're the missing prince. Is—is it true?"

"No. It's not."

"Nides was yelling it in the barracks. And he told the Archpriestess."

That dirty traitor.

Jaime quickened his sprint to Champion's Square.

Hida pleaded him to stop. The Free Guards chased after him, stumbling down the ragged, weed-strewn streets. His lungs were going to explode any second now.

Hilaris was already on the pyre.

Jaime bit down a scream.

Two soldiers held his brother down. His arm was stretched out over a wooden block. The Archpriestess snicked his brother's flesh with a knife. Hilaris's mouth twisted—he was struggling to bite down a cry.

When she finished, the Archpriestess lifted up his arm.

The Air Emblem was carved onto it, a mocking display of holy reverence to the God of Air. Her free hand clenching Hilaris's wrist, she wiped his blood over his forehead. Her milky eyes closed.

Jaime's chest rose and fell raggedly.

The night the Archpriestess arrived, the elders whispered she knew black magic. It was how she was able to feel out if a boy had the powers of a Sage—by feeling out their *avai,* the energy burning in all living things, and invading it with her own.

Cursed woman, they would whisper. *She is no priest of our god. Evil spirits infect her.*

Her eyes split open.

She yelled, "He hath not the blood of a Sage! Therefore, for belying His Holiness's Royal Decree, thus committing high treason in earnest, by the grace of our true God of Fire, he is guilty of death!"

Jaime stepped out, but Damias grabbed him.

"What are you doing?" the young man hissed. "She's baiting you!"

He glanced at the square below him. The entire royal army surrounded it, spears ready, bows slung.

Two soldiers dragged Hilaris to the stake, tossed his chains through the ring, fastened his arms above him.

Hilaris breathed hard. Jaime recognized the shock in his eyes— the only thing keeping him silent.

Strategos Reizo, on ground level, passed the Archpriestess the torch.

Time slowed to one long, dragged out heartbeat. Soldiers shoved Lord Gaiyus at the front of the crowd, forcing him to watch. The old man's eyes were closed, his lips moving in a low, useless prayer. His politicians stood behind him, togas ripped. And there was Nides, mounted and helmed, a smirk splattered wide across his face.

The royal banners whipped at all corners of the pyre.

Jaime glanced back at his mother.

Her damp gray eyes reflected his rain-stained face—she saw what he was about to do. One of her sons would live, and the other would die.

I love you, Mamá.

And he turned back around.

"Stop!" Jaime shouted.

The torch paused over the wood of the pyre.

Fingers gripping his breather, Jaime stepped into full light of the square. He took a breath.

No air went in.

"Let him go, and I'll come with you. I'm the one you're looking for."

Those milky eyes locked on his. An invisible draft froze his insides—and he saw it again, briefly. White mist leaching out of her body. But it had to be another trick of the flames.

Every bow shifted, pointing at him.

"Let him go, I said!"

The Archpriestess shrieked with laughter. "Thou art in no position to command *me*, my cripple Prince."

The nearest soldiers moved in to seize him.

The Archpriestess's fingers released from the stave. The flaming bundle crashed onto the pyre, bouncing once.

Jaime screamed.

He wasn't the only one. All of Townfold broke into cries.

Jaime leapt towards the pyre to get to Hilaris. Soldiers gripped his arms tightly. Shoved him backwards. Despite the rainfall, oil licked up the flames eagerly.

In seconds, the entire platform was alight.

The skin between Hilaris's brows creased. He struggled against his chains, but they held tight against the stake.

"Jamie—"

Black smoke rose over everyone's heads, bending to the wrath of the storm.

"Please, don't let them—don't—"

Coughing swallowed up his words. Already, it was difficult to see Hilaris through the waves of heat.

Jaime yanked against the soldiers, choking.

"I won't let them, Hilaris! I won't—"

But the soldiers wouldn't let go. Heat flared up Jaime's body. Every vein seethed, until his heart was trembling. His eyes were on fire. He could see nothing but the flames.

Jaime let out a scream from the well of his body.

A loose spear of fire devoured the air above the Archpriestess. She ducked in time, tumbled off the pyre's edge.

The soldiers released him.

The next time Jaime could see, both men twisted on the ground, crying out. Their cone-shaped helmets glowed a furious red. Cooking their faces from the inside out.

All of Champion's Square stared at him.

I didn't do that. I didn't just raise a fire current. The King is—I'm not a Fire Sage—

Hilaris's shrieks broke his focus.

Once, when Jaime was eight, Rimas Vulcas hamstrung a young goat and threw it into a cauldron. He lit flames under it, heating the water slowly. As the kid boiled alive, its screams mangled the morning silence—you could hear it from the other side the mountain.

That was what Hilaris's shrieks sounded like. Pitchless. A noise of nightmares that curdled every drop of his blood.

Jaime's mouth fell open.

His brother was no longer visible. In his place, a glowing bull shape of yellow kicked and thrashed inside the flames.

He's gone.

CHAPTER SIX

Cassie appeared where the fallen soldiers were, leading a saddleless gelding by the reins. Hilaris's horse. He looked at the mute boy numbly, not understanding.

"Jaime!"

Across the square, Julias Markus raised his spear.

"*Go!* You must live—duel the King and kill him! For us!"

The Archpriestess's shrieking voice clawed him awake. "Stop him! Stop him, stop him, you imbeciles—"

Cassie mounted the gelding and tugged at his himation. Jaime wobbled on behind him.

How does Cassie know how to ride?

No matter. Nothing mattered, nothing was real anymore.

As they broke into a gallop, the kingpines melted away into the rain. The gelding levelled the scraggly fields of wildflowers.

Arrows flew over their heads.

Strategos Reizo followed close behind them, a single-edged halberd with the New Jaypes pennant bleeding against the air.

"*Osei!* Prince!"

The roar of rapids gradually drowned the forest. The Estos River winded ahead of them.

Downstream from that were the falls.

"Please forgive, your brother has his honor now. But your life is of tantamount—eh, paramount? Of paramount importance! If I may please explain—"

Cassie reined them parallel to the banks. Mud flew into Jaime's eyes, spattered everywhere.

Reizo's destrier was catching up to them.

Cassie glanced back at Jaime.

The mute boy's mouth opened—Jaime swore he heard a word come out. *Sorry*, perhaps? It was impossible to hear over the river and the storm—and he shoved Jaime off the saddle.

The Strategos cursed in his native tongue as Jaime crashed into water.

Cold zapped him awake.

He paddled, fighting to get to the surface, but the rapids pulled him down. Jaime desperately kicked his feet. His left one made contact with rock. It sliced into his sole. He thrust upward. Burst back into open air.

Jaime gasped for a breath.

Two things happened before he reached the falls: Reizo grabbed Cassie, who also leapt into the water.

And he saw the curve of the river, the steep drop into darkness that marked the end of beloved Mount Alairus.

Everything he knew.

Jaime never heard his own screams.

He fell over the edge, and the dark of the world beyond swallowed him up.

PART TWO

CHAPTER SEVEN

Something licked a cut on his forehead.

Jaime opened his crusty eyes.

His head bobbed against a mud bank. Gray daylight slumped through foreign pine branches. Thrushes and larks twittered above him.

The Estos River brought him to a shallow ford.

A golden shape hunched over him, watching him with big eyes.

"Murrow?" it said.

A tomcat.

Only this one was the size of a young goat—the biggest cat he'd ever seen—and gods, its *eyes*. Otherworldly light glowed behind its retina, flickering like a lamp made of green flames.

Jaime picked himself up, stumbling back onto shore.

Sick skies.

His head—heavier than a boulder, pounding like a thousand donkeys trampling over him. As he splashed, the cat darted back under the weedy brush. His legs felt like sticks of suet.

I'm dreaming, I'm dreaming—

He batted his cheeks.

Wake up, Jaime. Wake UP!

His feet touched the banks—and he stumbled into the grooves

of mud. Landing on his chin. Pain whited out his vision.

Mamá was never responsible for the soldiers that came to town. I was. I raised a fire current—gods, I am a Sage. I killed Hilaris.

He reached into his pocket for his breather—

Panic spiked up his chest.

Nothing.

He must have lost it somewhere in the river.

His lungs heaved. He sounded like an old man, the way viscous air wheezed out of him. His panic swelled. His eyes watered. His asthma hadn't been this bad for as long as he could remember.

Jaime breathed in desperately. The coughing sobs burst free from his throat.

"I'm sorry!" he screamed. "I'm sorry! I'm SORRY!"

He couldn't stop coughing. He couldn't breathe.

You can. Breathe deeply, Jaime.

His mother's voice.

Jaime dragged himself upright and took deep, ragged breaths. *One, two, three, four.* Releasing.

Gradually, the attack withdrew, leaving only his sobs behind.

Jaime stared blankly at the marbled skies.

I'm sorry, Hilaris. I shouldn't have let my jealousy turn us into strangers. I shouldn't have stood there while they burned you.

I should've…I should've…

What?

What could he have done to stop the Archpriestess?

Just before Cassie helped him escape, what did Julias Markus say?

You must duel the King and kill him! For us!

He wheezed out a laugh.

The commander really believed he could challenge the King in a battle of the elements—and win. Even if the King *was* his father.

No.

The Air Alliance could deal with deposing the King. Jaime wanted nothing to do with Usheon Ottega.

But his mother was still out there, and he would fight to protect her as long as she was alive. Family before the Kingdom.

Even if it means the rest of the cursed Kingdom has to burn.

The giant tomcat reemerged from the trees, rubbing against his ankles. Jaime wiped away his tears.

"You're not real."

He stepped back, but the cat curled around his leg. Purring. With a shaking hand, he reached down to pet its fur.

Nothing happened.

No bolt of energy zapping off his hand. No burst of fire from its green lantern eyes.

The longer Jaime looked, the more it seemed to self-consciously shrink, shrink, shrink into a normal-sized cat, till the supernatural light was gone from its big, sad gaze.

"Mew?"

Dreaming.

Jaime turned away. He was dreaming. He shook his head. "I'm going back home," he declared.

The cat blinked up at him.

I still have the medallion. If I need to, I'll bargain with the Archpriestess for Mamá's life.

He stripped off his wet himation and sagging exomis, squeezed the water from them. Threw them over his shoulder. Then he crawled onto his feet, stumbling up the slope to get to higher elevation. The trees cleared at the top. Jaime's mouth dropped open.

Forested mountains rolled into the horizon in every direction he could see.

The Krete Forests.

He'd heard from the elders that this was the largest expanse of forest in Jaypes.

No sign of the cloud-covered Mount Alairus. He didn't have any idea where he was, or how to get home.

"Mew?"

The cat bunted his ankle. Jaime bent down and rubbed its throat. A new set of purrs hummed against his skin.

"Are you coming with me?"

"Mew, mew."

"Okay." Jaime stood. "Let's follow the river back to Townfold."

But before noon, the Estos split into two, and the rivulet he followed split into more tributaries. By twilight, he was completely lost.

⁓ ✺ ⁓

The stormy skies passed light and shadow over the pines so many times that Jaime lost track of the days. It rained off and on. Cold and dirt sapped his energy.

Still, he forced himself to keep walking.

At first, the constant climb across the mountains bloodied his knuckles, but over time, they grew shell tough. The muscles in his thighs hardened. Jaime scaled across slopes that would have once knocked the breath out of his lungs. His exomis began to recede above his knees until it resembled an oversized shirt.

Yet the further he trekked, the more the wild chestnuts, hazel, and eggs he foraged grew tasteless.

He missed that wretched smell of incense that choked his lungs. He missed the songs of thrushes as his mother weaved outside at the vertical loom.

The tomcat faithfully kept him company, but his spirit grew heavier with each passing day.

I'm going to be trapped in these forests forever.

And when the hour came that he could no longer bear the empty expanse, he collapsed on a mound of decayed leaves.

"Help," he croaked into them. "Someone, please help…"

As if in response, something rolled out of hiding. Nothing he could see—only feel. The hairs on his arms stood straight up.

We help you.

The high-pitched baby whispers tickled his ears. Jaime grappled the leaves, pulling himself upright.

A finger of mist trickled over the surrounding spruces and pines. The crows fell dead silent. This looked like the same white mist that came out of the Archpriestess back at Champion's Square.

"Hello?" he shouted, hackles rising.

Follow us.

He struggled to his feet. His companion dozed on a log several steps away, ear twitching, a patch of gold against a screen of white. The cat didn't seem to hear a thing. Jaime squinted through the trunks.

Over here, Jaime. We can help you.

Instinct warned him to move.

Jaime took his first step. The dead leaves at his feet suddenly exploded, a frigid blast that nearly knocked him aside.

Just a gust!

He forced air down his throat, willed himself to calm down. His mind was a twister of emotions.

Kuurjal hzajdi gûl…

This new voice was many octaves deeper. Even the baby whispers went silent. Its presence splintered him into raw fear.

The cat suddenly snapped up its head, hissing. As Jaime took another step forward, it bounded ahead into the mist.

He, too, broke into a run.

No such thing as strange creatures. Hilaris never mentioned a thing. Or the elders.

The mists grabbed at his ankles. He peered over his shoulder, holding back a scream.

White patches raced ahead of him from the corners of his eyes. His lungs contracted. The whole forest roared from sudden winds, attacking him.

Red spots appeared and blurred over his vision. The ground broke off into a steep ravine—Jaime skidded to a halt.

Something breathed cold air onto his clammy neck.

"Kuurjal hzajdi gûl, Jaime."

His blood turned to ice.

Turn around, turn around. It's behind you.

Trembling, Jaime rolled his head over his shoulder.

A plume of white rose above him. The most toxic, putrid stink assaulted his nose—it smelled just like the night Hilaris's flesh burned.

His lips pulled back into a scream.

The little tomcat suddenly bounded into view, the fur on its back prickly straight. It squeezed itself in front of Jaime. Bared its teeth at the shapeless monster. The cat grew in size, grew till it was larger than a goat, larger than a mountain lion—

"Gods!"

Jaime lost his balance, staggered backwards—only for the layer of mists to clear. A sharp ravine appeared behind him. But it was too late.

His heel slipped.

The last thing he saw was the mist hissing at the cat before it rolled away, vanishing. Twigs dug into him as he rolled—and then he landed flat on his belly.

Jaime gasped for breath.

A cat just saved my life! From a mist-monster? But I don't think that was a cat! What would that thing've done to me if I didn't escape?

His thoughts shut off when he saw the body next to him, lying facedown. Jaime bit down a shriek.

A dead person!

The ground muffled the man's low mumbles.

A living person!

Jaime took a step forward to grab him, shake him, and swallowed another scream.

Four round eyes stared at him from atop the man's back. A little hairy spider the size of Jaime's thumb.

The body mumbled into the ground. "By gods, I'm gonna beat those Jaypan dummies silly..."

Mustering his courage, Jaime scrabbled for his medallion and threw a warning swing at the spider. But it stayed planted in place, blinking up at him. Jaime took a step closer and swiped again, this time for a killing blow.

Get off, get off him!

The Air Emblem glistened against the skylight. This time the spider leapt off, scurrying into the brush.

Jaime shook the body, hysterics shaking his breath. "Hey! Wake up! You got to get out of here—"

The body snapped upright and tackled him to the ground. "How's this for a Kaipponese spy?"

"Are you crazy?" Jaime wheezed under his weight. "Get off me!"

As his vision refocused, he narrowed his eyes at the face looming above him. Not a man—a teenage boy, about his age. Shoulders hunched in. Body blubbery. His black, gibbous eyes opened to the size of pomegranates.

"Did you see those mists?" Jaime puffed. "Or hear that voice? On the other side of the ravine—"

"A what where?"

"*Mist-monsters!* They were chasing me, and then my cat—I found this cat—it tried to protect me, it was like the mist-monster was afraid of it! But then the cat transformed—"

The boy tilted his head.

Jaime stopped in mid-breath. "You didn't see anything?"

The boy scrutinized Jaime's dirt-crusted body before fixing his gaze on the medallion resting over Jaime's chest. Jaime quickly shoved it under his himation. The boy cleared his throat casually.

"You leave your brains in the forest or something?"

Jaime's fear vanished into a glare. "No. I know what I saw. Get *off* me."

As the weight lifted, Jaime crossed his arms over his waist. The boy had a mass of curly brown hair, a bouncing pot belly, a big flat nose jutting above his cake-round cheeks. But the wings at the edge of his eyes, big and amply lidded, gave him away.

"You're Kaipponese," Jaime exclaimed.

"'Course I am, dope. What do I look like, Glaiddish?" The boy shrugged. "So anyway. Where you headed?"

He hesitated. *I can't tell him I'm the Prince. I can't tell anyone.*

"I don't know. Somewhere away from the forests."

"You're better off in those forests, buddy. That City-State I was in—"

"*City?*" Jaime cut in. "There's a city here?"

And then he heard it—barking dogs, laughter, deep shouts. It was faint. Townfold Village used to sound like that before the Archpriestess came and built the pyre.

Jaime dashed past the boy and skirted the pines until the foliage opened up. He skidded to a halt before a steep cliff.

A brick wall below him marked the edge of the Krete Forest. Beyond it, a valley of terracotta rooftops tucked itself inside mountains of cypress, palms, and olive trees. There had to be more people there than ten Mount Alairuses combined. The Estos River reappeared to the east, snaking around a tooth-shaped akropolis.

The Estos River!

Those same coursing waters that had saved him from the royal army—it even cut through the same lands as home. The familiarity of it stirred both comfort and unease into his belly. But the akropolis here—gods, it had to be a thousand feet long and at least a hundred feet tall. On top of it, sand-colored shrines and monuments wrestled with the sky.

A City-State.

His mouth fell open. The remnants of his terror faded into the background.

Hida Pappas once said a dozen City-States existed in Jaypes: strongholds of civilization where Jaypes's greatest lords governed from. Some owned seaports that gave them access to all the Four Kingdoms. Others held open marketplaces as colorful as mosaics. Hektor, her husband, came from a City-State in the far south.

The vibrancy of this one was blinding. The boy bobbed to a stop behind him.

"I'm going there." Jaime pointed. *They'll be able to tell me how to get back to Mount Alairus.*

"*There?*" the boy cried. "You can't go there—the people are crazier than cave bats! They thought I was a royal spy and chased me out." He rubbed the side of his head. "Now that I think about it, one of them might've hit me with a pan."

"Well, *you* might be a spy, but I'm not. Go away—"

The boy grabbed him by the scruff. "Look, kid"—his sour breath coated Jaime's face—"you don't get it. That place is dangerous. Seeing as you're running around with nothing but that ugly stone, this entire *Kingdom* is probably dangerous for you—"

"Let me go," Jaime snapped.

The clouds above them raced faster. The winds snarled, razor-sharp against the blades of wild grass under his feet. Jaime barely noticed. But Toran peered at the gusts and quickly let go, backing away.

"Sorry, man. It's just that we're both lost in a giant turd of wilderness, and I ain't stepping foot anyplace without me grog." He paused. "A royal army separated me and my best friend, and until I find him, I'm on my own. I don't know how to survive out here by myself. I don't even know the way home."

"Okay," said Jaime. "We won't go inside, but I still need directions."

"From...them?" The boy pointed to the guards on the curtain wall.

Jaime followed his gaze. They weren't wearing the crimson mantles of royal soldiers, which meant they were loyal to the local lord.

But the boy had a point. How much difference did that make if there was a bounty on Jaime's head?

Suddenly, his gut clenched.

He's right. You approach that wall, they'll ask you questions. What'll you say? I was helping Mamá transport cloths to...to the east coast. For trade. But bandits robbed me and stole my donkey. And, um, I'm lost. Can you point me to a trader who's travelling to Mount Alairus?

It was believable, but risky.

Well, if you lumber through those forests anymore, the mist-monsters will eat you alive. What choice do you have?

As Jaime took his first step, the boy stepped in line with him. His face split from a grin.

"Toran, by the way. Toran Binn."

"You can just call me Jaime."

They shook hands.

As soon as their dirty soles hit the ground, Toran's fat fingers shook him.

"Juno, they see us."

On the parapets, the sentries on duty roused the rest of the gate command. The double gateway of the eastern entrance groaned open. Two mounted city guards clopped out between the crack, shortspears in hand.

"Told you they ain't friendly," Toran whispered.

The guards blockaded Jaime.

The silver swifts on their pennants seemed to take to flight. Gray daylight cut through Jaime's eyes as he looked up. High on their saddles, they looked like god statues.

"Our streets have enough tramps," the left one said. "What business have you inside Arcurea's walls, beggar boy?"

"I'm not here to beg."

"Then what are you here for?"

The other guard's hard gray eyes fell on Toran, who casually looked up at the sky. Jaime told them the bandit story he'd come up with. He couldn't feel his windpipe.

"Can you point me the way back to Mount Alairus?"

The stares of the guards were so intent that at any second, he was sure he would shatter like clay pottery. The guard to the left murmured something to his colleague, who nodded. The latter reined his courser around and cantered back into the gate.

"Wait here," the first guard ordered.

Jaime tried not to fidget beneath the guard's stony stare. His eyes darted to the spear's point, then to the guard's shortsword hanging off his steel corselet. When the seconds seemed to drag out too long, Toran shuffled closer.

"So, uh, I think now would be a good time to run."

"Run?"

"You're the missing Prince, right?"

Jaime's mouth dropped.

"How do you know?" he hissed back.

"The city's chockfull of notice boards with your face on it. The stuff I told you on the overhang? I assumed it'd be pretty smart to have a Fire Sage at my back. You can raise currents, right? Like the King?"

Panic surged through Jamie's blood.

"Um."

Toran gawked. "You can't raise currents?"

Before Jaime could explain, a dozen mounted guards poured through the gates. One of them held a New Jaypes standard. Another one unfurled a throwing net.

Jaime swore in his head and raced back in the direction of the forests. Toran was already partway up the ravine, shouting curses. But it was a lost struggle. He took seven short strides before the coursers caught up and circled him. The net slammed him onto his back.

"Let me go!" he screamed. "You don't understand! I'm not your enemy!"

He thrashed against the net; it only tightened around his body. Jaime bared his teeth. The other soldiers dismounted and shoved him upright.

Jaime wrenched his arms from them. No use. The net came off. Rough twine chafed his wrists.

One more guard galloped back from the ravine to join them, a muffled Toran roped tightly to the saddle. The rest of the soldiers lowered their tough, ox-hide shields. Barricaded them in.

The lead guard pointed through the gates. "Bring them to the Lord Mayor. He is expecting them."

A blindfold slipped over Jaime's eyes. Someone lifted him up onto a saddle. The courser's jolting gait hurt his thighs. Hooves pounded around him like drums.

I won't let them keep me from finding Mamá. I raised fire on Mount Alairus. I'll do it again.

The next time the blindfold lifted from his eyes, a great fire-lit theater surrounded him. Twenty-some legislators in official white togas sat on three sides of tiered steps. On top of the bowl-shaped ring, guards leaned against their spears, watching vigilantly. Something slapped against the high winds—the snarling white dragon of the New Jaypes Emblem. It ruled the night from atop the flagstaff.

CHAPTER EIGHT

"Councilors of Arcurea: The Prince has been captured!"

An elder man climbed onto the center plinth, pointing a halberd at Jaime. Unlike Jaypan spears, its curved blade was massive and single-edged. *Kendao*, they were called.

Although he was lean, his frame was shorter and smaller than most male warriors Jaime was used to. The edges of his black eyes were winged, unlike the full-shaped gray eyes of a Jaypan.

Kaipponese.

Jaime slowly turned around in full circle.

Expressions of shock blazed against the other politicians' faces. Some murmured it was impossible that the fabled Prince from the prophecy could've showed up outside their city. "It's a blessed sign!" one man cried. But a younger one swore it was a curse. A curly haired politician wondered how Jaime got here. And still a gaggle of bearded elders wrongly assumed he had died after his escape.

Holy skies, how long was I in the forests for?

"Let us hand him over to the Archpriestess!" the Kaipponese man bellowed.

"I'll not call that bloodstained witch to our city for anything," a bald councilor muttered.

Several murmurs of assent.

"How do you know he is the Prince?" someone else shouted.

"That is simple. He wears the brand of the crippled—just as the royal reports described. And he came to us with the Temple Relic." The Kaipponese man held the stone symbol up to the firelight.

Jaime jolted—the guards must have seized it from him while he struggled against the net.

"I would choose my son's life—I would choose the wellbeing of the Lord Mayor and his family—over the life of that coward who calls himself our Prince. Would not you?"

The assembly remained in murmurs.

"Would not *you?*"

Coward?

When his mind flashed back to his last night on Mount Alairus, his fury broke through the clog in his throat.

"I'm not a coward!" he yelled at the Kaipponese. "You weren't there when Hilaris burned! You don't know what that was like. I tried to save him!"

A vein of lightning severed the sky behind Jaime.

The theater gasped. Some of them sharply backed away. Hands went up to their squinting eyes. Even when the mighty light receded, ethereal fire charged the air.

The black-eyed Kaipponese moved in to grab his wrist.

"No, Sojin," the curly haired councilor cried. "Don't touch him! Didn't you see the lightning?"

Still, the Kaipponese man dragged him across stage, the *kendao's* blade shrieking against the stone pit. Jaime dug his heels into the ground. It wasn't until they were at the upper steps that he yanked himself free.

"This is why we will hand you over," the foreign man hissed.

To the west, a sheet of limestone rock dropped off just beyond the city. Below it, thousands of balls of light glittered into the dark distance.

Fire.

Fire burned as far as Jaypes Kingdom spanned.

"A fortnight ago, these lights did not exist. Then, reports spread of a cripple boy who woke a banestorm that opened the sky itself. The King heard all about it. But so have the people—all of us *felt* that energy wave. The return of their Sage-Prince restored hope to thousands who have risen up to fight in your name."

Jaime's head spun. "They're fighting for me?"

"Look well, boy. Look at all of those good people fighting and dying because of you. They forget that you are the cause of the Royal Decree."

Jaime blinked up at the dark maw of the skies. *A war broke out while I was in those forests?*

Disgust clouded the Kaipponese's eyes. He turned back to face the stage.

"My councilors, let us not make the same error! After all, where has this Prince been for the last fourteen years as our sons were seized and killed? Where was he as Lairdos Ascaerii's bondlords were massacred in the Storm of Flames? Where was he when all of Jaypes echoed with the tortured cries of our children? Where has he been as all corners of this Kingdom burned!"

Jaime's eyes flashed.

It wasn't my fault. I didn't know I was the Prince any more than you *did.*

"The moment we hand him to the King, it will be finished," the black-eyed Kaipponese continued. "No more boys will be murdered, and the Kingdom of Air will have peace again!"

"And it will be the same tyrant that stole our sons and denied our friends burial rites that will sit on the throne," a female voice said.

The Kaipponese's jaw tightened. The Jaypan woman who spoke had a voice like a kithara. She was the only woman seated at the wooden tables in front, and the only one he'd ever seen wear her tresses freely over her shoulders. Black charcoal emphasized her eyelids. White lead brightened her face. Her beauty made him swallow.

"Will all of you be able to live, to sleep, to look at your own sons and daughters knowing you betrayed a child to a fiend? And not just any child, but our own chosen Prince!"

A new wave of murmurs followed. The Kaipponese grit his teeth, but a firm voice cut him off as his mouth was opening.

"Enough!"

Someone crossed the stage, taking hold of a pennant with the city sigil of a silver swift. A strip of purple dye cascaded over his right shoulder—the same kind Lord Gaiyus wore on Mount Alairus. But he was hairless, the youngest of all the councilors present.

When he reached the plinth, he held up his free hand for peace. "Sojin."

Though hot fury undulated out of the Kaipponese, he bowed his head.

"Councilors of Arcurea," the young man said, planting the pennant's stake into the ground. "The Lord Jaypes is our true god, not the Lord of Fire, and certainly not our King—"

"*Aye!*" the theater roared.

"I serve him, and him only. I follow the light of his Air, not evil. And never the spirit of fear. Nay, never fear! On the greatest plinth or bare beneath bathing waters, I belong to him—"

The angry cheers of his politicians grew louder.

"So I will do honor and glory unto the savior the Holy Lord has sent to us. For I believe truly, with my whole heart, the Prince is his chosen one. This was spoken by the airpriests of the High Temple."

The young councilor's piousness made Jaime's insides roll. The former raised the sigil of the swift with one hand, and held out the other to him. He was a whole world away from where Jaime stood on the upper ring.

"My Prince, will you fight with us?"

"I can't." His breath came out dry. "I don't know how to raise currents. What happened on Mount Alairus with the fire current was a mistake. I can't kill the King—I won't last in a duel."

"You will find a way. Lord Jaypes will help you."

Jaime shook his head in a frenzy. *No! Lord Jaypes isn't even real!*

Instead, he whispered, "If I stay here, I'll never find my mother. The Archpriestess has her. Hilaris already died because of me."

"This is beyond your mother, or you, or any one of us. As long as the King lives, your mother will never be free. If you do find her and decide to stay in hiding, more Jaypans like her will die."

"But..."

"We cannot reverse this war. The only way through it is forward, into the storm."

Jaime took a deep breath.

What if that councilor is right?

He knew it ever since he woke up in the river, but his fear and love for his mother kept him from accepting the plain truth: he *had* to kill his blood father or the burnings would never end. No one—not that wretched Kaipponese man, not even the Archpriestess—deserved to endure what Jaime had with Hilaris.

"Okay."

Adrenaline raced through his chest. The stormwinds seemed to rise with him. Several councilors glanced at the sky where lightning struck, wringing their wrists. The banestorm seemed to rumble with his next words.

"I swear to fight with you."

CHAPTER NINE

That night, the councilors concealed him in the upper floor of the Stoa of Lord Jaypes.

Jaime shivered in his bed. Three layers of wool blankets weren't enough. Every time the young Jaypan woman—the one who stood up for him in the theater—tried to light the hearth, he pleaded, "No!"

She came over to his bedside and felt his hands.

"You're so cold," she said. "At least allow me to light a candle by your pillow."

"No," he whispered. "No fire."

After she left, and the world went dark, he saw Hilaris burning again.

Jaime's screams spilled into the night. He leapt out of bed. Pounded against the shutters of his window.

Hilaris! Hilaris! Hilaris! he screamed.

Just as he was about to reach the pyre, the woman burst inside his nightmare and pulled him away.

"Prince," she cried. "Wake, sweet, it is only a bad dream—"

"*No fire,*" Jaime screamed, throat bled raw. "*No fire, I said! Let me go, I have to get to him! Hilaris—I'm SORRY!*"

He didn't remember how that night ended. But his last dream

was of guards drugging him, and the Kaipponese yelling that he would wake the whole city, and the woman cradling his head, smelling of lavender.

She hummed a familiar melody deep into his spirit.

~~~❦~~~

"What is a Fire Sage who fears fire?" someone said.

Jaime opened his eyes.

His head throbbed from another awful headache. Jaime gripped his temples, sorely wishing he had his breather. But he threw off his covers and peered through the door.

Two rows of pillars roofed the second floor. White tapestries of the Arcurean swift spilled behind them. Stone pedestals stood at attention in the foreground. Today, their offering bowls were empty.

"…more than fortunate the daimyo missed yesterday's spectacle. He will be here any hour now."

The lovely woman from last night peered at the dying flames of a terra cotta firepit. The Kaipponese man continued to pace. The young councilor sighed.

"For now," the councilor said, "we plan in secret. Perhaps even rid ourselves of the daimyo."

A scornful laugh.

Across the pantheon, past the frescos of ancient Jaypan heroes in battle, scarred with the light and shadow of the fires, was an airpriest.

Jaime sucked in a breath.

No mistake—he wore the same white robes and maroon stripes as the Archpriestess. He was much older than the others. A piebald beard grizzled his jaws. His deep-set eyes were like dusty windows in an abandoned farmstead. The medallion rolled off his fingertips.

Jaime pulled himself back in, his chest thundering.

An airpriest, there's an airpriest here—

"Did any of you notice the boy's lungs last night?" the Kaipponese said. "He is sickly."

No one answered him.

The Kaipponese grunted, "It is folly to hide the Prince in our city. This will be the end of us."

"It is decided." The young councilor peered sideways at them. "Until our messengers receive word from Senator Gaiyus, it is too dangerous to take the Prince to the High Temple. Therefore, Achuros, you must train him here."

Achuros?

That airpriest was *Achuros?* Hadn't Commander Julias told him to find a man in the south named "Achuros"?

"What now?" The airpriest caught the stone medallion by its chain and moved into the firelight. "Nothing is decided, Florin. After the Queen's death, I swore never to take on another apprentice—you know that. But piss on the past! I *especially* refuse to train the son of Usheon Ottega."

With the exception of the black-eyed Kaipponese, the others groaned.

"Not this again." The young councilor stared up at the frescoes. "It must be you. No one else in the entire Kingdom can."

"The Archpriestess can."

The Kaipponese laughed. "My Lord Mayor, no one can force an airpriest against his will. That would be sacrilege."

"*Thank you*, Sojin," the priest said.

The youngest one—*the mayor?*—glared at them. The airpriest stood up and turned his back to them. The trains of his white sleeves clasped together.

"I have prayed to Lord Jaypes," the priest murmured.

Immediately, the others hushed.

"…to ask what in the high hells His Holy Lordship was thinking. All of you saw that boy. Not only do I refuse to train him, so will the Temple priests when they see what an undersized little fig we have standing between us and a Fire Sage who, by the way"—he scratched his scraggly beard—"levelled a rebel *city* with his fire currents alone."

His words lanced through Jaime's heart. He marched away and pressed himself against the door.

Breathe. Breathe. What if the priest is right? How can I save them when I couldn't even save Hilaris?

Jaime didn't notice the stoa's silence, or the footsteps approaching his door until the heavy stench of stonemist incense drowned the room.

"Prince?"

He looked up, trying not to choke.

The Lord Mayor stood in the doorway. At this distance, against daylight, he looked even younger than Jaime remembered. Long, hemp-brown curls framed his round face, his downturned eyes locked into permanent seriousness.

Jaime hurried to bow his head.

"My lord."

The mayor's sterling eyes frowned at the bannister. "Please do not take offense at anything you heard. Achuros has a good heart, but he has yet to release himself from tragedies of the past. If you would forgive us, we would speak to you about our plans."

Jaime breathed deeply. "Okay."

When they were back on ground level, the Inner Council rearranged themselves. The pretty lady—the Lord Mayor's wife—clasped her hands neatly in front of her. She redid her hair today: the top half fitted into a tight bun, falling in dark waves past her shoulder blades. The small Kaipponese hunched against a pillar, his wiry arms crossed. And the priest sat cross-legged by the firepit, his bare feet showing through the folds of his robes.

Jaime tried smiling at the priest. He received a curdled look back.

The mayor placed a fist against his chest and bowed. "Prince, a formal greeting on behalf of the City-State of Arcurea. This is my beloved wife and lady, Prescilla Menander." The young woman curtsied. "Sojin Tadamora, Captain of the City Watch." The black-eyed man offered no bow at all. "And honorable Achuros of Temple Jaypes." The priest didn't look up. "I am Florinokles Menander, the Lord Mayor—or simply Florin if you wish. The Lord bless you, Your Highness."

Your Highness.

He dizzily tucked himself away on the furthest bench. "I'm Jamian." After a pause, he added, "Pappas."

Florin's gaze brightened. "Yes, your name is familiar. Senator Gaiyus sent news of you before . . . well . . . the incident on the mountain. All the Lords of the Air Alliance received his report. It was stunning."

The Air Alliance. Didn't Lord Gaiyus say the Alliance was the remnant of an old rebellion that opposed the King's invasion?

"So you *are* part of the Air Alliance," Jaime said.

Mayor Florin nodded. "Gaiyus was an old friend of my father's before he passed."

"Is Lord Gaiyus okay? And my mamá—Hida Pappas—and Commander Julias, and the others in Townfold, are they alive?"

Florin crossed the room to a bowl of incense. "We don't know. I have sent a few letters, but nothing has come back since the Archpriestess's attack."

Jaime's shoulders slumped.

As Florin lit incense, Lady Prescilla gently took her husband's arm. "My love, if Gaiyus Sartorios were captured or dead, the whole Kingdom would know. The Air Alliance would, certainly."

The others nodded in agreement.

"So what now?" said Jaime.

"Our province is covertly loyal to the Alliance," Florin said, "but we pay tribute to a local daimyo—"

"A vassal lord to the King." Sojin glowered, like it was Jaime's fault.

"—and he has heard of unrest in his regions. Haigen Namoto will be making his way to our town soon. Prince, if he discovers you are in Arcurea, all of us will die and you will stand in chains before the King. We must be cautious with your lodging."

"Okay," Jaime said, "but we have to look for my family too. I have to know if they're alive."

"There are bigger evils we face than harm to your peasant family," Sojin snapped.

"Like *you*?" Jaime shot back.

Sojin snarled and lunged, but Florin left the pedestal and slipped between them.

"Enough, both of you!"

Jaime sat back down. The Kaipponese did not.

"We will speak of your family tonight, Prince, and I will order my bondlords to comb the south for news of them. Now, what plans did Senator Gaiyus have for you?"

"I don't know. We didn't have time to talk about it. But before I escaped, Commander Julias said..." Jaime paused. "He said I had to get training from an airpriest."

"If your eavesdropping did you any good," Sojin hissed, "then you know going to the High Temple is out of the question. Since your fire show on the mountain, the royal patrols have doubled."

Florin rubbed incense dust off his fingers. "Yes, you will have to be trained here."

"By him?" Jaime shot the priest a glare.

"Achuros is a senior airpriest and former advisor of the Old Senate. He will teach you to defend yourself, and to fight. A few months from now, you will duel the King."

"A few *months* from now?"

Sojin waved away a curl of stonemist smoke. "I thought Sartorios was proceeding with the original plan."

"Things have changed," Florin said. "Senator Gaiyus's base is in flames, and the Holy Lord knows if Julias Markus's forces stand a chance against the royal armies. The Senator would trust us to steward the Alliance in his stead."

"I vote my life on the original plan," muttered the priest.

This sparked a heated debate between the councilors. It looked like someone was going to sever off a head. Jaime stepped into the turmoil, throwing up his hands.

"Will everyone PLEASE tell me the original plan?"

Everyone quieted. Sojin glared in another direction. Lady Prescilla took a scroll curled on top of another pedestal and unfurled it over the ground.

"The Colosseum," she said.

It was an ancient map. He inched towards it, his eyes wide.

Wow.

Once in awhile, a coastal merchant would visit Mount Alaeris and talk about the world beyond the mists: how Jaypes was a mountainous island-Kingdom, how the Kingdoms of Air, Water, Fire, and Earth spanned four of five continents.

Despite the impatience of the men, Lady Prescilla paused their political dialogue and pointed to the smallest continent in the middle of the map.

"This is Jaypes, our Kingdom," she said. "And these are Glaidde and Kaippon, the Water and Fire Kingdoms."

Two continents, connected by a thin peninsula, fell vertical in the West. Jaime heard those two had been warring longer than he'd lived. The Skyrros Ocean divided Jaypes from them, fortunately.

And to the Far East—Larfour, the Kingdom of Earth.

It was larger than the other three Kingdoms combined. While Lady Prescilla named the various seas around it, Jaime stared at its giant shape. According to legend, Larfour was Guardian of the Four Kingdoms, charged with keeping the peace of the elements. During the ancient days, all the other Sages would kneel to its High Kings, Earth Sages who could raise whole mountain chains.

It was completely empty of labels.

Before Jaime could ask her more about Larfour, Lady Prescilla's finger fell to the north.

"And the Fifth Continent," she said.

His eyes opened wider. This one was bigger even than the Earth Kingdom, separated from the other Kingdoms by a narrow sea of water Prescilla called "the Dragonstail Sea." When he rearranged them in his mind, the other four continents fit like puzzle pieces against its shores.

A giant continent outside Jaypes!

The thought hurt his head. Up on Mount Alairus, Jaypes Kingdom once felt like the whole world.

"What's on the Fifth Continent?" Jaime asked.

Prescilla ran her fingers along giant peaks that layered its borders. "No one knows, Prince. Otherworldly energies thicken the air there. Mankind stopped trying to scale its mountains ages ago. Those energies would make them go mad and kill themselves."

"Cool," he breathed.

Sojin slammed a scarred hand over the pedestal. "We are not here to give the boy a geography lesson."

"He is our Prince," she said, unflinching. "He should know."

Her blunt stare made Sojin pull his gaze away. The others kept silent and let her continue.

"We were speaking of the Colosseum."

"Uh-huh," Jaime nodded, eyes big.

"Every century, on the second full moon after the summer solstice, the greatest of the Jaypan athletes gather there to compete. This is called the Greatsporting. It's one of our oldest traditions."

The mayor said, "Yes. Usheon will be there—"

"To dedicate the games to himself," the priest interrupted. His bedraggled face twisted. "Originally they were to honor the Ascaerii. The Holy Lord's divine representatives."

Jaime gasped. "What do they compete for?"

Florin rekindled the incense. "The Greatsporting consists of wrestling, foot racing, spear throwing, climbing, and charioteering, lastly. All of Jaypes's greatest sports. What they compete *for*, however—"

The mayor stopped, his round cheeks reddening.

"What?" Jaime said. "What's the prize?"

The priest dug his iron eyes into him. "Under an Ascaerii's reign? A golden amphora. This year, it will be the privilege to personally burn you at the stake."

His fingers seized the nonexistent breather in his pocket. Lady Prescilla took the priest's arm, pulling him away with a hushed rebuke. Jaime looked away, trying to maintain indifference despite the flush of his chest.

"And you're sure Usheon will be there?"

"Certainly," said Florin. "The Kingdom's greatest powers would kill to watch the Greatsporting live. A pity we won't."

"Yes," Sojin butted in, "and while our tyrant King squanders our tax money on useless traditions, the Alliance will merge and seize the silver mines of Mount Mynati. We do not need the Prince for that."

"Hold on," Jaime said. "I don't understand—"

"It will never work," Lady Prescilla snapped. "You know the state of the Alliance. No two City-States will agree on anything."

Jaime circled away from the incense, his eyes watering. "Why not?"

The priest laughed bitterly. "The Air Alliance is in havoc: twelve arrogant lords more interested in annihilating each another than serving you." At Florin's frown, the priest dipped in a bow. "Excepting you, my good lord. And now that the Head Senator is missing, no central command unifies them. The King will crush those imbeciles while they bicker over their wine and women."

"So there's no real resistance?" Jaime cried.

"There is a resistance," Sojin hissed. "The Alliance *will* come together and march on Mynati. Without silver, the King cannot import grain to feed his soldiers. There will be no need for a siege on the Capital. We will force him to surrender."

"What naiveté," the priest muttered.

They shot each other dirty looks. But Mayor Florin stayed tall as a spear.

"Everything they say has truth, Prince," he said. "Arcurea has many enemies, even among the Alliance. But we will discard our plans with Mynati. After you appeared in our city, it was apparent the Holy Lord's prophecy would truly come to pass." Jaime raised his brows. "Our god kept his promise by delivering you in the final hour. None of us expected this. And I believe Lord Jaypes will keep his promise to help you depose Usheon."

"It must happen by September first." Prescilla nodded.

Jaime blinked. "Why?"

Florin explained, "The prophecy states the Prince will overthrow Usheon Ottega in the fifteenth year of his reign. September first is that day. It also happens to fall on the day of the Greatsporting. This is not coincidence, but holy intervention."

Gods, the incense. His throat squeezed shut. He made a note to wash himself in the Estos River later. "So you're saying I have to duel him in the Colosseum?"

"If you do not, a Fire Sage will reign on in the Kingdom of Air, and the divine banestorm above us will blot out our Kingdom. This is Lord Jaypes's will." The mayor nodded, as if pondering to himself. "It is apparent."

For once, the priest nodded too. "An imbalance of elements, hence the banestorm. Yes. Just like ancient history."

"Hold on! *I'm* a Fire Sage!" Jaime cut in. "So how can *I* rule the Air Kingdom, or even overthrow the King?"

"You are different." Florin's face stayed solemn. "You are Lord Jaypes's chosen."

"Great," Jaime muttered.

Lord Jaypes can solve everything.

Without announcement, the airpriest strolled out of the room as if he didn't realize a meeting was still in session.

Jaime clenched his fists. *Hold on, give my medallion back!*

Everyone looked up but no one stopped him. Sojin turned his gaze to Florin. As his eyes narrowed, the wings on both ends extended past his dark eyebrows.

"That boy is a danger to my son. When the daimyo comes, I will inform him we have the Prince."

Florin sighed. "Sojin—"

The City Captain bowed curtly. "Lord Mayor."

And he began to march away.

"Don't mind him," Lady Prescilla told her husband. "He is a dragon without teeth."

Mayor Florin pinched his hairless chin. "We will debate later. I'm off to write Lord Haigen a welcome letter. It will be very warm indeed. Prescilla, my love, will you see that the Prince's stay is comfortable?"

They whispered at length, but Jaime barely listened. His eyes were riveted on the map. Something drew him back to the Earth Kingdom.

"What about Larfour?" he said.

He turned around. The others froze like busts outside the stoa's pillars.

"Everyone talks about Kaippon and Glaidde and the War of the West. But what about Larfour? The Earth Kingdom?"

The stares he got back was like he just announced Lord Jaypes was God of Sausages.

Something between a laugh and a scoff came out of Sojin. He briskly skipped down to the lower floor.

Finally, Florin said, "Prince, the Earth Kingdom shut its borders fifteen-hundred years ago. No one has seen a Larfene since. We know nothing of them, or of their High King, or if they are even still alive. It has long since been the Three Kingdoms."

"Oh." Jaime looked away. *Hilaris would know that. If he were still alive.*

Florin Menander shook his head. "And soon, it will be the Two Kingdoms after your father consumes our posterity."

CHAPTER TEN

Jaime barely stepped through the threshold of his new home, the rickety box where Lady Prescilla grew up, when low drums beat through the early morning air.

The lady's face went paler than goat's milk.

"What is it?" Jaime whispered.

They were gathered in the foyer—him, her, and Toran, freshly departed from the stoa. Her guards waited for her outside. More on the terracotta rooftops of the perimeter. Everyone taut as twine.

Lady Prescilla suddenly squeezed his wrist. "Stay here. Don't let anyone see you. I must find Florin."

"But—"

"No one, Prince. *No one* can see you."

With barely a curtsey, she streamed back out, a hand to her forehead. The sound of snorting horses and low murmurs buzzed from the other side of the door.

Jaime and Toran stared at each other.

"Let's go see what's happening," Toran suggested.

They raced each other to the second floor. Made of mud and clay, this house had sparse furniture and earth floors that chafed against Jaime's feet. A slew of other rickety boxes like it surrounded them. The agora, only three blocks away, blanketed their alley under noise.

Toran threw open the shutters of their bedroom. The coil in Jaime's chest twisted tighter.

Even without Prescilla telling him, Jaime knew the truth.

These were the same drums that played the night the royal army posted their banners all over Mount Alairus.

"Must be the daimyo everyone keeps talking about," Toran sniffed.

On his way to the window, Jaime rammed his knee into a three-legged stool. He swallowed a curse. Grabbed his pocket for his breather. Remembered he lost it. And this time, let the curse out.

"I'm going to go outside to look," he said.

Toran poked out his head. "Hello? Didn't you hear what the lady said?" His brown curls trembled against the stormwinds.

"I don't care. Move over." Jaime shoved his way past the hill of Toran's belly. "I'm not going to hide while the King's men come and burn people. I made that mistake before. If they want me to fight for them, I need to see who my enemy is."

"I don't know, man..."

Jaime fitted himself through the window and crawled onto the roof. Toran watched him, fiddling with his fleshy fingers. Most of the roofs here were made of terracotta tiles, unlike the flat, thatched, or mud-clay roofs at home. Twice, he almost slipped.

Gods. I wish I was home.

It wasn't hard to track the royal army. It was like some great twister was sucking the people out into daylight. Workers in only their loins. Beggars holding empty bowls. Clusters of women in thin, sleeveless peploses, murmuring to each other as they set down their clay jugs of water. Bodies clogged the banks of Panathea, the fifteen-foot main road.

Jaime slogged out of the alley, soaked to the ankle with mud, slop, and household waste. *Ugh.* He tried not to grimace. But no one noticed him—he fit right in with the crowds twisting their way up to the akropolis.

The propylaea, the columned gateway, cast diagonal shadows over the steps. Panting hard, Jaime broke away from the other bodies and climbed up a pillar of scaffolding to get to the roof.

Two standard-bearers stained the sandy uniformity of the akropolis with their albino dragon banners. The hundred riders that followed wore the standard Jaypan army wear: steel corselets and greaves half an inch thick, wooden shields gilded with bronze, throwing spears, and shortswords at the belt.

But his eyes were glued to the Kaipponese foreigner in the front.

Deer horns twisted out of his helmet and nape guards hung over his shoulders. In place of flesh, his face was black lacquer molded into a ghoulish grin. Leather plates served as his thigh guards and sleeve armor. A seven-foot-tall *kendao* in a decorated silk cover was strapped to his back.

Jaime swallowed.

The Council was already gathered outside City Hall, bowing in their white togas. Sojin was in full Jaypan armor, but as much as he was also Kaipponese—born in the Kingdom of Fire—his lower lip twitched. Chori, his fourteen-year-old son, fidgeted beside him.

Mayor Florin stood at the front, curls freshly oiled. He exchanged glances with Prescilla before the latter squeezed his hand and let go.

The Lord Mayor kneeled before the giant coursers, placing a fist against his chest.

"The City-State of Arcurea sends its warmest greetings, Lord Haigen. We have prepared food and drink for your men. Please, will you join us inside?"

It was so quiet that the only noise was his father's bloody banners whipping against the high winds.

Sojin took a step forward. "My lord, there is something imperative we must discuss."

Lady Prescilla slung a dirty look at him. Jaime's heart skipped a beat.

He means to tell the daimyo I'm here.

His eyes darted to the freckled, full-eyed boy at his waist. Jaime understood. Sojin's son was of age. Somehow, Chori Tadamora was exempt from the Royal Decree—maybe he was crippled too. Or maybe the sons of royal officials got special rights.

But if something went wrong—if the daimyo found out Jaime was here—Chori would burn.

Fortunately, the center rider, the daimyo, waved Sojin off. The City Captain obeyed with a bow. Jaime shoulders sagged in relief when the daimyo removed his mask—he *did* have a man's face. The skin under his dark, beak-shaped eyes sagged.

"Do you know why I am two days late, Mayor? You will never believe what is happening out there."

His accent was crisp, and his laughter slit the air. One by one, the other councilors laughed along nervously.

Florin began, "Pray, tell—"

"All the lands I am charged with in this cursed province have fallen to anarchy."

"Anarchy?"

"Because of the return of that little Sageling *choku* who calls himself the Prince." The daimyo turned aside and spat. "Fourteen years he has been missing, good gods! And I hear rumors that Arcurea is quietly supporting the rebel alliance, eh?"

Sojin started to open his mouth, but Florin deliberately interrupted him. "I assure you, my lord, Arcurea plays no part in this new war. We remain neutral as always."

"Neutral?"

"Loyal, my lord. To the true King."

Haigen smiled. "Of course, of course. Please forgive my ill mood, Florinokles. You must understand, I lost my sister's son in the riots. He was but twelve years of age."

"Mercy gods. I am sorry for your loss—"

"Say, is your pretty wife well?" Those inky eyes fell on Lady Prescilla. "How is your son? What is his age again? Fourteen?"

"Turning fourteen next month, my lord," she said evenly.

"Eh, yes. Born in the Prince's year, isn't he? Where is the boy? Is he so tactless that he would not come out to greet me?"

Florin smiled tightly. "He is unwell. I sent him off to his grandaunt in the north, where the air is cleaner."

"Of course you did." The daimyo leaned forward in the saddle. "Why do Jaypans conduct themselves with such bad manners?"

"My lord?"

"How is your bow to your liege lord?"

The councilors pursed their lips and turned away. When Lord Haigen continued to wait, Florin gritted his teeth and lowered himself onto his face, his white toga stamping the dirt. The standard-bearers behind the daimyo—also Kaipponese—curled their lips into sneers.

"Now, please, pronounce your fealty to His Holiness the King! Louder! Or I will cut out your tongue if you cannot make use of it."

Lady Prescilla stormed between them. "Lord Haigen, what have we done that you humiliate my husband without provocation? Our loyalty is with the King. You know this. Or shall you stand us before His Holiness to show our parts and play the flute?"

The Kaipponese handed their banners to two Jaypans and dismounted. Florin lifted his head from the dust. One of them seized his wife. The other drew his *kendao*. The formation of councilors broke, and Florin bellowed—but the halberd's blade stopped against the surface of Prescilla's throat.

"Or shall I cut out your tongue, you horrible snake?"

"Lord Haigen!" Florin rose, struggling to keep his voice civil. "As I said, there is *food and drink—*"

"Get back on your belly! The only food and drink I prefer in this pit of misery is your wife. I shall ease the hysteria of her lower parts since you seem unable to do so, Mayor."

Jaime's eyes widened as two Jaypan soldiers seized Florin. He leapt off the cornice to get to ground level. The standard-bearer drove a stake into the ground, and a lard-faced Jaypan drew his shortsword. Prescilla screamed. They hacked off Florin's toga and tied him naked against the standard.

"You there!"

Lord Haigen pointed two fingers in Sojin's direction. The Captain shifted uncomfortably. Not him. Chori, who stood meekly at his father's hip.

"Take this horse's droppings"—the daimyo tossed him a burlap sack—"and give the mayor a wipe, please."

"Lord." Sojin reached for his *kendao*. "I object—"

"*Gozai'masu, baikan!* Any commissioned Kaipponese who whores around with Jaypans should lose his head!"

Chewing his lip, Chori glanced at his father. The elder man gave a curt nod. Jaime's nails dug into his palms as opposing gales tore his mind—one screaming at him to step in and fight, the other warning him to stay hidden or get them all killed.

What'll Lord Haigen do to this city if you run in front of Florin to protect him?

Chori dragged the sack and stopped before the Lord Mayor, kneeling. One hand closed around a tiny turd.

"*More!*"

The boy flinched, and he scooped up a handful. He wouldn't

look at Florin. Chori whispered something to the mayor. Florin's eyes were low, but he nodded.

Hands trembling, Sojin's son rubbed wet dung against the Lord Mayor's chest. The royal army broke into roaring laughter. The Arcurean councilors clenched their fists and forced their gazes away.

"His face!"

Chori froze.

"*His face*, boy!" Lord Haigen reined his horse forward. "Open your mouth, Lord Florinokles, and orate! Or I'll stick your wife's throat."

Laughter clapped and rolled over the akropolis. Lady Prescilla dropped her eyes, but they blazed with fury.

Hunched over, one hand to his belly, the daimyo yelled, "So, Captain! What is it you needed to discuss?"

Jaime's heart leapt into his throat. *It's time. He's going to hand me over.*

Sojin held his steel gaze steady. "Taxes, Lord. The people are not equipped to meet the rising rates."

Taxes?

Jaime wheeled away into an alley, pressed himself against the propylaea.

He didn't give me away. Why?

Suddenly, he realized these high lords were as powerless as him. Actually *more*, since they weren't Sages. It was so clear now. So long as he refused to lead the war, *this* would continue to happen forever. Traitor airpriests and petty constables forcing humiliation, and pain, and death on thousands of Jaypans—just so the King could punish him.

Jaime's breath shallowed.

Earlier that day, Lady Prescilla had told him, "Priest Achuros lives on Chikos Pagos Hill, on the southside of the akropolis."

He knew what he had to do.

⁓⌘⁓

Overhead, the blustery sky darkened into early afternoon. Wind turbines hummed furiously as Jaime climbed a wooded outcropping across the akropolis. The winding path ended at a small square temple.

Melancholy song notes eddied through the olive trees.

The eerie melody stirred up ancient memories from his past. It was the same song Lady Prescilla hummed to him his first night at the stoa.

Where do I know that from?

And there he was—a white-robed, shaggy-maned shape on cracked steps of the temple, peeling fingers moving across a wooden flute. The medallion sat across his lap.

"Your Grace?"

The song continued.

"…Achuros?"

The priest lowered the flute. Jaime shuffled forward. "How do you know that song?"

A soft snort. "It's a Jaypan lullaby. When Lairdos Ascaerii was King, any Jaypan would have known it." The priest's eyes thinned as Jaime sat down beside him. "What are you doing?"

"I want to learn Air."

The priest's eyes narrowed even more.

"Look, I get that I'm Usheon's son. But this is about more than us. Didn't you see what they did to Florin today? And did you hear the awful things Haigen said about Lady Prescilla?"

"I did not. I prefer not to involve myself with worldly affairs."

Jaime clenched his fists. "Then I'll *tell* you about it! Or do you want me to tell you about the day my brother burned, what that was like?"

The priest rose. "You're a Fire Sage."

"I can learn Air." He clenched to the medallion. "It responded to me before, on Mount Alairus. I raised a banestorm—"

"Tch. Tomorrow morning, first light."

CHAPTER ELEVEN

The King's daimyo departed that night. But the Menanders were nowhere to be seen. Neither did they send word about his training.

It's not unlikely that they're dead.

Soon as blue dawnlight waxed against the earth floor, Jaime shoved off the blankets. A chiton awaited him inside a strongbox under the window, a single white sheet of fresh linen. It was there when he first arrived at his new home. But it cut his heart to consider shedding off the exomis his mother handwove for him.

After a pause, he stripped off his old clothes, slipped it on, and fastened the leather belt around his waist. The sandals came on last, strapped up to his calves. This was the kind of thing Hilaris used to wear.

Jaime glanced across the room. Toran was in the other bed, his eyelids fluttering. Low pleas escaped his mouth.

Toran Binn also had nightmares.

About what?

He stepped forward to shake his friend awake—and stopped. A silhouette the size of his fist was slinking down the wall above Toran.

Spider.

Four owlish eyes, a tuft of hair standing straight up from its head. It didn't stop until it was on Toran's bed. As if sensing Jaime's gaze, it lowered its hairy pincers, blinking at him.

Jaime's breathing quickened.

It looked like the first spider he saw on Toran the first time they met in the Krete Forests. Only this one was slightly bigger. The size of *two* thumbs put together.

One, two, three, four...

Counting. His breathing uneven.

Jaime glanced around the room for an object to smash it with. But the second it settled onto Toran's chest, his friend's desperate murmurs went silent. The nightmares faded into tense sleep.

Jaime stared at the spider. The spider stared at Jaime.

You'll be late if you don't get going. Toran can help you kill it later.

He forced his back to the disgusting thing and hurried out the door.

It took less than ten minutes to reach Chikos Pagos with a brisk jog. Today, the private courtyard was empty. Jaime slowed his pace, glancing at the dried fountains, the headless bronze statues of Jaypan heroes guarding the temple with their crumbling spears.

He climbed the steps, stuck his head between the pillars.

The single-roomed temple, stale and musty, smelled like a long-forgotten past. Old charcoal crusted the empty firepits. At one time, the frescoes of great Jaypan orators and scribes must have been a brilliant sight; now, they were faded, covered in sloppy scrawls.

His sandal stepped on a loose panel. Jaime glanced at the ground. *What is that?*

"You're late."

The voice behind him startled him around. A shape stood between the pillars, face shadowed, blocking out the daylight.

"No, I'm not!" Jaime cried. "You're early."

The priest circled him.

He tapped a fan against his palm—it was the length of Jaime's arm, two tassels of dyed purple cascading from a gilded handle. The individual panels were tipped with the ivory from elhorn antlers.

Where could a deadbeat like Achuros have gotten something as extravagant as this?

"Sallow complexion, small as a goat—what, were you the runt of your family?"

"Were you the drunkard of the High Temple?" Jaime pointedly glanced at the open bottles of wine stacked behind the firepit. The priest glared at him.

"Outside."

His new teacher took them to a wide, paved step at the edge of the cliff, where the land dropped off sharply into wild country. No barricade, no walls, nothing to keep him from falling to his death.

For a flash second, Jaime's heart panged. This rock hill reminded him of the steep escarpments of Mount Alairus. He wanted to see the silver skies again, smell the minty nips of the frostwinds.

No, you don't.

Accept it. You'll never see home again.

"Learning to control any elemental energy takes enormous discipline," said the priest, "which I suppose you lack. The best Sages spend hard years training into adulthood—mighty Kings like Viro Tazuga of Kaippon. Gildas Brennte of Glaidde. Like your bloody father." His hard eyes fell on Jaime's. "In the pitifully dragged course of my life, I have *never* seen a Sage master his element in less than a year. It is impossible."

"I can do it."

"We'll see." The priest turned away. "Before we begin, I require, as sworn airpriest of the High Temple of Jaypes, that you make an oath."

"An oath?"

"We of Temple Jaypes train Sages—"

Jaime raised his hand. "So we can learn how to fight—"

"Precisely *not* to start fights." The priest slid the fan open. "The gods gifted their bloodlines with the gift of the elements. Nothing"—his voice fell low—"*nothing* must compromise the unity of Air, Water, Fire, and Earth. That is what the Sages and the four High Temples protect: the Unity."

Jaime blinked. "The Unity."

"Do you know The Legend of the Four?"

That's the same tome Hilaris gave me before he burned.

The Legend was the origins story of the Four Kingdoms, chronicling how the four warrior-heroes—Jaypes, Glaidde, Kaippon, and Larfour—became gods. It was through these gods that the first Sages were breathed to life.

Jaime knew little of ancient history. After Usheon received Lord Jaypes's prophecy, he burned every Jaypan library his armies could find. Then he forbade anyone from learning any history prior to November 24, 2981, the day he established New Jaypes.

Of course, Hilaris was well-versed in Jaypan literature and philosophy. Lord Gaiyus kept a secret library somewhere under his villa. The nobility swore that books nowadays were more valuable than silver, but Jaime still preferred a himation or a filling bowl of stew. More utility.

"No," Jaime said. "Not really."

The priest pulled at his lower eyelids. "I hope you at least know the state of our world prior to the birth of our gods?"

"I don't. No one taught me."

"Well, *I'll* teach you. Banestorms tore up the earth and drowned the valleys with rain. Tidal waves flooded the coastlands, fire fell from the sky, earthquakes swallowed up entire tribes." The priest squeezed his fan between the soft flesh of his palms. "That is what will happen if one element falls out of balance—" He closed his hands together. The fan's folds bowed and snapped under the pressure. "The Four Kingdoms as we know it will collapse into darkness and destruction."

So dramatic.

Jaime glanced at the sky. "Isn't it already happening? Lord Gaiyus said when I touched the medallion, it started a banestorm."

"Yes, boy. Sartorios is right."

"Will it pass?"

"Not so long as a Fire Sage sits on our throne."

"But I'm a—"

"Florin already told you, you are Lord Jaypes's chosen." Even as the priest spoke, hesitance drawled out his words. "All the Ascaeriis are dead. If our god did not want you on our throne, then this storm would have already consumed the Air Kingdom."

I don't believe in gods. If the gods were real, Lord Jaypes wouldn't have let Hilaris die.

But Jaime bit his tongue and said instead, "What's the oath you mentioned?"

"Kneel," the priest said. "We shall speak it in Ancient Empyrean, the language of our gods and ancestors. It has much power."

After a pause, Jaime obeyed.

"*Mì*, Jamian Ottega, *Zan Jefes*—"

He repeated and stammered over his surname.

"*Anyitta ìn hijal taksen n'quélaan*—"

Jaime held up his hands. "Wait. What are you saying?"

Priest Achuros continued. Jaime sighed and repeated until they finished. Then the priest translated:

"I, Jamian Ottega, Prince of Jaypes, swear by the Church of Holy Sages to uphold the Unity of Air, Water, Fire, and Earth, by serving as Warden of my element, and Peacekeeper of my Kingdom, wielding sword and shield to protect the people, until my last breath should fail me."

When Achuros finished, Jaime nodded quietly.

Wow.

Every Sage in history spoke that same oath, dating all the way back to the first Sage-Kings of the Four Kingdoms. The blood in his body coursed to life. Somehow, he felt bonded to these old Sages.

Did Usheon take that oath too when he became King?

Priest Achuros's voice quieted. "Good. Now sit."

Jaime obeyed.

"There are two steps to mastering any element. The second is known by everyone: mastering the mind techniques to manipulate your element. The first step is cared for by few."

His eyes shone. "What is it?"

"Meditation."

His shoulders slumped. "What? Really?"

"The success of this step distinguishes Sages from the masses of mediocrity. Countless royals were unable to discover their inner power because of impatience. Most, in fact."

"Okay, so what do I have to do? Just sit here and think about nothing? For how long?"

"Until you form a bond with your element. In other words, you find a way to tap into The Empyrean."

Jaime blinked.

The priest slapped his head. "The spirit realm. Gods, boy, did they teach you nothing on that mountain of yours?"

"Lord Gaiyus taught my brother, but I was selling my mother's textiles in the marketplace every day," Jaime snapped. "So no, I know nothing."

Priest Achuros clasped his flaking hands together, his temper cooling. "The Empyrean is where all elemental energy originates from. It's made entirely of *avai*, the energy inside all living things. When man bonds his *avai* with The Empyrean, he awakens his greatest powers." The priest glanced at the clouds passing the skies. "Mm, I cannot explain it, but you will know when it happens. The ancient scribes say the way you perceive the world will change forever."

"But...I never felt any bond when I drew Fire."

"Well, I am an airpriest, not a firepriest."

"Well, I thought only Sages can use the elements, not priests."

"Not if we hold this." The priest held up the medallion with a sharp sigh. "Each High Temple has its own Relic. Air will never respond to me the way it did to Lairdos and his kin because I am not an Ascaerii. I can raise gusts; an Ascaerii can raise banestorms."

"I'm not an Ascaerii," Jaime snapped.

"No, you are an Ottega, unfortunately."

They exchanged venomous looks. Jaime crossed his legs the way the priest did, both feet balanced on his thighs. The medallion dropped tersely over his chest.

"Clasp your hands in front of you."

Jaime stiffened when the fan rapped his back.

"You are a Prince, not a Kaipponese rice noodle. Sit up straight. You only need to break into The Empyrean once. After the first time, it will become easier to tap into its energy. Now, let's see if there is truly a Sage in you."

If my father made the bond, I can too.

He huffed out a breath. "Can you at least tell me what I'm supposed to look for?"

"Clear your mind. Of your emotions, your senses, your thinking. Try to focus on your breaths."

"But that's focusing on something."

No answer this time.

Focus on breathing.

Of all things, why breathing? The one thing he'd struggled with for a lifetime. It seemed that the more he tried to be Prince, the worse his asthma became.

Breathe deeply, Jaime.

His mother's voice.

Somewhere in the distance, a dog barked. The hill turbines hummed against the gnashing winds. The brand mark on his wrist itched madly. Then came an eagle's cry, the clanking of construction, coarse laughter—the city was waking. *Gods.* And something stank. The airpriest—he smelled of livestock and sour wine. How long had both of them sat out here already?

His breathing turned ragged the more he focused on it.

One, two, three, four…

Counting like Hida told him to do whenever his asthma tried to squeeze his throat shut.

Where was his mother? Was she still alive? Was she hurt? Was she worrying about him, or cursing him for the destruction of the Pappas family? Trading her blood son for a monster's spawn—did regret ever crossed her mind for saving him that day in the foothills of Mount Alairus?

Jaime rubbed the melted flesh on his wrist.

The morning after a royal official branded him, Hida took him to Jaypes's Pantheon. Jaime was five at the time, maybe six. At the altar, she offered Lord Jaypes grain, a flask of olive oil, honey, and the silver pendant Hektor gave her on their marriage night. It was all she owned at the time. Hida had worn that pendant under her peplos every day for as long as Jaime could remember.

She dropped to her knees, pressing her forehead in the grime where hundreds of feet had walked.

"Protect him, Holy Lord," she murmured. "Take the air in my lungs and give it to him. Heal him."

Tears gathered in her eyes like liquid glass. One by one, they stained the ground.

As the memory faded, Jaime's thumb circled the same brand his mother had prayed over. Jaime saw it now: so many sacrifices on his behalf, beginning the day she plucked him out of the freezing wilderness. Fourteen years of putting him first. Hida Pappas was the only reason he was alive.

She was like air: steady and constant, imperceptible when she was there. But the second she was gone, he was suffocating.

A hand gripped his shoulder.

"Boy."

His eyes snapped open. Dampness was trickling down his cheeks. Jaime quickly turned and wiped them away.

"Sorry. The winds are stinging my—"

"We are done for the day."

"What?" Jaime planted his rear against the ground. "But it's not even afternoon—"

"Before both of us shrivel from your woolgathering. Gods, making a bond on the first day! Go get some bread, or cereal, try to come back tomorrow."

Priest Achuros's blasé tone needled him in the chest.

His lungs burned for his breather. But he refused to bow to panic and have an asthma attack in front of this stinking old man. So he picked himself up, started walking—and forced the air out of his throat.

"I'll try to come back tomorrow if you try to give more of a shit."

The airpriest went rigid.

A twister of cedar leaves leapt up and gnashed at them with the colors of fire. For a second, it looked like the old man was going to apologize. But his iron gaze steeled. He peered up at the sphere of thunderclouds breathing whole mountains into shadow.

"The days of the Sages are over," the priest murmured. "And both of us are already dead."

CHAPTER TWELVE

Jaime barely made it to the base of Chikos Pagos Hill when someone tugged him aside.

"Hey, man. We gotta talk."

Toran's face was barely visible in the falling dark. Jaime wrenched his arm away, unable to look at him. But Toran blocked him with his belly.

"I saw what happened with the priest, man. Don't listen to him. He's a sour chunk of cheese."

Jaime sank his hands into his face, struggling to hold down the storm in his chest.

"Why don't you *ever* mind your own business, Toran? I need you to just *leave me alone.*"

As soon as those words came out of Jaime's mouth, he immediately regretted them.

Toran's face was unreadable, but he felt hurt flickering through his friend's silence.

"I'm sorry." Jaime turned away. "I'm just—I need sleep."

"I bought us a surprise from the marketplace. It's by the river. Wanna come with me to get it?"

A weak laugh.

"Toran, you wouldn't be able to pay for a grape if your life depended on it."

"Wrong, man. I've been picking olives in the mayor's orchards and crushing them at the mill. They pay me nice."

Jaime raised a brow.

Toran crossed his arms. "What the hell do you think I've been doing while you've been out? Lying around, gobbling up pomegranates and wine?"

Jaime rubbed his chest. It still stung from Priest Achuros's jab. Any second now, his knees would break. Hida could well be hamstrung above a firepit while the King barraged her with interrogations and torture. Toran didn't know how close he was to falling apart.

But somehow, Toran, of *all* people, could feel this. In that moment, Jaime realized he needed a friend.

"Okay," he whispered. "Let's go."

They cut around Chikos Pagos, avoiding the one-hundred-foot cliffs and their bordering fortifications. The streets thickened as they approached the agora. City guards shouted at muleteers, sweat pouring through their helmets as they attempted to direct the wagons. A few workmen, wearing knee-length singlets, lingered on the scaffolds of two-story apartments. Jaime kept his face hooded from all of them.

The evening light waned. Indoor oil lamps and temple firepits flickered to life. As they drew nearer to the Estos River slithering under the northern gate, the city lights faded behind them.

Toran sat down under a plane tree and pulled a sack out of a patch of shrubs. "Here."

Jaime peeked inside.

Two folded sheets of paper, made of mulberry fibers, rubbed against his fingertips. But there was even more: a set of brushes, a stick of black ink, and an inkstone at the bottom.

"What's all this stuff for?"

"Here, lemme show you."

Toran took the inkstone and filled the square depression with a layer of water. Then he rubbed the inkstick against the stone until the water turned black. Jaime watched in growing fascination. Toran set the papers side by side. Dipped the brush into ink. Several letters swam to life across one of the papers.

After he finished, Toran unfolded it, a proud grin on his face. "A lantern. Kaipponese-style."

Jaime felt around his papery edges. "You found all this in the marketplace?"

"Yeah, and I knew you needed one too." He fished out two candlesticks from the stack. "When I was a kid, before the war separated me from my family, my ba and ma would buy these on festival days. You're supposed to write a single character on it, or draw a picture if you can't write." Toran pointed at his word. "That character's supposed to represent a wish or prayer. My parents always said your lantern would find its way to the family's guardian spirit. If you were in favor with it, it would make your prayer come true."

Jaime's eyes brightened. "Cool."

"You got any family spirits?"

"I guess we'll find out. What's your lantern say?"

"'Light.' In Moderna. I don't know how to write in Kaipponese characters."

Jaime studied the individual strokes of the letters. "What's 'light' supposed to mean?"

Toran pulled out a separate bag and offered him a round, fried pastry. "Honey nougat?"

"What do we do with those?"

"Eat it, stupid." Toran shoved it into his mouth. "Write a prayer on your lantern." Jaime began to protest that he didn't know how to write Moderna, but Toran said, "It's okay, just figure out what you wanna write, and I'll show you how."

Jaime stared at the blank canvas of his lantern, thinking.

What do *I want to write?*

His mind flitted back to his memories with Hida—her deft fingers on the loom, the wrinkles on her face as she prayed to Lord Jaypes at the Air Pantheon, her smiles in the kitchen as toddler Jaime jabbered away about the goats he'd chased with his best friend Peri Kreed.

When Hida Pappas smiled, the house blazed to life. Not like the oil lamps, or even the fires of the outdoor braziers where elders told stories of Old Jaypes—brighter. Something in her burned much, much brighter.

"'Sun,'" Jaime said.

Toran cocked his thick brows.

"My mamá told me about the sun a few times," he explained. "Before Usheon became King. I want to see what it looks like. And bring it back for her."

His friend nodded. Jaime took hold of the brush. Toran gripped the upper tip, showing him how to dip it into the inkstone. Together, they drew three letters onto the thin paper.

"*Sun,*" Jaime whispered. He looked up. "What do we do with it now?"

"Unfold it." Toran expanded his into a spider-shaped oval. "Like this."

Jaime mirrored him. Toran helped him place candles inside. Lit them. The black letters on Jaime's lantern flared to life.

Toran knelt on the riverbank, lantern in hand. "Ready?"

"Let's release them on four," Jaime said. He counted: *one, two, three.*

And on *four,* they let go.

Their lanterns bobbed away downstream, side by side. Little blossoms lighting a course through the night. Suddenly, the distance didn't seem as vast and dark as before.

"So"—Jaime tilted his gaze—"what's 'light' mean?"

A new pastry tumbled into Toran's mouth.

"I think you and I are alike, Juno. We're both walking through the dark. I don't know where I'm going, not really. I don't know why I'm here." Another pastry. "Some days, it feels like I'm dead-walking through the same things—wake up, try to get through the war for eighteen hours, sleep. Do it again. No purpose. No light along the way. Just one long night of *forever.*"

Jaime fixed his eyes on Toran's lantern, bobbing its way through the dark, winding path of the river.

I don't know anything about him.

The realization hit him like a cold splash in the water.

"Toran," he said, "what happened to your family?"

"Some nights, it gets so dark, I worry I won't ever wake up. I can't stand looking in mirrors." Another pastry. "And sometimes, I hear things."

"What kinds of things?"

Pause.

"Just nightmares. I have a lot of them."

"I know." Jaime lowered his voice. "I've heard."

"I wake you?"

"I've probably woken you and the whole city with *mine,* according to Sojin."

Toran laughed dryly. "I get what you're going through, 'cos I think I'm going through something similar. Only my war is mostly in my head."

"I'll ask Lady Prescilla for a mirror. We'll put it across from your bed. I'll show you, you're not *too* horrible looking."

"Any worse looking than you?"

"Not as fat as you."

A snort of laughter. "Not as tiny as you, little man."

"You know, I didn't want to say it, but I'm glad I'm not alone."

Toran Binn held out his hand, his large, double-lidded eyes finding Jaime's in the dark. "Let's find the sun together?"

"Yeah," Jaime whispered. "And the light."

They shook, their hands sealing onto each other's tightly.

CHAPTER THIRTEEN

Lady Prescilla came several days later, announcing that Lord Florin wanted to invite him over for dinner—but the fresh bruises on her wrists made Jaime freeze.

"Prince, is everything alright?"

He stood at the center of the staircase. When she followed his eyes, she abruptly pulled the train of her sleeves higher.

"I should ask you, my lady."

"I am fine." She looked away. "Will you come?"

Florin wouldn't...would he?

His head whirled. Suddenly, he remembered the night the Archpriestess's soldiers took hold of his mother. The way one son of a bastard struck her face. Jaime trembled with fury.

"Who?"

"Please." She smiled uncomfortably. "Let the matter alone."

"Did Florin—"

"I said, let it alone."

The steel in her voice cut through the heat in his shoulders. Jaime relented, nodding without a word.

"It would honor my husband and me greatly if you join us tonight."

He forced a smile. "I'll come to dinner, my lady."

A small skiff awaited them on the Estos River. Together, they sailed away from the agora and into the northernmost outskirts of the town, where the garbage-filled roads drained into airy pastures. An array of poplars saluted them as they passed. The warm breezes carried the earthy smell of the Lord Mayor's horses, grazing quietly, their coats as burnished as the moon.

Gods.

The foreignness of this city pulled his chest taut all over again. Reminding him how far away the wild kingpines of home were. The way the whole mountain whispered as frigid airstreams passed through their branches. A selfish part of him wanted that back. He was done with the huffs and snappy comments of an airpriest who despised him.

Lady Prescilla's soft hand fell on his shoulder, as if she understood his thoughts.

Half an hour later, the Menander's villa glowed on the opposite bank. Pink bougainvillea flowers hugged the colonnade. But despite its pastoral beauty, gloom hung over their jetty.

A servant greeted them at the doors, and another led them through the fountained garden that opened up before a colonnade walkway. The sky was warm. Silver moonlight limned the clouds.

Jaime's mouth fell open.

It was like walking through a dream. The frescoes on these walls showed a shy, boyish Florin offering a peony to Prescilla. This swept into an autumn painting where both lovers rode together on a white stallion into a storm of windflowers.

He stopped and drank in the fresco.

Jaime ached for *this*.

True love.

You'll never have it. You chose to give up everything to fight the King. You know you can't defeat him. And that's okay. At least you'll die trying. That's more important than something as childish as true love.

He forced himself to walk on.

As soon as they stepped into the andron, mouthwatering smells liquified his senses. Infinite dishes glittered on the center table: dates and figs the size of his eyeballs, mussels and rare Kyros eels basting in cumin. The center plate flourished pig's belly roasted in fragrant silphium and vinegar. Dessert was flat cake drizzled in steaming honey. He'd never experienced a formal dinner in an andron—that was reserved only for politicians, famous philosophers, and nobles. Hilaris probably had plenty back in Lord Gaiyus's villa.

Something groaned loudly.

"Sorry." Jaime's ears warmed.

Lord Florin smiled, rising from one of five couches positioned in a *U*. "We are honored to have you, Prince." He bowed. "It is long past due for a meal together."

Lady Prescilla curtsied. "Long past."

He stayed in place, wary, the lady's bruises still in the back of his mind. But Prescilla seemed to sense this, and she offered him a smile to put him at ease.

Finally, Jaime bowed low. "Thank you, my lord and lady—"

"No need to bow to us, my Prince." Florin offered a hand to the vacant couch in the middle of the *U*. "Please."

He took his place, wobbling over the formalities of the Jaypan upper class. Nobles ate reclining.

So weird.

At home, Jaime and his mother always sat at their table for meals.

Everything looked right: Florin wore his white mayor's toga wrapped in a sash of silver and purple, which complemented his wife's lilac dress. Lady Prescilla led polite inquiry about how he was liking Arcurea.

Nothing overtly out of place.

Except Prescilla didn't mention his training at all. And more incense was burning than usual in the holder at the center of the table. Florin's smiles were scarce. Pursed lips, sagging eye bags. A noticeable physical distance walled husband from wife. It was a glaring contrast to the way Jaime first met them—always holding hands, always standing close together. The air seemed pregnant with thunder.

Jaime wiped his mouth. "No more about me. How are both of you? That day with Lord Haigen—"

"The past is the past," the mayor said. "I understand Lord Jaypes has higher purposes for his ways. Forgive my manner, my Prince. Our minds and hearts have been absent. We have not been serving you as we should—"

"No."

They stared at him as he breathed into his hands.

"Can we…just be honest with each other? What Haigen did was my fault. Sojin's right. I'm responsible for the Royal Decree."

Florin looked away. "My love, why don't we bring it out now?"

Prescilla whispered sharply, "It is not to give, I told you."

"We already discussed—"

"*No.*"

Jaime sat awkwardly as Florin abruptly stood and called for the servant. Lady Prescilla seethed in silence.

What in the four gods is going on?

After a moment, the servant returned with a long, narrow box. Florin took it and held it out to him.

"Come closer, Jaime. Silla and I wanted to give you a gift."

"A…gift?"

Jaime swallowed a lump of goat cheese and opened the lid.

A translucent cloak glittered inside, its sleeves wide and airy. He lifted it up. And coughed on his cheese. The cloth cascaded down to his knees, fine and light as cattle-skin parchment.

"Thanks, but what is it?"

"A windcloak," said Florin. "During the days of the Ascaerii reign, when a child came of age, his parents would bestow him with one. It enabled him to ride the Kingdom's air currents. Most were mapped out by our ancestors long ago; there are thousands. Every time you see an airmarker, it means a current is nearby. They look a bit like headstones."

Jaime's eyes lit up. "I've seen a few of them before. There's one outside Townfold, by my foster papá's grave."

The mayor nodded. "And there is a marker outside our city. That is for Luna, a local current. Travelling by current is faster than any horse in the realm."

"Good skies, Florin." Prescilla shot to her feet and tossed out an arm. "Look outside at the air currents. Fourteen years it has been since any child could wear a windcloak without getting shredded into pieces. And now, with this banestorm that's smothering the Air Kingdom—"

"My love." Florin grit his teeth. "You are embarrassing us—"

"Embarrassing us? Does the city know I write your speeches—or would that embarrass them?"

Florin slowly rose to his feet. Prescilla's whole body was shaking. The mayor crossed the room and took her arm.

Jaime sucked in a breath.

Prescilla Menander burst into sobs. Her husband took her other shoulder and gently led her to the doorway.

What is going on?

Florin called one of the servants to take her upstairs. As her choking cries faded, the mayor relit the incense on the table, cupping his face into his hands.

"I am so sorry, Prince."

The sudden blossom of incense wracked his lungs, but Jaime came to sit by him. "What happened, my lord? Is it…something I did?"

"It is nothing you did." The mayor stared at an invisible stain on the ceiling. "You are a Sage, perhaps Jaypes's last. We feel very pressured to help you succeed."

Jaime reached over for the gift box and handed it back to Florin. "I can't take this. This belongs to your son…doesn't it?"

Florin shook his head. "Aulos is your age, but he is not our Holy Lord's chosen emissary. It would honor him for you to have this. Prescilla too. I apologize that it has been a difficult week for all of us."

All of us.

Suddenly, he understood why they invited him for dinner. They knew about what happened between him and Priest Achuros. Their mutual refusal to talk to each other.

The weight of the gift pulled at the strings in his chest.

My family.

Jaime used to think "family" meant the people you shared blood with, or in his case, the people he shared a house with. Hida was once his entire family, but now she was gone. Hilaris left him for Gaiyus. His blood father left him for the throne.

All this time, Jaime thought he was alone.

But love for the Menanders swelled deep in his heart, hurting every fiber of his skin. For the first time in his life, he realized he could have more than one family. It was a gift that he had been born an orphan—because he could *choose* his family. As many as he wanted.

"Thank you," Jaime whispered.

Florin's towering height left the couch and came down to his eye level.

"There is an old legend. It goes like this: A warrior-hero named Jaypes Ascaerii told his tribe he was going to ride out to quell a banestorm. They laughed and sneered at him. His chieftain told him, 'You cannot overcome this storm.' And do you what the warrior said?"

I know this story.

Smiling through his tears, Jaime quoted Hilaris the night before his death: "He said, 'I am the storm.'"

Florin nodded. "You are the storm."

"I'm sorry about what I said."

Jaime's sandals stopped outside the temple, but all he saw was Achuros's back to a pillar.

"I want to try again."

A long pause.

"Sorry is not enough," the priest said. "You are not ready."

Jaime circled the pillar till they were face to face. "Look, I was upset over what Lord Haigen did—and a lot of things that happened since last fall. But I'll stay here and meditate every day till I make the bond—"

Priest Achuros held up a hand and turned away. "Boy, all you have shown me is that you neither understand or respect the elements. You are not ready."

"Well, what about you?" he seethed. "You don't care about anyone but yourself. You were out here playing the flute and drinking while Lord Haigen forced Florin to eat horse manure—"

The priest's voice flared. "You come to me expecting help, then throw accusations my way. You're no better than the entitled whoreson who sits on our throne! Gods have mercy! I'll hang myself if you're truly the one Lord Jaypes chose to replace him!"

Despite the urge to strangle the priest, Jaime sighed.

"You know what?"

The priest was already storming back into the temple.

"You're right."

Priest Achuros stopped.

Jaime fell to a kneel and bowed his head. "When I promised the city I would stay to learn Air, I knew I had to make this worth it. For my mother's life." He lowered his eyes. "I don't know how to be Prince, but I want to learn. I *need* to. From you."

The priest's iron brows furrowed.

Suddenly, the medallion thrummed against his chest. Jaime startled, taking it out from under his chiton. Something compelled the priest to reach out and take it. As soon as the old man's hands touched its vibrating energies, an image flashed across Jaime's vision.

A young boy with dark hair and stormy eyes kneeling before the airpriest, in the same way, saying similar words, in another time and place.

The vision vanished the next second.

Jaime blinked.

Priest Achuros stumbled backwards.

"You saw it too?" Jaime breathed.

"Who are…?"

Jaime stood. "Who what?"

"You remind me of someone I use…used to know." The priest gripped the fan tucked in his sash. Then he shook his head. "It was a long time ago. Never mind."

The priest's fingers were shaking slightly.

"Very well, let's try again. Sit."

Jaime obeyed. Priest Achuros looped the medallion back over his neck.

"Left hand gripping your right thumb. Good. Now tuck both hands in your lap. Perhaps I should have begun our first session with clearer instructions. Today, try focusing on nothing but the wind. We'll pick up from there."

Jaime closed his eyes and levelled his breathing. It was easier to shut noise out since Arcurea was quiet today. Still, his legs went numb after twenty minutes, and his breathing grew strained the more he paid attention to it. The priest was merciful enough to allow him to take a short break and move after the second hour.

"Your Grace," he said.

"What am I, a bloodstained arch-wench that you should address me that way?"

"Achuros." Cough. "What's going on between Florin and Prescilla?"

"She carries Lord Haigen's seed."

Jaime stopped in mid-stretch. "*What?* How do you know?"

"I am an airpriest." Achuros snorted. "By the grace of Air, I felt another *avai* pulsing in her."

Jaime shook his head. "But that means—"

"That means Lord Haigen will be back in the spring to take what he thinks is his. Child and mother."

Suddenly, Jaime understood the bruises—and the tension between both Menanders last night.

What would Florin do to the daimyo?

What *could* Florin do without breaking his disguise of loyalty and jeopardizing Jaime's life? So long as Jaime trained with Achuros, no one could know he was here, especially the royal authority.

"I'll help Florin kill him," Jaime vowed.

The airpriest smiled wryly. "Unless you make the bond before then, Haigen will kill *you*. That you can be sure of."

CHAPTER FOURTEEN

On the way home, a surprise awaited Jaime in the agora.

His stomach plummeted.

A hundred mounted city guards were amassing outside the civil buildings. They lugged supplies onto wagons yoked to oxen, fitted on their cuirasses, kissed their lovers goodbye. There was talk of sea travel to the west coast to avoid Jaypes's mountains.

He had to find out what was happening.

Jaime skipped behind a clothesline hanging behind the apartment stores.

Chori, Sojin's son, was at the edge of the marketplace, mounted on his own black gelding. The boy was fully armored and bore the military honor of carrying the royal standard. Even with just his small *kendao*, he looked enviously impressive from up high.

Jaime cleared his throat.

Chori's eyes darted to the square of diaphanous cloth, then to his skinny legs below it.

"Where are you going?" Jaime said.

The boy reined his gelding closer. "Oh, it's just you. Lord Haigen is out crushing rebellions in the central plains, and we offered to bring him reinforcements." Chori raised his head smugly. "I'm going out to fight."

"I thought Lord Haigen's our enemy—"

"Keep your voice down, you fool." Chori glanced at the motley bodies clogging Panathea Way. "That's not *really* why we are leaving. My father's going to meet an old friend, the Lord Mayor of Korinthia City. When we come back in the spring, we'll be leading five thousand men."

"Why?"

"Why do you think? You've been nothing but a liability ever since you came. My ba's not going to wait on the Air Alliance anymore. Lord Gaiyus is dead, he has to be. After Ba petitions our allies in Korinthia for an army, he's going to lead the march on Mount Mynati's silver mines himself. We'll force the King to surrender and end the war without you."

His chest spiked. "The mayor's allowing this?"

"Sure." Chori sneered. "You're disposable. After we come back, Ba's handing you over to the Archpriestess—"

"I don't believe you."

"Believe what you want. While you're burning in the Capital, that'll buy us more time to prepare. The King's eyes will be on you, not us. It's a perfect plan." Chori threw up his head and gaggled. "Gods, may the Ottegas destroy themselves!"

Jaime shoved the clothesline aside. The gusts suddenly picked up, snapping at their heels. Jaime was about to lunge when a shadow fell over them.

"*Gozai'masu*, Chori!"

Abruptly, the laughter stopped.

The City Captain towered above all the agora's heads. His white mantle cascaded down his destrier's flank. All of the Kingdom's skylight seemed to glint off his sculpted breastplate.

Sojin Tadamora flicked his head to one side. Chori dipped his chin a few times in guilty apology and dashed away.

The elder man's face was barely visible in the diamond shape of his helmet, plumed with magnificent black horsehair. But Jaime could feel a scorching glower behind the eyelets.

He refused to balk.

"Chori told me everything. If you ever lay hands on me again, I'll kill you."

The captain's laugh was deep and throaty. "We shall see. If you cannot draw Air by the time I return in the spring, I will make you the Archpriestess's chattel."

Jaime balled his fists.

A sudden gust, sharp as a spear, rose above the rest. It threw off the City Captain's helm. Bronze and steel clanked loudly, rolling away against the cobblestones.

The creases and wings on the edges of Sojin's black eyes extended.

With Jaime's every breath, the banestorm above them rumbled louder, like a growl lodged in a mountain lion's throat.

"Captain!"

A Jaypan officer kicked his courser in their direction, snatching up the helmet from the ground.

"All are present and standing by for your departing order, sir!"

Sojin's eyes flickered back to Jaime.

"I will see you in the spring."

The City Captain swiveled away and snatched his helmet from the officer, his horse's tail flicking behind him. Sojin Tadamora raised his monster-sized *kendao* in the air. Barked a command. Everyone obediently fell in line.

The great company thundered down the agora.

"Why's Sojin so bent on getting rid of me?"

Jaime peered up at the sky, his knees notched to his chest. The last hour of meditation was nothing but circling thoughts of his spat with the City Captain earlier that morning.

"Hmm." Achuros sat against a temple pillar, scribbling away in his ledger.

"You know what Chori told me today?"

Jaime recounted everything that happened, the tips of his ears steaming. Achuros continued writing.

"Those two talk bigger than the size of their own heads," the airpriest said. "You needn't worry about Sojin."

"Not worry?" Jaime twisted his head around. "How can you say that when he's been threatening to chain me up since the day I got here!"

"The Mayor of Korinthia is Florin's friend. Decades ago, Prescilla helped Romulus's wife deliver her first child. She was a midwife before she married the mayor."

"What's that got to do with anything?"

"Romulus's wife had many miscarriages before Prescilla. That couple will do anything Florin asks."

"But Sojin said he's going to replace me with an army—"

"Our City Captain talks nonsense just to make himself feel important. Florin ordered him to bring back the army."

"Why, Achuros?"

"Because, you fool, he is ready to fight back against Lord Haigen. Florin is preparing a full-scale rebellion. The time for hiding is over. And I am telling you, boy, our Lord Mayor is a religious man. He will never give you up."

Jaime breathed down a gust. "Sojin doesn't like Florin, does he?"

Achuros slammed his ledger shut. "You won't just cork that spigot of yours, will you?"

"I just want to protect myself."

"Don't speak of things you don't understand. Sojin throws his temper at anyone who does not see things his way. He and Florin disagree on many things, but that is all. Sojin Tadamora swore to serve the Menander bloodline so long as he lives."

"Why?"

Achuros huffed. "*Because*, years ago, Sojin came to Jaypes with the King's host. After the Royal Decree was issued, Sojin's orders were to seize every Arcurean boy born in the Prince's year. But Florin's father crushed his forces. After Sojin was captured, he fell in love with a Jaypan woman inside these walls."

Jaime blinked. "He did?"

Achuros tilted his head.

Understanding coursed into Jaime. That's why Chori looked so distinct—he had a Kaipponese's ink-black hair and irises, but the round, full-shaped eyes of a Jaypan.

He's a half-blood. Like me.

"What happened?" Jaime said.

"Sojin deserted to our side, obviously. Rheia gave him two sons. But Lord Haigen didn't think well of that. He punished Sojin's disloyalty by locking his family in his home and setting it to fire. Florin's father is the only reason Chori is still alive. Benetto wasn't able to save the others."

Jaime shivered. "Oh—I didn't know."

That's why Sojin hates me. The same thing that happened to Hilaris happened to his wife and first son.

"Well, what about Lord Haigen? He still lets Sojin serve as Arcurea's City Captain?"

"Haigen's clever, boy." Achuros pinched a scraggly patch of beard on his neck. "He saw that Sojin had great influence over our City-State, so he put his former vassal in charge of keeping the peace. If Sojin failed, Lord Haigen would burn the very place he loved to the ground."

"Not if I burn Sojin first."

"Sojin is our true hero, not Florin or Prescilla or any councilor breathing in the south. Sojin is the one who keeps this great stinking hovel standing. The Arcureans are his wife's people."

Achuros retreated behind the firepit and retrieved a bottle of wine. Without turning to look at Jaime, he pulled the cork and guzzled.

"You two are more alike that you realize. One day, you'll see that. In war, enemies are really your friends. Friends are your enemies."

"Sojin will never be my friend."

His mentor laughed, choking as tears of blood-red wine ran down the bulge of his throat.

"You'll see, boy. You'll see what I mean. And on that day, may Achuros of the High Temple be dead."

CHAPTER FIFTEEN

Four months later, in mid-February, a banestorm of a surprise disrupted Jaime's training.

A heavy book slammed down at his feet. Jaime jolted out of meditation. The front cover bore the symbol of Jaypan classic architecture: a pillared marble temple.

Priest Achuros stared down at him severely.

Jaime stopped breathing.

"Is that a book on…Jaypan architecture?"

A smile twitched across the priest's face. "It includes a copy of the Colosseum's plans. Gods know you'll need it."

"But—what about meditation?"

"It's obvious we'll need more time for that, which we have little of. From today onward, we will spend the morning meditating and the afternoon learning the mind techniques needed for currents. I might just throw in some history, philosophy, and music to culture you."

Jaime's chest swelled. Achuros was offering him the same gift Gaiyus Sartorios offered his brother eight years ago.

"I thought you said the days of the Sages were over," Jaime quipped.

"Did I? Hmm. I can't remember."

Jaime smiled. "Guess I can't remember either."

"What you truly need is hidden in the Library of Nandros, outside the city proper. The mayor granted us permission to leave the walls. We'll study there until springtime."

Without thinking twice, Jaime dropped the books and threw his arms around the priest's neck.

Achuros widened his eyes, nearly toppling over.

"Thank you," Jaime whispered.

"Alright, alright, before I change my mind." The airpriest handed Jaime a fan much smaller than his own. It was tatty, the folds sparkling with a flamboyant pattern of cows.

Jaime looked up in dismay. The priest grinned.

"Before Usheon's reign, we used to give the young Air Sages fans when they began their training at the High Temple. Once you learn to draw air currents, it will focus your power."

The back of Jaime's mouth went dry. They'd nabbed at each other for so long that he didn't know what to make of this.

Achuros waved him along. "Come on, let's go meet Thunderman."

"Thunderman?"

A playful smile tugged at his mentor's mouth just before he vanished into a one-stall stable behind the old temple.

~c⊱❦⊰ɔ~

They rode Achuros's silver mare to the edge of the Krete Forests, just outside the south gate. An ancient two-story structure slumped under a tunnel of firs and pines. One gate dangled off its hinges. On the other gate, the Air Emblem eyed him through its splintered wood.

The airpriest led him through the courtyard. Jaime lagged behind. His eyes lingered on the rotting awnings, the piles of shattered pottery, the stillness behind the archways.

Invisible wisps of energy scampered away from him, teasing him to follow.

"Can you feel that?" Jaime whispered.

The priest skipped up the chipping steps. Jaime turned his head around, the surface of his skin tremoring.

"Achuros!" he called. "The air feels funny here. Can't you feel it?"

"We are standing above a reservoir of Empyrean energy," the old man replied. "Pockets like this exist all over the Four Kingdoms, little tears in our world that connect us to the spirit one. Most of our libraries and temples were built on these pockets."

Jaime peered over his shoulder. He didn't like not being able to see the shafts of energy. They were quick and impish as game darting under forest brush. Like they were alive—as alive as *him*.

Priest Achuros stopped at the top of the steps, observing him closely.

"It's good you can sense them. Most people cannot. That means your bond with The Empyrean is getting stronger."

Jaime stuffed his hand into his pocket, aching for his breather.

If the spirit world is real, are the mist-monsters real too?

"I don't like this, Achuros. I couldn't feel any of this stuff on Mount Alairus."

The airpriest's iron eyes grew unreadable.

"Boy…"

Jaime turned around to look at him.

"A whole *world* exists out there that you don't know about. If your goat shepherds could see the things I've seen, their spleens would come retching out of their throats." Jaime swallowed. "This is a world meant only for Sages, and a few others."

Pause.

It looked like Achuros was about to disclose something important, maybe even a heavens-upturning secret. Jaime held in his breath. But the priest's lip pursed.

"For you, it begins with the books in this library."

Then the airpriest turned around and disappeared into the darkness between the crumbling columns.

With one last shiver, Jaime raced up the stairs after him.

It was dark inside. Occasional shafts of skylight broke through the crumbling ceiling. Great arches and corridors stretched above him, guarded by marble statues watching him between the upper-level pillars.

"Who are they?" Jaime said, keeping close to Achuros. His voice echoed off the rows of empty bookshelves like a ghost.

"Great scribes of the ancient world."

They cut through the circular floor of the center hall. Ancient Empyrean characters were carved into the center pillar. Achuros recited it, and translated: *"Wisdom is knowing you know nothing."* He tugged at the footstone. Jaime flinched. The entire library echoed from the noise.

His breath flowed loose when Achuros turned back around, two massive tomes pressed to his heart.

"This"—he handed Jaime the first—"is *The Legend of the Four.* Our history. Very, very precious."

Jaime caressed its gritty goat-skin cover.

"Its author is unknown," Achuros cooed, "but in my opinion, Sutta wrote it. The greatest of my kin, the ancient scribe-priests. They say he saw Jaypes Ascaerii in his mortal body before he became the God of Air. Can you imagine? Living and breathing in such an epoch?"

"My brother—" Jaime began, but the priest, carried away by passion, blustered on.

"*The Legend* is a total of six books, but alas, alas, Books Five and

Six were lost a long time ago. We can only surmise how the rest of our origins' history ended. So many speculations. Yes. Many, many theories from the best academics. The truth is dangerous. You realize history can shape our culture, place certain mortals in power? It can transform our *entire* system of government!"

Jaime mumbled, "Hilaris, my brother, gave me a copy the night we were supposed to run away from Mount Alairus."

"What a remarkable brother!" Achuros exclaimed. "Hilaris—was that Gaiyus Sartorios's ward? He gave you Book One? And all the other books?"

"I guess just Book One."

"What an illustrious gift! Only a few copies survive in all the Four Kingdoms. Where is it now? Or did you regift it to the Archpriestess?"

All he could remember was throwing himself at Hilaris, and spitting fury that his brother would give him a tome couldn't read. Now he felt like a pile of manure.

"Yeah." Jaime looked away. "She probably took it."

"A shame. Well, no matter. We'll use this copy to practice your reading." Achuros handed him another book. "And this—this is just as precious. The magnum opus of House Ascaerii."

Jaime's arms sagged under its weight. Numerous pages stuck out between its binding like loose teeth.

"The Queen entrusted it to me when I was still living in the Capital." Achuros gave a ghostly smile. "Only the Air Sages of our divine House are permitted to write in it. It's a compilation of every air sequence known to man."

His heart skipped faster; he almost dropped both books.

"This belonged to Lairdos Ascaerii," Jaime breathed.

"You will meet Thunderman in there." The priest nodded. "He is best friends with every Temple apprentice who ever graced our loving Kingdom. Come, let's study outside—"

"Great!"

Jaime dashed ahead, setting the books down and perching on the library's top step. He flipped to the first page.

The wizened parchment revealed a sequence of three images: the first was of a man, the second a short tunnel of air spiraling away from the man, and the third was a direct hit at a sackcloth fifty meters away.

"Thunderman never misses." Achuros slouched down beside him.

"How do I create this current?"

"You memorize the sequences."

Jaime blinked. "That's it?"

"After you make the bond. Once your *avai* is connected to The Empyrean, you recreate the current in your mind."

Jaime flipped to the next page. The ink stains formed a similar current-sequence, but now Thunderman's target was one hundred yards away.

"This tome is organized by difficulty," Achuros explained. "Easiest currents in front, advanced ones in the back. We will spend our remaining time mastering the first few pages."

Jaime kept flipping through till he reached the last entry. The final picture displayed Thunderman in control of a banestorm. His heart sank into sick dread. The entire mind sequence was fifty-one *pages*.

"As I said, we have only until springtime to learn Air," Achuros said with a sniff. "This sequence would take the best Air Sage half a century to master."

"Could Lairdos control them? Banestorms?"

The priest looked out into the crumbling horizon.

"He was the one who wrote this entry."

Jaime ran his fingertips over the ink, imagining the precious moment in time when Lairdos Ascaerii handwrote these pages for his descendants. The individual steps were mind intensive; you had to keep your focus on multiple points of the storm all at once, while shifting strings of air across a boundless expanse of sky.

Gods, how much physical energy would it take to do this?

"Alright. Start memorizing the basic air current." Achuros pulled out his ledger to begin his scribbles.

Jaime propped his hands against the ground. His chest was thundering with renewed excitement.

"Can you tell me more about the King? What should I expect if I'm dueling him?"

The priest rolled the quill between his peeling fingertips. "Are you familiar with the ritual of the duel?"

"What does that mean?"

"Of course not. I should assume you know nothing. There are two rules: a Sage cannot refuse another Sage's call to a duel. And both Sages must fight to the death with their element only."

Jaime stared at the tome tucked in his lap. "What if they break the rules?"

"You cannot break the rules, boy." Annoyance flashed over Achuros's face. "They are written in the Sacred Codex. The international laws written by the Church?"

"I don't think Usheon cares for the Church."

"I don't think Usheon cares for anything."

As Jaime was opening his mouth in a reply, Achuros shut off their conversation by resuming his scrabble in the ledger. Jaime sat up straight and began memorizing.

The day flew into evening.

That night, after two bottles of wine forced Achuros into slumber, Jaime slipped fleeting glances at Lairdos Ascaerii's entry on the banestorms.

CHAPTER SIXTEEN

Jaime was so deep in meditation at midnight of the following day that he didn't feel the light on his cheeks at first.

Slowly, his eyelids parted.

Off in the distance, smoke curled over the dark pines. A plume of yellow tore the sky open, spilling light over the expanse of forest.

Fire!

By habit, his hand darted to the breather in his pocket. Hilaris's screams flashed back into his head. Paralyzed him. A cold tide of fear rose high, higher into his lungs—the air wouldn't come inside. It was six months since his last asthma attack, two seasons since he last used his breather, but suddenly, he forgot how to—

Breathe. Breathe deeply, Jaime.

The familiarity of his mother's voice calmed him. After a few deep breaths, he climbed off the steps and bolted inside Nanos Library.

Please, please, don't let it be the Archpriestess!

"Achuros!" he screamed. The airpriest was sprawled over the center hall, on ragged blankets like a beggar. Jaime bent down and gripped his shoulders.

"Wake up! There's a fire outside!"

His mentor's eyes opened.

"The medallion." Achuros stretched out his hand.

Jaime fumbled, lifted it over his neck. Achuros's fist closed over it.

"With me," he ordered. "Stay close."

After the airpriest helped him onto his mare, they galloped out of the courtyard and into the direction of the flames. Jaime swallowed down his stirring nightmares. *Not now.* He couldn't have an asthma attack right now. The priest looped one arm protectively over Jaime's midsection.

They reached the wall of fire. Terror twisted inside Jaime's chest.

Dozens of the City Watch were already there, hollering, passing around buckets of water. One of the pines was completely swallowed in flames, its seething branches torching the surrounding trees. This would be impossible to contain—fire was about to bury the southeast.

Achuros dismounted, the medallion's chain wrapped around his palm.

Breathe, breathe . . . one, two, three, four, breathe.

Jaime clambered down and held onto the reins to keep the mare from bolting.

A longspear split through the dark. The sigil of the silver swift fluttered from the pennant. Prescilla Menander. Her belly bulged and she wore no cosmetics tonight. Sweat formed the dark hair around her ears into curls.

"My lady!" Achuros yelled, face glowing from the flames. "You shouldn't be here!"

"Florin ran into the fire!" she shouted back. "Achuros, you have to find him!"

The trees belched flames. The guards cried out, fell backwards. All of their buckets empty now.

Jaime clenched and unclenched his sweaty fists.

You're a Fire Sage. You raised fire once. Now crush it, help them, do something!

But when his mind searched for The Empyrean to tap energy from, nothing existed but pounding panic and heat.

Achuros stormed up to the line of seething fire. Blue light radiated from the medallion. The edges of the airpriest's body blazed, outlining him. The night thrummed with energy. One thrust of his palm—

A blade of air sliced through the flames' cowlicks.

Jaime's mouth dropped.

Achuros's hands formed an open *V*—a tunnel of air charged headlong at the burning pine. The fires hissed and shrank in anticipation.

And the current made impact.

The sheer energy of Achuros's air current thrust Jaime backwards. His heels dug into the dirt, forming grooves over ten feet long. The mare screamed and galloped away. A whirlwind of air currents swiped out the rest of the fire.

The forests instantly went dark.

Jaime's chest pressed against the ground. Heaving for air. The other guards let out sighs of relief, but his eyes stayed frozen wide.

So that's what it's like to control Air.

Achuros glanced at Prescilla. No words exchanged. Together, they marched into the charred shrubs.

Jaime wrestled to his feet and raced after his mentor.

Florin's bay gelding was off to the side. A circle of longspears formed behind the remains of the burning pine. The airpriest shoved his way between them. Jaime skidded to a halt behind the guards.

The mayor was in the middle, gripping the ear of a writhing shape. Toran.

Jaime hurried to his side, coughing, eyes watering from the flecks of ash. "What's going on?"

"You might ask him yourself, Prince."

Fury scorched Florin's graphite irises. The surrounding smoke overpowered the whiff of stonemist incense on his toga.

Toran threw his hands up. "I told you all, it was an accident! I swear it. I was out here camping, and the fire got out of the pit somehow!"

Camping? What's he doing out here camping?

"You nearly started a wildfire." The round edges of Florin's jaw trembled. "If His Honorable hadn't put it out, all of South Jaypes would be in flames by morning."

Achuros spoke up. "What was the boy doing outside the gates, Lord Mayor?"

Jaime grabbed his best friend and pulled their faces up close. "Toran! Why'd you burn up the forest?"

"It was an accident," Toran snapped back. "You know I wouldn't try to hurt anybody."

"But *why*—"

Toran shoved him away and turned back to the adults, though his eyes stayed down. "I was just lonely with Juno gone, okay? I snuck out here to look for him. When I couldn't find him, I lit a fire to keep warm. Let's call it a night and go to bed?"

At Florin's nod, the guards seized him.

Toran's brows bounced up.

"Hey! Juno, tell them to let me go! I said it was an accident!"

Jaime's belly twisted. He turned to the mayor. "He's my best friend—"

"These forests belong to the King. The penalty for arson on royal property is death. He will be tossed into the barathron. Sojin will carry out the sentence when he returns."

The barathron.

That was the deep pit west of the akropolis. And Sojin—he would be back any day now; the Kingdom's air currents were now sweltering by midday.

"Florin"—Jaime clamped onto his arm—"have mercy—"

Achuros hissed in undertone, "When will you learn obedience, boy? Bow your head!"

"Then exonerate him, Prince," the mayor replied, "and explain your decision to our region's royal watchkeepers. They will be investigating the meaning of this burning."

Jaime balked, startled by Florin's coldness.

But as his gaze drifted to the hard faces of the Jaypans, he understood. Lord Haigen already attacked Florin and his wife over the mere suspicion that Arcurea was an Air Alliance sympathizer. What would he do if he found out the Arcureans *were* the rebels?

Jaime turned away from the others, closing his eyes tightly. The night of their lanterns flashed back in their mind.

Light.

Sun.

The shaking of their hands. They'd made a promise to each other. And Jaime would give his life to keep it.

He turned back around.

"I'll find a way to free you," Jaime whispered.

The guards dragged him back in the direction of the city. Toran blanched.

As Achuros murmured with the mayor, Jaime threw one more look back at his best friend. His eyes were round as moons, full of crisp fear. Toran wasn't stupid. And he certainly wasn't drunk.

He burned the trees on purpose.

But why?

~·❦·~

The next morning, instead of training in the library, Achuros walked them to a hill at the western edge of Arcurea.

This dry, rocky hump was nothing compared to the mountains

he'd cut across in the Krete Forests. But he hadn't fallen asleep yesterday until the final hours of night. The slightest slope drained his energy.

"Where are we going?" Jaime panted.

"Climbing."

"Climbing?"

"If you're to raise mighty air currents one day," the priest said, "it will require much physical and mental stamina. We must keep your body strong. The best way to do that in Jaypes"—he smiled grimly—"is to climb mountains."

When they reached the top, Jaime was panting hard, his thighs burning. Snowy clouds shrouded the rest of the Kingdom. Their hill of daisies was the only thing that towered above the white.

Mamá is somewhere out there. And the King.

What else existed out there?

He needed to find a higher hill to climb so he could see. The Townfolders back at home had a slew of sayings about mountains:

"Your vision is clearest on a mountain's peak."

"It is when you make it to the summit that you understand why you climbed."

"The measure of a Jaypan hero is not how many valleys he conquers, but how many mountains he defeats."

But most Jaypans never made it to the top of any mountain. It was too trying. And nobody had the time. Jaime didn't either. The Kingdom's northeastern alpines were too lofty, too steep.

Maybe that's why Jaypans dreamed up poetic sayings instead. Why no one on Mount Alairus could ever see past the shivering fog that surrounded the mountain, why they could only speculate what existed in the King's lowlands below. And what existed above Mount Alairus's clouds, in the direction of his mother's god?

No one could say either.

One day, I'll know. One day, I'll see everything.

Later that day, while Achuros scribbled his fingertips raw with his quill, Jaime floundered through meditation. After a few minutes, Jaime turned his head around.

"We have to talk about Toran—"

"No," the priest said flatly. "That silly cornpone is under the Lord Mayor's jurisdiction now."

"But he didn't do anything wrong—"

"He is guilty of arson. In your friend's home Kingdom, that's a serious crime, punishable by summary death."

"It was an *accident*."

Achuros clasped his hands slowly, tilting his head in Jaime's direction. Those shrewd iron eyes. Since they moved out of the city, he smelled less of livestock and manure, and more of torches and ink.

Why doesn't he ever smell like stonemist incense? He's an airpriest. I've never even seen him pray.

"Boy?"

"Yes?"

"If you are concerned about saving your friend, the best way is to learn Air."

"I *know*—"

"Do you? When you can summon currents at will, then you may command high lords and the city watch. Until then, you are just a boy. And my apprentice, unfortunately."

Jaime rolled his eyes, returning to meditation position. *I would be hiding in the mountains if I didn't want to learn Air.*

The shadows of the clouds folded into late afternoon. Jaime shifted his focus into memorizing air currents, but every few minutes that went by, he imagined Toran stooping in the stink of the city prisons.

Achuros is right. Gods, he's always right.

After another hour of studying, Jaime glanced at the stone airmarker his mentor sat behind. Ancient characters cut into its rock face, just like the one he saw outside Townfold marking the Northwind Current.

"What's that one say?"

Achuros kept scrawling. "*Galīdha.* 'Sun,' for the Solstice Current."

Sun.

The same word he'd written on his lantern, of all words. Tingles rushed up Jaime's limbs. Perhaps it was a sign.

"Have you seen the sun before?"

"Ah, it was always summer when Lairdos and Sarendi reigned. Scarce ever could you see a cloud in the sky. Back when I served in Aeropolis Capital, the wind chimes sang the dawn into our *avai*, all in unison. A man would wake bathed in the sky colors of grapes and windflowers." He closed his eyes. "Now, with Ottega on the throne, Air tells me the chimes have gone silent."

"What did the sun look like?"

Pause.

"Lairdos Ascaerii was the sun." His voice thinned with the gusts. "My King would wake before the rest of the Old Senate. Each morning I found him, he was aloft the tallest parapet, singing to the blazing, heavens-bright skyline. He had a voice that made even the great eagles fall silent. In those days, the night was so bright, so short, I began to believe mankind had no shadow."

Jaime started when the old man's eyes misted.

"And he always told me, 'One day, when my firstborn is here, Sarendi and I will teach him to catch the sun.'" The priest lifted his hand and cupped his gnarled fingers into a sphere. Today, the gap between them showed marbled clouds. "'If you can do that, my son, this Kingdom of Song, and the hearts of her people, will belong to you.'"

Achuros slumped forward, his hand pressed to his brows. "Gods, how I miss those times. The day the last Ascaerii died, daylight left this Kingdom, and all the Kingdoms, forever."

This was more words than he ever heard the priest speak altogether.

Achuros does *care about something, after all.*

The weight and depth and height of the old man's pain smothered Jaime—he knew *this*. *This* is what he'd felt the first morning after Hilaris's burning. And the way it was bleeding out of Achuros urged Jaime to sprint away and hide behind the pines where no one could see him cry.

But Jaime stood up, wrapping his arms around the priest's shoulders.

A pause.

Achuros reached up for one of Jaime's wrists, holding on tight.

"I should have been there to stop him," his mentor whispered. "I saw him walk off the cliffs from the other side of the palace. And the Queen—" Bright beads bled from his eyes. "I left her alone in the Capital two months before Ottega's invasion. She told me to go. I shouldn't have. I should have stayed behind to protect her."

"Lairdos's death wasn't your fault. Or—" Jaime closed his eyes, swallowing. "Or my blood mother's. But I'll bring them back."

"They are dead. You can't bring them back."

"I can. I'll bring them back for you, Achuros. I'll do it by showing the families of Jaypes what the sun looks like again."

Jaime let him go.

"If Usheon didn't become King," he added, "I never would've met you."

Achuros shielded a hand over his eyes. "Ah, what a mess I am. No more talk, boy."

"It's okay to admit you care about something. Or someone. I

cared about Hilaris, a lot. I just didn't know until after he was gone."

The priest fell into a silent contraction. After a long silence, when his mouth could form words again, Achuros said, "I haven't been treating you as I should. I am sorry, Jaime. That your father is Usheon Ottega poisoned my behavior."

Jaime glanced away at the sky. His chest hurt. The tears stayed stuck in his eyes, but he wouldn't let them fall. The winds did not cry, and he wouldn't either, not anymore.

"I forgive you, Achuros."

He turned around, forcing a grin.

"But only if you let me hit you on the head with that fan of yours."

The old man broke into a gale of laughter.

That night in the library, as Jaime lay down for sleep, the airpriest drank double his dose of wine until the quill he held to his ledger flailed and fell flat to the ground. And while Jaime pretended sleep, Achuros stumbled into the woods.

In the deepest hours of night, the trees echoed with the unending howls of sobs.

CHAPTER SEVENTEEN

Jaime dreamed he was careening over the southern edge of the akropolis.

Shackles immobilized his arms. The barathron waited for him a thousand feet below. In the deep darkness of its pit, bodies of executed criminals writhed, festered.

Cold beads gathered on his skin. He glanced behind him. The Archpriestess's blank, milky eyes stared back at him.

"Jump."

Her voice was hoarser than dry winds blowing through a crypt.

Jaime turned back around. His mouth opened in a scream—

Sojin, now in front, shoved him off the akropolis.

His innards lurched up into his throat. The pitch-darkness of the barathron grew closer, closer—till a sheet of hellfire exploded into life. Hilaris, reaching up from under, skin melting off the bone, hot white eyes pouring out of his sockets, formed a soundless word with his mouth.

Juuuuuuump.

Jaime's hands transformed. Enlarged. Instead of seeing himself reflected in his brother's eyes, an older man fell in his place. In his dream state, he instinctively knew who: Lairdos, the last of the Ascaeriis, who committed suicide by jumping off the cliffs of the royal palace.

He woke upright.

Sweat drenched his chiton.

He rolled over and shook Achuros awake.

"We have to save Toran! *Please!* Before Sojin gets back—"

Eyes flicking open, his mentor's hand shot towards the medallion. "Holy Lord Jaypes! What—"

"I said, we have to save Toran—"

Achuros slumped forward, pinching the bridge of his nose. "Go back to sleep."

"I can't."

"Yes, you can."

"No, I *can't*. Every time I close my eyes, I see Hilaris in the fire. I thought—I should be over it by now. Why can't I get over it, Achuros?" Jaime buried his face in his hands. "The nightmares are getting worse. Toran can't die—" The memory of his dream suffocated his body under shivers. "If they make him jump, I'm jumping with him. They made King Lairdos jump too!"

Sighing, the priest pressed him into his shoulder. "Shh. Just your dreams. Where is the oil lamp?"

"No—no, fire!"

Only then did Jaime realize he was hyperventilating.

"Alright, alright," Achuros crooned. "Don't panic or you'll panic yourself right into an asthma attack. Easy. Can you breathe with me?"

Jaime blocked out the images from his sleep. Counted to four. They did this together, a set of five. Breathed deeply.

"That's it." Achuros counted with him.

After a few minutes, the nightmare's claw-like grip on his lungs let go.

"Okay. I—I think I'm okay."

Achuros helped him to his feet. "Let's go on a walk together.

Bring your books—the Ascaerii tome, and *Legend*."

"Why?" Jaime let out a shuddery breath. "Where are we going?"

"The forests."

"*Now?*"

"I thought the Empyrean energy under the library might accelerate your ability to bond with air. But too much can make a mortal go mad. Nightmares are a warning sign."

Achuros rapidly packed their things.

"We will not be coming back."

⌘

The Krete Forests felt different than when Jaime first trekked through them months before. They were heavier, much heavier.

And too quiet.

It was the way daylight fell over the leaves—more shadow, less evergreen, like the darkness in his dreams was spilling into real life.

Mist-monsters, Jaime suddenly remembered, for no apparent reason. Frigid cold crawled up his body. *It feels like the mist-monsters are coming back.*

"Can you feel that?"

"Ah, yes." Achuros parted the vines. "A southern summer is coming."

"I'm not talking about the heat."

"Lord Jaypes, I still don't know how the lords of the south put up with this stinking humidity."

"Have you ever seen weird things in these forests, Achuros?"

"And the flies. Holy Lord, the flies! You don't know a southern summer until you put up with the houseflies."

The airpriest ducked a branch and vanished into the foil ahead of him.

Jaime bit his tongue.

Stop being a kid. Mist-monsters aren't real. The only real monster is your blood father.

But Jaime secretly hoped the mist-monsters *would* show up. At least then he'd know he wasn't going mad.

He lingered behind, glancing over his shoulder. Scrutinizing the gaps between the canopy and the trunks. The breezes were mild, lazy. Hundreds of cicadas chirped all around him.

Nothing emerged.

They climbed over moss, tree roots, and rubble, until they emerged before an archaic gateway. Three crumbling arches loomed overhead. Lush beeches surrounded them, blocking out the skylight. This must have been an old temple site centuries ago.

Without any talk, they separated. Achuros hunched against a pillar and pulled out his ledger. Jaime hunkered down on the third and topmost step under the middle arch.

In this vast, timeless silence, he started meditating.

A few hours later, the breezes cleansed off the worst of his nightmare. Peace ebbed into his lungs. He studied a chapter on the Colosseum's architecture until his eyes watered. Jaime stretched out his legs for a short break.

Achuros was in the exact same place as before, sitting cross-legged and barefoot, ledger propped against one arm.

Jaime said, "What in the skies are you always writing?"

"Shut your mouth and meditate."

Jaime stifled a grin and dived for the ledger. Achuros snarled at him, but Jaime moved quickly. He zipped around the center pillar twice, Achuros chasing after him, before crossing the gateway into the other side of the forest. The priest's bellows were claps of thunder in this wilderness. Jaime riffled to the last entry.

Although he couldn't read well, the first thing Achuros taught him was his name.

His name appeared on almost every page.

"This is your diary." Jaime widened his eyes. "You're writing about me. I'm blushing, Your Honorable."

Achuros's growl melted into a snort of denial. This time, Jaime didn't duck when the priest swiped the ledger back into his hands.

"Never touch this. *Never*. Do you understand?" His anger lashed the smile out of Jaime's face.

"Okay, I'm sorry. But why's my name all over there?"

"I am writing history," the old man puffed. "It falls on the priests of the High Temples to record the times. If I do not, future generations will not know who Lairdos and Sarendi truly were." He paused. "Or you."

A southern summer was indeed here, because flies tickled the entire wall of his chest.

God, I hate how he does that.

Changing directions like the gales of a storm. Prickly and naggy at one moment, serious and sincere at another. Lately, it was more of the latter. And a whole lot more bottles of wine.

"Can I also write an entry in there?" Jaime said.

Achuros snorted. "Why?"

"I want the world to know about you too. A Sage is only as good as his mentor."

The creases fell out of the old man's face. He opened his mouth. Closed it.

The next time he opened it, something whizzed through the trees—piercing the tree trunk just above Achuros's head.

An arrow.

Both of them froze. Achuros's mouth was still open, unsaid words hanging on his tongue. Jaime's heart felt like a falcon plummeting into a dive.

They abruptly split apart, swiveled behind the opposite side of the trunk.

"Jaime," Achuros said under his breath. "Listen to me."

"No! We're not separating—"

"*Jaime.*"

He stopped breathing.

"Pass me the medallion. Run as fast as you can westward. Avoid the city. Don't trust anyone, don't let anyone see you. And don't look back—do you understand me?"

Jaime shook his head, his throat thick. "I'm not leaving you, Achuros."

It's got to be the Archpriestess. I lost Hilaris and Mamá and Commander Julias and everyone on Mount Alairus. I'm not making the same mistake again. Not with him. If they kill Achuros—

"We'll see each other again. Boy, we don't have a lot of time."

Jaime breathed deeply. "Promise?"

"Yes, alright—"

"*Promise,* Achuros."

The old man took his shoulders, his hold firm as a father's, and looked him in the eyes. "I promise, Jaime."

No one could promise anything in this Kingdom when humans were killed more often than cattle. But Jaime lifted the medallion over his neck and passed it to the airpriest. Their breathing fell heavy.

Then, Achuros hissed, "*Go!*"

Jaime sprinted in the opposite direction. His sandals had long become an extension of his feet, but still, he tripped over several tree roots. His lurid vision reeled in and out—one second he saw the gnarled branches of pines, the next a burning pyre.

Arrows screeched through the air. His breathing accelerated. The row of trees in front of him flashed into imaginary tapestries of fire—

Jaime tripped over a shrub, flew into the dirt.

He whipped his head around.

A comber of horsemen crashed through the arches he'd meditated under. Their broad, two-handed swords lowered towards Achuros. Terrifying shapes. Calf-high leather boots clamping their thighs. Chainmail jangled over their broad chests. Threadbare caps covered their heads. None of this the neat, polished armor of standard Jaypan military wear.

Forest barbarians?

Achuros wrapped the medallion around his left hand. Without so much as a blink, a breath of air knocked them backwards.

Jaime held in a gasp.

The coursers shrieked, lobbed off their riders, crashed to the ground. Men went flying helter-skelter.

"Sage!" one of them squealed. "An Ascaerii is here!"

The forests echoed with unsheathing steel. More of them were coming. The grounds under Jaime trembled from pounding hooves.

His mentor calmly stood in place, but sweat dripped down into his beard.

No more running. I don't care if he cusses me out. I'm not leaving him.

Jaime dug his heels into the dirt and zigzagged between the pine trees. Burning with anger. It was almost spring. How did he not know how to draw air? He had to learn. He *had* to break the bond.

Achuros pivoted forward. A blade-thin air current fractured their lines—

Two barbarians smashed against the trees. Three more collided into each other, legs in the air. Snarling, frothing at the mouth. They picked themselves up, huffing, puffing, forming a circle around the priest. Foreign swords hacked at Achuros.

Whing.

Whong!

But the air currents curled around the blades, hurling them out of their masters' grips.

"Bloody bastard!" a barbarian roared. "He's an airpriest!"

Jaime's chest raced until he could no longer feel. He was only a few trees away from his mentor now.

Achuros's air currents kept headbutting the lumpish barbarians away. But more replaced them, a never-ending sea tide of bulky bodies. The old airpriest bent his body backwards to evade a falling axe. His head twisted around. Eyes widened when he saw Jaime approaching.

No! his expression said.

One of the hulking barbarians, hoary hairs showing a liver-spotted head, yanked a small pouch from his belt.

A shelf of air slammed into the barbarians directly in front of Achuros. But Achuros was too preoccupied drawing new air currents to see the bald barbarian chucking the pouch at him from an angle.

A cloud of barley exploded into the air.

Jaime's mentor's eyes watered and shut. That was all the time the bald barbarian needed. The butt of his giant broadsword rammed into Achuros's temple. He crumpled.

In a half second, Jaime snatched up a fallen sword and dragged it across the dirt. The muscles in his arms screamed. It had to be twice, three times the weight of any Jaypan spear. He leapt in front of Achuros, lifted it up against the bald barbarian—

As it was making contact with the barbarian's sword, the barbarian grabbed his wrist. Slammed the heel of his paw-sized hand against Jaime's chin.

Jaime crashed to the ground.

The pine trees all doubled. His vision sank beneath a watery surface.

Rough snakes slithered across his wrists, binding them together. Vaguely, he sensed scores of giants circling him. Their silhouettes stared at him from the other side of consciousness's surface, above shore. One of them gaped at the bald barbarian.

"The Lady. Do you think he's the Prince?"

"We'll find out."

And Jaime went out.

CHAPTER EIGHTEEN

His eyelids parted in slits.

Everything was upside down. The sky was an infinite sheet of marble and a valley of silhouetted pine trees made the ground. The last light vanished over the dark skyline.

Jaime groaned, sitting upright.

People the size of trees surrounded him, just like the forest barbarians did before he lost consciousness.

No. Not people.

Pillars. He was back in the Library of Nandros.

"Achuros?" he croaked.

Gripping his head, he turned around, squinting through the dark.

His hands were immobile.

That was when his sandal splashed into water, and the shallow pool appeared as an irregularity in the darkness. Its reflection showed a hooded shape staring back at him.

Jaime jolted backwards. "Who are you—"

His captor didn't answer, not at first. He was about a head taller than Jaime, and wiry, but not much bigger. A shortspear clung to his back.

"Where is Toran?" Seething heat pilled out behind that hood.

"Toran?" Jaime coughed.

He peered over his shoulder. Boots shuffled outside the doorway of their chamber. *Forest barbarians.* Their meaty bulks stood guard. His nails dug into the soft flesh of his palms.

"*Toran* is behind this?"

"Are you deaf? *Where* is he?"

"Where is my mentor? The airpriest?"

Calf-high boots crossed the pool and yanked him into the water. "You don't get to say what goes, Your Highness," his captor hissed. "*You're* the prisoner, and I swear on the four gods, if you don't give Toran back, I'll stuff your pissface into a box and deliver you to the King."

"What's wrong with you?" Jaime yelled. "Have you *seen* what Usheon's done to everyone—"

"I don't care about your war." He drew his spear, pointing the tip at Jaime's advancing shape. "Back off."

"*My* war?"

"Last chance. Tell me where Toran is—"

"No wonder your men fight your battles—a barley stalk has more substance than you!"

"At least I know how to wear pants!"

The shape wrenched back his hood.

Jaime gasped.

A girl.

"You Jaypans who wear your tunics so high, the world can see the crack of your ass when you bend over. I do hope your front is less wanting."

His cheeks burned. "What would you know when you are—"

"*I* am Lady Eridene, firstborn of Berold Swansea, Highlord of Rainmere!"

Jaime was used to seeing lank-haired, hollow-eyed girls that were so pale from Jaypes's stormy skies. But *this* girl had limbs like a mountain lion ready to spring. Her hair, braided into a brown cord, revealed a raindrop-shaped face. Skin bright as honey cakes. And eyes sharper than the wasp sting he got four years ago, when he'd dozed under a hive in the forests—

"Are you listening to anything I'm saying?" she said.

Saying?

What was she saying?

Her eyes were bluer than Mount Alairus's snowy rivers. Not the Jaypan gray. Or the Kaipponese black. Which meant—

"You're *Glaiddish!*" he exclaimed. "From the Water Kingdom!"

"No, moppet, I'm from the Earth Kingdom." Her voice was acid.

This doesn't make any sense. Didn't someone—Lord Gaiyus, maybe—say the only foreigners allowed in our seaports are Western Kaipponese merchants?

Jaypes's soil was too poor to sustain enough grain for the entire royal armies, so the King was forced to import it from the Fire Kingdom, where he came from.

How did these Waterfolk get in? What're they all doing in Jaypes?

"…make a fine hostage," she was saying. "With you, I can bargain for anything I want."

Jaime snorted. "I thought you were one of the King's officials. Puh, there's no danger at all."

The spear sank into the flesh of his neck. His throat swallowed on its own, but his glare stayed.

"Shut your sass. You aren't anything I expected the Prince to be, just so you know, and in my opinion, you Jaypan doves with your pitchy accents wouldn't know war from poetry anyway."

"You sound like you have constipation."

"I sound like I am civilized, as all the people of Glaidde are." Her face slowly extended toward his, until the dazzling starburst in her eyes overpowered the screen of his vision. "If you don't hand me Toran Binn, I will personally see that you burn in the Capital."

"You wouldn't."

"Are you so certain, Your Fiery Highness?"

"I couldn't even if I wanted to, Your Watery Ladyship," he spat. "Toran's guilty of arson. He almost burned down this forest! I'd have to go against the Arcurean Council, which I can't do. They're my allies."

The lady didn't blink.

"Then we're going to the Capital."

She let go of him.

Enraged, Jaime pulled against his bonds, but when they wouldn't budge, he stormed forward.

"Hey!" he hissed. "I want to get Toran out of prison just as much as you, probably even more. He's my friend too, okay?"

"Then tell that to your Lord of Arcade—"

"It's *Arcurea*, stupid—"

"And if he doesn't listen, I swear by Lady Glaidde—"

"But hand me to the King, and millions more people will die. Do you know how many Jaypans he's murdered? Do you have a heart? And either way, your stupid threats are the last thing that will free Toran!"

The girl bit her lip, but only for a second.

A dark shape flickered from the corner of his eye. One of the patrolling barbarians outside the doorway suddenly went down. By the time the girl noticed the distraction in his eyes, it was too late— she swiveled around the same time light-footed Jaypan mercenaries streamed through the doorway.

Sojin was back.

CHAPTER NINETEEN

"Thank you," he breathed as a Jaypan mercenary sliced his bonds free.

A dozen more Jaypans blocked off the library entrance with their spears. Their trunk-hard arms and thighs were bare of armor. A white tyto flew with outstretched wings in the center of their blue shields—a sigil he didn't recognize.

Their thrusting spears circled Lady Eridene. A bulky mercenary bound her wrists.

"My father is Highlord of Rainmere, righthand advisor to the Glaiddish King!" she bellowed. "You're declaring war on House Swansea and all of the Kingdom of Water if you touch me—"

Jaime cupped his hands together. "Hey, sea swan!"

Lady Eridene bared her teeth.

"So my answer's no, I'm not helping you!"

He started to dart outside when the same Jaypan mercenary who cut his bonds gripped his shoulder.

"Not so fast, boy."

His face fell.

The mercenaries shoved their smaller bodies through the library gate. Jaime caught eyes with Eridene. She shot him a smirk of triumph.

The warm night air suffocated his lungs—the last person in the Kingdom he wanted to see was the City Captain.

Achuros appeared instead.

"Jaime!"

His mentor shoved his way through several more Jaypan mercenaries. Jaime scanned the forests. No horses in sight. Their coursers were probably hidden somewhere in the pines. And so were their archers—they shot at a few foolish Waterfolk who continued to fight.

"Are you alright?" said Achuros. His wrists were chafed, his white robes sullied.

Both of them were sweating by the pitchers.

"I'm okay," Jaime replied. "You?"

Before the priest could answer, a scream split the air.

"Stop, stop!" Lady Eridene yelled, her bound hands pressed to her face. "Sons of Glaidde, lay down your weapons!"

They didn't need to be told twice. The Glaiddish straightened, dropping their swords at her command.

Four riders appeared through the shadowed trees: Lord Florin, Lady Prescilla, and a fully armored officer with a black-plumed helm. Only one man in Arcurea had a helm like that.

Sojin.

If he was back, how many mercenaries from their ally City-State—Korinthia, Jaime recalled—rode behind him? More and more gathered behind him, slinking out of their hidden campsite, awaiting his command.

Jaime swallowed.

What was the last thing Sojin swore to him?

If you cannot draw Air by the time I return in the spring, I will make you the Archpriestess's chattel.

A round, fat shape writhed in the fourth saddle.

"Beanie!"

An Arcurean guard held him tightly by the tunic.

Lady Eridene dropped her wrists. "*Toran!*"

She started to rush forward, but two of her guards lowered their spears in front of her chest.

"What happened?" Florin shifted his eyes to Achuros, now at Jaime's side.

Sojin's dark eyes scoured over the lady's barbarians. Stinking men, with mops of stringy hair and full beards and belted jackets like the skin peeling off a snake's back. He ripped off the cap of the nearest one.

A unanimous gasp.

The hair beneath it was an undyed, bright yellow. The City Captain spoke in a hush. "Glaiddish."

"Seamen?" Florin blinked. "In southern Jaypes?"

"Well," Achuros muttered, "I heard Glaidde has a fervor for discharging its seamen over every virgin land."

"I do not presume to know your business in Jaypes," the captain continued, "but you shall answer to the royal authority for it." Sojin turned to the mayor. "Tomorrow morning, you will prepare the barathron. These seadogs will be executed."

Achuros knit his brows. "Are you mad? You will ignite a war with the Water Kingdom."

Toran raised his hand. "I'm not Glaiddish. Do I still count?"

The heat in Jaime's chest ebbed. He didn't know what this Glaiddish ambush meant—or what Toran had to do with a highborn lady from the Water Kingdom—but Jaime made a promise. They were going to find the light and the sun together. He wouldn't let Toran die.

"Sojin," Jaime forced the words out, "let them go—"

The captain swerved around.

"*You,*" he snapped. "What have you done for our city in the time I have been gone? Besides letting these mongrels of the sea lay hands on you and your endearing mentor?"

Jaime's face flushed with sudden heat. "I've been mastering air sequences. Aren't I going to duel the King in the fall?"

The lines on Sojin's face tightened. He faced the other leaders with the vigor of a horned dragon breathing fire.

"Why should we keep the Prince here any longer? He is useless! Every day he stays, he endangers all of us!"

Florin sighed. "Truly, Sojin, he is the Lord's chosen—"

"I will hear that no longer!" Sojin roared. "I put aside my judgment last time, but this time we are doing things my way. In the morning, I will sentence him to the barathron myself. So the Royal Decree will end, and justice will be served for the deaths of our children!"

Jaime took in a dry breath. His dream of the barathron flashed back, coating his forehead with sweat. *Fire.* Hilaris. *Please, don't let them.* Burning in flames. Soon it would be his turn—

"This is not Kaippon." Achuros slapped his forehead. "In your home Kingdom, you may take human lives at will, but we are in Jaypes. The boy is a Sage—"

"Lord Haigen has laid a bounty on my head!"

The hysteria in that scream stunned them to silence. The veins on the City Captain's temples bulged.

"While I have been negotiating for a force large enough to defeat him, while I have risked my life and *my son's* on this voyage of hell, this so-called Sage cannot even protect himself!"

"Sojin," Florin murmured.

"An Ottega is an Ottega." The captain wiped the sheen from his face. "I will rid Jaypes of them all."

"Gods." Achuros sounded unimpressed.

"Be silent, priest!" Sojin shouted. "You have disgraced this Kingdom as much as *he* has."

His mentor went stiff.

Jaime winced at Sojin's jab. Never in a day of his life had he heard anyone rebuke the old airpriest.

Achuros stormed forward, batting aside the captain's single-edged *kendao*. Their faces were a hairsbreadth away.

"I do not fear you, Sojin Tadamora! I speak for everyone when I say I've had *enough* of your colicky tempers." Achuros shoved his finger at Jaime. "To assault my honor is one thing, but it's quite another matter to put up with your constant harassment of our future King. That boy saved my life when I commanded him to run, and he came defenseless! But put aside his recklessness, I'd like to see any of you step up and learn Air! He cannot hold a pole weapon, perhaps, but in two seasons he has memorized techniques that would cause a grown man years of mental constipation. *Buzz buzz buzz!* Go away, you gadfly! O, before I smack you with my flyswatter!" The city leaders struggled to keep their faces deathly straight. "We've all sacrificed and lost loved ones! Don't any of you smile—I speak to all of you!" Achuros whirled around to face the growing crowd. "All of you halfwits who forget that he learns not shield, nor bow, nor those manmade play sticks you all swing around, *but a holy element that is not even his own!*"

Jaime nearly fell over.

Was this the same old man who once swore never to train the son of Usheon Ottega?

Against Achuros's broiling glare, Sojin was the first to break eye contact.

"If all that you say is true, let him show us Air. Let him prove he is a worthy Sage, and he may keep his life."

"Come to your senses, will you? He cannot draw elemental

power. It's been under a year—"

"Then it isn't worth keeping that prince of pusillanimity. As our children die in his place, he hides and hides."

Pusillanimity?

Politicians and their big, stupid words. This one he knew from reading with Achuros. Jaime bit his tongue so hard that he tasted blood.

"You accuse me of being a coward…" The winds around them picked up, surging past the pine branches. The forests hissed at them in sibilant whispers. "But what about you?"

Florin peered at the sky, murmuring a low prayer. Achuros doubled back and gripped Jaime's arm.

"Boy, stay out of this—"

"Let go!" he yelled. "All of you think you know me, but you know *nothing*." His chest heaved. For a second, lightning whitewashed the skies. "Where have you been for the last fourteen years as thousands of boys like my brother were seized and murdered? Where were you when Lairdos Ascaerii's bondlords bled in the Storm of Flames?" His throat thick, he screamed, "Where were you as Chori wiped manure over our Lord Mayor, and the daimyo dishonored the Lady you swore to serve?"

The city leaders around him gasped.

Worst of all, the captain's own words hit home.

Snarling, Sojin wrenched his *kendao* into both hands. He slid off his saddle and lunged at Jaime.

Jaime slung his head backwards only by impulse.

A puff of breath clouded the massive whetted point that hovered over his nose. His own terrified reflection stared back at him for one heartbeat before the blade withdrew.

Sojin pivoted and lashed again. Jaime twisted his body to the side. None of the City Watch moved in to protect him. Achuros's eyes were wide in alarm. He wedged himself between them.

"Oh you fools, stop!"

But the captain thrust the priest aside and lunged again. Half a dozen Jaypan men rushed out of the way, another two helping Achuros up. Sweat formed a river down Jaime's neck. Every time he dodged, the blade missed him by mere hairs with each thrust. It *breathed* on him every time it shaved off strands of air above his nose. When Sojin spun around again, Jaime was still caught in a rushed backflip, and the angle and speed that the *kendao* was coming at him was all wrong.

Florin threw himself in front of Jaime.

"Enough!"

Gasps and screams. Sojin pulled to a halt—at the last second.

His *kendao* grazed the surface of the mayor's speckled cheek. Blood trickled down his chin, splattering onto the dirt. Florin glowered at the smaller man, unflinching.

A ragged breath escaped the captain. The fury in his black eyes flickered out, replaced by horror. He lowered the weapon and staggered backwards in a bow.

The mayor's hard gaze fell on Jaime.

All around them, the giant pines continued to sway. Their tips trembled. Giant wolfs of wind bolted westward in the skies, tossing the land in shadow and light.

"Do you believe you are the Lord's chosen?" the mayor said, peering at the unruly winds.

Jaime wet the roof of his mouth.

"I…"

"For years I have prayed," Florin murmured. "I pleaded the Holy Lord to deliver us. Fourteen years, he was silent. But the second you came to our city gates, I knew. You were the one he sent."

Water broke from the young mayor's eyes. He fell to his knees.

"You *have* to be."

Jaime took a deep breath.

Until tonight, religion was a stench to him—gods, how the incense clinging to Florin's toga suffocated him—but in this second, as the power of Florin's love, welling from the love he had for his god, penetrated Jaime's *avai,* Jaime saw a sliver of Lord Jaypes's spirit in that man.

Gradually, more Jaypans took after the Lord Mayor, falling to their knees, bowing to him, until the only men left standing were Achuros, Sojin, and the Glaiddish.

Tears blurred his eyes.

"I am," Jaime whispered.

Suddenly, he was as certain of it as his heart hurt. He took the mayor's hands, tugging him upright.

"I am, Florin."

The stormwinds around them began to ease, and the Krete Forests shivered back into tranquility.

Lady Prescilla pointed at Sojin.

"That man has betrayed House Menander and the Council of Arcurea. Arrest him."

Hold on—what?

Jaime jolted.

The combined Arcurean and Korinthian spearfighters obeyed her without question, turning on their commander.

CHAPTER TWENTY

Sojin's teardrop-shaped eyes widened into full moons.

The trains of Lady Prescilla's wisteria dress washed over the hindquarters of her towering courser. Two standard-bearers with the Arcurean sigil flanked her as she emerged into the moonlight. Despite her belly, a round apple over her lap, power blossomed from her presence.

It hit Jaime—with all the male leaders on foot, and Prescilla Menander mounted above them all—she held true power over the combined army, and thus the council, the city, his life, and the fate of the Kingdom of Air. Jaime shivered. *She* was his righthand in this war, not Florin or Lord Gaiyus or any man in the Kingdom.

All of them had miscalculated her, Sojin most of all.

Lady Prescilla raised a letter into the air. "Last night, a guardsman on night patrol delivered this to me."

Its broken wax seal was a swift flying above a crisscrossed spear and shortsword. That was the official signet of Arcurea's Captain of the City Watch.

"Our guards also brought us the messenger." Her cold eyes fell on the captain. "Dead now. But alas, the recipient remains at bay; the letter was addressed to Her Grace the Archpriestess."

The silence erupted with gasps.

"She knows the Arcurean Council gives sanctuary to the Prince. Damasia will be here within the fortnight."

Invisible hands were closing around Jaime's throat. Air leaving his lungs. *One. Two. Three. Four.* But counting didn't help. In a puff, he was that knobby-kneed, wheezy little kid on Mount Alairus again, fumbling his pocket for the breather. Without it, he didn't know how to inhale air.

The Archpriestess.

The King made the decrees from his throne, but she rode out and delivered—the single woman who had killed the thousands of boys born in Jaime's same year. The face who murdered his brother. Jaime's own burning wouldn't be on Mount Alairus, no, no, but in the Capital, on Jaypes's largest pyre—

Lady Prescilla bellowed, "What have you to say to this, Sojin?"

The City Captain shook his head, his face white.

Behind him, tears glistened down his son's face. Sojin opened his mouth, then closed it, then opened it again.

His voice was hoarse.

"If you believe I would ever betray you, my lady, then I have failed to serve House Menander."

He didn't put up a fight as two broad men of the City Watch seized his *kendao* and shackled his wrists behind him. As Sojin passed his mayor, he opened his mouth again. But nothing came out. Florin's dark eyes averted as they marched his captain away.

Achuros squeezed Jaime's shoulder and gestured his head at the white mare waiting for them.

The sky felt upturned. He was walking the earth upside down. Though Sojin would no longer be a threat to him, Jaime's belly writhed and turned.

For some reason, he felt no satisfaction over Sojin's arrest, only a growing storm in the pit of his *avai*.

When Florin announced in City Hall that he was going to throw a pepkos, a citywide festival to worship the God of Air, Jaime was the only one who didn't roar in assent.

Hida used to tell him about the pepkosi she celebrated every year as a girl. This was before the Temple prophecy, before Usheon declared a New Jaypes. In the ancient days, their Jaypan ancestors hosted pepkosi before going to war to please their god and ensure victory.

"Lord Jaypes will help us destroy the Archpriestess's armies," Florin orated. "And this season, I will kill Lord Haigen. The time for hiding is over. The Lords of the Air Alliance have wavered, but Arcurea will step up and take her place as the Lord's Holy Spear. When the other City-States see us, they, too, will fly their pennants behind us."

The hall broke into crashing applause. He glanced at his wife sitting silently in the corner of the front tier. *How am I doing? Okay?* The gray in his eyes were blazing with life again, its sheen enraptured with love for her.

Jaime caught everything.

She nodded, exchanging a smile, though Jaime understood now she was the better orator. It was her gift. Not Florin's. But the public theater only had one plinth, and she willingly stepped aside so her husband could take it, thus giving great power to them both.

Wow.

For a second, he almost prayed to Lord Jaypes that one day, he would find *this* sort of true love, and a woman like Prescilla, or else he would die—but he caught himself in time.

You don't believe in Lord Jaypes, remember?

"Prince Jamian is our god's chosen," Florin called. "The Holy Lord delivered him to our gate—this is unequivocal. We, my councilors, were handpicked to serve him. Let us refuse to be fettered any longer; let us march into a red dawn of courage and strength. The Temple prophesized that with our Prince, Usheon Ottega *will* fall. In a fortnight, so it will begin with Archpriestess Damasia, the traitor airpriest."

More roars.

You're all wrong.

Nausea crawled up his mouth. He still couldn't draw a *breath* of air since his training, and worse—they didn't know that he not only didn't believe in the gods, but he *hated* their supposed God of Air for pitting him against his own father.

"Jaime," said Florin.

He shook his head into the present. The assembly was adjourning.

"You will be our guest of honor. Prescilla and I have something special planned at the end of the festival. Will you join us in the akropolis tomorrow night, twelfth hour?"

His heart fell. Despite his affirmations last night, he didn't want to have anything to do with worshipping Lord Jaypes.

"Is it something I said, my Prince?" Florin bent down to eye level. "You are upset."

Jaime looked away. "No, I—I'm fine. I just don't think openly throwing a pepkos is a good idea, my lord."

"We mobilized an army under the Emblem of Air; we cannot go back to slavery and subjugation now."

"I know." Jaime forced himself to meet the mayor's face. "I'll be there tomorrow night. What's planned?"

"You'll see." Florin smiled.

The next day, Achuros went missing. Jaime resolved to meditating and studying the tomes on his own since his mentor left him with no direction. *Probably advising City Hall with the pepkos.*

But the banestorm's winds were ferocious today, and the lump in his stomach wouldn't go away. The more Arcurea broke into reckless celebrations and athletic competitions, the more he felt as restless as the gusts.

Something was in the air—the currents were all blowing in wrong directions today.

With half an hour left before Florin's surprise, Jaime rushed back into the city proper. The City Council was giving out free porridge in the agora to the masses. Jaime insisted on starting at the end of the line, and when his bowl was full, he brought it over to the city prisons.

Somewhere in here, Sojin's in chains.

Jaime kept his head down.

Please, please, don't let me run into him.

It stank powerfully of sweat and leather in here. His eyes watered. Jaime stopped outside the cell he was looking for.

Toran leapt to his feet. "Juno! Aw, man, you brought me food?"

As soon as they were standing on opposite sides of the bars, Toran's eyes bright, his smiling mouth open, Jaime dumped the porridge all over his face.

The entire cellblock went quiet. Several Glaiddish heads turned in his direction. And suddenly, Lady Eridene broke into roaring laughter behind him.

Toran unfroze, shooting him a glare of death. "Gods—I'm gonna beat you into pig lard—"

"That's for lying to me," Jaime said. "And for pretending to be my friend."

"Hey! I was your—I still *am* your friend!"

"Why did you burn the forest?"

"That doesn't matter, man—"

"*Why*, Toran?"

A short huff.

"Before we ever met, Beanie and I got separated at the west coast.

I was trying to find her. But then I met you." Toran pinched his moon-round forehead. "I thought it would be a good idea to stick around with a Sage 'cos I didn't know my way around this turd Kingdom. But then you wanted to stay here. And I saw how much your own war meant to you, and that mattered to me.

"But then guilt started eating at me. I had my own war I had to get back to—the one at home that Beanie's trying to end. So I looked for a way to find her—"

"That's why you burned the forest?"

Toran's breathing grew flustered. "Yeah."

"You're not telling me everything—"

"I'm telling you the truth." Toran balled his fists. "The Bean and I agreed that if we ever got lost, we'd send fire signals to each other. I just felt bad abandoning you, especially after our promise and all. And I was kind of scared of setting things on fire. So I kept putting it off—"

Jaime grit his teeth. "You're not telling me everything. What're you doing in my Kingdom?"

Lady Eridene shifted her glare to Toran. *Don't you dare talk.*

Toran quickly said, "It doesn't matter, Juno. By the time I sent the fire signal, I was so sick of rock-hard barley rolls and stinking mountains that I just needed to go home."

"Poor moppet," the lady muttered from the cell corner.

Toran showed his teeth. "Stuff it, will you?"

"No, *you* stuff it." She marched over and jabbed her finger in his chest. "You're the one who got us into this mess in the first place."

"Me?" Toran whined. "Now that's cruel of you, Beanie. What have I ever done?"

"For starters, the royal authority wouldn't have found out who we really were if you didn't gorge on so much grog and practically *tell* them we were from Glaidde—"

"Man, that's not what happened—"

"And I was worried to death searching this gods-forsaken island for you! Do you realize what I had to go through to find you?"

"Jaypes's ass?"

"Not funny!" Lady Eridene slammed her boot down. "The mercenaries almost refused to ride into Arcurea's lands in case this stupid attack failed—and where are we now?"

"And this's *my* fault?"

Jaime glanced between them, senses perked. They looked like they were about to rip each other's heads off.

"I never wanted to come along anyway," Toran whined. "You know I prefer sausages and your uncle's delightful company."

"Oh moppet, your story will make a fine Jaypan tragedy. Perhaps they will even perform it in a theater after you're martyred."

"Okay, that's it. Take your Water Court missions and go away forever."

"Ha! *You* begged me to take you with me—"

"Fart, fart, fart, what'd you say? Fart, fart—"

Jaime pointed to them and called to the guard, "I want them freed."

Both of them halted in mid-sentence.

Florin was planning to hold them hostage until the end of the war, but Jaime knew that when the Archpriestess arrived, she would light Arcurea City into a bonfire. Even if Toran was withholding the entire truth from him, he was still Jaime's friend.

And they had made a promise to each other.

The master-of-guard stepped in and crossed his arms. Jaime recognized him. Achillus Kyrossou, the new City Captain.

"The Lord Mayor gave strict orders to keep them behind bars," the captain said. "They only go free on his authority."

His gaze hardened. "They're my friends."

"But the mayor said—"

Jaime finally lost his patience. "Or do you prefer me to interrupt the festival so I can take it up with the mayor? His wife assembled an army under the Air Emblem." He pulled the medallion from under his chiton, pointedly displaying its sigil. "*I* am the Prince of Jaypes, not Florin or Prescilla or anyone else in this Kingdom."

Captain Achillus brusquely turned away to avoid a bow. "Very well, Your Highness. Just for tonight."

"Fine."

As soon as a guard unlocked the door, Toran burst out and threw up his arms. "Freedom!" he whooped.

Jaime waited for Lady Eridene. She stayed sitting in the corner, inspecting a curl of dark hair.

"You're free to go," he growled.

"I wouldn't go anywhere with a sugarplum pretender like you, even if my life *depended* on it."

"I don't *believe* this!"

Toran skipped to his side. "Don't worry," he whispered. "Beanie's got more cock than a capon. She'll come out when it's time for a good piss." He burped. "Buddy, I'm starving! Whadda they got at the festival?"

Jaime pulled Toran to the exit. "Come on," he growled. "I'm running late. We need to get to the akropolis."

Once they skipped outside, Jaime stopped short. The banestorm's gusts drowned out all noise.

Gods.

The procession was already starting—or really, ending.

Panathea Way led from the agora to the akropolis and would finish at the Pantheon of Air, the largest holy monument in the city. He joined the tail end of it, struggling to keep his head down. Despite the weather, older citizens stood on the marble steps of the agora's administrative buildings, reciting famous lines from Jaypan epics. Flute girls and merchant daughters stood at the thresholds of their own homes, tossing windflowers onto the streets. All the while, children in garlands passed the edges of the procession, waving Arcurea's banners, singing holy hymns.

As if the roaring winds of this banestorm didn't exist.

Reckless. So reckless.

Toran opened his mouth, catching the sweet cakes the women and elderly uphanded at the crowds. Jaime tensed when Toran's elbow jabbed him. "Why are you so uptight, man?"

"Why *aren't* you?"

Infinite bodies squeezed Jaime into a grain of barley. The sooner he was out of these crowds, the better. He was about to kill someone.

When they finally made it to the akropolis, Jaime almost collapsed in relief.

The highest councilors stood on an altar in front of Pantheon of Air. The city had erected a marble statue of Lord Jaypes and clothed him with a wool himation.

Jaime shivered.

That was *exactly* what he wore the day the medallion awakened his Sage-power.

The Menanders stood at both sides of the statue, accepting offerings with warm smiles. Lady Prescilla's belly drooped over her waist.

Achuros wasn't in the akropolis either.

Weird.

His mentor hated this kind of stuff—festivals, big crowds, merry cheer. "Hoopla," Achuros called it. But the old priest wouldn't wander off if his mayor was dedicating a festival to Lord Jaypes...

Would he?

Jaime stood off to the side with Toran while the final part of the pepkos played out in bursts of classical songs so lyrical, they made his shoulders shiver. A score of girls—none as pretty as Lady Eridene—carried baskets of barley meal to the altar. A toddler offered Florin a wooden figurine of Lord Jaypes, and the mayor accepted it with a hearty embrace. All other citizens offered variations of wool, fruit, wine, and oil flasks—the way his mother did when she would pray over his asthma.

"You know"—Toran chomped at a handful of grapes—"I heard the Ascaeriis were gifted with song. You should go up there and sing something."

"I'm not an Ascaerii."

"So? They're practically treating you like one."

He rolled his eyes, but his chest swelled. Toran was right. This wasn't just a festival. As much as it *was* a bad idea, this was a gathering of *avai*, an amassing of all different classes and ages and people as varied as the leaves in fall. Never had he seen such unity among Jaypans. And even though Jaypes might have been the smallest of the Four Kingdoms, *gods,* Jaime was so proud to be Jaypan.

The night drew to a close when Florin's household servants brought in a fat bull. Lady Prescilla sang a final song, her voice falling over her people like stardust. Then, Lord Florin stepped up to the bull with a knife in hand. He spoke a prayer to Lord Jaypes. All heads bowed.

This isn't right. Achuros should be here. He's an airpriest. Why isn't he here?

The akropolis broke into thunderous cheers as Florin finished the sacrifice. It was difficult to make out the words over the gusts.

"Hail Lord Jaypes!"

"Praise to the Holy Lord of Air!"

Treason, this is open treason, they're asking for it—

He jumped when Toran's hand dropped on his shoulder. "Too uptight, buddy."

"We have faith our victory is sealed," Florin shouted. "Now, on this night, I wish our city to look upon the one whom our god has sent us."

Jaime went rigid.

"The Council has seen him grow much over the seasons, and to mark his passage into adulthood, it is customary that his household bestow him with his first drink of wine."

Toran bent over and choked on a grape. "Gods! You never had *wine* before?"

Florin held out a hand to the crowds. "Prince of Jaypes, if I may have the honor."

Calves numb, Jaime stepped forward. His fingers started to twitch as thousands of heads observed him for the first time.

You still can't summon currents. You don't even believe in Lord Jaypes. What if they find out you're faking all of this?

Jaime scoured the crowds. Captain Achillus was here now, his face tense with lines, the winds gnashing at his white mantle. Dozens of his mounted City Watch surrounded him. Despite Jaime's throbbing chest, no one laughed or said a word.

A councilor helped him onto the altar. Jaime nodded in thanks since he didn't trust himself to speak.

"Prince." Prescilla greeted with a smile. Jaime hugged her. She kissed him on the brow, her ringlets whipping behind her like a dark pennant. "Our city stands behind you."

"And I stand behind you," he whispered back.

Florin handed him a chalice, gripping it with two hands to keep the stormwinds from tearing the wine from him.

"I was nervous on the day of my passage," Florin whispered. "But you shouldn't be."

"Is it okay if I am?"

The mayor laughed. "It is okay if you are."

As Jaime lifted it to his lips, his stomach clenched. The air currents felt wrong again—very wrong.

He peered at the multitudes. Jaypans smiling at him in anticipation. Jaypans half drunk. Jaypans clinging tight to their himations, the easterly winds buffeting their faces. He studied the Arcurean banners somersaulting across the akropolis, the way the breezes wheezed as they passed through wool and linen clothing.

Not cloth. They're passing through metal plates.

The wine crashed from his hand. Jaime swiveled around and shoved Florin flat to the ground.

An arrow skewered the spot where the Lord Mayor stood a second before.

The crowds erupted into gasps. An elder councilor tore off its pennon and flipped over to the sigil: an albino dragon.

"Lord Haigen," the councilor breathed.

"Florin!" Prescilla screamed.

But a storm of fire arrows pelted the altar, separating them. Jaime flipped off his belly onto all fours. Captain Achillus yelled his first order—

An arrow sank into his throat.

The civilian crowds shattered into shrieks and screams.

"Stay down," Florin whispered. Bodies crashed all around them, faces, limbs, backs splintered with arrows. They looked like grotesque pine trees from down here.

Jaime dug his knuckles into the altar. "They killed Achillus. No one's commanding the City Watch or the spearfighters from Korinthia."

The young mayor closed his eyes. "I will."

He helped Jaime up.

Enemy soldiers crashed into the akropolis. Their longspears blockaded the exits, forcing the flailing civilians back. Gold standards with the albino dragon of New Jaypes snapped in the gusts—the royal forces were here.

But *how?*

How did this many bodies sneak through Arcurea's fortified walls unnoticed? Where was the City Watch? No one heard them coming?

Jaime grit his teeth at the sky.

Well, with this banestorm, a giant could smash through the gates and no one would hear a thing.

"Jaime!"

He plummeted back into the present. Florin was gripping his shoulders, bellowing over the tempests.

"Protect Prescilla. Whatever happens, don't let them hurt her. Promise me!"

Jaime swallowed and nodded. "They won't. I promise, my lord."

As Florin rallied the City Watch with shouts, Jaime crawled his way over to Prescilla. She was reaching over to lift a fallen guard's shortsword. Her mouth stretched open from the exertion.

"No, my lady!" Jaime placed his hand over hers.

"They are going to kill Florin—"

"We have to get away from the fighting! Let's get to the City Hall—"

A new spate of screams forced him around.

The rear ranks of the unarmed crowds fell like mud-clay bricks crashing down from the sky. Outriders cut them down to make way. Someone else was coming.

His lungs shrank.

A fresh century of heavy infantry swept into the akropolis. New Jaypes standards, fitted on gilt staffs, rattled high over their heads.

The rider in the center had a shaved head, lips darker than blood.

The Archpriestess.

To her left, Lord Haigen was buried under full Kaipponese battle armor. A smirk spilled from under his lacquered helmet.

But this wasn't why Jaime's blood froze to ice, nor the fact that his brother's murderer had arrived two weeks early. It was the rider to her left, in matching white robes, grimace barely visible under the snarl of his beard. And suddenly, it hit him that Sojin was never the traitor.

His own mentor was.

CHAPTER TWENTY-ONE

The drums from the royal ranks drowned out the thudding of his heart.

The Archpriestess turned on the daimyo. "Where is the boy?" she demanded.

"Your Grace, so sorry." Haigen bowed, the bridge of his nose crimping like a pig's snout. "I told you, I never knew the Prince was here until I received your letter."

"He is close." The winds brought Achuros's gravelly voice to Jaime. "That boy won't abandon the mayor and his wife to die."

Reining her horse around, the Archpriestess bellowed to the army, "Search the akropolis! Burn down every wretched building until I hath the Temple Relic in mine own hand!"

The first raindrop spattered onto the altar. Achuros withdrew from all of them—galloping away in the direction of Chikos Pagos Hill.

Prescilla shook him. *Jaime, Jaime.* Calling him several times. Jaime blinked the hot tears out of his eyes and turned around to face her.

"There is a tunnel under City Hall that will take you back into the forests," she whispered. "Arcurea has several. Achuros must have led them through one of our postern gates."

"I'll—" He breathed out. "I'll kill him."

"No, Prince. *I* will."

Jaime took her hands and helped her up. "We're going together."

They dashed into the City Hall's outer colonnade, Prescilla hobbling as she held onto her belly. They passed the first pillar. A hand shot through the darkness, gripping his ankle.

Jaime bucked his legs by instinct.

A low groan.

Jaime gasped. "Toran?"

The stocky boy tottered to his feet, rubbing his bloody nose. "You didn't have to kick me, you dummy." One hand holding a half-eaten cake.

Prescilla's eyes narrowed. "Not him."

"Toran"—Jaime yanked him closer—"we don't have a lot of time. You have to tell the prison guards to free the Glaiddish."

"Wuh-why?"

In the background, someone played the sharp notes of a flute. Jaime glanced at the fiery courtyard below the City Hall steps. Florin was mounted on his white gelding now. At the sound of his notes, the City Watch regrouped, filed into prickly barricades of shields and spears.

Jaime turned back around.

"Arcurea's forces won't stand a chance against both the Archpriestess and Lord Haigen. I need you to convince the Glaiddish to fight for us."

Toran gave a shaky laugh. "Beanie's never gonna fight for you."

"Tell her"—Jaime clenched his jaw—"if she doesn't, we all die."

Clanging corselets and the smell of rain-soaked iron raked the air.

The soldiers were drawing closer.

Jaime took Prescilla's right arm; Toran took the other. Lightning flashed against the sky. The lady directed them into a small room behind the Assembly Hall. At her instruction, Jaime and Toran pushed aside the marble altar. A narrow tunnel groaned open. Toran's wrists swung like weights in front of him as he skipped through.

Jaime offered a hand. "Come on, my lady."

She breathed hard, sweat trickling down both ears. The noise of crashing flagstaffs and furniture penetrated the other side of the City Hall. Toran hissed at them to move.

"The baby is coming," she whispered.

Jaime croaked, "No—"

Toran swore. "Empyrean hell, not now!" He took her other hand. Together, they supported her through the tunnel.

A ten-minute hike turned into a half hour of wading through darkness. Jaime's instincts screamed at him to leave Prescilla behind; shutting out those animal voices drained his energy. The weight of his chest grew heavier. At their halfway point, Prescilla lagged, wheezed. Toran offered to squat over into a makeshift chair so she could sit down for a minute.

"Leave me," she said huskily.

Jaime interrupted, "No. I promised Florin—"

"They are already inside the tunnels. We will never make it."

He was grateful the darkness hid his expression. Time was slowing to a crawl. Every footstep, voice, pulse of his heart, was an explosion in his ears.

"Juno, wake up." Toran slapped the side of his face. "We gotta get to the nearest exit. Where is it?"

Prescilla clenched her teeth, lifting herself back up. "I will show you."

They resurfaced five minutes later. Jaime recognized the unpaved street by the dim light of the firepits—they were just a few blocks away from Chikos Pagos. His training ground was one of the few places in the city still completely dark. It would suffice as a hiding place. For now.

"Toran," he panted, "the prisons!"

His friend saluted him and dashed into the labyrinth of the slums. Jaime helped Prescilla up the rocky hill. For two seasons, he had climbed this every day, but tonight his thighs were weak. They had to take breaks every minute. The lady shut her eyes.

"The child is coming," she gasped. "Lord Jaypes—"

You all paid worship to Lord Jaypes and now look where it got us. I knew something like this would happen! None of you listened.

Jaime took her into his arms and practically carried her the rest of the way. The city air smelled like an overburnt pot of meat by the time they reached the top.

He laid her against a temple pillar. Her silk peplos was drenched through. Prescilla gripped her belly, holding down a cry.

Gods, gods, what do I do now?

She murmured something to him. He bent down closer, afraid to know what it was. The frescoes around them seemed to be watching and whispering.

Something hiccupped under his sandal. Jaime peered downward.

A loose panel of stone.

This was the same panel he stepped on the first day of his training. Achuros was hiding something under it. But he didn't have time to move it over and look under it—a knife emerged from Prescilla's peplos.

She pressed it into his hand.

"Go."

"I can't leave you behind." Jaime forced the words out. "I promised Florin."

Her eyes closed. "You made a promise both of us knew you could not keep. This is Lord Jaypes's will, Jaime."

He took the knife and forced himself to march away from her. Jaime stopped at the edge of Achuros's temple, the spot where he had meditated every day during his first few months in Arcurea. It took everything to suppress the urge to hurl his medallion into the night.

I don't care. I'm staying. I'll fight, kill, die before I leave her behind. I won't let more people die like Hilaris...

Before him, Arcurea's flaxen expanse suffocated under sickly light.

This isn't Lord Jaypes's fault. They're dying because of you. Just like Hilaris did. Just like all the people on Mount Alairus. Just like Mamá. All the boys who died under the Royal Decree—all because you couldn't stop it.

A shadow caught the corner of his eye.

Jaime stiffened.

Achuros stood at the foot of an olive tree, peeling fingers pressed to its bark, heaving up the night air. The other hand was pressed against his beetled brows. His back was turned to Jaime.

The grip on the knife tightened.

Jaime marched to him.

They were ten steps away from each other when Achuros seemed to suddenly register the fallen branches crunching under Jaime's sandals. The old airpriest turned around.

"Jaime..."

Rainwater coated Jaime's vision. The fires turned into watery yolks dripping against the darkness.

"I trusted you."

Achuros pressed his back to the tree. "It's not what it seems. If only I could explain—"

"They all trusted you." His lip trembled, but Jaime bit down on it. "Florin, Prescilla, Sojin, the Arcureans—*gods,* even Commander Julias, my uncle. And my blood mother, the Queen."

"Jaime—"

"*Why*, Achuros?"

"I am *not* on Usheon's side—"

"Aren't you?" he screamed, pointing at the burning city. "Is that what you tell yourself when you betray your friends?"

His mentor opened his mouth, but a round of clapping split the coiled air.

"Thou hast found him. Very good, Achuros."

The Archpriestess now stood between the dry fountain pools, a century of mounted soldiers cantering up behind her. Their torches spilled firelight over the courtyard.

High winds tossed thunderclouds over them, pregnant with the earsplitting shrieks of stormwinds.

Hot shivers rippled Jaime's flesh. The nightmares haunting his sleep for so long—always with *her* in them—paralyzed his limbs. He was that mountain boy frozen before Hilaris's pyre all over again.

No. I won't run this time.

He turned around and met her eyes. Her eerily blank gaze fell to the medallion around his neck.

"Bring him forth, loveth, prithee," she lilted.

Achuros closed his eyes. When they opened again, his mentor shoved Jaime behind him.

"That I cannot do, Sia." Achuros turned to him. "Give me the medallion," he whispered.

"Why? You think I trust you?"

The Archpriestess tossed up her head. Broken pieces of metal chafing against each other—that was the sound that came out of her mouth.

"*Of course.* Thou lovest the knave. Nay, he is more than that to thee—how fitting! The most disgraced disciple of the Kingdom shouldst apprentice the Prince to himself? A frail, coughing cripple whose fate has liketh been sealed by the gods? Ah! Hallowed art thee, Achuros."

"We crossed paths once," Achuros murmured, "and it didn't end well. Let us not make that same mistake tonight."

Her laughter shut off, and her eyes became blank again. "Nay, we shalt not. Crosseth me once, and I forgive under the probity of a priest. Crosseth me twice, and thou shalt die."

Achuros hissed, "The medallion, boy!"

"No!"

She extended her hand, unblinking. A soldier rode forward, placing a spear in her grip.

"What a pity you ever tried to love again," she said in plain Moderna.

Her heels dug into her horse. The palfrey galloped forward.

The Archpriestess lowered the blade.

A scream broke through Jaime's throat. His feet moved forward by impulse, but his mentor shoved him aside. Jaime crashed into a hedge of bindweed. Achuros didn't move out of the way. The palfrey streamed past them towards the temple steps in a smear of white. The next time the spear's nose lifted back up, the Archpriestess was out of range.

Achuros stayed standing, his back facing Jaime.

The seconds grew insufferably long. A second pair of heartbeats pounded in his ears.

"Achuros?" Jaime whispered.

His mentor crumpled to the ground.

A dark splotch grew from a point above Achuros's waist. In seconds, it pooled the entire front of his robes.

"*Achuros!*"

A laugh crackled against the sky. The Archpriestess looped around, kicking her horse forward. The stained spear dropped again for the final kill.

Jaime squeezed the medallion. His knuckles trembled. The fires, blades, faces grew blurry.

After Hilaris's death, Arcurea had been the last thing holding him together. *Achuros* was the last strand holding him together, his true family, his last family, the man he loved more than anyone else in this cursed and horrible world.

And now, the Archpriestess was taking from him again.

She was taking away *everything*.

Jaime threw his head up and screamed a cry. It twisted into the heart of the banestorm above him.

A sharp whinny rang in the air. Someone gasped.

Jaime opened his eyes.

The palfrey was galloping away. And the Archpriestess—she was on the ground, gripping her shaved head with her claws. Blood trickled down behind her ear.

"Jaime…" Achuros's eyes glistened against the storm.

Cool energy rushed through his veins like the icy strands of Mount Alairus's air currents. The walls of his mind collapsed. Suddenly, his *avai*, the energy field of his body, felt as limitless as the skies.

Jaime gasped. "What's happening to me?"

"You made the bond, *finally*."

Despite the blood pouring out of him, Achuros's grin stretched all the way up to his ears.

CHAPTER TWENTY-TWO

His dimension of reality cracked.

It was like the mortal world was merely a glass painting all along. As the trees, the dark skies, the limestone temple fractured like hardpan, vibrant rays of light blazed through. Jaime squinted at the otherworldly dimension behind it. Infinite vertical characters floated against a backdrop of ghostly blue. *Ancient Empyrean.* The language of the gods.

The Empyrean—the spirit world, skies—it's real.

The Kingdom's currents rushed through his matted hair in a screaming storm. Jaime glanced down at his palms. Light was bursting from his skin—the same radiant light pouring through the spirit dimension.

Holy skies, I see it now. The mortal world is an illusion. The Empyrean is real. Inside The Empyrean, anything is possible.

Jaime breathed in its infinite power, his wide eyes landing on Achuros.

The airpriest returned silent words through his gaze: *Remember everything I've taught you.*

Jaime closed his grip around the medallion, blinded by the shards of light radiating from his body. The mounted soldiers behind the Archpriestess backed away.

He turned to face the her. She stiffened. Jaime saw something in her eyes he had never seen before: fear. Of *him.*

"No more," he whispered.

The element of Air locked onto the images he drew in his mind, reproducing them almost in exact time. A current, compact and sharp as an arrow, awakened in front of him—

He discharged it at the Archpriestess.

She cried out. Lifted herself onto her feet, but she wasn't quick enough. The current wrapped around her ankles. Tugged her backwards. Her Grace splatted flat on her face.

Achuros broke into gurgling laughter. "Ah, there's my apprentice!"

The thrill in Jaime's spirit welled. He threw up his hands.

"I *am* a Sage! Yes! *Yes!* YES!"

He snapped out his tattered fan, held out the medallion in the other. As he advanced, the Archpriestess crabbed backwards.

"No—no—no—"

Jaime thrust out his fan. "Hah!"

The Archpriestess stumbled to her feet, yanked a soldier off his horse, and clambered up the saddle.

Jaime held onto the steady focus of his *avai.* His mind brushstroked another series of currents, the same combinations he'd studied for so many months with Achuros. A new current slithered against the ankles of the Archpriestess's ranks.

The horses panicked and went totally amok.

Whinnies, hoof beats, crashing steel pounded the air. Smaller air currents battered them from all sides, breaking through their shields. A squat soldier hurled a throwing spear at him, but an air current bucked it aside. The soldier gasped and fled. Thunder chuckled above them. Jaime dropped a final whorl of air into the center of the squad, expanding it until the royal unit was on all fours or rolling off the edges of the hill. Once Jaime decided they had enough, he let go, and they routed back to the city streets, bawling.

His brief glimpse into The Empyrean dimension vanished. The courtyard fell dark.

Jaime's skin vibrated with energy.

It was only when Achuros groaned that he spun around and hurried back to his mentor.

"Achuros—"

He dropped his fan, propping the priest's head against his arms. The old man's eyelids fluttered open.

"I'll get you out of here." He struggled to lift Achuros upright. "Come on! We have to go—"

But the priest laid a hand on his.

"No, Jaime. Help the mayor."

He shook his head. Achuros tightened his grip on his wrist.

"He needs you. Don't worry, I'm not going anywhere." He coughed up blood as he laughed. "Go on, my Prince."

The sheen in their eyes reflected their rain-stained faces.

Slowly, Jaime nodded. "I'll help him. Lady Prescilla is in the temple—she said the baby's coming."

"Gods help us. I will watch over her. Here, take this." Achuros pressed his own magnificent fan into Jaime's hand.

He ascended to his feet.

"I'll kill you if you die," Jaime swore.

Achuros's bubbling laugh echoed behind him as he stormed down the hill they trained on for so many seasons, perhaps for the last time.

The bulk of the fighting had shifted to the agora. Most of its civic buildings were smoldering.

Jaime traced the surface of the writhing mayhem.

The Glaiddish were among the Arcurean forces, lugging their big swords at the royal soldiers. The enemy forced Florin back, swiping at him behind the pedestals of statues, around the trunks of cedars. Florin's scraped knuckles held onto an ivory-hilted shortsword. Half of his toga was in ribbons. He fought with a limp. Blood spilled from a gash over his unarmored thigh.

Any second now, the royal soldiers would find an opening and kill him.

If the medallion is what the Archpriestess wants, then the medallion is what she gets.

Jaime focused on the pulsing energy of his *avai*. Shutting everything else out. Just the way Achuros had taught him during his meditations, and his mother on Mount Alairus.

Breathe, Jaime.

Time vanished into the present. He found The Empyrean again. His Sage-vision shattered the world back into vivid light.

Air flushed into his lungs, light and cool.

One, two, three, four.

It was easy to breathe now, so easy.

Every blade's edge was sharpened and clear, even at this distance. The thrusts and slashing seemed *sluggish* now.

The ridges of Achuros's fan became his sights. Jaime aimed with his mind. The soldiers chasing Florin shifted to the center of his vision. His mind painted a current slashing through them, another bunting the two at Florin's side.

Breathe.

Air obediently materialized his sequences.

A third simultaneous current sent a cluster of soldiers tumbling off a narrow stair. Florin was free of his foes, for now. The mayor panted hard, nodding at him in thanks.

Jaime birthed a larger thundercloud of air—aimed—released energy at the eastern edge of the agora. Clay jugs, abandoned baskets of cucumbers, and loose awnings went flying.

Exclamations of surprise.

"The Prince…!"

"Four gods, a *Sage* among us—"

"An Ascaerii! Great House Ascaerii lives!"

This larger current, requiring far more of his energy, rebelled against his control. Jaime gripped it with both hands, crying out as it dragged him along the cluttered streets. The tidal wave of air bowled the royal soldiers into each other. A unit of archers lost their bowstrings and fled. Their nearest colleagues saw and panicked, following after them. This larger group absorbed more and more men until an entire section of the agora was crashing into the merchant stands, thundering towards the gates.

"Prince!"

Jaime turned his head.

"Prince Jamian!" Chori panted, pulling up close to him. Sojin's oversized *kendao* sagged in his hands. His lanky body trembled. The boy pointed to the burning prison.

"My ba is still in there. *Please*, you have to help him!"

Jaime nodded. "Come on, let's go."

He led the race across the agora. Several soldiers materialized out of the sea of awnings. Threw themselves at him. A trunk of wind clobbered them into a stand of terracotta wares.

Air poured into his lungs. Jaime gasped. Adrenaline pumped them wide open.

Breathe, breathe, I can breathe again.

Jaime ducked his head as they tumbled inside the prison entrance. Sweltering air burned his throat. Chori cried out—a flaming beam crashed behind them. His eyes watered, but he forced them to search the empty cells.

No one on this level.

Jaime dashed up onto the second floor—

Sojin appeared, first cell to the right.

Shackles from the walls stretched his arms and body into a tight Y. The mud bricks above them swelled into a feverish red.

"Keys," Jaime coughed. "Do you have the keys?"

Chori shook his head, a hysterical sob bursting out of his lips.

Jaime studied the rock walls of the cell, pressed his chiton to his nose. Closed his eyes. His mind searched for the right current. Achuros had instructed him to focus on the basic ones, but in his spare time, Jaime memorized most of the intermediate and advanced ones too. Just in case.

Thank the skies I did.

Jaime took a heaping breath. Refocusing. His mind wrapped around The Empyrean's threads. His *avai* pulsed, grew with energy. All of his senses screamed, *Let go, NOW!*

But he held on, building the threads, biding the current until the energy in the center of his being was so strong, so massive, his heart felt crushed. Didn't Achuros once warn him drawing too much Empyrean energy could kill him?

He gasped and released.

A giant current of air smashed itself at the left cell wall. The floor under their feet quaked. The iron bars caved in. Chori jumped inside, throwing himself around Sojin's chest.

"Ba!" he cried. "Ba!"

Jaime aimed the folds of Achuros's fan at the cuff points for precision. Hurled two more currents at them—*snap!*

The cuffs released Sojin.

The elder man pressed Chori's nose against his chest, shielding him from smoke. He took his eight-foot *kendao* with his other hand.

"I did not betray the mayor," Sojin panted.

"I know," Jaime said. "The royal army is still outside. I can't fight them all, and Florin needs you. Will you help me?"

Sojin bowed his head in reply. Jaime's lips formed a small smile.

They flew downstairs, staggering out of the prisons. A second later, the front section of it groaned. The two-story building collapsed into a molten pool of timber and flames.

Sojin set his son down and pressed a kiss to Jaime's head.

"Look after him for me," the elder warrior said. "I will handle Haigen."

"I will," Jaime whispered.

And Sojin let him go.

Jaime waved Chori to the eastern edge of the agora. Together, they built a makeshift fort with the fallen timbers from stands and scaffolds. Jaime shot currents at any soldier who dared get too close.

Lord Haigen's bellow pierced through the clamor.

"Stop, you *baikan*! Cowards of dogs! I'll have every deserter burned!"

The daimyo fought on the incline of a burning temple. He drew back his *kendao*, plunged the spear-like blade into the nearest Arcurean guard. Blood dripped a crescent moon over the stone panels as the Jaypan gasped—but another *kendao* ripped through his back, out of his stomach.

Haigen's eyes stretched wide.

The single-edged halberd dropped from his grip. Jaws trembling, he peered down at the steel sticking out of him.

Sojin stood behind him, outlined by the fire, gripping the other end of the *kendao*.

A shudder passed through his body. Haigen Namoto collapsed. As the blade slid back out, an urgent cry tore across the agora.

"All royal units, retreat! Fall back!"

In one massive crashing wave, the remaining soldiers threw off their opponents, scrambled onto their horses, and galloped into the dark shelter of the Krete Forests. Those on foot stumbled to follow.

An Arcurean guard threw his bloody spear into the air.

"*Victory!*"

Jaime blinked.

Impossible.

But the shout was as real as the winds at his fingertips.

The rest of the ashen, weary warriors of Arcurea raised their weapons. Jaime joined them in a united roar.

CHAPTER TWENTY-THREE

Pimples had sprouted on his face overnight.

Everywhere—two on his chin, one on the right corner of his lip, one below that, three more along his forehead like a swollen constellation.

Jaime rubbed them in the dark of the Pantheon of Air. He hadn't noticed them until now, after the Battle of Arcurea had quieted, and the bodies, both Arcurean and royal, were cleared from the streets.

They hurt.

He gazed up at the empty altar high above him. Squeezing his medallion, he sank onto his knees.

"Lord Jaypes," he whispered.

His voice echoed.

Lord Jaypes…

Jaypes…

Though no stonemist incense was lit, a mysterious whiff of it tickled his nose. He closed his eyes, breathed it in.

"I—I'm sorry."

Wet beads gathered in the corner of his eyes, but he kept his lids shut, resisting them.

I understand now, Lordship. The Arcureans were never fighting for me. They are fighting for you. They saw you in me all along. Even though I couldn't—I didn't want to.

The dead Jaypans on the streets flashed through his mind. Blank gazes. Breathless bodies. Friend and foe—all his people.

Jaime let out a breath.

In the isolated darkness, tears spilled over the new bumps on his skin.

"If I'm going to take more lives…" He bowed his head the way he saw his mother do so many times on Mount Alairus. "Help me be strong, Lord Jaypes. Help me end this war."

Jaime opened his eyes, fixing them on the altar.

Help me do this for Mamá.

At dawn, he left his prayers, and his tears, in the pantheon. A myrrh-like aroma lingered on his skin. The medallion hung openly from his chest. No longer would he hide it away under his chiton.

Gold streaks of dawn lightened the sky.

By the time Jaime arrived home, he collapsed into bed without changing out of his sandals or stained clothes. For the first time in months, he slept dreamlessly till late afternoon.

⁓ⱻ⧉ⱻ⁓

They held a makeshift assembly in Florin's bedchambers. Prescilla was propped up against the pillows. Jaime raced to embrace her.

"My lady!" he cried, half laughing. "You're okay!"

She gripped him tightly, her arms against his head. The roundness of her belly was gone.

But where is the baby?

Jaime glanced at the windowpane, where Florin sat absorbing the wan daylight. His sterling eyes were wet. Jaime tilted his head, puzzled. But the mayor closed his eyes. Tears spilled free, rolling down the cuts on his face.

Jaime's heart stopped.

He peered back at Prescilla. But she refused to look at him either. *Gone.*

His vision blurred.

"Prince."

Sojin stepped out into the daylight. Blisters plagued both of his arms. Like the Menanders, he hadn't taken the time to bandage himself properly.

"We must speak," the City Captain said.

His throat hurt, but he swallowed and nodded.

The only missing member of the Inner Council was Achuros.

Sojin took the initiative to order hot bread into the chambers. Everyone silently took a roll. But when the basket returned to the elder warrior, he passed.

Florin forced words through his watery voice. "You must eat, Sojin."

"My indigestion." The City Captain placed a hand on his belly. "I will eat later."

Jaime stared at them. *Sojin and indigestion. Prescilla and lavender oil. Achuros and his extended naps, his bottles of wine. And Florin? Well, Florin always smells of incense, which means he's always praying.*

It dawned on him for the first time—stress was crippling these Jaypan leaders. Even the most powerful of Jaypes's lords and ladies were as scared and exhausted as him.

And now, Jaime and his pimples.

He placed a hand to his chin in embarrassment.

"So." Lady Prescilla forced a smile. "Sweet prince, you saved our home. Lord Jaypes knows no boundaries of our gratitude."

The men nodded.

"Thanks." Jaime coughed. "But now what?"

Florin dug his thumb into his knot of bread. "The Archpriestess will not forget her defeat. Now that she knows your whereabouts, you will not be safe here. As soon as you are ready, you must depart for the High Temple."

"But…the King's patrols—"

"Will have tripled by now." Sojin spoke up. "It troubles me that Reizo Kita was absent last night. If we know anything about that Arch-wench, she does not travel far without the Chief Strategos's protection. One child may make it past a legion of soldiers undetected, but not our mobilized armies."

They want me to go alone.

His mouth grew dry. "But…I don't know the way."

At the Lord Mayor's nod, Sojin unfurled a map and spread it across the wooden table. "Temple Jaypes is here, at the highest point of the Lunar Peaks." He pointed far north, further than even Mount Alairus. Then his middle finger slid three-fourths down the map. "You are here. Head northeast to the hills beyond town. You will see a marker for the Solstice Current."

Jaime nodded. "I saw it once when I was training with Achuros."

"Take it and use the winds to navigate. They will help you bypass many mountain trails."

"Wait—you want me to ride a current?"

Prescilla squeezed her husband's arm. "The currents are out of control, Florin. They could kill him."

"Travelling by horse or foot is out of the question now, my love. The Holy Lord will protect him." The mayor turned back to Jaime. "Prince, do you have the windcloak we gave you?"

"I think it's in my room."

Sojin continued. "When you take Solstice to the bottom of the cliffs, you will transit onto Northwind. Take care to ride it but northeast for two days until the scrublands change to forests of kingpine. A marker for the Silverwind current will await you across a ford. It will be the last you take before you reach the base of the northern peaks. The stone path will take you up into the heavens. When you are at the gate, announce to the airpriests who you are, and you will be admitted."

The longer Jaime stared at the vastness of the Kingdom of Air, the more he felt like the size of a water vole.

"I've never travelled so far on my own before."

Florin left Prescilla's bedside and placed a firm grip on his shoulders. "You have done far greater things only yesterday, Jaime."

"But what about all of you?" Panic needled his chest. "The King will burn Arcurea now that he knows you're on my side. And the Air Alliance—will they help you fight?"

"No matter the Air Alliance. To give our lives for yours would be our highest honor to His Lordship."

The others nodded. His belly clenched.

This war's just starting.

Now that he knew how to control his Sage powers, every high place in New Jaypes would plot to kill him. Every dirt trail he walked, every hamlet he entered, could be his last.

"What about Achuros?"

Everyone's eyes flickered away. When Jaime couldn't stand it anymore, he said, "What will happen to him?"

"He is in the infirmary," Florin murmured. "The Council will pass sentence the day after tomorrow, when order is restored. If you have any last words, it is best you say them before your voyage."

"Hey, kid."

Jaime stopped outside the infirmary's doors, turning around.

Toran stood in the middle of the pavement, arms hanging awkwardly. At the corner of agora, the Glaiddish mercenaries were assembling for departure.

"Toran." He blinked. "You got my message to the Glaiddish yesterday."

"Yeah, I did. And now I'm waiting for that royal feast you've prepared for me as thanks."

Jaime laughed. Toran's hand vanished behind the unruly curls dangling over his neck.

"Well, I guess this is goodbye forever."

Jaime raised his brows. Toran shrugged. "Now that I'm reunited with The Bean, maybe we'll be able to finish up here and go home soon." He grinned. "I miss fried eggs, and sausage, and buttery muffins, and grog for breakfast. All the standard fare for a Glaiddish." He patted his Kaipponese gut. "I bet Beanie does too."

His belly was in freefall. One more person he would never see again.

"You can't go. I made a promise to help you find the light."

"You already kept your promise, man. You freed me from Jaypan prison. It was damn dark and smelly in there."

"You're still not going to tell me why you're in Jaypes?"

"Maybe another time."

"See you never again, Toran." Jaime moved to embrace him.

"Don't touch me—I'll punch your ugly face—"

But Jaime threw his arms around him anyway. "The next time we talk, remind me to tell you about these crazy spiders I saw."

Toran slapped him back. "Juno?"

"Yes?"

"Nice pimples."

Jaime let go. "Shut up, pork lions."

Lady Eridene cantered into the alley, white skylight outlining her atop her stallion. Her dark hair fell in a messy braid over one shoulder. At the cock of her head, his best friend tottered away and mounted his own gelding.

Jaime locked eyes with her. His body suddenly tingled with heat.

But she didn't smile or speak. The lady reined herself around in one lithe tug. Without so much as a command, the Glaiddish men poured down the hill behind her with all the force of a waterfall.

Jaime gave a crooked smile.

Lord Jaypes, please, please make it so that Lady Eridene and I meet again.

⁓◦◦◦⁓

His insides squirmed at sight of the infirmary. Jaime took several deep breaths and pushed his way inside.

The stench gagged him.

All of the beds were occupied. Men of the City Watch were missing limbs, fingers, eyes. One man's intestines dangled out. The southern heat drew flies to the raw chunks of his flesh.

Jaime pressed a hand to his mouth.

This is what Sojin meant when he said people are dying for me. Gods. I'll kill you, Father. I'll look into your eyes and watch the blood drain from your face when it's finally your turn.

A nurse led Jaime to Achuros's bed.

He swallowed.

The airpriest's eyes were closed. Rust brown stained the bandage around his midsection. Jaime lifted it with quivering fingers. A gaping hole appeared past the ripped flesh: raw meat and roiling puss. No one would survive that wound.

Jaime let go of the bandage and turned for the doors.

"Leaving without saying goodbye?"

He went still, turning around. Achuros's eyelids parted into slits.

"Lord Jaypes, how much of a stinking corpse I am. In the end, that's what we all are, eh?"

Despite the stone weights on his feet, Jaime knelt down. He

pressed his head against his mentor's shoulder. The tension beneath the old man's skin seemed to loosen. The priest let out a quiet sigh.

"I'm going to the High Temple tomorrow," Jaime said.

They both pretended to ignore the shackles on Achuros's wrists.

"I heard. I wager I'll be a carcass before the Council hurls me into the bloody pit. But there are things you should know." Achuros tilted his head back. "Damasia—the Archpriestess—I had a plan in motion to kill her. The Council won't believe me, and rightly so—my letter was supposed to draw her to me. I would never betray you—"

"It's okay, I don't want to talk about it." Jaime pulled the tasseled fan out of his sash. "Here, this is yours."

Achuros looked at it for a long time, then shook his head.

"It isn't mine."

"What do you—"

"It belonged to Lairdos Ascaerii."

Jaime stumbled and threw open the fan, his eyes wide. "Lairdos? But—how do you have…"

Memories danced like ghosts over the old priest's eyes. "He was my apprentice once, a long time ago. The Temple weaved it for him. I presented it to him on his first day of training."

Jaime dropped his jaw.

"After you became my apprentice, you reminded me of him so much. Both of you hot-headed, stubborn, ego bigger than a horse's cock. He was the last Sage of redoubtable character, I believed." Achuros smiled. "Until I met you."

"*You* mentored a King!"

"I served him in the Capital until the night of his death. Before I left, your mother gave it to me with her blessing." The airpriest's smile lifted skyward. "Keep it. You earned it."

Jaime suddenly grew conscious of the medallion around his

chest. His heart fell as he rubbed its edges into his thumbs. "I don't know, Achuros. Isn't this the only thing making me what I am?"

"Boy."

His mentor lifted up his chin.

"That trash Damasia said about your fate—did you also hear the part about how she's an ugly old slattern? Or did I leave that out?" Jaime laughed. "Destiny is a choice. You have never been more ready for the High Temple. Gods—look at you."

Jaime blinked.

"Have you heard none of the idle chatter among those councilors? Your voice is deeper. The blubber has left your cheeks. And I even see you've sprouted some pretty boils, eh?"

He cupped his chin, his face hot. Achuros squeezed his arm gently.

"Jaime, Jaime, how much you've grown. Sarendi would be proud—if only your mother could see you know."

Jaime locked onto Achuros's hand, afraid to let go. "Tell me about what it was like in the Capital. Back when Lairdos and my blood mother ruled Jaypes." Fighting fresh tears.

"Well. We had a common saying in Old Jaypes." Achuros closed Jaime's hand over the medallion. "Lairdos sang it before any of us in his court would embark on a long journey."

Little rills glistened down the old man's cheeks, as he, too, sang:

"Let the winds lead you, and you shall find your feet…"

Jaime was in the middle of a nap—the kind one took right before a long journey—when a tremor rippled across the dark.

He sat upright.

Thud.

Thud.

Thud.

He had heard those drums before, the night the Archpriestess and Strategos Reizo came to build a pyre on his home.

Fear pricked the sleep out of him. He rushed down the stairs of Prescilla's home. Now, as his sandals pounded down the stairs, it echoed from emptiness.

His oversized knapsack drooped over the kitchen table. Jaime tossed it over his shoulder and tucked his new fan under his sash. The windcloak the Menanders gave him—where was it?

Panic rushed up his limbs as he groped through his pack, under the table, inside drawers.

Nowhere.

He wouldn't be able to follow Sojin's escape route without it.

No time. You'll have to leave it.

Jaime crossed the doorway—then stopped.

That night when he helped Lady Prescilla up the hill, his sandal shuffled against a loose stone in Achuros's temple.

You never found out what was under it.

It would only be a matter of time before his bodyguards arrived to guide him out of the city. If Jaime never found out what Achuros was hiding, he would toss and turn till the day he died.

His thighs burned by the time he was back up Chikos Pagos Hill. Jaime hurled the knapsack over his other shoulder, bending down before the stone. His teeth gritted as it gave way. A pool of black, dusted with dirt, reflected the firelight.

His eyes widened.

Ledgers. A dozen of them. Achuros's most recent one—its leather cover weathered from writing—rested at the top of the pile.

But why is he hiding them?

Well, no matter.

These pages recorded decades of precious Old Jaypes history. It was the last thing he could remember his mentor by.

A second after Jaime skidded back in front of Prescilla's house, two standard-bearers and four guards escorted him to the akropolis.

It was deep in the night. Arcurea's streets stirred with unrest. Merchants ushered their children onto unsaddled mules, wives kissed their husbands in the City Watch a final goodbye.

They reached the summit of the city. By habit, Jaime shoved his hand at his thigh, where he used to keep his breather. In the distance, a river of torch fire glowed against a black sheet. Horns fell into a single note, nightmarishly deep, dragging through the skylight's dregs. Strategos Reizo's legions were here.

"Prince!"

Lord Florin, Lady Prescilla, and several other councilors hurried out of City Hall. Tonight, the New Jaypes flag was torn from its roof. Even the silver swift of the Menanders—taken down.

The Air Emblem, the gold-and-white sigil of the Ascaerii, replaced both, flying higher than any pennant before it.

My sigil.

Sojin dismounted from his black destrier and passed him the reins.

"Quickly, take my horse."

A thousand words lodged in his throat. All he could remember was the way Cassie helped him up a horse on Mount Alairus, how he rode away from a pyre on a different night, never to see his home or family again.

He couldn't do it a second time.

The City Captain helped him off the lead guard's courser and onto his own towering saddle. The rest of the Council folded their hands in somber silence. Prescilla stepped forward, bundling her eldest son's windcloak over him.

"You forgot this," she said. His heart leapt in relief. She folded three coarser ones into his knapsack. "In case you lose it."

"I won't lose it," Jaime whispered. His eyes switched between Florin and Prescilla, the single couple who would command his armies as he rode to train at the High Temple. "You can't stay here. They'll kill you. I've *seen* what they did to the people on Mount Alairus—"

"There is no time." Sojin stepped back, joining the Menanders. "Keep your promise to us, Prince Jamian. Fight for our children, and protect the people of this Kingdom."

The destrier threw his head, restless against the echoing cries and drums. Jaime tightened his grip on the reins. Another first—he'd never ridden a horse on his own before.

"This war *will* end." Jaime's voice cracked. "I'll see all of you again, soon, so I can return Aulos Menander's windcloak."

Lady Prescilla said, "Let the winds leads you."

"I shall find my feet," Jaime replied.

She dipped her head. The others followed. His gaze blurred. He kicked the stallion forward.

The heavyset pounding of feathered hooves blended in with the drums. Gradually, City Hall, and the rest of Arcurea, smeared, bleeding into the distance behind him.

The second he was level with the Krete Forests, an arrow shot past him. He ducked his head by impulse.

"Skies!" he gasped.

Scouts from the royal armies galloped in from the west. Jaime struggled to grasp onto The Empyrean. The horse rattled his brains up and down. He couldn't draw air—his focus was entirely on the Arcureans.

The hillock he meditated with Achuros on rose in front of him. The shadow of an airmarker stood high above him like a cloaked watchkeeper.

A jolt.

The gelding shrieked—an arrow burrowed into its neck. Jaime cried out. His mount furled him high in the air. By impulse, he twisted his body into a ball, broke his fall with one roll, two, three.

Royal outriders streamed towards him.

Jaime clenched his medallion. He would never make it to Solstice Current in time.

CHAPTER TWENTY-FOUR

"Jamian!"

The unfamiliar shout caught him off guard. He turned around, knees bent, mind flustered as he fished for The Empyrean. *Come on, come on.* Two shapes charged towards him at a sharp angle, intercepting the royal scouts.

"My lady!" he cried.

The sight of Eridene Swansea and Toran Binn nearly made his lungs collapse. The lady pulled up at the base of the hill, glaring from the saddle.

"Would you like a ride, Your Holy Highness, or are you going to stay there on your ass?"

He sprang up and snatched his fallen knapsack. "I've got extra windcloaks. Just ride to the top of the hill."

Toran chucked rocks at the scouts. With that brief distraction, Jaime climbed up behind Eridene. The shouts behind them swelled. Something about "in the name of the King."

Lady Eridene muttered, "I poop on the King's name," and slapped the reins.

Toran laughed, whooped, "There's my Beanie!"

The winds stung the crusts around his eyes. Jaime blinked hard. Glanced over his shoulder. The Solstice marker was disappearing behind them.

Alarm spiked in his chest.

"Stop! We're going to the wrong way—we have to go back!"

They galloped over the spine of the next knoll. More arrows flew overhead. One whizzed past his ear.

Lady Eridene clenched her teeth. "Too late."

The ghostly shadow of another airmarker fast approached from the north. As they surged past it, Jaime twisted his upper body parallel against the stallion. His fingers brushed stone.

Lunas, the winds whispered to him.

Not Solstice. I knew it. We're riding into the wrong air current.

Jaime looked up—saw what lied ahead of them. His breath stopped.

An ocean of clouds had blanketed these hills the day he last meditated on them, but tonight the skies were clear. Steep cliffs dropped off into a narrow, fertile plain that stretched into the horizon, interrupted by glitters of flame and limestone mountains. Wild rivers blazed unnavigable paths through deciduous forests. No highways. No milestones. Only ancient trails stamped into the earth by travelers and their pack animals; the land was waiting for him to carve his own road.

The lady slid off the saddle. "Here we are, just as you wanted!" she shouted above the roaring gusts.

Toran pulled to a halt behind them. Jaime scrambled for his pack, dumping out the other windcloaks.

Eridene stared at him in disbelief.

"This is your plan—an ugly wardrobe? The royal army's going to capture us, Your Highness! What a stupid idea, I knew I should have never left camp—"

Jaime shoved a windcloak at her and handed one to Toran. They went white as he took a long, deep breath, poking a sandal over the hill's edge.

"The kid's crazy!" Toran cried. "We're gonna die!"

The wind currents swirled around him, tossing every which way. He closed his eyes. *One, two, three, four.* And then he felt it: a steady current brushing his arm, twisting over the cliffs.

"Now!" he yelled, and jumped.

For one terrifying moment, he was trapped in freefall. Darkness nipped and gnashed at him. The crags zoomed in fast.

Abruptly, the wind caught the feathery folds between his arms and legs. A sharp jerk—

He swooped forward like a bird of prey, wings outstretched in a dive.

Screams echoed over the canyon. Toran and Eridene tumbled into jagged flight. The winds clawed at them, tossing them up and down. Their screams turned into shrieks of terror.

For the love of Lord Jaypes!

Jaime gauged the airstreams with his *avai*. Then he tilted his outstretched arms like an eagle in flight and looped himself around. The current dropped him behind his friends. Jaime extended his hands.

Eridene and Toran fumbled to grab them.

"You have to trust the winds to hold you!" he yelled. "Don't be afraid or you *will* fall!"

Arrows punctured the air.

Jaime ducked his head. "Come on! Spread out your arms!"

"Easy for you to say, Your Holiness of Air!" Toran gasped.

Lunas thrust them forward, although his friends were falling fast. The winds refused to support them. Jaime clenched his teeth, searching for The Empyrean—

Got you.

At his mind's command, Lunas broke into smaller currents. Jaime lifted his friends back up with air.

The enemy arrows fell out of range. Royal soldiers pull up sharply at the cliffs, figurine sized, as Jaime led the sail ahead.

He gulped in a breath.

Far below him, the toy villages and patrols he saw so many times from the akropolis passed him in a smear of battle flames. They were crossing a wide fissure now—away from northeast, and south; away from everything in Jaypes he had come to know and love. Out here, dark clouds obscured whatever awaited him in the west.

Jaime crossed into the greater world of men: Usheon Ottega's world, and civil war.

PART THREE

THE

BANESTORM

CHAPTER TWENTY-FIVE

At the break of dawn, they crashed into prickly shrubs. Jaime swore he had seen all of Jaypes. Beside him, Eridene giggled out her innards.

"Now *that* was the best time of my life."

Despite the sting of his wind-bitten ears, Jaime wheezed, "Me too. We flew—" He windmilled his arms.

Lady Eridene hiccupped a laugh. "It was like—"

Jaime collapsed onto his back and stared up at the sky. He couldn't form whole words. His head felt lighter than the fluffy clouds that always obscured Mount Alairus's peak.

Toran popped out from his windcloak, rubbing down his explosion of hair.

"Will you shut up?" he growled. Eridene giggled harder. "I mean it, if you don't, I'll…"

He leaned over and vomited.

The lady's laughter faded.

Wiping the water from her eyes, she crawled over to him. "Seas, Toran, are you alright?" Eridene pinched her nose. "Lady Glaidde, what did you eat."

Jaime studied the lands beyond them. The forests he came to know so well were gone. Now, ashy clouds blotted out all skylight.

Not a single mountain to climb. An infinite plateau swept into the horizon, devoid of life.

He squinted into the distance, hoping to find the peaks Sojin spoke of, but gnarled crags and unruly cypress trees populated space. The ground was a flat sheet of purple knotgrass.

Am I still in Jaypes?

"Oh, this is horrid." Lady Eridene cupped her face. "No roads, no rivers or *any* source of water, no bodyguards for hire. No proper toilets, nothing."

Toran mumbled, "Is that a bad thing?"

"It's okay, let's start with finding water." Jaime shuffled through his pack for his map. "Let's see where we are…"

He flipped open the map—and froze.

So many labels spattered the parchment, so many unfamiliar towns and geographical regions he could've been holding it upside down and it wouldn't make a difference.

"Um."

Eridene glared at him.

Sighing, Jaime folded the map. "It's okay." He grinned. "We'll just use the winds to navigate."

⁓⋅⊱⊰⋅⁓

The clouds swelled into a cancerous yellow.

Jaime stayed ahead, his senses perked. The air streams spoke to him in whispers of Ancient Empyrean, guiding his way through the knee-high wild grasses. Somehow in his *avai,* he could feel which way was northeast.

Toran fell behind, batting away mayflies, clouds of pollen swelling his eyes shut. After another few hours, he declared with a sneeze, "Alright, I've had enough of this place. I ain't taking another step without a few decent hours of sleep."

Jaime wanted to keep going, but when Lady Eridene sided with Toran, he sighed.

"Okay. Let's find a place to camp."

At twilight, they burrowed inside a gorge. Now that his giddiness was gone, the dry emptiness of this place widened the hole in his heart. He missed Achuros's nagging. The trill of his flute. His huffs and short sighs as Jaime stumbled over the modern translation of *The Legend of the Four.*

Toran started a campfire with flint and stone. Lady Eridene wandered off to take a piss, although in her words, it was to "pray alone with the Holy Lady."

Jaime handed out the stale biscuits Prescilla had packed for him. Neither of them talked.

His legs twitched. He'd climbed up slopes with Achuros every day to strengthen his physical energy and mental discipline. The lack of resistance in these plains was driving him mad.

When he couldn't take it anymore, he stood up.

"I'm going to go for a walk."

Toran grunted, absorbed by the shape he was absently drawing into the dirt. Something with multiple legs.

A mini foothill rolled out west of their camp. Jaime started scaling. Rocks tumbled. His sandals crunched under wildflowers and grasses. Charred blocks of clay scattered the landscape. A battle must have raged here, years ago. His last night in Arcurea flashed across his eyes.

A rock cut into the sole of his foot.

Jaime stumbled.

Abruptly, an old memory flashed in his mind: the autumn he climbed up the base of Mount Alairus with Hida. It was his sixth birthday. To celebrate, she insisted they climb to the cave temple two-thirds up the mountain. That way she could pray for his asthma in closer proximity to the God of Air. On that day, they were as sure-footed as Sokrates, their pack donkey.

"Lord Jaypes lives on Mount Alairus," she told him, "above the clouds. No one has ever reached the top. It is not terrain meant for human feet."

"Then how do you know he's real?"

"Because he gave you to me," she replied.

"But Mamá, Peri Kreed says you have to *see* things first. Or you can't believe them." Jaime's little hand tugged at her peplos. "I'm tired. This climb hurts."

Hida Pappas bent down and lifted his right foot. Blood and dirt crusted his soft soles. She took a rag from their pack, pressing it to his wounds.

"One day, my son, you will climb Jaypes's highest mountain, and you will see everything."

The memory faded. Jaime's face was buried in a clump of heliotrope. He stayed there, head bowed. Musky clouds passed overhead.

His eyes dampened as he thought about the sturdiness of Hida's faith. Even when the Archpriestess began building the pyre in Townfold, she didn't stop believing.

Lord Jaypes, what is Jaypes's highest mountain? Is it the Lunar Peaks, where the High Temple is? I've climbed small hills and cut across alps, but Mamá says it's impossible to reach the top of a great peak. There's not enough air up there. I have a feeling my father is on the other side of Jaypes's biggest peak. Help me make the climb...

"What by the great gods are you doing?"

The voice startled him. He stopped in mid-prayer.

Lady Eridene stood on a boulder below him, her shadow falling on his shoulders. He snapped upright.

"Nothing! Just—just resting."

She gave an indifferent shrug and started her way back to camp. Jaime's heart jumped. He was alone with her for once. He *had* to keep it that way. Just for a little longer.

"Thank you," he blurted.

The Glaiddish lady turned around, her eyes narrowing.

"For, you know. Helping me back at Arcurea."

"It wasn't my idea. Toran saw the royal armies and insisted on helping you. You're lucky he's on your side."

"Oh. I thought you—"

"I'm only here because circumstances forced me to come with you, but once we find a city or seaport, we separate."

The resentment in her glacial eyes made it clear they were not friends. His throat grew lumpy.

"Oh—yeah, I know." As she was turning again, he shuffled forward. "Wait. I wanted to ask...you're from Glaidde, right? The Water Kingdom?"

"What in The Glens' hells do I look like, a Kaipponese?"

He glanced at her dark waves. *Well, yeah.* Didn't all Glaiddish have yellow hair? But he sensed he would lose his eyeballs if he asked her about it.

Instead, he said, "Does the sun exist in your Kingdom?"

The defensiveness blinked out of her eyes. "Yes. We have few storms where I'm from. But a lot of snow."

"What does the sun look like?"

Eridene glanced back in the direction of their campfire. At first, he was sure she would shove him off.

She shuffled over to sit by him.

A thousand cicadas buzzed against his belly.

"I never really thought about it before." She reached for the stone charm hanging around her neck, a seven-pointed star made of glittering blue gems. "The sun is..." Pause. "True love."

Jaime laughed. "Really?"

"I know it sounds stupid, okay?" she snapped. "But it's always there for you, even if you don't notice it. Sometimes, it hides behind squalls and blizzards. But there are the days when the skies are clear, and I'm walking along the snowbanks of the Eirewood, and Uncle has a letter from the House of Lords. He tells me we lost another sea town to the Kaipponese Emperor. And I start to believe the war will never end. And Toran will never get to go back to Kaippon to see his family."

"How do you and Toran—"

"But then you feel it." Eridene closed her eyes. "Winter's daylight washing your face clean. The elwood leaves are limned in silver. And suddenly, you look up into the sun's white light, and you know."

"Know what?"

"Somehow, everything's going to be okay."

"You think…it's going to be okay in Jaypes?"

She paused. "People come and go. They say they'll be there for you, always—" The charm fell from her fingers. "But they aren't. People lie. And die. The sun is always there, though."

"I wish I could see it." Jaime took a deep breath. "Sometimes I think I never will."

"You'll die before you ever see the sun."

Hurt prickled his chest, but he quickly covered it with a mask of indifference. "Why would you say that?"

"Because I've been in Jaypes long enough to know you aren't your father. You're so much better than him."

Then she stood up and marched away.

CHAPTER TWENTY-SIX

Two days later, the morning after the winds led him to a river, Jaime woke to Lady Eridene's screams.

He flipped himself upright.

No. The royal soldiers can't have found us all the way out here.

His sandals bound across clusters of origanum till his feet smeared and he couldn't remember when he started running.

Protect her, protect her, his senses screamed.

He made it to the riverbank, pulling to a halt, blood rushing in his ears.

"Get it away from me!" she shrieked.

A spindly ball crept out from under a rock. Gods, it was the size of a mountain kid. *Spider.* Nearly half the size of Jaime himself. Legs hairy and thick as a wolf's paws. Eridene was backing away like a crab towards the water, screaming her innards out.

Despite the fear and disgust roiling through him, Jaime stepped between them.

"Don't worry, I'll kill it!"

He squeezed his sweaty palms together, racing to find The Empyrean with his mind. The winds started to pick up—

"No!"

Toran jumped in front of the living nightmare, the black in his eyes dilating wildly. "Empyrean hell do you think you're doing?" he cried.

Jaime cried back, "I'm killing it!"

"What has it ever done to you?"

"Don't be stupid! It's gonna eat her!"

Eridene shrieked and shrieked as both boys bellowed at each other.

Gusts swirled around them. Just as Jaime was about to release a spear of air, Toran turned around.

"Come on, you," he cooed.

The spider backed away, one crawl at a time. Toran bent over as if to pet the hairs on its head.

"*What are you doing?*" Eridene screamed.

"Protecting it from both of you," Toran said defensively. "It doesn't deserve to die just 'cos *you* don't like it." Then he chided the spider, "Shame on you for scaring them. Go back to your hole."

It squealed, its fangs quivering furiously as it disappeared back under the ground.

Eridene cupped her mouth and bolted for the river. A second later, Jaime heard the noises of retching.

He glared at Toran. "That's disgusting, you know that?"

"I always liked spiders as a kid." Toran turned away and sneezed from the pollen. "They never hurt me." Then he tromped off to the river.

Jaime shuddered. Back on Mount Alairus, he was bit plenty by house spiders. "Where are you going?"

"I'm sweaty, stuffy, and need a bath. Shut up."

"But we can't stay here—"

It was no use. Jaime swiveled around as Toran's pants came flying off. The lumpy boy gave a manly shout and jumped in.

Jaime stopped beside Eridene to make sure she was still

breathing. She wiped her mouth, her face green.

"Well," he muttered, "I suppose it's a good time for breakfast."

Jaime scoured around the rocks to study the plants. One of them, at least, was familiar—rock lettuce. It also grew on Mount Alairus's lower altitudes. Hida used to take him down there to pick the tangled purple flowers and mix it into a salad. A fresco of related memories appeared in his mind: clanking of clay pots. The minty smell of kingpine. The way she shook olive oil and bits of goat cheese into their bowls. It would always happen in that particular order just before she called him to dinner.

Jaime!

He could almost hear her voice in the winds, swishing through the blades of grass.

Eridene bent down beside him. "What are these?"

Jaime blinked back into the present, forcing the shakiness out of his voice. "This? Rock lettuce."

"Rock lettuce," she repeated. She called to Toran, "Hello, spider brains! Food! Come and help us pick some rock lettuce!"

Toran blew a raspberry. "Rock lettuce? Give me my *meat!*"

He peeked at Toran. The Kaipponese boy wasn't exactly the skimmest cheese on the plate, but he certainly was proportionately *big*. Which wasn't fair when their ages were so close. Jaime had always been skinnier than an olive branch no matter how much barley meal he ate.

Toran's bellow echoed across all of Lord Jaypes's creation.

"Come on in, you wimps, join me! Juno, answer before the River King! Duel me with your Air!"

"Sweet gods," muttered Eridene.

Their heads were inches away from each other now. Jaime peeked at her. It annoyed him that she was half a head taller than him, but the feeling puffed away when he absorbed the glow of her ocean blue eyes. She had two small dots on her right cheekbone he never noticed before.

I wonder if she's betrothed to anyone.

His crotch tightened—and panic prickled his whole face.

Lady Eridene turned her head slightly. Jaime pulled his head away, scrambling for something, anything, to fill the silence.

"I meant to ask you."

She raised a brow. "Yes?"

He took in a deep breath, too afraid to ask her about a betrothal. "Why are you in Jaypes? And how do you know Toran?"

"It's none of your business."

"I kind of think it is if I'm letting you along."

Her face twisted into a sarcastic smile. "You wouldn't understand since you don't know about my war."

"Sure I do. It's called the War of the West, isn't it? Your King's name is—" He frowned at the sky, recalling his assemblies with the Arcurean Council. "Gildas. Uh, Brennte. And the Emperor of Kaippon is Tazuga."

"It's Viro Tazuga, stupid."

Jaime rolled his eyes. "How did the war start?"

Eridene stood up and faced the river. "It doesn't matter. Not to *you*. The Glaiddish and Kaipponese Courts feel that way about your war, too. They're obliterating each other without a second glance at Jaypes. You're about as good as a dead trout to them."

Jaime stood up too. "Great, because I feel the same way about you and Glaidde—"

"But *I* think it's foolish of them to think that way." She shook off her boots and dipped her feet into the river. "I think you're important." Quickly, she added, "In a utilitarian way, of course."

"What's that supposed to mean?"

"Emperor Viro's fire is unstoppable." She paused. "I believe we need something else on our side to tip the scales. Not more armies. Not more warships. We need another *Sage.*"

"Me?"

She slipped deeper into the river till the water was up to her ankles.

"Why don't you ask my father to help you?" Jaime said.

"I think your father is a filthy heretic who deserves to be hung from the gates of Temple Jaypes."

"So you came to Jaypes to convince me to join your war."

She waded through the water, keeping her back turned.

Jaime furrowed his brows. Considered the full battle gear of her mercenaries, Toran's flightiness in the Arcurean prisons as Jaime questioned him.

He suddenly understood.

"You were going to kidnap me!" he exclaimed. "The whole thing in the library was a bluff. You weren't ever going to hand me to Usheon. You were going to sail me to Glaidde!"

Lady Eridene didn't turn around.

"Don't you have a heart?" he bellowed. "I watched my older brother burn at the stake! He was screaming my name, and I couldn't help him. That's why I'm fighting, so that the same thing doesn't happen to thousands more Jaypans—"

"It only started out that way, okay?" Water plashed into a rainstorm as she swiveled around. "Why do you think I let you go after the battle at Arcurea?"

"You didn't have a choice!"

"I always had a choice," she roared. "You snivel about you war, but this is *nothing* compared to what's happening back at home—"

"Why'd you help me escape those scouts? Are you going to lead me to your sellswords so you can dump me into a cargo ship after all?"

Eridene stormed out of the water, ramming herself into his chest. "I don't have to be on this malodorous island of puke, but I am! So I can help *you!*"

"Why!" He shoved her back. "Why do you care what happens to me?"

She grinded her teeth together. Jaime glanced at Toran floating in the background.

"I get it," Jaime seethed. "You think that if you help me, I might return the favor—"

"No, *Toran* thinks that way. Because he's a true man. Too bad he thinks you are, too—"

"I don't need you—"

"I don't need you either, Prince of Pimples!"

Toran noticed them and cupped his hands together.

"What did she say?"

Jaime called back irritably, "She likes your ass."

"My what? Eridene's talking about my gas?" He waded through the water to get to them. "You mean the mouth or butt kind? Come on, tell me! I *knew* girls were all about it!" He pleaded and whined at them until Eridene took them all by surprise—she tackled Jaime onto his back.

Toran's eyes bulged.

"Wowie, Beanie! Are you *wrestling* someone? I've taught you well, young apprentice!"

"Apologize for foul talk," she hissed in his ear.

"I think you should apologize for how foul you *smell.*"

She yanked him forward and punched his nose.

He gasped. "You punched me!"

"Yes, I—"

He bit her arm. Eridene cried out in furious surprise. Yanked his ear. It wasn't until Toran leapt out of the river, grabbed them both, and shoved them apart that they stopped murderously grappling for each other.

Eridene breathed heavily. Jaime held onto his nose. It felt like it was swelling to the size of a grape cluster.

"You're both more dope than the dope that's ruling this Kingdom," Toran said. He slipped his shirt back over his head, glancing into Jaime's knapsack. Scowled down at the gnarly bunch of rock lettuce. "Next person who starts a fight, I'll beat 'em up. Now go make me lunch."

"Go put on your pants," Eridene snarled.

She and Jaime exchanged a fiery glare before they stormed off in different directions.

~~⚜~~

For the next three days, Jaime and Eridene avoided each other—until Toran noticed the cottage.

It sat on the other side of the plateau, squeezed into a rocky alcove. Candlelight flickered through one of its sleepy windows.

He clenched his medallion. This was the first sign of life they'd seen since they landed in western Jaypes.

Toran's swollen eyes opened. "I can't believe we didn't notice it earlier."

"Prince Jamian might have if he wasn't so engrossed by himself."

"No, I'm just grossed out by your screwy temper."

"Okay, shut up, both of you." Toran jogged downhill. "Let's go find the cottage. Maybe they'll have ah—ah—ah—" He sneezed. "Food."

They followed after Toran, Eridene keeping at the front, Jaime travelling a few feet behind them. When they drew closer, his sandals juddered to a stop.

It was the strangest structure he'd ever seen: a dark roof with strange, curved eaves. Two stories high. A signpost hung under its door with the emblem of a white, pillow-shaped object.

Eridene groaned. "I don't believe this."

"What?" Jaime said. "What is it?"

"Toran"—Lady Eridene grabbed his slab of arm—"don't you think we had enough dumplings at the seaport? If I have to eat another one, I will throw up on *you*."

"You kids do what you want, but I'm getting me some yum-yum." Toran broke into a full-out sprint and tossed his arms into the air. "*Yaaaaah*, dumplings! *Ashi'maga*, Lord Kaippon!"

"What's a dumpling?"

Eridene pinched the bridge of her nose, ignoring him.

"I don't think this is a good idea," Jaime said.

He still didn't entirely trust Kaipponese foreigners, and if there was one doing business out here, in the middle of nowhere, that could only mean a royal garrison was stationed nearby.

Jaime said, "We better make sure he's okay."

They closed the final distance across the plain until they were outside the dumpling house. Toran was pounding hard on the sliding door. A stream of Kaipponese words rushed through his teeth.

Jaime stopped beside him. "What's going on?"

"The dope won't let me in." Toran glowered at the door. "I know he's in there. I saw him peeking at us through the window!"

An old man cried out in a tinny voice, "Go away! We *closed!*"

Lady Eridene took her friend's shoulder. "Leave him alone, Toran."

A passing draft swept the grit at Jaime's feet. He tensed. They whispered Ancient Empyrean words to him that he couldn't understand, only feel.

Something was wrong.

Jaime took two steps back. He drew out a basic attack current in his mind. The edges of his medallion glowed.

He released a strand of Empyrean energy.

Swush!

The door smashed in.

"Jamian!" Eridene exclaimed. "What are you doing?"

Toran patted his back. "My man." The older boy kicked through the splintered hole, shoving his body through.

Jaime's sandals smacked onto a thin rush mat. The walls were made of wood, not mud or clay.

Weird.

And there was the dumpling owner—a toothless old man with no beard and hoary wisps of hair on his liver-spotted head. He was small and cute. And probably older than the island's oldest tortoises.

Jaime dropped his guard, suddenly guilty. Had he heard the winds wrong?

The owner hobbled in front of a black curtain hanging over the kitchen's doorway. "*Aiyee*, what are you doing? You kids stir up big trouble!"

Toran stomped up to the Kaipponese. "Why you toying with my hunger, grandba?"

Eridene tugged him backwards. "Toran, *leave* him alone." To the old man, she smiled in embarrassment. "I'm so sorry about this, mister. He's just hungry, but we'll be leaving now. Right, Toran?"

Again, the winds whispered to him.

Help. Help...

Jaime slipped through the slitted black curtain. The old man shrieked.

"No, no! No, go—"

A basket strainer laid toppled on the earth floor. Half-chopped vegetables hung over the wooden sink. A chopping knife was stuck in the wall. Two metal boilers spilled half-cooked rice and steaming water over the mortar stove.

It was the most bizarre kitchen he'd ever seen.

He started to believe it was empty—but his heel kicked against iron.

Jaime swiveled around. A cage was set against the back of the kitchen, big enough to hold a fat swine.

Only a human body was in it.

"Lady Glaidde," Eridene whispered behind him.

Both of them bent down and peered through the hood. A *boy*. Maybe sixteen or seventeen. Jaws unruly with stubble—he must've been on the road for awhile. His dark brows arched downward like the curve of a hawk's talons. Jaime shivered. But the most striking thing of all was the flushed gold of his skin.

That can't be right. There hasn't been any sun in Jaypes for fourteen years.

His hair was dark as umber, so he wasn't Glaiddish. Glaiddish had blonde hair—except for Lady Eridene. But the boy didn't have the fair, pale complexion of a Jaypan, or Toran's tear-shaped black eyes. Two small hoops of steel pierced the boy's right ear.

Which Kingdom wore hoops like that?

Toran burst through the door. "What's happening?" he sniffed. "Beanie? Why's it so quiet in here?"

Lady Eridene sharply backed away, knocking into Jaime.

"He's a *Larfene!*"

CHAPTER TWENTY-SEVEN

"Leave *alone!*"

All of them spun around.

The little old man blocked the door, a rusty butcher's knife trembling in his hand. Jaime held up his hands for peace, but the old man kept advancing. Poor Moderna sobbed out of his throat.

"He evil, he evil. I should have kill him, chop up him inside my dumplings and feed to *guaimon*, evil spirits! Make them all go away from Uji house!"

"*Ew!*" Eridene and Toran cried together.

The man swiped his knife at them. Jaime drew his fan, slashing it out an arc to guide the precision of his air currents. A blade of air knocked the knife out of the owner's hand.

Jaime leapt up.

Caught it.

Eyes shooting wide, the old man tried to hobble out in an escape. Toran blocked the curtained doorway with his belly.

"Not so fast, buddy."

"Help! Help, Prince of Jaypes!" the man cried. "*Eeeeeeeee!*"

Jaime pointed the knife at the cage. "Where did you find him?"

"*Not my fault!*" the man croaked. "I minding own business, then *guaimon* came in demanding food. I told him we closed, but he gave me evil eye! So I, very, very scared, offer him dumplings. When he not looking, I powder his soup! Please, it self-defense!"

Jaime blinked. "Powder his soup?"

Eridene crossed her arms. "Hold on, a Larfene would never act so dishonorably."

"Not this one! He dangerous—stink of black blood like demon!"

"What were you going to do with him?" said Jaime.

The dumpling owner covered his face. "Please, I too afraid to kill him. His blood is cursed. Bad luck. I swear on your Jaypan god!"

Toran bellowed something in Kaipponese.

"Please, no hurt Uji! I only going to sell him in the black markets. You know, ones around the western coast. Get rid of him fast. I imagine His Excellency the Shogun would pay a fortune and put him in a garden cage, where he belongs. Let Shogun take care of bad *guaimon*—"

"He's not a *guaimon*," Lady Eridene insisted. "He's a *Larfene*. You'll curse yourself for caging one like this."

The man covered his face in despair. "I no know what to do— afraid take him out of cage!"

Jaime spoke up. "I'll let him out! Okay? Just don't tell anyone the Prince of Jaypes was here!"

The dumpling owner nodded, crying silently. "*Suki, suki*. Please, quick."

Jaime turned around to survey the cage's lock—and started.

It was empty.

But the lock was still bolted.

"He's gone!" Jaime cried.

"That's impossible." Lady Eridene spun around. "We were standing here the whole time!"

"Wow," Toran exhaled. "Grandba was right."

The old man blanched. "See what Uji tell you! He demon! *Guaimon!* He murder us all!"

His friends split, Toran behind Lady Eridene as she snatched the butcher knife out of Jaime's hand. The old man hung little silk-enclosed charms around all doors, clasping his hands, sobbing out prayers in Kaipponese.

Jaime's hackles rose.

No one had ever said anything about Larfenes and magical abilities. But didn't he see evil things in the Krete Forests? And what did Achuros say their first day inside the Library of Nandros?

A whole world exists out there that you don't know about.

He hurried back to the entrance. A man-sized hooded shape flitted behind a cluster of boulders. Perhaps it was the trick of the slate evening light, but the Larfene's shadow was warped like a bear's—or perhaps a large feline's.

Jaime held onto his medallion tightly, put one foot out the threshold.

"Wait!"

Every heartbeat a tiny explosion in his head.

"I'm the Prince of Jaypes! A friend."

The air dropped in temperature. Infinite blades of grass swayed. It was like the winds were bowing—or cowering—before whatever hid in front of him, something stained with blood and death.

His animal instincts squirmed at him to flee.

What if the dumpling owner was right, what if you should've listened—

The stranger stepped back out.

The passing clouds washed jagged shards of light against a sword and a quiver of arrows strapped to his back. Neither were there earlier.

Eridene and Toran jogged to catch up to Jaime's side. The Larfene eyed them one by one. His gaze rested on Jaime last of all.

"Nimzh jadi im'jin?"

Tendrils of energy stirred in Jaime's *avai*.

Ancient Empyrean.

Achuros once said that was the forgotten language of the spirit realm—a language of power.

"Lady Glaidde, Lady Glaidde..." Eridene pressed her hands to her head. "We're talking to a living, breathing Larfene. It's like we're living the Legend again."

Jaime took a deep breath. "The old man—he didn't mean you any harm. He was just afraid. You're safe now."

"I know."

All of them gasped.

"*Mimi.* Thank you."

Jaime scrambled for words. "The old man said you tried to attack him... Is that true?"

A cunning smile glinted behind the hood. "You tell me what you think is true, Prince of Jaypes. I appreciate by sword and blood if you tell no one of this encounter. Now I must be going."

The young man swerved around to leave, but Eridene surged forward to block him. Jaime tried to pull her back by impulse and missed.

"Wait! What are you doing here? Who are you? How did you get here? Are there others of you in Jaypes?"

The stranger paused. "No, my lady. No other Larfenes here. Too cold."

The humor in his voice broke the tension. Jaime inched forward and patted his chest.

"I'm Jamian." He pointed to his left. "That's Eridene—"

"*Lady* Eridene of the House Swansea," she corrected. "The Highlord of Rainmere is my father."

"—and Toran Binn of Kaippon. They're my friends."

The stranger glanced at the rippling clouds for a second.

"I am Arrys."

"Wowie," Toran whispered. "Grandba was really afraid of you. What'd you do to him?"

"Do you mean, what did he do to me?"

Jaime butted in, "How'd you end up in that cage?" He swallowed when those flashing green lanterns locked on him.

"That old man not used to visitors." Arrys smiled. "Or armed strangers in cloaks. I sensed his fear, but I did not foresee him drugging my food. Alas, I let my guard down. My pride. My mistake."

All of them nodded, their breaths held.

Toran wiped running mucus from his nose. "And, ah, what are you doing all the way out here, man?"

"Hunting apples." The cunning glint flickered back in his eyes. "We do not have any in Larfour. Selling few will make a man many coin. You are lucky, you Westerners."

Jaime said, "*They're* Westerners. I'm an Easterner."

"You are not a Larfene."

"No, but—"

"Then you are Westerner." Arrys brushed a hand over his dark stubble. "Where are you travelling to? A Larfene is bound by Earth to repay the favor of a friend."

Jaime's eyes fell on the blade. He guessed it was around forty-five inches long, about half the length of a Jaypan spear. Its bottle-shaped hilt was patterned with half suns and ornate palm fronds. The spread wings of a sand phoenix made the cross guard. He didn't know much about swords, but this one was probably worth his weight in gold.

Arrys noticed his stare and drew the hilt behind his cloak.

"I'm headed to the High Temple," Jaime said. "We're going to stop at the nearest town or seaport." He didn't look at Eridene. "We're parting once we find one."

"Korinthia."

"What?"

"You can reach the city in seven nights."

Korinthia. Isn't that the same City-State that lent troops to Prescilla?

"My *syrai* is yours until then, Prince of Jaypes. I will scout ahead for royal patrols."

Before he could stutter that the winds were already leading him, the Larfene flitted ahead. Vanished over the scraggly hills. He'd never seen anyone move so fast—not even Achuros the day he drew air currents against the Glaiddish.

A long silence.

Jaime finally said, "Should we follow him?"

"I dunno," Toran croaked. "I have a bad feeling about him—"

Lady Eridene cut in. "I'm not waiting around for royal patrols to come at us with fire and stakes. If I'm going to bet my life with anyone in this Kingdom, it's *him*." She broke into a brisk jog in the direction of the falling light.

Jaime glowered. *You just like him because he's dark and mysterious.*

Toran sneezed over his shoulder. "We better not lose her. I don't like being alone in the dark." When Jaime stayed in place, he scratched his butt. "What?"

"You feel it too, right?"

"Feel what?"

"His energies. Something about him is..." *Dark. Very dark.* Jaime fumbled for another word.

Together, they said, "Off."

Jaime nodded, glancing in the direction of the dumpling house. He lowered his voice. "What if the old man was right? What if Arrys is dangerous?"

"Well, I guess he's a Larfene."

"So?"

"Aren't Larfenes supposed to be Guardians of the Four Kingdoms or something? I don't know, you're the Prince. You should know more about the Legend than me."

I should. But I don't, because I never had a chance to finish Book One before the Archpriestess spat fire all over Arcurea.

Toran placed a hand on his shoulder. "Tell ya what, Juno." He moved his head closer to Jaime's ear. "With all these patrols around, maybe Beanie's right. We're safer with him. *But...*"

"But?"

"If you believe he's out here hunting apples, your brain is mush."

CHAPTER TWENTY-EIGHT

Arrys the Larfene jogged ahead of them, hood covering his brows at all times, recurve bow clasped in his left hand.

Lettuce weed and wild daisies streamed under Jaime's sandals. The plateau was rising into clay-brown mountains again. His eyes darted to their peaks constantly, looking for torches or iron gates or New Jaypes banners.

It had been too long since his last encounter with royal soldiers. His *avai* wriggled against the walls of his body.

As day circled into night, and back into day, they kept a single course at all times—towards a scraggly mountain jutting out of the horizon.

The night they reached its base, they stopped to build a fireless camp. Eridene sat by Toran, murmuring lowly. Toran kept sneezing from the pollen and batting away the moths. Arrys left to scout their surroundings.

When the others weren't looking, Jaime dug through his knapsack till he felt Achuros's ledger.

He pulled it up to the moonlight. Flipped through the pages. The rough pads of his fingers pressed against the precious black ink.

I wish you were here, Achuros. I barely know how to read books. You would know how to read Arrys.

The memory of the priest's piebald beard, the easy cock of his brow, his warm grip on Jaime's wrist—

His heart clenched.

Jaime flipped till he caught an entry with his name. He practiced reading in his head:

Today Jaime convinced me to teach him swordplay. He found a big stick and came at me first, right against the arm. Hells, it hurt. But I was not to be defeated! I swiped up another stick and parried. In four strokes, mine landed against his throat. Alas, but he did not know I learned weapon-fighting from the Queen's brother himself. We aren't just lazy winebags, we airpriests...

A smile curled over his lip.

He kept riffling. In another entry, Achuros replicated the cripple's brandmark on Jaime's wrist: an X overlapping a circle. More writing beneath that. The strokes curt and angular.

Riffling.

Another symbol caught his eye: a vertical line, intercepted by an upturned crescent; below that, two horizontal lines in descending length. Four of them duplicated in circle. The longer he stared, the space inside the center square started to shimmer...almost as if a cursed shape, or an eye, was forming . . .

Jaime sensed someone's gaze on him. He looked up.

Arrys was back, staring at him across camp.

No, not him—at the black ledger.

Jaime shut it and stuffed it back into his knapsack. For some reason, he didn't want anyone to know about Achuros's ledger.

The hooded Larfene waved at him.

"What is it?" Jaime breathed when they were noses apart.

"Do you have your windcloak?"

"How do you know about—"

"I saw you riding air currents a few times, from a distance." Arrys lifted his head. "Lady! Toran!"

The two stopped in mid-sentence, inching around, eyes wide.

"Let me show you something." He glanced back at Jaime. "It will be a long climb. Bring the rest of your things."

Mystified, Jaime obeyed and relayed the directive to his friends.

Late afternoon washed into early twilight. The conical shadow on the mountain shifted towards the east. In the time it took for a stick of incense to flicker out, Jaime's thighs began to burn. The familiarity made his tendons buzz with pleasure.

This was the kind of slope he used to climb regularly with Achuros.

"I see you were reading earlier," Arrys said ahead of him.

Jaime stuffed his hands in his pockets. "A book my mentor gave me on air currents. We used to practice my reading with *Legend of the Four.*"

"What do you know of the Legend?"

"Not much." Jaime panted, "I just started the last third of Book One."

"Hmm." Arrys glanced back at Lady Eridene and Toran. "And both of you? How much of the Legend do they teach in the West?"

Eridene clomped over the rocks, her panting loud and strong. "I haven't actually read the Books—really only our scholars and professors do that. Although my father has, all four. He's read every great tome in the Four Kingdoms. My governess taught me the Legend by word."

"I probably know less than—an—an Juno." Toran sneezed.

Arrys grimaced. "No good. It seems history has been forgotten in the West. History is power, yes?"

Didn't Achuros say the same thing?

"What's in the other two books?" Jaime said. "Books Five and Six? My mentor said they were lost."

They held their breaths as Arrys lifted the hood over his head, the hair over his neck flat with sweat.

"Book One begins as such…"

"'*In the beginning, all things were one, and the Four Kingdoms were one,*'" Jaime recited.

Arrys kept his eyes high to the sky. "Yes, very good. Three thousand years ago, all things were one. *Ilaqua.* The name of our mega-continent. One day, massive tremor opened the lands in the north. *Uhélaan.* The Great Rift, it is called. That day, waves of energy from The Empyrean, the spirit dimension, surged across the mortal realm."

"Is it real?" Eridene interrupted. "The Rift?"

Arrys didn't have to turn around. He walked several more steps, his arms swinging in time with his body, shoulders square, head held upright. Saying nothing for a second.

Eridene shrugged defensively. "History says that The Rift is as wide as Jaypes Kingdom."

Jaime snorted. "Impossible!"

"It is true," Arrys said.

"But how can you know if no one's seen the Fifth Continent?" Jaime said.

"This history is real."

Jaime cut in, "What happened after?"

Arrys continued. "Many clans of men walked *Ilaqua,* but these energies made them see illusions, made others kill themselves from madness. Most were afraid. But a few obsessed to control these energies, and so, control their enemies.

"And few discovered how. Mages, they were called. Those who could harness air, water, fire, earth, at will. Warfare broke out across the land as mages tried to conquer the other clans."

Lady Eridene nodded. "I knew all that."

Toran's eyes watered. "Sure ya—ah, ah—" Sneeze. "Did."

"And then what?" Jaime said.

They were halfway up the mountain now. He struggled not to peek at the way Eridene's wiry thighs were molding into her leather riding pants.

"More mages warred, more the elements warred on the lands. Many disasters: earthquakes, walls of sea, volcano bursts, even fire raining from the sky, slowly obliterating mankind. And many *yupalu*." Arrys nodded at the sky. "Mammoth rain and wind."

"Banestorms," Jaime murmured.

"But four young warriors from opposing clans joined to stop disasters swallowing the mortal world."

Jaime took his hands out of his pockets, reciting: "'*Their names were Larfour, Kaippon, Glaidde, and Jaypes. And they said, let there be unity on earth and the firmament.*'"

"Good!" Arrys gave a firm gesture of his hand. "This Prince is a scholar."

Jaime smiled. "My brother's favorite part was when Jaypes Ascaerii told his chieftain he was leaving. The chief replied: 'You cannot overcome this storm.' Line 1312. Hilaris recited it to me the night before he died."

"And he said, 'I am the storm.'" Arrys nodded. "Line 1313. Yes. Larfour leading, the four trekked across *Ilaqua's* broken earth. End of Book One."

"Gods, man, you know this stuff like I know a feast," Toran sniffed, his shoulders hunched from exertion.

Arrys continued. "Book Two: a spirit-warden of The Empyrean met them at Kazadûr Baen, his gateway, and guided them to the mouth of The Rift. The warriors climbed into layers, many layers, of The Empyrean, until they reached center.

"And they met a new spirit: *Dhaemûlaan*, king of the sky and earth. In order to stop the disasters, he said, they must overcome him. Book Three: The Great Battle. So the warriors fought him. But their mortal weapons were poor against his great energies. To stop the deaths of his friends, Larfour offered his life for theirs.

"He was touched so by his sacrifice that he gifted them with air, water, fire, earth. 'Serve me as wardens in the mortal realm,' he said, 'and you shall have power to quell the disasters. And you will watch over the Unity, peace between the elements, to ensure war does not break out again.'

"Book Four: the four emerged as gods. Before their clans, they quelled the elements and restored the Unity. Larfour split the lands into five, one for each of them, and the fifth for the spirits. Under him, the four named their first descendants Kings, bestowing them with the gift of their Continent's element. Thus, the Sages and the Four Kingdoms were born."

Jaime spotted the top of the hill from here. Daylight was just sinking over the horizon. This was the highest mountain he'd climbed yet.

"And Books Five and Six?" he panted. "What happened in them?"

"Destroyed. It has been the mission of many priests to find them, but I believe they are gone."

"What is there else to know?" Lady Eridene stomped with her legs wide apart, arms swinging like she owned the air. "After Book Four, here we are, in present day. Maybe there never was a Book Five and Six."

Arrys repeated, "Maybe…"

The footholds scattered. From here, reaching the pinnacle meant climbing onto final precarious humps of rock.

Toran shook his head, wiping at his raw nostrils. "Uh-uh. This's as far as I'm going."

"I agree. This is dangerous." Eridene thumbed her charm. "Why are we up here, Arrys?"

"It is time. Where are your windcloaks?"

Toran's face went white. Arrys grinned and climbed onto the final splinter of rock. Once he made it to the top, he offered a hand to Jaime.

Jaime's heart jolted. The plains and scattered corktrees below him were a world away. Even his flight off Arcurea's cliffs had been half the height he stood at now.

But despite the gnawing in his belly, thrill made him take Arrys's hand.

Jaime planted his sandals tightly onto the mountain's point. The winds were cold, but so clear up here—the air like silver washing into his lungs. Ahead of them, to the west, layers of mountains rolled over the land like dark ocean crests.

Is this Jaypes's highest mountain?

Jaime took all of it in, his mouth open.

Arrys smiled. "Have you ever flown before, Prince of Jaypes?"

"I used to think so, but maybe I was wrong." Jaime grappled though his knapsack for Aulos Menander's windcloak. The spare, folded neatly, still laid at the bottom.

Jaime offered it. "I have an extra."

The smile rose into the Larfene's eyes. He took it, his grip sturdy.

After he draped Aulos's windcloak over his own shoulders, Jaime took a deep breath.

Gods, if only he could share this view with Achuros. The old man would've broken into song and tears. And if only he could tell Hida: *Mamá, I think I made it to the highest peak. The air isn't so bad up here.*

"Ready?" Arrys said.

Jaime swallowed. "Ready."

He backed a step, took a running charge—and leapt.

Freezing winds battered hair from his face. The plain below him rushed up close. His lips flapped, his mouth stayed open. Any second, he was about to vomit up his innards.

Jaime screamed.

The Kingdom's air currents caught his folds—and he was falling parallel to the great expanse of sky.

Adrenaline spurted into his blood in place of terror.

Jaypes Kingdom expanded beneath him, bathed in the light of evening. Hills, gorges, the river he'd crossed with Toran and Eridene, so far below. Leagues of pristine lands untouched by the King's fire. He was flying *above* clouds. Above Usheon's bloodstained Kingdom, untouchable in this space. Never had he felt so many emotions at once.

He spread out his arms, his lungs inflating with delicious air.

My asthma—gone. It's never coming back. Not up here.

"*Yeeeeeeeeah!*" he shouted.

Lady Eridene and Toran's screams echoed behind him. But they laughed through their terror, diving left and right behind him.

Somehow, Arrys flew lither than them all, cutting through the air like a bred hawk.

He caught up to Jaime. Their four silhouettes neared each other. Arrys held out his arms. Jaime reached, took hold of his left hand. Eridene gripped onto Jaime's right.

They shouted at Toran, "*Reach!*"

"*Aaaaaah!*" he yelled back, and locked onto their circle.

They spun like that, linked together. Jaime sensed a deep bond sealing their lives together, as mighty and supernatural as The Empyrean itself, rippling across time, into the past and future, as their laughter spilled color over the open canvas of the skies.

CHAPTER TWENTY-NINE

Within seven days, as promised, Arrys took them out of the sizzling plateau. Toran pinched his runny nostrils shut and cried hurrah.

"Gods-damned Jaypan summers!"

But things had drastically changed in the lowlands. The royal bounty for Jaime's capture went up to fifty thousand decara—one lifetime of paid wages. Soldiers now watched every causeway, village, and stinking hole in the ground.

After a day of darting patrols, the hills rolled off into dark shores. On the opposite side of the gulf, the bright lights of a city spilled across the skies like stars.

"Is that the *ocean*?" Eridene cried.

She tossed off her riding boots and ran down the sandy slope towards the shoreline.

Toran sniffed. "Glaiddish and their oceans."

Jaime's chest soared. Gold-dusted clouds touched the misty indigo horizon. Overlaying it was a great City-State. Korinthia. The fireflies of its lights scattered the coast. Briny winds battered its pennants, bearing the sigil of a white-chested tyto. Beyond the sea, a cluster of dark islets laid in slumber. *So this is what the ocean looks like.* Despite the wall of fiery warships blocking off the open ocean, the coast stole his breath.

Here Jaypes Kingdom *ended.*

Did the Royal Decree exist out there, where the gulls were flying?

Were there other boys like him fighting for their people, and their freedom, out in the West?

Far below, Eridene and Toran dipped their ankles into the tidepools, nattering secretively. Probably about their Western war, as usual. Jaime stayed on the cliffs. Korinthia's fires filled him with a renewed sense of time.

How did Arcurea and her southern allies stand? Were Florin and the others even alive?

A soft thud.

Arrys's hooded shape prowled behind a palm tree. He threw off his bow and quiver, thrusted his sword in the dirt. Jaime watched him kneel before it. His lips moved in a soundless prayer.

Jaime bent down to study his sword, the distal tip of the blade, the boat-shape of its pommel.

What kind of sword is this? Not the chopping shortswords the City Watch wear. A longsword? Greatsword?

His hand closed around the half grip—heavy. An unaccustomed three, maybe four pounds.

The older boy lashed out and grabbed his wrist.

"Never touch another Larfene's weapons." Arrys's direct eye contact jolted him. "Unless he has been defeated in battle."

"Sorry," Jaime whispered, dropping it.

A smile broke through Arrys's thick lashes. He let go, chortling. "Why go so pale like that, Prince of Jaypes? Do you think I'll cut you up into cubes and sacrifice you to sand gods?"

"I don't know, will you?"

"Mm…maybe."

"How did you get past the King's blockade?"

"Larfenes like no questions from Westerners."

"I told you, I'm not a Westerner, and I know you're not here for apples—"

"*Nòs kivhan.*"

"What does that mean?"

"'No questions.'"

"I get *one*. Why did Larfour close its borders?"

Arrys turned his back to face the glowing sea. After a pause, he spread his hands.

Jaypes's stormclouds ended just beyond Usheon's warships, but their dark entrails spread far into the horizon. Jaime went still. Listened. The royal garrison overlooking the strait released a prisoner's scream into the starless sky. Somewhere across the Skyrros Ocean, a second war was ravaging two larger Kingdoms.

"To shield ourselves from this," Arrys finally said.

⁓ᵕᦊᵕ⁓

Eridene let out a loud yawn, waking him from his nightmares.

"Lady Glaidde, today is the day."

The hems of her riding pants were still soaked from yesterday's beach excursion. She tried to rise, and stumbled. "Oh, my leg…it's gone all numb."

"Let me help you, lady."

Arrys materialized out of the dark in his ghost-like way, holding out his hand. Eridene smiled in pleasure and took it.

Seeing them touch stirred up gusts in Jaime's insides.

He stomped across camp to shake Toran awake. Toran's belly spilled from under him as he grabbed at Jaime's ankle.

"Mm…mutton," he drooled.

Jaime tried to shove him off, but he wouldn't let go.

"Toran, apple pie!"

His friend flubbered up. "Where?" As soon as he saw the clumps of grass and dirt sticking to their clothes, he sighed and collapsed. "Ugh, gods. I can't believe I'm still in Jaypes."

Arrys cocked his head at the forested villages far below them. "We escort the lady to a hostel?"

"Yeah." Jaime stuffed his hands in his pockets. "But we should stay outside Korinthia, just in case—"

Toran broke in, "Fishing villages are my favorite places in the world. C'mon wimps, let's go find something to eat!"

He bounded down the mountainous slope, wrists flying behind him like tails. Jaime called him to stop.

"Hey! We have to be careful—"

Eridene galloped after him with equal excitement.

Arrys started down the rocky path, casual but brisk. Jaime swallowed down his irritation, following behind Arrys. After a second, he discreetly tried to imitate the elder boy's pace. Tugged his shoulders back. Freed his hands from his pockets, though the natural swing of his arms felt stilted compared to Arrys's.

They reached the nearest wharf. Korinthia City loomed across the gulf. Warm winds brought him aromas of roasted nuts and baking flatbreads opposite the boardwalk.

His belly rumbled.

Skies. It feels like I've been eating biscuits since the day I was born.

Shopkeepers were folding up their shutters, builders adjusted their awnings in preparation for the day's heat. Traffic was already thick. He nearly bumped headfirst into a smaller boy wheeling eels, mackerel, and clams. Jaime was about to pinch his nose—but *there*, gods! Soldiers stood under New Jaypes colors fluttering at the intersection.

He dashed behind the cart.

The little Jaypan behind the wheels raised his brow. Jaime placed a finger at his lips and glanced over his shoulder.

Toran was openly devouring a flaky fig pastry outside the marketplace. On the opposite side of the unpaved street, Arrys swiped an apple from a stand, munching contentedly under the shadows. Outside a sweet stand, Eridene eyed a vibrant array of honey sticks from the Koiphi islets, where purple dye was extracted from sea snails—probably the same islets he could now see with his own eyes.

Jaime rolled towards Eridene and pressed himself behind a wooden crate.

"Toran and Arrys are stuffing their faces," he growled, "but you, Eridene? Even you?"

She glanced down at him, raising her brows. "Why, of course. We're in a fishing village. Why aren't *you?*"

"Because I'm not a girl, I'm of age under the Royal Decree, and I'm Jaypan. The last thing we should be doing is eating right now!"

Sighing, she returned the honey stick. "Okay. I'll go look for an inn."

"You shouldn't go by yourself."

"I'll ask Arrys to accompany me."

They faced each other awkwardly, the remnants of their fight by the river lingering between them. Lady Eridene twisted the end of her braid.

"Well, I suppose this is farewell."

Why did those words gut him in half?

"What're you going to do next?" he said.

"Sail home, I suppose. My mercenaries won't look for me for long without pay." She looked away.

Jaime scratched self-consciously at his chin pimple. "Let me, um, watch over Toran till he's done eating. I'll be right here. Then we can say goodbye. When you're back."

Lady Eridene smiled. "Okay."

"Great. Then actually, I'll see you soon."

"See you soon."

"Soon," he repeated.

He stood up and nodded feverishly, a crooked smile on his face—and stumbled over a pile of crates. Face flushing, he swiveled around, marched towards Toran before he could see Eridene's expression.

You idiot!

When he dared turn back around again, his eyes fixed on Eridene's receding curves. He sank into a dreamy daze—till someone punched him in the jaw.

Jaime stumbled. "Empyrean hell! What was that for?"

"You were gawping at her ass," Toran said.

"I *wasn't*—"

Toran tilted his fat head. Jaime turned even redder.

Hasn't he ever looked at her before?

"Ya know, plenty of men have stared at Beanie like that. Adulterous pricks. Old wrinkly grandpops. Little kid-boys whose dads are asshole constables. Usually they look at her tits."

"Toran—"

"Shut up." He pulled up close. "You have no *idea* what she's been through. The way high lords—even her own family—talk about her at court. And I'm telling you now, you aren't the one."

Fire prickled Jaime's face. "You're just saying that because you're jealous."

"She's my best friend. You know that."

"And you think I'm not the right one because what?"

"Because." Toran pulled up so close that Jaime tasted his warm, sweet breath. "Eridene doesn't want any man."

"She's a girl. All girls want—"

"You don't know what girls want. The last thing you'll ever know is what Beanie wants. Don't you see the way she talks and walks?"

They glanced at her vanishing shape. The wide strutting of her steps. Her heavy stomping. Her bellowing voice, and loud, snorting laughter as she bantered with a foreign beer merchant.

"She didn't get like that by accident," Toran said. "She's trying to protect herself."

"She's not betrothed."

Toran snorted. "You think she'll ever marry *you* when you're still trying to figure out your own heart?"

"Shut up, you sap."

Jaime started to pull away, but two slabs of arms grabbed him, shoved a half-eaten fish pastry in his mouth, and patted his back.

"Juno, you know I'm your friend."

"Mmpf, you know *nothing*—"

"That's why I'm telling you the truth now so you don't have to find out the hard way."

Toran grinned at him.

Jaime spat out the fish and tossed it at him.

He stormed through the marketplace, keeping sights on Eridene. A few minutes later, the air brought him low moans and cries of pain. And roaring cheers. From the east side of the village.

He skidded to a halt.

What's going on out there?

Under the roars, the choked noises grew louder. It was like the cries the young bulls would make when Lord Gaiyus publicly sacrificed to Lord Jaypes in the Pantheon back at home.

Someone was dying.

You're a Sage. Remember? It's your *responsibility to stand up and fight.*

His earlier anger puffed out of him. Temporarily, he let Eridene out of his sight and accelerated his pace. Swarms of mosquitos hovered over rainwater pools. Jaime smacked them away. His sandals splashed into turbid water. He grimaced, but didn't stop sprinting through the gravelly roads till he passed under an archway. The clay buildings vanished into cypress trees. A hillside ahead of him dropped off sharply.

Below him, a full audience sat in the orchestra of a theater. Some one hundred Jaypans.

His belly writhed.

Men in togas, striped with the blue colors of Korinthia, sat on the lower tiers. Councilors. They guzzled wine, lifted their fists with shouts. A small civic building with tyto tapestries loomed behind them.

Six spearfighters circled the arena below. Their shields, helmets, and corselets glinted in the daylight.

They surrounded a broken shape.

The prisoner held his spear at an angle like it was too heavy for him. Ankles bowed. Ears cut off—the same way the Archpriestess had cut off the ears of Townfolders who were caught worshipping Lord Jaypes. His gray eyes a bleeding, bloodshot mess.

Jaime pressed his hands to his mouth, swallowing his vomit.

He would recognize that face anywhere: Nides Doupolous. The young Townfolder who had flaunted stories of the King's fire before Julias Markus backhanded him.

Here. Alive.

Well—just barely.

The spearfighters jabbed at his legs. One of them impaled his left thigh. Nides sobbed in pain, falling to one knee.

Roars of delight erupted over the stands.

Jaime swallowed.

By all rights, this man was a traitor. The moment he had left Mount Alairus to join the King's army, he betrayed his hometown.

And he had openly stood at the Archpriestess's side as Hilaris burned at the stake.

Nides deserved to die.

But his suffering cries pulled the strings of Jaime's *avai*. He was so sick of this, so tired of the lawlessness and murder that would go on forever so long as this war existed.

Despite the screaming of his senses to stay put, he raced downward, dodging the spectators, shoving past the shields of the spearfighters, till he was side by side with Nides.

"Stop!" Jaime yelled.

The stench of sweat, dirt, and feces infiltrated his nostrils. Nides sobbed quietly behind him.

A swarthy, middle-aged councilor in the front stands stood and raised a hand to his guards.

"My name is Jamian," he shouted. "I am the Prince of Jaypes, and I *command* you to let him go."

Adrenaline coursed hot through his blood.

With his back turned to Nides, the latter could have impaled him at any second. Townfold's greatest traitor probably hungered to.

Finally, the swarthy councilor said, "Prince Jamian. That man betrayed all of Lord Julias's hidden bases to the royal armies. My bondlords captured him at the base of Mount Alairus. We are friends of Senator Gaiyus, our leader of the Air Alliance."

His shoulders uncoiled. *Commander Julias led a battle? Lord Jaypes, there was a battle after I escaped?*

"Nides Doupolous participated in the slaughter of thousands of Alairans. He deserves to die in the arena, in disgrace—that is the Jaypan way."

"The royal authority will find out," Nides interrupted. Tears carved trails down his filthy face. "They'll burn you. They'll burn all of you maggot-infested rebels!"

A few heads turned away in disgust. Jaime closed his eyes. In another lifetime, he would have demanded Nides's head.

But he turned around, looked Nides in the eye. *Gray.* Both of them had the same Jaypan-gray eyes. The young soldier turned away first, unable to bear the shame of his mutilated face.

Despite the knot in his chest, Jaime forced the words out.

"I forgive you," he said. "For fighting on the King's side. For fighting against my uncle. For yelling to the Archpriestess that I was the Prince, for being part of the royal force who came to burn my family at the stake. I forgive you for all of it." Jaime cupped the taller man's face. Nides flinched. "I'm sorry for what they did to you."

Several Korinthian councilors shot to their feet in fury.

"You mock us!" an elder councilor hissed.

"No," Jaime snapped back. "This"—he nodded at Nides's mangled face—"is Usheon's way."

"Many Jaypans died in your name—"

"If you host cruelty and murder in my name," Jaime interrupted, "you aren't fighting for me. As your Prince, I'm mortified."

The jaws of the elder councilor started to tremble. The arena blazed with hateful gazes.

What are you doing? You could completely undo the following you have.

But Jaime kept his shoulders square, glaring back at them.

The surrounding spearfighters glancing at the head councilor for orders. Nides sobbed quietly behind him.

The Korinthian Guard never received their orders.

A host of royal soldiers brimmed over the top of the theater, their spears and shortswords brandished.

CHAPTER THIRTY

"*Jamian!*" someone screamed.

Lady Eridene streamed through the parados, the side entrance behind him. A few seconds later, she was guzzling air by his side, a stolen spear raised.

"What are you doing?" she said. "Announcing you're Prince like you own the world? Are you trying to die?"

Adrenaline pumped him with giddiness. He breathed, "I would only die if you did."

"Funny," she hissed.

Skylight radiated off her honey skin. A strand of hair, loosed from her messy braid, fell down the curve of her neck. His senses went berserk. He wanted to kiss her there.

You're so perfect.

"Bring me the Prince!" their commander hollered. "Alive, by order of the King!"

The councilors scattered, crashing into each other. Nides's eyes stretched in manic ecstasy. "They're all rebels!" he bawled. "Part of the Air Alliance—they confessed it!"

Jaime swiveled around.

"Go on, you're free," he hissed. "But if I ever see you again, I'll kill you myself."

Nides started to smirk a reply, but Jaime backhanded him.

Eridene gawped.

Mouth falling open, the young soldier hobbled away, tears welling in his eyes. A second later, he vanished into the fray.

One of the Korinthian guards leapt over the lower tiers, drawing his spear. A silver pin similar to Sojin's—a flying tyto with a sword and javelin in its claws—glistened above his heart.

"Protect the Lord Mayor!"

Jaime's glanced at the swarthy councilor in surprise. *Lord Mayor?* Was that man Lord Romulus, the same Lord Mayor who had lent Florin and Prescilla troops?

"No!" the mayor bellowed in reply. He gestured in Jaime's direction. "Protect our Prince!"

Their eyes met.

This high lord, three times his age, wearing blue dye worth more than everything Jaime owned, lowered his bare knees into the sharp gravel.

Bowing.

Several of his councilors breathed out gasps. Relief coursed through Jaime's blood. Six months ago, such a sight would've made him stumble off a mountainside.

Florin and Prescilla might be gone, but you're not fighting this war alone.

Jaime straightened his shoulders.

"Let the winds lead you," Lord Romulus recited.

Jaime returned a nod. "I shall find my feet."

Eridene tugged at his arm. Soldiers were forming a ring around the theater, pouring into the stands. Fifty of them. In less than a minute, they would block the parados. Their last chance of escape.

It would take unshakable focus, and a well of *avai* energy, to stop all of them.

"We have to go, Jamian."

Eridene nudged him again, but Jaime shook his head. Dug his sandals in the ground, facing the oncoming tide.

"You're mad!" she cried. "You can't defeat them all!"

The first sounds of clashing steel rippled across the theater. Jaime drew a current in his mind—a gyre of air. Focusing his *avai* energy at the soldiers' middle lines.

And released.

Back at the Battle of Arcurea, several seconds would lag between the currents he drew in his mind and their manifestation. Today, they were instantaneous.

The wheel of air knocked the enemy's center off balance. Soldiers exclaimed, crashed down the steps, shields colliding into spears. Only the front and rear lines, and the edges of the company, were still advancing.

The Korinthian Guard formed a protective line in front of Lord Romulus, but their Lord Mayor roared, "I said, *protect the Prince!*" He stretched out one arm. "Spear!"

His City Captain tossed him a shortspear, its pennant flying with the blue and white colors of Korinthia.

Lord Romulus thrust it at the nearest soldier.

An arrow whirred in Eridene's direction. Jaime clamped onto her hand, spun them around. *Avai* swelling with energy. He discharged a shaft of air. The archer, fifty feet away, crashed onto his nose. Jaime caught her before she could fall.

Her back nearly touched the ground. Jaime's body dipped in her direction, their faces only a breath away from each other.

"Thank you," she whispered.

"I'll take out the rest of them," he whispered back. "Watch."

He pulled Eridene upright again, turned back to the soldiers. The front lines were crossing into the arena now. Eridene sprang back into the fight, huffing and grunting as she swung. They crashed against the Korinthian Guard, lightning against thunder.

Jaime focused.

Small bursts of currents fired at individual soldiers, needle accurate. The Korinthians panted in surprise, their spears half raised.

In a final offensive, Jaime sprinted forward, powering his *avai* energy. Rolled past a soldier's thrust. Snatched up a spear. Leapt onto the first tier of seating, slammed the butt down.

A shockwave of air blasted across the orchestra, levelling every standing body at full force.

The last of the soldiers smashed into the stone seating. Helmets crashed against steel plates. Wine spilled everywhere. No one got back up. Several of the councilors were also on their bellies, moaning.

Oops.

Jaime dropped his arms to his sides, a crooked smile on his face. "Sorry."

The Korinthians left standing, including the elderly councilor who had spat at him, went silent. Their jaws nearly touched the ground.

"Gods," the City Captain murmured, "he fights like an Ascaerii."

The elderly councilor broke into laughter. "If only the rest of the Alliance could see this!"

"They will." Lord Romulus staked his spear against the ground. "Send out our owls. Rally the bondlords who have pledged themselves to Romulus Biros. Tell them our true King lives."

Eridene squeezed his arm. "Jamian, he's rallying all of the west for you."

"The south and the northeast are also on my side." He stood straighter. *At least, what survives of them.*

He forced himself to look at her.

"We should get you to an inn. It's too dangerous to stick around me any longer. You need to sail to Glaidde tonight."

The smile vanished from her face. "But I can't just—"

Before she could finish, a horn blared across the western expanse of Jaypes Kingdom. A long, single note. So deep, the sky seemed to shatter.

Both of them turned their heads in the direction of the strait. It was coming from inside Korinthia's citadel.

"A breach," the captain murmured. "The royal authority knows the Prince is here."

Jaime clenched his fists. "I'll stay and fight—"

Lord Romulus turned around. "No," he said sharply. "Is your final destination Korinthia or the Lord's Temple?"

"I saw the royal armies march on Arcurea." Jaime bared his teeth. "I won't let it happen to another City-State—"

"Florinokles was my friend also, Highness."

"I *know* how to fight—"

"Your battle is with the King, not these royal dregs!"

Eridene whispered in his ear, "He's right, Jamian. It will take some time for your King to send an entire army here. By then, western Jaypes will be mobilized to the teeth."

His nails dug into the tendons of his palms, but he met Lord Romulus's incisive gaze. Nodded. He touched Eridene's arm and led them in a sprint.

The din of marching shields, armor plates, and boots on grass tingled his spine. More soldiers were coming. The City Captain yelled orders. The Korinthians followed their Lord Mayor in a retreat back to their city walls. The tips of enemy spears began to appear over the top of the theater.

When Jaime and Eridene were halfway across the theater, Arrys and Toran cut through the parados. Arrys's hood shadowed his face.

His recurve bow was strung, a deadly arrow notched in place. Toran's eyes bulged as he drank in all the fallen bodies.

"I brought you some friends," Toran called.

Jaime panted. "Friends?"

"The rest of the fishing village. I told them it was your birthday."

Gods.

And there they appeared, behind the descending lines of soldiers. Several of them commoners he had seen in passing. The little boy with the porgies and mackerels carted his wheelbarrow alongside the crowd.

"Merry birthday, Prince Jamian!" someone shouted.

"Merry, merry birthday!"

"Hark! There is Lord Jaypes's chosen one!"

The soldiers paid them no attention—until they started to pelt smelly seathings, bruised fruit, and stale barley bread at the soldiers.

The theater fell into a greater storm.

"You're crazy," Jaime half laughed, half cried to Toran.

The royal commander, cowering behind the rear ranks, cursed them. "Anyone who raises a hand against the King's authority is guilty of treason! Do you hear—"

"Long live King Jamian!" the City Captain interrupted.

Roars followed this.

Adrenaline pounded his heart. It took everything in him not to turn around and release a slew of air currents to protect them.

This isn't your fight. You can't fight every fight in Jaypes Kingdom or you'll never make it to your duel with the King.

Arrys released an arrow. A soldier swinging against an unarmed fruit merchant snapped backwards.

"Go!" the Larfene yowled. "This is our parting!"

Jaime nodded. With the heartbeat of the Korinthians pounding in time with his own, the three of them escaped out of the parados and into the free winds calling him northward.

CHAPTER THIRTY-ONE

To Jaime's relief, the Korinthian Guard gifted him with three of the Mayor's best coursers. As western Jaypes trembled from growing mobilization, Jaime galloped into the winds.

The weight of his shoulders felt so heavy.

The three of them didn't stop flying across rocky plains of fennel and prickly lettuce till the Skyrros Ocean vanished from sight.

"I had a nightmare," Eridene told him the next morning.

She peered through the crumbling pillars of the cylindrical tholos they camped out in. White clouds drifted above them. Speckled slopes covered the horizon. The growing stormwinds leveled the firs, beeches, and oak trees.

Toran was somewhere out there, harvesting wild beans. For once, Jaime was thankful his best friend wasn't here.

"What did you dream of?" Jaime said.

"You."

He returned his gaze to the shadows of their camp.

"I see you facing your father in the Colosseum," she whispered. "And you're burning…" A small breath echoed against the walls. "I hear your screams, but they're like my own. They vibrate inside my bones, and I feel them behind my eyelids, and my whole body is melting."

"That's so dramatic." He laughed without humor.

"Maybe that's all this is. Jaypan theater drama."

She stood up.

"I have nightmares too," he said.

She paused.

"I failed to keep my promise to you." Jaime turned away to face the gusts. "We were supposed to find you an inn. And now you're back on the road with me. The King will kill you—"

"Jamian, I *want* to go to the Temple with you. I know you don't trust me—"

"Why would you say that?"

"I'm sorry I wanted to kidnap you to Glaidde."

Although nervousness was about to tear his chest open, he took the frame of her shoulders. At this distance, her hair smelled like the wind. That urge again to kiss the curve of her bare neck zapped his sanity.

Toran's voice filtered in: *Eridene doesn't want* any *man.*

Jaime felt a tiny tremor ripple under her skin where he touched her. Toran had to be wrong.

"Run away with me," she whispered. "The lords of Glaidde will protect you. You'll be safe there."

"You know I can't."

A quiet sigh escaped her mouth. Gently, he took her back to the ledge, and they sat down by each other.

He stuffed his hands in his pockets. "I'm tired of being afraid," he admitted.

"Everyone is afraid of something," she said.

"What are you afraid of?"

She clutched her charm, her thumb rubbing the seven-pointed star.

"You can tell me anything, Eridene."

Her eyes fell.

"I just…I can't stop thinking about the war at home. I'm worried about my father and uncle. I keep having dreams—Emperor Viro spiking their heads on his palace gates. I see the Kaipponese breaking through the Border Wall, and—and—selling me. Uncle says we'll win the war, but Jamian…I'm so afraid."

Sweat was forming pools in his hands.

"Can Toran help you?"

"Toran is my father's prisoner of war."

Jaime beetled his brows. "I thought you were friends—"

"We are. But Toran is a peasant from the enemy Kingdom. He can't stop the Imperial armies from storming the Wall."

"How do you know each other?"

"It's not important—"

"It is to me."

She sighed. "My father's bondmen invaded the other side of the Wall nine years ago. They looted the rice fields and demanded coin. Toran fought them. He wanted to protect his family, but he gave them such nasty blows that they brought back him to our castle. The marshal demanded his head. I pleaded Father to let him go."

"And he did."

"He did." Eridene tucked her fingers around the loose curl of hair on her neck. "Toran can't go home, not as long as our war stands."

"Why?"

"Prisoners are treated like deserters under his Emperor's mandate. If you leave Kaippon for any reason, you're a deserter. The Imperial Court beheads deserters."

"But that's not fair—"

"Nothing is fair," she interrupted. "Toran wants our war to end as much as I do, maybe even more. It's been nine years since he's seen his family."

Jaime breathed, "I had no idea."

"He's afraid, too. Of many things."

"Really?"

"He…" She paused. "Never mind."

"You said you trusted me," he teased.

She sighed. "You *have* to promise not to tell. Toran's really sensitive about it." When he nodded, she lowered her voice. "In Kaippon, they draft any boy older than twelve. They'll behead you if you try to avoid the Imperial Conscription. Toran hates his Emperor. I think it's why he let my father's bondmen capture him when they stormed his village. He says he didn't have a choice. But…I think he's afraid of dying."

Jaime lifted his head in astonishment.

"I—I thought I was the only one," he croaked. *I thought I was a coward for feeling that way.*

"You're not."

Compelled by her honesty, he whispered, "I've never told anyone this before, but…I'm afraid to do what everyone expects of me. They think I can just kill my father because Lord Jaypes wants me to, but—" He raked at the growing locks of his hair. "Eridene, I've never had a real father before. I've seen the terrible things he's done, but I still love him."

"It's okay—" she began, but he shook his head, fighting to keep his voice steady.

"That makes me weak, doesn't it?"

"You're not weak, Jamian."

A horde of cicadas buzzed against the walls of his chest. He couldn't sit still. He couldn't keep it in anymore, so he leaned in towards her face. Forced the words out.

"Eridene, I—"

"Juno!"

Jaime whipped around. Toran closed his grip around his shoulder and yanked him backward.

"You're awake! Look at all these beans I found!"

The joy in his friend's voice was stilted. He dumped out a knapsack of green pods.

Jaime seethed.

He's doing this on purpose. To keep Eridene and me apart. Why?

Every tendril of his body screamed at him to blow Toran off the hillside. But his mother's voice filtered into his head.

Breathe. Breathe, Jaime.

"We should probably get going." Toran fought the congestion in his voice. "Put some distance between us and the royals before a storm comes."

Jaime glanced at Eridene, his jaw clenched.

Are you on my side, or his?

She avoided his gaze and squeezed her friend's fleshy shoulder. "Toran's right. We should go."

Toran's right.

The cicadas died in his chest. Jaime walled the emotion from his face and marched out to untie his horse.

Toran was *not* right. Toran would never be right. Eridene *did* have feelings for him. He was sure as the storm clouds pulsing over the hills.

⁓ತ⚜ತ⁓

For two months, they rode through slopes of wild manna, poppies, and heliotrope until dark peaks appeared over the horizon. Jaime raised his head, his breaths coming out light and fast. Sojin mentioned peaks would appear just before he reached the High Temple.

The final stretch of their journey was coming to an end.

It felt like he'd swallowed a stone. It sat in his belly, growing heavier and heavier. First of September. The date of the prophecy was less than a month from now.

What could the airpriests possibly teach him in a *month*?

By noon the next day, the summer heat grew frigid. This was the same northeastern air he grew up with on Mount Alairus. Home was close. But he veered away from it, riding further north.

Nostalgia squeezed his heart.

On the third day, the shadowy foothills of the Lunar Peaks appeared through thick mist. By evening, just as Sojin has promised, a shallow ford intercepted their path. A storm of purple blossoms snowed over their heads. Windflowers. They raised their heads in awe.

"We made it," Jaime whispered.

He led them across over the ford. A new airmarker rose above the reeds. Jaime bent over, touching its stone.

Silverwind, the medallion whispered.

He took their windcloaks out of his knapsack, and without a word, they rode the new current for an hour. It kept them low, never more than twenty feet above the ground.

Within the hour, they reached the base of the peaks. A narrow stone path vanished into the first row of pine trees marking the end of Usheon's world, and the beginning of the untamed north.

The three of them climbed.

At midday, Jaime swore this was the most grueling part of his journey yet. Sweat lathered his armpits and thighs. His legs crumpled from burns. The air grew icier the higher they ascended, until not even birds flitted within the isolated wilderness.

On the fourth day, Toran started lagging. Jaime stopped to wait for him. Dark patches sagged under his friend's eyes.

"How are your allergies?"

"What?"

"Are you okay?"

Toran's shoulders hunched more than usual. "Just tired, and kind of homesick."

One week later, Jaime was the first to climb all the way up the side of the tallest peak. He helped Eridene up, then Toran. Thick mist obscured whatever lied ahead. The medallion hummed against his chest with energy. His insides fluttered.

Together, they took hands and stepped forward.

A suspended bridge led them into a network of mountains that stretched into the horizon.

Jaime gasped.

The skylight was an ethereal gold. His eyes darted to find the sun, but all he could see was the moon—a massive crescent falling through a bath of evening clouds.

"We're in the sky," he said in awe.

His friends were staring too. Jaime closed his eyes. The air was thin and stale here. It was hard to breathe. *Strange.* Hadn't he climbed plenty of slopes without a problem?

Perhaps we're too high in the sky. Didn't Mamá say it was impossible to breathe on high mountaintops?

He forced his panic down.

As windflowers fell, air currents slithered over his shoulders and away into the distance like they didn't know him.

This range is even taller than the one Arrys took me on. So I haven't climbed Jaypes's highest mountain yet.

Eridene pointed. "Look, Jamian. There it is."

Temple Jaypes rested on the crest of the middle peak. Jaime took the lead and crossed the ancient bridge. Only clouds sprawled under his sandals. His belly squirmed.

The skies grew dusky by the time they arrived at the Temple gate. Jaime glanced at the dazzling crescent. It loomed over him, larger than ever. He shivered. For some reason, the symbol he saw in Achuros's ledger—and the eye in the center—flashed back.

Eridene held onto his arm for comfort.

He took in a deep breath, and shouted: "I am Jamian Ottega, Prince of Jaypes, and I request to be admitted!"

He waited.

The winds whispered through the pomegranate trees, laurels, and fields of wild hyacinth. The gates stayed shut.

His friends exchanged glances.

"Maybe you didn't say it loud enough," Eridene said. But when he tried again, nothing happened.

Toran sighed curtly. Eridene pointed to their right.

"What's that?"

He followed her finger to a large hole in the side of the stone wall. Water trickled out of it, cascading into the open clouds below.

"Looks like a storm drain," she said.

"Let's give it a try."

They formed a human tower, with Toran on the bottom, and helped each other clamber inside. The walls were barely big enough to fit a child; Jaime's shoulders were cramped in. The way ahead was dark, but he focused on the present and tapped into his Sage-vision. Violet color illuminated the walls, sharpening every clay brick. All of them groaned as they sloshed knee-deep into water.

"Ew, what's that smell?" Eridene scrunched her nose.

It hit him in a wave—Jaime almost fell over. The smell of a rotting carcass. All of them went quiet as they passed a dead rat, and then another, and then another, until a trail of them floated out of the tunnel ahead.

His skin prickled. Whispers bit his ears as they winded deeper into the dark. But these weren't coming from air currents. They were half-formed words; the same whispers he'd heard in the Krete Forests just before the mist-monsters appeared.

When they rounded a bend, a ladder stretched up into a manhole. Jaime splashed forward.

"I think I see an exit!"

Eridene exclaimed in relief. Toran kept silent. Jaime groped for its slippery edges and lifted it open. Daggers of skylight cut into his eyes.

He was standing in a giant *city*. The sky soaked the tips of the white parapets with fiery light. All of these structures were slender and taller than the highest beacon towers in Arcurea. Ancient cobblestones formed a winding river of roads that snaked infinitely into the horizon of Jaypes Kingdom.

The High Temple was completely deserted.

Whispers licked at the sweat on his neck. Jaime shut his eyes, but he couldn't wall them from his mind.

Kuurjal hzajdi gûl.

"Do you hear that?" he said.

Eridene blinked. "Hear what?"

He met eyes with Toran. Sweat rolled down his best friend's temple. Toran's coal-black eyes darted away.

Somehow, Toran could hear the Voice too.

But how?

And suddenly, Jaime remembered the night of their lanterns— hadn't Toran mentioned he often had nightmares?

Jaime had never asked what kind.

Oblivious, Eridene stepped past them and looked around. "Where is everyone?"

"Maybe they're all dead," Toran said.

Jaime sharply turned on him. "Don't say that."

"Why? Gods, will you grow a cock?"

"*Shut up!*"

Eridene started. "Jamian—"

It was the whispers—they were cornering him into the edge of a sheer cliff he couldn't see, only feel.

Toran stormed over and jabbed him in the chest. "Look here, meathead. We're all frustrated and tired, and you're not dragging us through another half of the Kingdom just so we can run from more soldiers." He turned around. "C'mon, we're leaving."

"Is that what this is to you?" Jaime cried. "Running around the Kingdom, playing Prince like I have nothing better to do? Do you have a brain, or is it all barley bread up there?"

Toran's eyes burst into hellfire.

But this wasn't anger—this went beyond anger, to something as black and hateful and murderous as the tunnel they had waded through—as the Voice that churned inside his head.

"No, Jamian, I've got no brain 'cos I'm fat old Toran who eats and drinks and burps out jokes. Is that it?"

"I didn't mean—"

"I've spent an entire year following you into banestorms. A *year* in this shithole Kingdom. I thought I'd be back in Glaidde by April, but it's past summer. I can't imagine how my family's working the rice fields another year without me. They've got tax to pay to the Emperor, unlike Your Royal Highness, and I swear I'll kill you if I have to do this for another month!"

"That's not fair. You promised—" Jaime swallowed. "You *promised* back in Arcurea you'd help me win this war. No matter what. Or was that all just a fart?"

"What've I been doing this past year?" Toran bellowed. "Wake up! And you tell me if *you* have a brain—"

"I'm doing the best I can—"

"And man, aren't you a Sage? Your people need your help, but all you do is hide behind peasants and unarmed councilors—"

Eridene interrupted. "Toran—"

But he pushed her behind him, eyes locked on Jaime. "I made a promise to you, sure, but you're the one throwing it away. If you had any balls, this war would've been over yesterday."

Something in Jaimeh finally snapped.

"What about you?" Jaime screamed. "What about *you*, Toran Binn? You're useless! You say I have no balls, but you won't even join the military to defend your own family! At least I'm trying to learn Air, but you won't even pick up a pike and be a stupid *foot soldier!* So who has the bigger balls, me or you!"

Toran went stiff.

Jaime realized too late what he said. Toran's eyes slowly passed to Eridene. She covered her mouth in horror.

"Jamian! You weren't supposed to—"

A sudden thrust into his stomach.

The world flashed red. For a second, he lost all feeling.

And then his senses rebounded back. It was like a building had collapsed on him. Jaime bowled over, heaving.

Toran reappeared. Shoved him flat against the ground.

At first, Jaime tried to protect himself. But Toran threw blows at his head with the sharp of his knuckles. Jaime started fighting back with equal venom. His nails dug into flesh. Twisted. He bit down on Toran's arm. Kicked as hard as he could. They screamed things at each other, cusswords Jaime had never used on anyone before— until Eridene yanked them apart.

Toran snarled. Jaime was about to lunge back in. Eridene stormed between them.

"That's *enough!*"

Hot tears brimmed Toran's eyes. Jaime's breath stopped.

Was Toran Binn *crying?*

In the heat of his own adrenaline, he noticed Eridene was struggling to hold back her own tears.

"Toran's right. It's time for us to leave."

"No," Jaime shouted, "I'm not leaving till I find the airpriests!"

"Then maybe it's time to split up," she said quietly. "Toran's right. They are gone."

Jaime's blurry eyes widened. Eridene took Toran's arm, gently easing his limp against the weight of her own body.

"We'll be waiting at the base of the mountain if you change your mind."

He stared at their crumpled backs, his shock blazing into fury.

"Fine! Leave! I never needed you anyway—"

He screamed at the sky and ran.

Thud. Thud. Thud.

His chest—all he could hear.

Jaime threw open the door of the nearest tower and sprinted up the steps. They ended into an empty spherical room at the top. Withered petals and laurel leaves littered the ground. He took Aulos's windcloak out of his knapsack and threw it over the ground, collapsing on it.

The sky grew dimmer, hurling his shadow against the wall. Jaime shut his eyes.

Forget it. Forget what Toran said.

He couldn't remember what had made them snap—only that his feelings of fear and despair were real.

He wrapped himself tightly into the windcloak and pressed the medallion to his chest. Temple Jaypes whispered to him lowly.

Kuurjal hzajdi gûl, Jaime.

And then there was quiet laughter.

CHAPTER THIRTY-TWO

Jaime tossed and turned.

He was falling, falling, falling, into a black hole where only nightmares and white mist existed. Dying screams clawed at his ears. Bells tolled desperately. Shadows flitted across sun-drenched streets in Jaypes's high mountains, but every time he stopped to look at their faces, they vanished.

His eyelids fluttered. Sweat drenched his face.

Kuurjal hzajdi gûl.

The low rumble, like that spoken from the belly of a beast, rose out of the grinning whispers.

You cannot hide from Me, Jaime...

His eyes snapped open.

Amber daylight, the color of Arcurea's firepits, diffused through his window. The winds swirled around his ankles, urging him to wake. A heavier, darker energy—not elemental—poisoned the air.

He rubbed the sweat from his face and closed his eyes. *Ugh. Just a nightmare, that's all. I've got to find the airpriests. I can't leave without them. Gods, Lord Romulus and the other Alliance Lords are warring for me. Where else can I go?*

Jaime tossed the knapsack over his shoulder and skipped down the stairs.

The heavy door moaned. He pushed past it and stepped onto the everlasting expanse of white.

It should have been morning, logically, but the hidden sun flooded the mountains with the blood-orange light of late afternoon. An upturned crescent loomed over Jaime as he wandered. He knocked on several doors and poked his head inside, but they were empty.

Where are all of you?

As the winds guided him up a slope, Jaime considered shouting. Someone was bound to hear him. But somehow, he sensed that would be a bad idea.

Come to Me, Jaime...

The Voice was returning, louder and clearer than ever before. Something cast a shadow over him from above. Jaime looked up. A bell tower blotted out the sky. Charred and cracked. The ghostly tolling from his dreams prickled his ears.

"Who are you?" he whispered to the Voice.

No answer.

Jaime walked up a new set of steps and into a vast courtyard overshadowed by the moon. A marble staircase led to an enormous temple structure, held up by a colonnade. The open sky framed the balustrades to their right and left.

He slowly bent down.

Dried blood smeared the pattern of stones. It was dark, but not faded—the blood was recent. His chest tightened as he traced the rusty stains to the opposite side of the courtyard.

There was an attack here.

The wind's whispers pressed him to run, but Jaime ignored them and climbed the steps. When he was at the top, he dragged his eyes over the courtyard. The smears of blood formed a vertical line with a crescent and two dashes below it. Four of them—aligned in a square.

This was the same emblem that Achuros drew into his ledger.

And the longer he stared, an eye began to form in the center…

Royal soldiers suddenly swarmed into the courtyard—tens, hundreds of them, until he couldn't count. In the time it took him to turn around, the Archpriestess was already standing behind him.

The clashing light of the hidden sun and the glowing moon silhouetted half her face. Her bottom lip was ripped. Jaime hoped someone in Arcurea had done that to her—Florin, maybe. Or better, Lady Prescilla. Now that they were standing face to face, Jaime noticed it: her irises had turned as poison-black as her pupils.

As their eyes locked, it felt like all of the Kingdom of Air was drawing a breath.

Her knife slashed across his eyebrow.

Warm blood spattered into Jaime's eyes. He stumbled backwards, temporarily blinded. An explosion of pain went off in his body.

The Archpriestess thrust out one arm—and he went tumbling.

Jaime crashed onto the stones and rolled forward a few times, sharp points digging into his face. His body finally woke from shock. It was a shallow wound, but Damasia hit a blood vessel. Warmth gushed down his face. Jaime bent onto his elbows, choking for air. His lungs heaved—*no, no, no.*

After four seasons, his asthma was coming back.

He landed in the blank square of the cursed symbol.

Raising her head to the sky, the Archpriestess bellowed, "Temple Jaypes is mine!"

Those foul words echoed across the silent expanse of the mountain chain, drowning the air. Jaime forced himself to rise to his feet. His eyes fixed on the Archpriestess, blurred by hatred.

"Kill him!" she shouted.

Jaime held onto the geyser of hate bleeding from his heart. He couldn't hear his heartbeats anymore, or the Voice. He heard, saw, and felt nothing but the swarm of arrows rushing at him across the courtyard.

Jaime twisted his body. A wall of air blew out the volley. The archers released their bowstrings again, but his lip contorted. He snarled at them. Another wall broke their attack. Before they could try again, he sent lashing currents straight into their ranks. Shouts of surprise. Bodies crashed into each other. Horses threw off their riders and streamed out of the courtyard. As the front lines cracked, the archers he wounded scrambled to get up—the flesh where his currents had struck bore bloody gashes, like whip marks. *Good.* The unspeared soldiers drew their swords and leapt over the fallen men. Tears streamed into Jaime's eyes, mixing with the blood of his face wound. Soon, the soldiers trapped him into a tight circle. He spun around and around in a blur, evading the jabs of spears. Thrust violent bursts of air at them. Each held the force of artillery. Several soldiers screamed as they tumbled over the balustrade. The sky swallowed them up. Others lay facedown on the ground, their eyes lifeless, their necks snapped, their noses smashed into their skulls. As The Empyrean's energies overpowered his mind, reality blurred. The evening sky seemed to transform into tar. Torches glowed like diabolical eyeballs of light. The soldier's shouts turned into fiendish laughter. And drums. They didn't look like men any longer, but vaporous bodies hidden behind white mist. They leered and jeered against the fire and smoke. Their whispers flooded the skies.

Kuurjal hzajdi gûl. Tee hee hee!

Mocking him.

Jaime struck down one soldier after another, but each time another one filled his place. There were too many of them. The strength of his *avai* energy rolled in and out. Gaps appeared in his vision. Air no longer entered his lungs. The flight with Arrys, Toran, and Eridene in the skies seemed like a distant dream.

Someone struck him in the head. A blade jabbed his left calf.

He collapsed.

The tide of soldiers parted as the Archpriestess approached him. Jaime looked up at her, chest rising and falling shallowly. The knife in her hand dripped a fresh trail of blood.

"Stand," she ordered.

They forced him onto his feet. His left leg stung. He shifted his weight on his right. Damasia seized the medallion. Then, she licked up the blood on his forehead with the point of her tongue.

"It was all too easy," she whispered. "My Air Alliance contact revealed everything to me. After you vanished from Arcurea, not even the King's bondlords knew where to find you. But I did. How sad Achuros died for nothing."

Jaime rasped, "It was you. You betrayed the airpriests."

She laughed.

Their faces blocked out the other soldiers, so none of them saw the flash of evil dilating the black in her pupils. This was no airpriest. No, this was a monster originating from the same hellworld as the Voice.

"Fare thee well, Prince of Jaypes."

He closed his eyes.

Cold steel bit into the flesh of his throat.

CHAPTER THIRTY-THREE

A storm opened out of the dark skies.

Jaime kept his eyes closed. He had completely lost his grip on reality. But the rhythmic blasts of air fell stronger and closer, and the soldiers' grips on him loosened. He dared open his eyes.

Gold the size of his head hovered between him and Damasia. A *beak*. It reflected his bloodstained face.

Slowly, he lifted his head.

Enormous wings beat the air. Dark feathers. A crest like the horns of a dragon—he was staring at a hawk, but this hawk was the size of Sojin's destrier.

It released a sharp, high-pitched cry.

"Larfour," whispered the Archpriestess. The black ink drained out of her gray irises. She backed away from its spear-sharp claws.

The soldiers shouted and scrambled for cover. The giant hawk dived. Half consciously, he slipped into Aulos's windcloak, pulled the knapsack over his shoulder, and staggered onto the balustrade.

Jaime fell.

Somewhere above him, faint bellows chafed against the hum of flying arrows. Glacial air burned his face. No currents existed up here to catch him. He fell through the clouds, fell in the direction of the mortal world, until the only thing that existed was the beating cadence of wings. The hawk had caught him.

His eyes rolled back. His head went limp.

Crackling fire. Wild wrens, owls, partridges.

Gods.

Partridges?

Their bird cries were little throaty clicks—a noise he hadn't heard since he escaped Mount Alairus.

Jaime tried opening his eyes, and immediately regretted it. They were so crusted. Like someone had dumped salt on his eyeballs, sealed them shut with honey, only to be torn back open with a prong.

He forced them open.

The world was blurry and distorted. The prickly trees swayed violently; stormwinds blew the alpine ferns and bluegrasses flat. Something smelled of cold mint.

Were those trees *kingpines?*

Kingpines didn't exist in the south or west. He was near Mount Alairus—near home!

Near Mamá.

Jaime grappled with his body until he was upright. A wool blanket blocked out the worst of the windchill. Someone had wrapped a thick pad around his left calf. The small fire struggled to stay alive.

In front of it was a pile of golden apples.

Gods—

Chomping noises from behind. Then a voice said, "What did the lord apple say to lady melon, say you?"

"*Arrys?*" Jaime cried.

The dusky young man gulped down his apple and said, "'Tis a shame we cantaloupe."

Jaime threw off the blankets. "You're alive! What—what are you doing here? How did you find me?"

"Master hunters are the Larfene."

Jaime shoved his hands in his pockets. "This is all wrong. I shouldn't be here. I have to…"

Have to what?

The skin above his right eye stung madly. One more gift the Archpriestess had given him—a scar he would wear for the rest of his life. It dawned on him that with the High Temple fallen, he had no idea what to do next, where to seek help from.

He covered his face. Arrys caught him as he was falling to his knees.

"The airpriests are dead. I'm a Sage, Lord Jaypes's chosen, but somehow, I'm always one step behind the King. I—I don't understand."

Jaime tried to push Arrys off. He kept his glistening face turned away from both his friend and the firelight. "I'm okay."

"I have known grief," Arrys said quietly. "The kind that parches great rivers and hides crop under cracked earth for an eternity." He paused. "My baba and mamah died in an avalanche. Always I see their faces in crowds, from the corner of my eye, when the torches are low. But when I turn around, they are gone. I mistake them for someone else. This is a wound that never heals."

Jaime refused to look at him.

"I understand, Prince. *Feel.* It is okay."

Arrys pressed his arms against Jaime's back. His balance caved. Jaime collapsed over Arrys's shoulders. The last time he embraced anyone like this was Hida, just a few minutes before Hilaris's burning.

"I need to get to Townfold—" he choked. "I need to know if she—if my mamá is alive."

"Prince, the Greatsporting is in three weeks."

"I don't care!"

"You have my *syrai*. It will be done."

Later that night, after Arrys left to a brook to wash, Jaime closed his eyes. Without his medallion, he felt like he was trekking the Kingdom naked.

As the darkness deepened, Arrys's shadow skulked across the scraggly forest floor. Through the slit of eyes, he studied the Larfene's steel hoops, his sunstruck skin, the glistening beads in his thick eyelashes. All of him seemed to capture the firelight.

Arrys turned his back.

Jaime stifled a gasp.

Black ink swirled over his tendons, down his upper arms. It looked like calligraphy of some sort, interwoven with ivy, jasmine, and the fiery remiges of a hawk. The details were dagger-sharp and delicate, down to the individual strokes.

Breathtaking and terrible as a pyre's flame.

Who are you, Arrys?

Jaime sifted through the energies of his *avai*, but they were murky, impossible to read—he detected tendrils of love, fiercer than what he ever felt in Hida. But he also picked up on fainter tendrils of bloodstain. They were buried under a long, dark past of murder.

Why are you here?

<hr />

Just when his eyes closed, someone urgently shook him awake.

"Time to get up."

Groggy from pain and exhaustion, Jaime rolled aside. "No. Go away—"

"I could," said the low voice, "but this camp is about to see a storm in fifteen minutes."

"A storm?" Jaime flipped upright, biting down when pain needled his calf.

The fire was out. Irate gusts gnashed at the needles of the kingpines.

Arrys pulled the hood over his head, a finger against his lips. "Soldiers. They are marching this way. Where is this Tenfold you spoke of?"

He closed his eyes and listened to the banestorm. Its winds were streaming in from the east. "Townfold is in the direction of this banestorm's origin."

"Mm, I feel it." Arrys narrowed his eyes. All of his senses seemed perked like a feline's.

Jaime checked his neck by habit—and started when he didn't find the medallion there.

The Archpriestess has it, remember?

They streamed across uneven slopes of broom and woodrush, familiar flowers nipping at his bare knees. A year ago, Jaime had raced through these same shrubs with Hilaris in a race to the barrows.

Arrys prowled. Jaime limped.

The gales battered away his drowsiness, blasted his hair flat. Branches whipped at his brows. The wind screamed at him. Every waking step was a nightmare.

In only a ten-minute window, Jaime smelled a menagerie of air currents: wild ones, wispy ones, some galloping across the forest in single-minded urgency, some diffusing tremors of massive energy greater than all the human *avai* of Arcurea put together. These made him stumble backwards and choke out a gasp.

"It's like the whole Kingdom's being ripped apart," he yelled.

Arrys said grimly, "Northeast Jaypes has been this way for several months now. Air has fallen from Unity. This Kingdom is coming to an end."

Jaime's heart accelerated.

The Legend is real.

He glanced up at the boiling clouds.

They were dark as metal, clashing and kicking and roaring at each other like giant rams. The boundlessness of its energy, the berserk wrath of the air currents—this was the kind of mega-storm the four gods tried to stop long ago during the preformation of the Kingdoms.

All for nothing. This would be Jaypes's final storm.

Eridene. I have to get to her. What if she's still waiting for me at the base of the Lunar Peaks?

He swallowed down his panic. The kiss of her sweet breath blotted out everything else.

An eternity later, the trees parted. The Estos River muttered under him—the same waters he had jumped into with Cassie. A mildewed bridge opened toward a valley of colorless slopes.

Jaime slid to a stop.

Lord Jaypes…

Where Townfold Village should have been a smoking wasteland. The lofty kingpines he fondly grew up with were splintered teeth sticking out of waist-high debris. Tattered New Jaypes banners flailed in the wind. No thatched houses. No arbors of grapevines, no porches shadowed by awnings, heirlooms passed down by generations of Alairan families. No sounds of clanking iron from Jorges's forge, or the taste of crusty barley in the air.

Jaime fell to his knees.

Tatty tents struggled to stay standing against the tempests. Perhaps fifty, perhaps less. This was all that was left of Mount Alairus.

"It's over," Jaime said.

Arrys placed a hand on his shoulder.

"My mother—"

"Go first," Arrys murmured. "I will follow close behind. Strange tracks on these paths trouble me."

Jaime didn't ask questions. By the time he staggered down into the valley and neared a shallow bend in the river, Arrys was gone.

The world went silent except for babbling water and the crunch of his sandals against dandelions. Thick mist obscured the way. His steps slowed.

Whispers.

Sweat crept down his neck. These weren't coming from the winds. It—whatever *it* was—was growing closer.

It was *hunting* him.

The pines formed tight clusters the banks, stamping shadows against the mud. They started to move and transform in the corner of his eyes. Jaime glanced behind him.

The bluegrasses around him were still.

A breeze tickled him behind the ear, warning him of death. The feeling was so strong, like a chariot smashing into his chest at full speed.

Swish.

Jaime whirled around, crouching his knees into defense position. He couldn't swallow. Several pine needles gyrated downward from something he couldn't see.

Animal fear fueled him into a sprint.

Thick mud slurped at his sandals. Jaime limped across the river, cutting his ankles over shallow rocks.

The things teased the edge of his sight—rolling clouds of white—chasing him from both banks. So many of them.

"*Arrys!*" he screamed.

Baby-pitched laughter in his ears.

Arrys, Arrys, they mocked back. *Hee hee.*

Jaime glanced over his shoulder for the Larfene's hooded shape, but as he turned back around, he crashed to a halt.

A spark of mist intercepted the river, blocking him from Townfold Village. Mini human-shaped outlines flashed in and out of the white smog. Their heads and arms were bent at grotesque angles.

His mind raced for Air. He grasped at his chest for his medallion. Without it, he couldn't draw his element.

Jaime backed away from them. *Splash. Splash.* Another wall of mist rolled to a halt behind him. Trapping him. A thousand whispers and baby laughter scraping his ears.

The mist-monsters *were* real.

CHAPTER THIRTY-FOUR

A spitting yowl forced his eyes open.

Jaime gaped.

A golden leopard twice the size of any mountain cat he'd ever seen bounded over the rear wall of mist-monsters—it looked exactly like the larger version of the lantern-eyed tomcat that followed him around the Krete Forests last fall.

Countless hisses echoed in his ears.

The fog broke formation. Flitting silhouettes, whiter than ghosts, appeared behind it. They moved too fast for him to make sense of what they were.

The leopard landed on its feet. Bared its fangs. Some of the mist-monsters accepted its yowling challenge with the sound of grinding iron teeth.

Jaime sprinted upstream. Pressed his hands to his ears to shut out the horrible noise. Water soaked him down to the marrow.

A mist-monster cut in front of him, giggling in delight.

It locked gazes with him.

For one breath, Jaime saw blistering, pupilless eyes—the color of human flesh burning in flames.

Those eyes set his mind alight. The stormy landscape vanished into a new dimension of infinite pitch-black. A doorway of burning light floated toward him, growing larger, larger. Its light drenched his skin in crimson.

Doorway into The Empyrean—

It was trying to drag him into the spirit world—into a layer of hell.

No!

Tongue frozen. Jaime screamed. No sound came out. Instinct told him whatever was behind that door would end in horrible death—

Let go of my mind! he cried.

Yum, yum! the mist-monster squealed.

The doorway floated ever closer, breathing heat against his face. It felt like a knife was severing through his brain—

A yowl split his eardrums. The mist-monster released him.

Jaime gasped. The mortal world rebounded back into view. Water streamed from his eyes.

In the next two seconds, the most bizarre thing happened: the oversized cat reared onto its hind legs—and morphed into Arrys.

Jaime released a scream.

Arrys gripped his sword, slashed a vehement arc over Jaime's head. The mist-monster shrieked. Shattering into white shards of light.

"Run!" Arrys roared.

Mud gushed into the bed of Jaime's nails as he picked himself up. The mist-monsters' numbers were growing on both banks. He resorted to his last option—

Jaime ducked into the deep end of the river.

The world under its surface was eerily silent. His heart drummed against his head as he dived further upstream. The rocky waterbed opened into a tunnel. *Please, please, lead to an opening.* His only other option was to resurface.

The seconds ticked away. His lungs bucked, screamed for air. Just as they were about to burst, glowing light shimmered over the surface.

His head shattered through water. He choked and wheezed for air.

Crystal rocks grew all over the walls, throbbing with a faint blue light. His *avai* sensed a well of spirit energy. *A cave.* Didn't Achuros once mention otherworldly reservoirs, scattered across the Four Kingdoms, leached The Empyrean's energies into the mortal world?

Jaime dragged himself onto shore. A monstrous headache wiped out his strength. If the mist-monsters tracked him here, he wouldn't be able to fight them.

Jaime listened, waited.

Seconds trickled away into minutes.

A minute turned into an hour.

No one came for him.

He breathed hard, counting to four. *Stay awake. Stay awake.* But the poisonous energy that invaded his mind sapped him. Jaime closed his eyes.

His head fell limp.

⁓⚜⁓

Splashing echoed in the cave. Jaime's lungs heaved in dry fear. No matter how much he grappled for air, it eluded him.

"Prince?"

Jaime stumbled onto his feet.

Arrys stepped out of the pool, his umber hair clinging to his neck. Jaime's knapsack hung over his left shoulder.

"You—you're—you're a leopard—"

The Larfene held up his hands in peace. Jaime trembled, his back pressed against the cave wall.

"Don't! Stay *away* from me—"

Arrys unslung the knapsack, offered it to Jaime.

"You were not meant to see that," he mumbled.

"What? That you can *turn into animals?*" Jaime's eyes bulged as he understood. "You—you were that cat that followed me through the forests! And that hawk that rescued me from the High Temple! *Gods*, is that how you got through the King's blockade? By turning yourself into a whale?"

"I flew," Arrys wearily corrected.

"Lord Jaypes! You've been watching me since the day I escaped Mount Alairus!" Jaime grabbed onto his cloak. "No more secrets! You've *got* to tell me who you are!"

"*Nòs kivhan.*" Arrys arched brows lowered even more. "No questions. But for our friendship, I will admit: I have been hunting the things you saw since—" He paused. "Since the death of my baba and mamah. For many years, I saw none in Larfour. But these dark energies are growing stronger in the West, and then I felt the stormwave in Jaypes. I knew a Relic awakened a new Sage. I have been following you ever since to see that the Darklings do you no harm."

Jaime rubbed the scar wound above his eye.

Darklings? Dark energies?

"You *felt* the stormwave," Jaime said. "How is that possible unless you're a Sage or airpriest?"

"There are many powerful beings in the Four Kingdoms. Inside my Kingdom, some know how to shape-shift into beasts. They are shaimans. I was born with this gift."

Jaime slumped against the wall. "Other powerful beings—what other beings? Why hasn't anyone in Jaypes—or the other Kingdoms—seen those mist-monsters before?"

"Before our gods formed the Four Kingdoms, the Continents crawled with dark things—"

"Is this part of Book Five and Six? Your version of the Legend on the mountain didn't mention any dark things."

Arrys thumbed his pommel. "They are a varied race. For example, the things you saw outside—banshi. I trust you understand what they do."

"What…" Jaime's voice cracked into a whisper. "What happens if they drag you through their doorway?"

"This, *nòs kivhan*." *No questions.* "You do not want to know. I have seen men devoured in terrible ways."

Jaime swallowed.

"And many, many more cursed beings. The Dark race is as old as the Sages, but fortunately, less powerful. In the days of yore, the High Kings of Larfour hunted them to extinction. Book Four."

Jaime closed his eyes. "I wish I couldn't see them."

All the times one had appeared behind him, he was afraid to turn around and look, but he would *feel* it, his hackles standing straight up, raw fear surging into all corners of his body, neck paralyzed, his chest about to burst, as he prayed, prayed, prayed it would go away.

"I understand," Arrys murmured.

"Who are they? What do they want?"

"As the Sages uphold the Unity, they try to destroy it. They lurk in the shadows, plotting, scheming, *whispering*." His grip tightened on his hilt. "Hungering for Sage blood. It is Sages who protect elemental peace. It was Sages who nearly obliterated the Darklings, and now they are back to do the same to your kind."

Cold crept up Jaime's spine.

"All think they are dead. No one in my Kingdom will believe me, but now…" Arrys peered at the pool where they resurfaced from. "I have seen them here, and so have you."

"What do they want?"

"Wipe out the Sages, and so bring back The Empyrean's

supernatural disasters on our world."

"But why?"

"This is a dark plan I cannot figure out. And perhaps, no why; simply because they are mischief. They trespass into the mortal world with growing numbers. Night is becoming darker in the Four Kingdoms. The other Kings do not see or feel. Not even the High King. But I am here to hunt, and bring a Darkling before the High Throne. Then, the Four Kingdoms will believe and unite as our ancestors in the Legend. We will destroy them for good."

Holy skies.

"How many of them exist?"

"A few hundred perhaps," Arrys said. "No more."

"That's why they're following me. They know I'm a Sage."

"*Elaa.* Yes. I am a Darkslayer. Like my ancestors, I hunt Dark blood under the cover of night. My *avai* felt Darklings in your Kingdom, but I did not expect to find so many."

Does Usheon know about the Darklings?

With trembling hands, Jaime reached for Achuros's ledger. Perhaps the old airpriest had written something about them. The cursed symbol—it had to be the Emblem of the Darklings. But the rumbling Voice—who did that terrifying Voice belong to?

He cried in dismay when he opened its pages. Its precious ink was bleeding into the water stains.

The second Arrys saw the foreign symbols, he snapped upright.

"May I see?"

Jaime gingerly handed it over. The Larfene's gaze darkened as his eyes skimmed over the vanishing words.

"*Hava Lashquélaan,*" Arrys breathed. "Who does this book belong to?"

"My mentor, Achuros. He was an airpriest." Jaime forced in a breath. "Why, what's it say?"

"Let me study. I will keep this."

"But—"

"This mentor of yours." Scarred, rough hands pressed the pages shut. "Where is he?"

Jaime swallowed. "Dead."

Arrys nodded and tucked the ledger deep under his cloak. "Lucky, as you Westerners say. Lucky for you, and me."

CHAPTER THIRTY-FIVE

It was Jaime who finally shook Arrys to leave the cave. As terrified as he was of the banshi, he *had* to find his mother. He had to know the truth.

Both of them climbed the scrubby slope that opened to the biggest of Townfold's network of villages.

Scattered fires were the only light on the mountain. Behind the collapsing palisade, squalid people wandered between the charred remains of their houses. Thatch, spilled oil, and broken pottery lacerated his feet. Town Hall was gone. Ptolemy's Library gone—all the historical buildings of their once great town, levelled.

All that remained of Champion's Square was the pyre.

Jaime stared up at the stake from the very same spot he stood a year ago. A heap of charred kingpine and debris loomed over him.

Please, don't let them—don't—

His brother's screams. Like Hilaris Pappas, it was as if Townfold Village—and the rest of the mountain—never existed.

Vultures circled above him. One of them screeched, waking him.

His feet shuffled toward the ragged slope of the akropolis. It was like time didn't exist, he was separated from his body, observing former Jaime Pappas from a distance. None of this was real. It couldn't be.

Jaime reached the pinnacle of Townfold, standing where Lord Gaiyus's villa used to be. The blood rushed out of his head.

Bodies, spears, and shields littered the ground as far as the eye could see. Somewhere out there, the vultures picked at Julias Markus, Commander of the Free Guard.

Everyone he knew, gone.

As Jaime turned, his sandal caught something on the ground. Rimus Vulas, the town bully—his eyes were wide open. Maggots writhed and squealed inside a tangle of intestines spilling out of his stomach.

Jaime crashed onto his knees and vomited. Arrys was back at his side, holding him.

So this is what war really means.

Suddenly, he understood why Sojin had hated him. Why Toran snapped at the Temple—even why Eridene wanted to smuggle him to Glaidde against his will.

"I have to get home," he said.

Arrys didn't seem to understand. Jaime's mouth couldn't form words. His lungs shrunk back to the size they were before Hilaris's burning.

Not enough air.

He needed his breather.

The cry of vultures grew louder as he trudged out of the main gate. The barrows loomed high overhead. He could almost see ghost projections of him and Hilaris skipping past tall broom and wild daises to get to Hektor Pappas's grave.

The barn was empty. Sokrates, their mule, gone.

Water drenched his eyes, falling over his clamped teeth. His sandals scraped against the beaten earth portico of their country house. The familiar tapestry of ivy crept over the south wall.

Empty.

Of course it was.

The sobs stayed lodged in his throat. As Arrys held him in their central courtyard, the banestorm's tempests passing overhead, a familiar scent trickled into his nose.

Stonemist incense.

Oh, what a sweet aroma! An outcropping of memories surfaced from his childhood. And as the scent grew stronger, Jaime lifted his head.

A blurry shape formed in front of him in the doorway of their kitchen.

"*Jaime?*"

Arrys let go of him. In the span of a breath, Jaime was pressed in her arms. His head now towered over her shoulder. The smell of stonemist incense washed over him, and his lungs inflated with air again.

"Mamá," he whispered.

His foster mother buried him in kisses. "My Prince. My sweet Prince, you're alive…"

"What happened after I ran?"

"They took all of the children. Commander Julias lead a small resistance south of here, but they were defeated. The royal army killed everyone else. Someone betrayed the Alliance's plans to the King."

Nides did, he thought bitterly. *But I let Nides go.*

"We had hoped that you…?"

A dying glint of hope lit her eyes. By habit, Jaime reached into his pocket for his breather, even though he knew it wasn't there.

"I can't fulfill the prophecy."

Hida did not answer. The tears in her eyes swelled.

"I'm sorry," he tried to say.

In the howling darkness of the banestorm, they wept.

The last light of the day died. Shouts rattled the alpines from the west.

Hida looked up from the dough in her clay bowl, honey cakes only half formed. Her eyes darted to the mantle, where she kept the incense holder. But when she hesitated, Jaime stood up and lit it for her.

"I'll go see what's happening," he said.

But she held onto his wrist, shaking. "Jaime, it's not safe."

"I'll be careful."

She wouldn't let go, not until he kissed her cheek.

Hida Pappas forced a smile. "Don't stay out long. The cakes will be ready when you get back."

Jaime stepped outside—and immediately pressed a hand to his nose.

Despite the distance of his farmstead from the battlefield, the vicious winds slapped the stench of corpses against his face. He swallowed a gag and jogged in the direction of the shouting.

A handful of the Free Guard stood at the edge of the dead sea. Trying to engage the Alairans, trying to find anyone who would listen. The soot-faced villagers blankly scavenged or turned their faces away.

"Hey!" Jaime sprinted down the sloped fields, now absent of wildflowers. "What's going on?"

The closest guards stumbled backwards. Jaime recognized the one at the head—Damias Demoulios. The last Free Guard he had spoken to before he escaped Mount Alairus. It looked like he hadn't shaved for a year.

"*Jaime Pappas?*" he exclaimed. "I mean, Your Highness—Holy Lord! The rumors were true!" He floundered into a bow. "Royal scouts—one of them alerted the nearest garrison of your presence. We didn't believe it at first, but we saw them. Two armies are approaching."

"How far?"

"They will arrive by dawn, Jaim—I mean, Your Highness. At least a thousand, to finish off the rest of us."

These people are farmers, shepherds, cheesemongers. But I get it, Father. You'll make them suffer, again and again, and make me watch. It will never be enough for you.

"Who's in charge here?" Jaime demanded.

"L-Lord Gaiyus Sartorios, Prince!"

"He's *alive?*"

Damias hurled his beard up and down.

"Take me to him!"

The young guard waved to the others. They raced through the field of dead. Jaime limped, struggling to keep pace.

Florin said the Air Alliance was scattered without central leadership, but his brother's ward had survived all along. Gaiyus Sartorios alone could unite the Jaypan high lords. Gaiyus would know what to do. The prophecy was three weeks away. There was time yet.

It's not over, Your Holiness.

Damias pointed to a lonely pavilion up at the barrows. "Over there, Prince!"

Jaime thanked him, breathless, and climbed up the shelf of basalt. The slope was slight, but he was panting hard by the time he shoved through the flaps.

"My lord!"

The lone shape turned. A coarse wool himation curled his shoulders in. Liver spots stained his hands and pate, more than Jaime ever remembered. His right hand squeezed the neck of a wine goblet.

He looks like a shriveled fig.

Even so, Lord Gaiyus spoke in his familiar gentle lilt.

"Hmm, Jaime? I did not realize you were back on our mountain. Or what is left of it…"

His wolf-gray eyes were still penetratingly sharp.

"One month ago, Julias Markus led the last of our forces in a desperate battle against Strategos Reizo's armies. But alas, we failed. No one answered our call; no one could protect us against the King's wrath." His former liege lord began to circle him. "You had been our last hope. And your brother's. He cried your name the night he burned, do you remember?"

Lord Gaiyus stopped at a wooden table and reached for something behind his back.

Slowly, Jaime said, "You already knew the soldiers were coming. You sent for them."

"What do you mean, child?"

He closed his eyes. Trying to quell the rising storm in his chest. This man. Hilaris's second father. His brother had loved Gaiyus as much as Jaime loved his mother.

"How long?"

"I do not understand—"

Not Nides, it was never Nides.

Jaime lashed out one arm. The goblet sailed out of Gaiyus's hand. Blood red splattered the linen walls.

"How long have you been in contact with the King?" he shouted. "Did you betray Arcurea, too? Did *you* tell him Hilaris forged his age?"

The old man's papery lips thinned in a smile. "What does it matter, anyway? The Lords of the Air Alliance are in chains. And that fool statesman Florinokles—dead. His head is spiked over Aeropolis's gates."

Jaime tremored.

"*I* sold their identities to the King. His Holiness knew of our plans to capture Mount Mynati long before you ever learned Air." Lord Gaiyus chuckled. "It is over. Let what hope you have die. By the end of this month, that banestorm outside will obliterate the Jaypan race."

Gaiyus abruptly uncoiled, lashing out his arm. The object behind him glinting—a knife.

Jaime ducked.

The Senator staggered forward in surprise. Jaime slid aside. Gaiyus crashed into his table. Fruit bowl, wheat bread, alabaster vessel of perfume all went flying. Jaime wrenched the knife away from him. Holding it up high. The old man raised both hands in fear.

"Pr—Prince—Prince, listen to me—"

"You betrayed Hilaris!" Jaime screamed. "He trusted you!"

"You do not under—"

"He called you papá!"

"I had no choice. The King espied my operations last fall." Tears vanished into Gaiyus's thick beard. "I was under duress to convince him of my loyalty. He would have accepted nothing but my ward. My son. It was the only way to buy us time to cover up the Alliance—"

Jaime grabbed the wine bottle, shattered it on the ground. "You should have burned in his place!"

"—but alas," the old man brooded, "there never was an Alliance, only a cesspit of feuding fools. I submitted to the Archpriestess after you escaped. Had I not, she would have killed your mother."

His brother, and all the people of Jaypes, betrayed by one man. *Hilaris loved him. You can't kill him.*

Jaime twisted the knife around. Thrust the hilt toward Gaiyus. Both of them screamed.

A loud *crunch.*

His nose smashed in. The old Senator moaned. Jaime hurled the knife aside and fled the pavilion.

⚜

Off in the mountain, away from the tents—away from everyone— Jaime sat on the edge of Estos River, at the same place he had jumped in to escape Strategos Reizo. He peered into the watery mirror. Rainfall distorted his reflection.

A giant hawk landed on the tree behind him.

"I swore to Sojin I would protect our people," he whispered. "*Gods,* Toran was right."

A long minute passed.

"Maybe the best thing I can do is to submit myself to the King. At least then, no one else will have to die."

The winds grew colder. The stalks of broom swayed. Dawn was here.

Arrys's low voice drifted through the rains.

"Prince."

It was faint at first: the noises of boots on bluegrass. As the rains pattered, it grew heavier, mixing with the tattoo of drums, falling hooves, the clattering of steel corselets.

Jaime raised his head.

The armies materialized above the hazy crests of the hills. Infinite archers, infantry, and cavalry surrounded him. On the overlooking hill, the commanding Strategos pulled to a halt. His standard-bearers flew the New Jaypes colors, blazing like spilled blood against the gray skies.

Gradually, the din drew the remaining Townfolders to the hills. They huddled close to each other, faces ashen. Hida stood on top of the highest crest. The sheen in her eyes captured the dark light of the banestorm.

"In the name of His Holiness the King, we are here for the one who blasphemes our monarch and calls himself Lord Jaypes's chosen!" the Strategos bellowed.

Briefly, Jaime's eyes met Arrys's. Despite his screaming right calf, he shifted onto his knees, lifting his hands to signal his surrender.

"Hold, boy—stop!"

Thousands of heads turned. Cassie raced past the cohorts, crashed into the river. Damias waved his hands, but Cassie wouldn't stop paddling until he reached the other side. When he was back on his feet, he gripped Jaime's hand. Pulled him to his feet.

Cassie the orphan. Cassie the mute—the boy who shared the same cripple's mark on his wrist; the boy who had helped him escape the Archpriestess that cold night of Hilaris's burning. He was the only reason Jaime was alive.

Had it really been one whole year since Jaime stopped Rimus Vulcas from drowning him?

Cassie lifted Jaime's wrist high into the air. His fierce eyes fell on the Strategos, and then the rest of the people of Mount Alairus.

This awakened something in the Townfolders. The storm gray in their eyes hardened to steel. More gathered around, holding scythes, pitchforks, butcher knives, anything and everything they owned. The mouths of the soldiers twisted in scorn—until Julias Markus himself appeared.

Jaime stopped breathing.

The late Queen's brother wore a weathered cuirass, the hems of his tunic shredded against his thighs, but he drew his shortsword and pointed it to the sky.

"The sacrilege of Usheon Ottega's reign has come to an end!" he bellowed. "No longer will you threaten us into submission; no more will Jaypans die as slaves. We will not yield our rightful Prince— today, we fight under the Emblem of the rightful King!"

The people roared. Jaime spun in a slow circle, staring. The booming of their unified voices thundered across the gray expanse of sky—perhaps across the entire Kingdom.

The Strategos shouted a command. The ragtag mass charged down the hills. The soldiers shifted formation, lowering their longspears perpendicular to their knees.

They believe in me.

Arrys's dark brows arched downward, and his lip curled up. "Tonight, I shall practice the sword. But for you, it is half and one fortnight till Sporting Day." He extracted one of his two steel hoops from his ear. "Take this. If a Larfene gives one to another, it means you are his blood friend. It is no an easy task, a foreigner befriending a Larfene."

Jaime turned his ear to Arrys, taking a deep breath. Eyes watering as steel cut through his soft flesh.

"Ow," he whispered.

"Now win the Greatsporting so you can give it back. I will be rather irritable with only one ring."

Jaime gripped his friend's hand tightly. "I'll see you in three weeks." He turned to Cassie. "Arrys will take care of you. I have to leave. I'm going to duel the King."

Cassie shook his head vehemently. His eyes seemed to say, *You can't. If you do, we will never see you again.*

Despite the well of infinite fear inside him, Jaime said, "Thank you again, Cassie. I'll be back. I—"

He hesitated, but the roars ascending his home suddenly made his voice strong.

"*I promise.*"

CHAPTER THIRTY-SIX

Jaime raced down the mountain, careful to stay off the paths, but a stray rider thundered behind him. He sucked in air. The banestorm's winds were everywhere, but he couldn't seem to breathe any of it. The limp in his calf dragged him down.

"Prince Jamian!"

The courser pulled to a halt, stomping against the wild grasses. Jaime skidded too, heart fluttering.

Slowly, he turned around.

Julias Markus stared down at him through his glorious plumed helm, his face barely visible behind his T-shaped visor. His sword hand held a stained spear. So many times during childhood, Jaime had looked at the Free Guard Commander, desperately wishing to one day become that man.

"Uncle," he said.

The commander threw down his spear and dismounted. In one swoop, he pressed Jaime up against his cuirass and kissed his head. He, too, still smelled strongly of incense.

"I have failed you, my Prince."

"No," Jaime murmured. "Mamá is alive because of you."

The commander let him go and fell to his knees, head pressed against his spear.

"One month ago, I led my men in a charge down this mountain. I was present as thousands of Alairans died under my command." Tears rolled down the elder man's cheeks. Jaime, perhaps foolishly, always thought Julias Markus did not know how to cry.

"Alas, but I know if things could have started anew, they would do it again. How avidly they fought and died for you, Jaime. We should have won. We should have ridden by your side a long time ago. I beg your forgiveness."

"There is nothing to forgive." Jaime lifted the heavy spear and extended it to him. "None of this was your fault. Gaiyus betrayed the Alliance to the King."

"That cannot be. He told us—" Julias took the stave, his calloused hands chafing Jaime's. "This whole time…?"

"I have to get to the Colosseum. Only, I don't know the way."

Julias frowned. "Jaime, the Sporting is in under three weeks. Even on the Kingdom's swiftest mount, it will take four to reach it from here."

"I have to try. If I miss the date of the prophecy, the King wins, and the banestorm destroys us all."

The Commander stood. "I will accompany you."

"No—Mount Alairus needs you. You're the only one who can protect them."

After a pause, Julias gave a brisk nod.

"Very well. The Colosseum is bound southwest, in the heart of the Central Plains." He gestured away from the mountains and the coast, in a direction Jaime had never been before. Julias handed him the reins.

"Take my horse, and fly."

As Jaime climbed onto the high saddle, the commander smiled grimly. "I will take care of Sartorios. If Lord Jaypes is on our side tonight, and we survive this, I will rally our last friends behind you."

"Protect Mount Alairus. And Mamá. Please...protect her, Uncle."

Julias Markus bowed his head.

"Let the winds lead you, my King."

"I shall find my feet," he whispered. Jaime kicked the courser into a new gallop and did not look back.

~~⚜~~

Five minutes into riding away from battle, Jaime pulled up short. His uncle said he would never make it to the Greatsporting on time—on *horseback.*

He glanced up at the sky. High winds flattened the broom, wrestled him on the saddle.

The currents are out of control, Lady Prescilla once said.

But he had to take his chances. He turned the courser around, riding back in the direction of his farmstead.

The only light on this side of the mountain flickered through his kitchen window. Jaime dismounted outside, rushing up the portico steps. Bright flames still kindled under the legs of their domed oven. He doused the coals and glanced through the mouth.

His mother's honey cakes were charred black.

Dashing upstairs. Swinging inside his bedroom. Snatching up his knapsack.

Aulos Menander's windcloak back in his hand.

Jaime spurred the courser back in the direction of Hektor Pappas's grave. The stone airmarker was just a few steps away from the spot where he first touched the medallion.

He brushed his fingers against the marker's engraved characters.

Northwind, an ancient power whispered.

Jaime wrapped himself into the windcloak and traced Northwind's current to the sheer cliffs.

It was the largest current he had ridden yet. Streams of energy splintered and raged against his *avai*.

He took a deep breath, sent a short prayer to Lord Jaypes, and took a running leap off the mountainside.

In one jerk, the folds of his cloak opened.

Northwind suspended him high over the landscape.

For a second, he felt like the golden eagles he occasionally saw, wild and free from the King's reign.

Jaime screamed out a whoop.

The banestorm's streams sent him in a dive three, four, five times faster than any of the air currents he conquered in the west.

Soon, the cloud-dipped peak of home vanished for the final time.

⁓᪥⁓

At twilight of the fourth day, he soared into rocky plains. Only the toughest of grasses existed out here.

Another airmarker appeared on the crags ahead of him.

Jaime hopped off Northwind before the ground below him could drop off. The mighty current swooped back to the northeast.

He brushed his hand against the new marker.

Aspasia.

It was a gangling current that would take him straight into the crimson-drenched plains ahead.

His frayed sandals inched over the edge.

A river of bodies stretched from the south—so many it stole the weight from his body.

They travelled on foot, on horseback, even some in curtained palanquins. He had never seen so many *bodies* before. Banners of all colors and sigils flaunted themselves at the winds. They were all meandering in the same direction—to a gigantic stone structure in the horizon.

The Colosseum.

Jaime let out a breath.

Spherically shaped, it had ten levels of arches glowing with the most decorated of firepits. Giant marble statues of the four gods, painted brilliantly, posed at the world on the upper levels.

Ten levels!

The mud-bricks—even the lime—used to build most structures could support two stories at most. Anything more, and buildings were prone to cave.

How had his ancient ancestors constructed *this? This* had to be hundreds of times as large as the theater outside Korinthia City.

I'm going duel the King in there.

He forced himself to count to four—and jumped.

Aspasia glided him down to plain level. A supply wagon stopped in the copper grasses so a Jaypan lady could relieve herself.

There's your chance.

He darted inside.

After it started forward again, he dumped the contents out of one of the strongboxes. A whole lot of silver pieces. His eyes grew to their size. Quite a modest tribute to the King.

He jumped in, squeezed the lid shut.

His body fell into judders.

The evening sky brightened to fire. No one entered the wagon. The late summer air was stuffy, unbearable. In the shadows, Jaime touched his aching chin—and noticed a new batch of pimples.

Great.

An hour later, it was time. The wagon passed through gods-sized pillars of painted marble.

Jaime kept his eyes fixed through the knothole in the wood. It was hard to see anything except the soldiers posted on ground level and every tier of seating above that.

Suffocating.

The air was suffocating him; he needed out.

A squad of soldiers checked the crowds, stopping anyone with anything more than sandals and a tunic on their skin.

The wagon rolled to a halt.

"What's inside?" a soldier asked the driver.

"Our supplies," someone else replied. "And a gift for His Holiness."

Jaime's hands poured with sweat. New pimples seemed to sprout by the dozen. Two more soldiers hopped in, shuffled around the crate. One of them lifted his strongbox. Knocked his head against wood. Salt dripped into his eyes.

Please, please, Lord Jaypes, don't let them open me!

The soldier put him back down and cleared the wagon. Jaime stifled a scream of relief.

The lady's guard emptied her supplies into an ornate hall of fountains and garlanded columns. They were under the Colosseum's lower ring. The din from outside fell to a stream of murmurs.

Jaime lay there for a minute before lifting the cover.

The King must be close. But where?

He recalled the Colosseum plans Achuros had drilled into his sleep. The first book he ever received was on Jaypan classical architecture.

Why couldn't he remember them now?

Breathe. Breathe! You know this place like Arrys knows the sword.

Arrivals.

He was in guest arrivals. The Colosseum's southside, nearest to the gates. The King's podium was on the northside, two tiers above the arena. This mighty Jaypan wonder had an entire network of underground chambers and rooms. So if he was looking for the King—Usheon would be right under his podium, in the Hall of the Ascaerii.

It was finally time.

Find him, and challenge him to a duel. Easy. He can't refuse you because of the Sacred Codex.

Jaime hopped out, walking as casually as he could to the enclosed walkway bordering the arena. As he moved clockwise, staying away from the firepits burning atop pillars, his belly clenched.

A ditch separated the stands from the arena. Torchlight drenched the grounds. It was total wilderness—his section began with a pit of sand for wrestling, which morphed into a field of dry grasses. Foot racing. Then an artificial river: swimming. And a gorge made of wedges that rose up from the ground like islands: spear throwing and climbing. The final section, the northside, was a rocky plain with deep pits. Charioteering.

A championship for Jaypes's most celebrated sports.

But his attention flitted back to the tiered seating. That tome on Jaypan architecture said the Colosseum could seat—how many?

One hundred fifty thousand.

A hundred fifty-thousand people would be watching his duel against his father. Already, thousands of New Jaypan officials occupied the first two tiers. They gorged on sea delicacies, slurped up autumn wines.

Jaime stopped and vomited.

When he was upright again, the judders came back violently. He walked faster, breathed deeper, but his whole body felt like it was going to burst—or melt.

A door rapidly appeared ahead of him, carved with the ancient Air Emblem. Usheon Ottega would be lodged behind it.

Jaime halted again.

The Archpriestess was making her rounds across the arena. The medallion hung openly over her white robes.

Jaime pulled himself between two columns, breathing hard. The aggregate murmurs of the Jaypan audience were pottery exploding in his eardrums. He waited a full minute before he poked his head outside again.

The Archpriestess was gone.

He jogged the final length of the walkway, his heart an unruly ram against his flesh, until he reached the double doors. Tossed himself inside. Pressed them shut behind him, wiping the vomit from his mouth. It was pitch-dark except for the torches lining the walls.

"Greetings, my Prince. It has not been long at all, has it?"

That voice—

Archpriestess Damasia stepped through a side door, her hands clasped together.

His calves broke from immobility. Jaime lunged at her. But someone caught his ankle in the dark. Yanked him backwards—

The carpeted stone floor slapped his face. His vision flashed out.

"I'll kill you!" he screamed. "I'll burn you for everything!"

More soldiers poured into the corridor. Blinded by pain, Jaime batted at their greaves. Legs rushed up around him. They tugged him upright. Foreign hands wrenched his arms back. Iron clamped them together.

Jaime screamed through tunics and steel plates.

They did the same to his ankles, too, linking them together with a short chain. A collar fastened around his neck last. It smelled of iron—of blood. So tight, he fought for air.

The soldier handed the leading chain to the Archpriestess.

Strategos Reizo, the King's chief military official, burst in behind his men.

"The Prince! He is—"

His eyes widened and he pulled up short.

"You have him already?"

309

The Archpriestess seized a soldier's short spear and slammed it down on the wound in Jaime's calf.

He crashed to the ground, biting down a scream.

In his ear, she whispered, "Just in time for the Greatsporting. Thou art the grand prize, didst thee hear?"

He stared up at her, eyes wet with pain, his shackles digging into his back.

"I'll burn you."

"Thou hast no idea what shall befall thee by the end of tonight," she said.

His brother's murderer tossed the leading chain to the head guard.

CHAPTER THIRTY-SEVEN

"Faster, boy!" a burly soldier snapped.

The chain yanked again, jerking his throat. Pain surged into his head. Jaime stumbled, fell in a fit for air.

The soldiers around him laughed.

"Hail, the Prince of Jaypes," the first one sneered.

Blinking.

Slowly.

Once, twice.

What am I doing here? It wasn't supposed to turn out this way. I don't understand, Lord Jaypes. Everything, all the deaths—what for? Was there any purpose to it?

Not a dream.

Thud. Thud.

He couldn't feel his chest anymore.

I don't understand.

A final set of doors appeared ahead. Reizo knocked. No answer. He knocked more frantically on the painted gilt, blaring out, "Your Holiness!"

Still no answer.

"Holiness, I understand you are occupied. Please forgive, it is urgent. I present to you: *the Prince of Jaypes!*"

The silence that followed was unbearably long.

...one, two, three four...

A low voice:

"Bring him inside."

Strategos Reizo peered at Jaime, gesturing his head at the doors. *Come along.*

Jaime obeyed without a fight. The soldiers sealed the doors shut behind him. The Hall of the Ascaerii stole away his jitters.

It resembled a Jaypan temple, held up by four great colonnades. Their capitals were bell-shaped swirls of acanthus leaves. The Air Emblem swept across the mosaic ground, embedded in Jaypan silver. *Maybe they're from Mount Alairus's old mines.* Winking like stars, even in the firelight and shadow.

And yet, it smelled like withered ivy in here. The statues guarding the painted walls—Thollos, Lybera, Agmon, Kleio, the first of Jaypes's monarchs—stared at him with hollow eyes.

And there, between the center columns, stood the King of Jaypes. His back faced Jaime.

Rich robes of damask—cut in the Jaypan toga-style—fell to his knees. A silk sash blazed crimson down one shoulder. *The Legend of the Four* was in his hands.

Head pricking upright, the King lowered it onto empty the altar, took a jeweled knife in its place.

The silence was so overpowering, Jaime forgot how to count.

Ushion Ottega turned to face him.

Jaime was tall now—taller than Usheon—but the King held himself like a mighty mountain, shoulders pressed outward. His presence alone felt like a great beacon blistering against Jaime's *avai*.

Yet unlike the high lords Jaime was used to, only the slightest scent clung to his skin. Cassia. A clean smell. Despite that his black hair was neatly cropped and oiled, nothing could hide his sagging eyes, the gauntness of his cheekbones. No crown on his head, no golden cuffs on his arms or wrists.

In another lifetime, he might have been very handsome.

It struck Jaime: he saw no resemblance of himself in this man.

Yet he blurted the first word that came through his lips.

"Papá—"

As soon as he spoke, someone echoed him.

"Papá!"

Two figures raced through a side door and clung to the King. Girls, both several years younger than Jaime. They had Usheon's long, round face and black eyes.

No one ever told him the King had other children in Jaypes. Impulsive envy burned his skin.

I'm your true blood, not them.

Usheon's left arm slid around the girls' waists. They looked at Jaime with fearful, teary eyes. The more he tried to diminish them as lower bloods, the more he felt, perversely, like a villain.

"Leave us," the King said.

He kissed the little girls. Reizo hesitated, but bowed low and took the children through the doors.

And they were alone.

"So tell me. Why do you wish to overthrow your father?"

His Moderna was accented, but articulate.

Jaime's aggression deflated. The answers he had rehearsed in his mind, all of the grandiose rhetoric he learned from Achuros's books, suddenly empty air.

One, two, three, four.

He took a breath.

"You've murdered the sons of Jaypes. You've destroyed thousands of families. *You* stared this war the day you decided to invade the Kingdom of Air. Lord Jaypes sent a banestorm over all of us because *you* broke the Sacred Codex."

"Is that how you justify yourself?"

Jaime's eyes flashed, fear dissipating. "If you have to ask, then you don't know about Hilaris. Do you know that name?"

No answer.

"Hilaris? My foster brother? Even Lord Gaiyus loved him—a *monster* loved him. I didn't realize how much I did, too, until I was forced to watch him burn in your fire. He was just a mountain woman's son. But you wouldn't know what that was like because—" He clenched his jaws. "Because, you were never there."

Silence.

The King turned aside, brushing his thumb over an old burn scar on his right jawbone. Burn scar. How was it possible a Fire Sage could have a burn scar?

"You are wrong. Countless nights I lay awake, thinking about your mother. About you. In the beginning, I believed there was a way to find you and make peace with your god's prophecy. After she fell on her own blade—"

"*You* killed her—"

"You were the last memory I had of her. But the rebels hid you and held onto you tightly. The more I fought for you, the more they fought; and when I crushed them, then you fought me in their place."

Jaime closed his eyes.

Liar. He's always wanted you dead. He killed Mother. Everyone said so. Why would he destroy Townfold if he cared about you?

"Now, here we are, you and I."

Usheon rubbed the silver pommel of the knife.

"My bondlords demand your execution. For a time, I reminded them you were my son, but the damage you have done to this Kingdom far exceeds mere treason. If I should pardon you, then I may as well pardon every criminal who challenges a Sage-King's divinity."

Jaime bared his teeth. "That's holy of you—"

"Yet *I* am King. Bow before me, boy, and relinquish your rights as Crown Prince. Then I will let you live."

"As a slave? So you and your Court can display me like an amphora, burn more children, behead more statues of Lord Jaypes, make me watch until we're all obliterated?" Jaime pointed his wrists at *The Legend*. "You're no Sage if you think that banestorm outside won't destroy us as long as you're King."

"So be it."

"I challenge you to a duel."

"You are in no position to invoke the Sacred Codex. And who shall strike me down if I refuse you, your god?"

"Let's end this war then. Now."

Usheon's grip tightened over the knife. He stepped forward. His father's breath fell on the sweat soaking Jaime's scalp.

Jaime clenched his jaws, preparing himself—

But standing so close to the King, Jaime saw it: grief broke over his eyes like water diluting ink, briefly.

He won't kill me.

He can't.

Jaime closed his gaping mouth.

But Usheon's expression turned cold again, impregnable. He shouted for the guards. They surged inside, their hands tight on their spears, ready to hack Jaime apart.

"Lock him in a cell. And hand him this." Usheon extended the knife to them. "Spare the King from another death. Let him choose his own fate."

The guards took hold of his neck chain and wrenched him out.

I don't understand.

This wasn't the monster the people of Jaypes had sculpted into his mind. If he peeled away all the fronts, he would see his real, raw papá underneath. *I did see him, for a second.* And he knew, from the ten minutes of being inside that chamber, that Usheon was a good papá to those little girls.

His chest hurt.

In another lifetime, I would've stood in their place.

Before the King's soldiers came to Mount Alairus, Jaime would have wanted that more than anything in the world.

In an adjacent corridor, a sunburnt Colosseum worker approached them. A straw hat clung around his chin, shielding his face. The soldiers only gave him a second glance, but when the worker passed them, the guard on the right groaned and fell to the ground.

"What in the gods—"

The other three guards swiveled around—a knife stuck out of their colleague's back. Jaime froze.

The stranger drew his sword. Slashed at the Jaypan holding his leading chain. Startled cries echoed the hallway.

The guard lifted his shortsword to parry him, but the stranger flitted aside. In four strokes, two more bodies were on the ground.

The last guard held up his hands, puffing hard.

And he fled the corridor.

Jaime gawked as the stranger bent over the portliest guard, wrenched a set of keys from his belt, and shoved it into his iron collar. One by one, the rest of his chains clanked to the floor.

"*Arrys?*" Jaime cried.

The stranger tipped his hat. "Good evening, Prince."

"What about Mount Alairus?" he cried. "The people—"

"There was great fire," Arrys began, but their reunion was cut short by a furious bellow.

Jaime hastily grabbed Arrys's arm for support.

"Um. We should probably run. There's a Fire Sage behind us."

Noises of marching beat against his eardrums, until it sounded like all of Jaypes's royal armies had been crammed into the narrow corridors. His father's shouts echoed against firelit stone.

"*Baikan!* Do not let him get outside!"

To their right, Reizo Kita burst in from a perpendicular hallway. Jaime's calf wound cramped. Arrys swooped in front of him, sword lashing out. His friend connected blades with the front lines.

The corridors sang like a kithara of steel.

Arrys's wild hair lashed against the fervid *V* of his brows. In a flurry of slashes, four soldiers were on the ground.

Strategos Reizo cursed in Kaipponese, drawing his *kendao*. "Who by great rice maggots are you?"

Arrys responded with the double-motioning of his blade. His sword seemed to grin.

Jaime swallowed down the dryness in his throat.

Once, he overheard Nides Doupolous swear it was impossible for a sword to win against a polearm.

"If you lose your spear in battle," Nides declared, "and you only have your shortsword left, you're already a carcass."

Surely a rogue teenage Larfene couldn't beat the King's righthand official, sword to *kendao*?

The Strategos swung first, a quick jab at Arrys's unprotected hands. Arrys slipped to close-guard stance—and caught it with the flat of his blade. For a second, the *kendao*'s blade locked against the sword's cross guard.

The bronze vase along the wall mirrored their firelit reflections.

Arrys slid forward along the length of the shaft. Bringing himself in, closer to Reizo. At any second, Arrys would cut past the lacquered plates of his armor, ending the duel.

Jaime clenched his fists.

Reizo made a small circular drop at the last second, disengaging. Thrust the butt end at an angle, down at Arrys's collarbone.

Arrys thrust up, beat it aside.

Reizo retreated backwards, but this gave him the advantage of distance again. His single-edged halberd came up perpendicular to his body.

Arrys backed away as well, assuming middle-guard position.

Jaime's heart pulsed louder. For a second, the deadly opponents stared at each other.

Reizo's weight fell forward, jabbing high. Arrys lifted his sword to parry—but Reizo's was a clever feint. With Arrys's guard down, Reizo pulled back, lunged low this time.

Arrys dropped to the floor, rolling aside to avoid the blade.

But that was a last resort defense. Now he was backed up against the wall. The chunky, black-eyed Kaipponese drew his *kendao* back, a buttery smile on his face, as he bided his energy for the final killing thrust.

No!

Jaime grabbed his fallen neck chain and whacked it across the Strategos's butt.

Reizo roared and pivoted around. It was all Arrys needed to launch himself to his knees.

Now they were back in close range again. But the Strategos sensed Arrys would get back up. He was already thrusting straight at the Larfene's chest.

Arrys did the unexpected.

He threw himself forward, towards the blade—and gripped the polearm's shaft with his hand.

Yanking.

Reizo cried out in surprise, his portly rolls tumbling from

balance. Just as the Strategos came crashing into him, Arrys thrust his knee in a swift, upward cut.

Right in the larger man's groin.

Reizo moaned and crumpled, his *kendao* falling with him. Jaime crawled out of the way. Arrys caught the polearm in midair and slammed the butt against the Kaipponese's temple.

His eyes rolled to the back of his head.

Reizo Kita went out cold.

Their gazes met, Jaime breathing heavily, Arrys smiling through the sheen of his sweat. The Larfene sheathed his sword.

"I owe you another life," Arrys panted.

Shivering, Jaime lifted up a hand. "Just help me out of here," he breathed. "I have to get outside and make an announcement."

Arrys pulled him to his feet, his bowman's hands sandpapery against Jaime's. They made a few limping strides together—

A fresh storm of soldiers appeared behind them. The door to the arena was so tantalizingly close now.

Suddenly, the Archpriestess pulled up at the front, blocking out the light of the fires. Not even Arrys would be able to hold all of them back this time.

But his friend released him and drew his sword again.

"Go!"

Jaime's eyes caught the Archpriestess's, then they fell to the medallion on her chest.

I just need to grab it, and I'll have Air again...

With Air, he would be able to fight off these soldiers and protect Arrys. But it would be risky—either he could turn around and grapple her for it, or run for the doors. He didn't have time to do both.

Arrys clenched his teeth, clashing against swords as the rest of the Jaypans surrounded him.

"*Go*, I said!"

Jaime shot the Archpriestess a hateful look and turned for the doors. She raised a current, but he sensed it before it hit. Ducked. A screaming tunnel of air battered the doors open.

He closed his eyes and collapsed flat onto the dirt.

The chatter of Jaypans circled through the Colosseum. Jaime was rising to his feet—

Another air current snatched his ankles, yanked him onto his back. A few eyes from the lower seating glanced down at him—then the soldiers came. Shoved him back to his feet. One held the chains Arrys had freed him from.

No!

"I am the Prince of Jaypes!" he yelled, but his lungs were weak. Airless. The Archpriestess was holding Reizo's fallen *kendao* now. She rammed its butt against his head.

"Shut your mouth!" she hissed.

The world burst into a bright expanse of stars. He fell onto his chin. Somewhere behind him, heavy boots kicked up a cloud of dust.

Usheon Ottega marched past the six spearfighters of his King's Guard. He whaled his men in Kaipponese, black eyes blazing. They cowered and bowed for forgiveness.

Arrys was gone.

Dead?

Too many dead, too many people gone. He knew what he had to do. The judders came back. He felt sick.

Jaime lifted his head up and tried one more time.

"*I am Jamian, the Prince of Jaypes!*"

And screamed this next part at the top of his lungs: "I CHALLENGE THE KING TO A DUEL!"

CHAPTER THIRTY-EIGHT

The world shimmered under the summer heat, watering Jaime's eyes as he lifted them upward, tier by tier. The audience of New Jaypes nobles and statesmen nudged each other, demanding to know what they missed. A tiny part of him hoped they hadn't heard.

All noise halted.

The King wouldn't be able to refuse his challenge in front of them. The duel was a sacred, gods-ordained ritual.

But then again, Usheon had already defiled the Church by crowning himself King of Air.

Would he dare do it again, and risk his own political legitimacy, in front of his followers?

The Colosseum's attention shifted to Usheon.

Sweat glinted off the King's calloused face. He glanced at the courtiers on every level, at the high lords measuring their liege lord against his son, at the Jaypan soldiers that served in his royal armies, a hundred of them on the upper circuit with bows trained on Jaime. They served Usheon because he was, undisputedly, the greatest Sage in Jaypes. Would the direction of their spears and arrows shift if he refused Jaime's call?

The black in his father's eyes narrowed to slits.

321

"I accept."

The Greatsporting's herald stepped between them and raised his silver-cuffed hands.

"The Prince of Jaypes has challenged His Holiness the King to a duel, and His Holiness accepts! All Greatsporting events are hereafter suspended for the night…"

Overpowering cheers rocked the Colosseum. Royal trumpets blared through the air as staff rushed to hang impromptu banners of Old and New Jaypes over the stands.

There hadn't been a duel in Jaypes for centuries.

What've you done? Without your medallion, you won't be able to draw a wisp of air!

The filthy airpriest now stood at the King's side. She pointedly tucked the medallion under her robes, her face smug.

As the trumpets changed to a lower cord, the herald impatiently waved at the King's Guard to get out of the arena. Nothing was to stand in it besides Jaime and the King.

He tried to steady his wobbly breaths.

Breathe deep.

But it didn't help. He stuffed his hands in his pockets. Desperately needed his breather.

While the Colosseum scrambled to settle into their seats, the herald prated off formalities.

"I want my medallion," Jaime snapped.

The herald furrowed his brows. "I beg your pardon, Your Highness, but did you not hear? By the sworn laws of a duel, no weapons or assets in any form are allowed—"

"Okay, forget it."

The King's forcible voice overrode the high trill of his herald's. "Let us test the strength of Lord Jaypes's prophecy. Let us see how powerful his chosen one is!"

More roars.

Jaime felt like he was standing before all of them bare.

Finally, the trumpets finished. The herald bowed and retreated into the safety of the higher tiers. Two workers in frayed exomises kept their heads bent and eyes lowered as they showed father and son to opposite sides of the arena.

As Usheon marched past him, he hissed, "*Baikan.* You do not know what you are getting yourself into."

Jaime trained his eyes on the path ahead of him, limping to the sand pit on the southside. Usheon took his respective place on the pockmarked plain above the royal seating.

When Jaime finally stood in place, the plain looked like an entire Kingdom away.

The riotous cheers shook him from the inside out. He closed his eyes.

This is a dream.

He was really back on Mount Alairus, deep in slumber. His mother was kneading honey cakes in the kitchen, and at dawn, Jaime would take her textiles to the marketplace to barter. He would do so well, he'd buy pomegranate seeds for her, a luxury—

The white flag between them rose.

Wake up, wake up…

Sweat washed down his brows, blinding him.

And sharply, the flag fell.

How foolish to think he was healed of his asthma.

Jaime breathed in, focusing on the present—on anything except his hunger for ephedra. But this was wasted effort.

He couldn't even *sense* the spirit dimension; he had no source to pull energy from.

On the plain, Usheon tossed the magnificent sash off his shoulder.

A year ago, almost to the day, Nides Doupolous told a story of the night he saw the King's fire obliterate Thessalona City. Jaime couldn't remember his exact words, but he remembered the way fiery light varnished the walls of his imagination. His chest soared with thrill. His belly twisted from dread.

That was how he felt now as a missile of fire blazed down the indigo sky.

Just before it made impact with the sand pit a few steps away, the ground trembled. A ripple of pure energy tore Jaime's world into a sheet of blistering light.

All sound went out.

His body sailed through a sheet of smoke. Sometime later, the dirt pit was gone. Tall grasses cut against his throat.

Jaime groaned. His ears were ringing.

Above the blanket of shimmering heat waves, what felt like another Kingdom across the sea, the Colosseum cheered. Something warm trickled down his temple. He wiped it and placed his fingers in front of his wavering vision.

Blood.

He struggled to his feet, started sprinting—where, he didn't know. Away from the open pit. Away from one stagnant spot. His calf screamed in protest. His panic screamed louder.

Lord Jaypes, where are you now!

The grasses transformed into riverbanks. More fire currents exploded behind him. He forced himself to jump.

Gasping.

It only went up to his nose, but the firelit waters felt like a wall of iron against his knees. Jaime shoved himself through.

Forward, keep moving forward...

His mind frantically sketched out air currents. Basic ones. The most advanced ones he'd studied in secret. The sequences he used against the Archpriestess in the Battle of Arcurea.

Why—why isn't it working!

The river ended, twisting away into a shallow gorge. Jaime bent over, choking for air.

A fire current pierced through the blanket of smoke. Diving at him. Jaime panted. Leapt onto the island wedges.

His ears trembled from the impact of the explosion. Flames lashed at him from the right. He ducked, but it singed the tip of his right ear.

Yelling out—

And another current. To his left—no, his right. More fire, until a rain shower of light barraged every patch of air.

How is he so accurate?

Jaime coughed, his lungs searing.

I can't see anything through this smoke—

Hopped onto the next nearest wedge. He sprinted toward the arena's northside, where Usheon was drawing him close. Forget fighting his father. His goal was only to stay alive now.

His eyes watered from the heat. A headache thrashed against the walls of his head.

Jaime raised his melting face to the sky.

The smoke had blotted out the stormclouds above him, the way they must have the night Hilaris tried to escape the stake.

Lord Jaypes, is this the end?

A stream of light materialized from the opposite side of the wedges, moving faster than an arrow from Arrys's recurve bow. Jaime widened his eyes. His limbs seemed to drag as he took a running leap off his wedge.

But the wound on his calf made him too slow.

In mid-jump, the fire current struck his heel. Swallowed up his right leg past his knee. Jaime's mouth opened in a soundless scream.

He was falling.

～◦❦◦～

Jaime awakened deep underwater.

Unworldly silence wrapped around his *avai*. The surface of the pool glowed from fires that were gradually consuming the arena. Jaime drifted there for a moment, half awake. Half alive.

How did this ever happen between Father and me?

Then he broke through the surface.

Air rushed back into his lungs—

A scream ruptured the lining of his throat.

Jaime kicked himself to shore, lugged his right leg onto soil. His lip trembled as he looked down. The entire upper section of his leg was wet pink. From his knee below, black charred his skin.

The wild cypress and poplars around him started to glow from green to red.

A silhouette emerged behind him. Usheon advanced past the trunks steadily, his damp skin absent of burns.

Forward. Keep moving forward…

But he couldn't. The pain in his leg blocked out all else. Moving it in the slightest triggered agony from his foot all the way to the center of his brain.

So he sat in place and bowed his head.

Don't be afraid. You're going to go see Hilaris, and Achuros, and your blood mother—Sarendi. They'll be in a place where the sun touches the earth.

As shadows and light danced across the forest floor, he accepted death.

Profound beauty glazed over the world. Fear's grip loosened over his heart. He couldn't feel his lungs, but it didn't matter. Nothing mattered now. How much grief, anguish, energy he'd put into every waking moment of the last year. But stripped of that, he saw the trees, the pond, the wedges—*Jaypes,* for what it truly was.

A larger shadow fell over him.

"You brought this upon yourself. I never wanted this."

Jaime forced the words out of his burning throat. "No, Father. The day you declared the Royal Decree, you did."

The silhouette circled around him.

Usheon Ottega's eyes were glowing rings of fire. His *avai* vibrated with such mighty energy, it was like standing before the mouth of Empyreal hell. And perhaps Jaime was.

CHAPTER THIRTY-NINE

The temperature in the air suddenly rose. Usheon's body glowed a blistering red. Fire birthed between his palms. This would be the final current.

"Stop! Let him go. You have the wrong Prince!"

The voice was unfamiliar. Speech heavy, slurred.

One, two, three, four...

In the haze, Jaime counted. Something splashed behind them. The seed of Usheon's hell-current vanished.

A small shape clambered onto shore, head beetled forward, arms flapping at his sides. "I am Kassios Ottega, and I demand an end to this false duel in place of one with myself!"

Jaime's blurry eyes widened.

Cassie, the mute from Townfold.

The King backed away from Jaime. The younger boy forced his gaze off the ground and fixed it on Usheon.

"I swear this Kingdom will see ruin if you refuse!"

The boy pounded out his scrawny wrists. A spear of flames discharged at the King. Usheon's mouth twisted in a snarl. A larger, faster current devoured Cassie's.

Jaime dropped his mouth.

This isn't real...

As the King advanced in a stark march, Cassie yelled, "Run, Jaime!"

He stumbled backwards and threw another fire current at Usheon—but the King met it with one of his own.

The forest exploded with energy.

It slammed Jaime onto his belly.

Cassie skidded away, his back rounding into a C. He raised another desperate burst of flame. Usheon snuffed it out, his broad shoulders staying square, his fiery gaze fixed upright. A blue-tinged torrent torched the surrounding poplars.

Jaime pressed his face to the ground, cupping his head against the unbearable heat. The trees shrieked, crashed. Cassie retreated deeper into the forest, escaping the falling flames. Arms flailing at his sides. The King flitted after him. The arena rocked from Sage energy every few seconds.

Get up, Jaime.

He shut his eyes. Bit back a scream from deep within his *avai* as he rose to his feet. Jaime limped as far as the first row of trees—and stumbled.

Come on, get UP!

Lifted himself back up. Jaws clenched. He staggered through the forest until the trees started to spread out.

Above the blanket of smoke, the upper levels of the arena materialized. Mouths twisted open in soundless cheers, roars, exclamations. An entire world away.

The gorge ended on an upward slope. The final section of the arena awaited him—the dry plain, scattered with deep pits.

Cassie and the King were already there, pivoting around the holes, exchanging currents. Every time their fire connected, the impact threw Jaime back on his knees.

He bit down waves of pain. Kept climbing upward. *Climbing—*

This he could do.

Sometime in the night, he reached the top of the slope. Jaime peered into the nearest hole. Not far ahead, a New Jaypes tapestry had fallen off the arena's rim, torn off its rod by energy waves.

As Cassie and Usheon fought, Jaime hauled it over the hole. Kept it in place by gathering rocks, placing them along its edges like paperweights. Kicking dirt and dust over it. Covering the tapestry and the pit.

High above him, Cassie released a dart of bright flames. His gray eyes darted to and fro, never able to meet the King's.

Usheon released his final current: a twisting dragon of searing white fire that wiped out Cassie's smaller current.

The boy disappeared into flames.

Jaime crashed flat to his chin again. The fires crackled. The smoke cleared.

The small body appeared several steps to the right of the hidden pit. Lying facedown.

He crawled over to Cassie, lifted him up. The boy's entire face was wet from blisters—melting, bubbling, the left half spilling down his neck. His eyelids were sealed closed.

Acid rolled up Jaime's throat.

Jaime forced it down. Hands trembling, he eased Cassie onto his back. The boy's lips gnarled into a murmur.

"Jaime…"

"I'm here."

"Please—don't let him—I don't want to burn…"

Hilaris's same screams for help—*that* night flashed back into his head. His body convulsed into fear.

But this time, instead of running away, Jaime clamped his hand around Cassie's. "I'm here. It's okay. I won't leave you."

Jaime mustered the last of his energy and dragged both of them to the south edge of the covered hole. The King's silhouette materialized in front of them on the other side. Usheon's flaming irises locked with his.

Jaime said, "Don't."

The King took one step forward.

"*Please.*"

And another.

The trap gave way. The King tumbled into a storm of dust and rocks, the New Jaypes tapestry swallowing him. Screams scraped against Jaime's eardrums.

He struggled upright, peering over the edge.

His father was at the bottom, his leg twisted at an angle.

Jaime lifted one of the stones from the ground, his arm shaking from the effort. It was nearly the size of his face. All he had to do was drop it on Usheon's head and his father's skull would cave in. The duel would end. The heat of the flames licked at Jaime's tears. His arm trembled from the weight.

But he couldn't do it.

The rock fell at his feet.

Tears spilled through his eyes. He gripped the edge of the pit, blindly feeling for footholds as he lowered himself in. Halfway down, his wounded calf buckled. He lost his grip on the rocks, crashing into the bottom. For a minute, he lay there.

Usheon would die here in this pit. Jaime had won the duel.

This isn't a victory.

Father and son had warred and destroyed their own House. Jaime decided. He would stay here till the Colosseum's fires consumed them both, till all memory of Ottega wiped itself from the Kingdom of Air forever.

Jaime crawled across the pit and buried his tears against his blood father's chest. The fires in the Colosseum raged, its smoke twisting into Lord Jaypes's banestorm.

Sometime in the night, the sound of wings flooded the skies. Jaime was only half conscious. The next time he blinked past the crust in his eyes, colors flooded the arena.

Not wings.

Banners.

Hundreds of horsemen flooded the lower circuits. Their shields and mantles were blue, stamped with white tytos. They led a charge of banners with sigils so varied, he recognized only a few from the history books he studied with Achuros.

Lord Romulus brought the Air Alliance.

Tears glistened down Jaime's face.

But the Jaypan forces were not the only ones here. The sealed doors of the arena burst open. Two riders galloped at the front, flanked by their standard-bearers.

One banner bore the black-horned dragon of the Fire Emblem. The other was pleated diagonally with cerulean and sea blue, sealed with the gold sea serpent of the Water Emblem.

Jaime knew these sigils well.

The Kings of the West were here.

CHAPTER FORTY

The gold-headed Glaiddish at the front lines crashed into the arena like a tidal wave.

"Get out of the way!" they bellowed.

A deep voice awakened from the rush: "By the power of the four gods, the sanctified High Houses of the Four Kingdoms do declare this duel suspended!"

A rope dropped into the pit. Someone helped him out. The raging fires glazed the dark-haired shape before him in light.

"Eridene," Jaime croaked. "How…?"

"Smarts." She tapped her temple. "I've been in contact with my uncle since we met. Uncle told my King who you were, what was happening here. And I told him if Glaidde didn't help you, a banestorm would wipe out the Air Kingdom."

She glanced at the destruction around them.

"This war is bigger than you and me. I see that now, Jamian. I just didn't expect King Gildas would actually—"

Jaime pressed his lips against hers.

The Glaiddish lady staggered backwards in surprise. But she did not push him away.

Her arms cupped his shoulders despite the blood crusting his skin. Setting Jaime alight. He brushed her hair aside, hand falling on her neck. Their tears mingled together. Like the foam of seawater, her presence washed away his wounds.

He would have stayed like that forever if not for the warriors of her court marching past them.

Jaime let her go.

"I love you," he whispered.

She gazed into his eyes. Her fingertips gently brushed the knife wound below his right eyebrow. So only he could hear, she said, "I love you too."

Jaime took her hand, and they stood side by side, hiding their entwined fingers behind them.

The towering Glaiddish placed Cassie on a canvas stretcher and tromped him out of the arena. A group of light-footed Kaipponese lowered more ropes into the pit where Usheon lay.

But his gaze fixed on the elderly Kings before him.

Everything about Gildas Brennte was *big*. A big grisly beard covered his big jowls, which made the lower half of his face look bigger than his forehead. Wheat-colored hair coursed down the back of his head in thick waves, mopping up his shoulders. The energy surrounding him was as mighty as Estos River's waterfalls— vaporous, blinding, and overwhelmingly powerful.

The shorter man to his right sat prim and erect on his black gelding. A jacket was layered over his crimson silk kimono, pattered with elaborate dragons. Viro Tazuga's head was shaved, leaving only a clean goatee bordering his mouth. Unlike the Glaiddish King, who stank of thoroughfares, black pine scented his skin.

Jaime was too stunned to bow.

The slits of Emperor Viro's black eyes passed over him, a dingy boy half naked in his chiton, and landed on the hole.

An Imperial officer pulled a limping Usheon forward. Even with his broken leg, the Jaypan King held himself like a mountain.

The Emperor peered at the burn scar on his jaw. "You were a useless daimyo, and even more deplorable general, yet you try to be King?"

The whole arena seemed to quiver as the Fire Emperor spoke.

"Ah, I will tell you what you are. You are a peasant of Kaippon Kingdom. By Imperial law, I declare your life forfeit for desertion and the highest sacrilege. Chain him!"

I'm dreaming.

The Glaiddish King's voice drummed the air.

"Usheon Ottega, unlawful ruler of Jaypes, is hereby under arrest"— the Jaypan soldiers dropped their weapons—"for blaspheming the gods, for crimes against the Jaypan commonwealth"—his father vanished under the fray—"and for the highest degree of contempt against our holy gods!"

As the skies crashed over Jaime, someone collided into him.

"Juno! You're alive!"

Jaime bit his tongue. Pain blazed through his body. Eridene snapped at Toran to be gentle. But laughter broke through his throat, and Jaime hugged his best friend as his wounded leg gave way.

"You're here," he breathed. "You both came."

Eridene looked away, tucking a loose strand back into her braid. "We felt awful about what happened. Toran and I decided if there was any Prince in you, you'd find a way to make it to the Colosseum. So we left the peaks to find you. That's when we saw the Western forces in the distance and followed them here."

"You knew they were coming?"

"Not at all. It was as much of a shock to us as anyone else."

Toran whispered, "You should've seen her. She actually *fainted* when she saw a Brennte riding with a Tazuga."

"What are you whispering about now?" she demanded.

Jaime peered between his best friends, his chest welling with warmth. To Toran, he said, "I'm sorry for what I said to you. Back at the Temple."

Toran rubbed his neck. "Yeah…you kind of were an ass." He paused. "I'm sorry about what I said too. I guess you aren't *too* bad of a Prince."

He grinned.

That was all Jaime needed to know they were alright again.

A six-foot Glaiddish giant—gods, the Waterfolk were so big—offered to take Jaime into the infirmary where Cassie lay, but he shook his head.

"I'm fine," he lied.

Why are the Western Kings here? Why now? *Usheon's reigned for fifteen years.*

He had to find out.

Shouting broke out between the two factions. A throng surrounded his father—or Cassie's blood father. Jaime still wasn't sure what to make of that. A black-eyed Kaipponese warrior hammered a nail into the wall. Another shoved Usheon under it.

"Viro—" Gildas boomed, but the Firefolk wrapped Usheon's chains around the nails and wrested his wrists upward. The Glaiddish King dismounted and marched his unkempt bulk straight to the Kaipponese Emperor.

"Viro! He is still a Sage!"

The Emperor murmured something to a bald warrior mounted beside him. If the Glaiddish were big, he was inhumanly tall; a repulsive scar ran from his left eye to his jawbone. The bald giant said in crisp Moderna, "The day he swore himself to the Imperial Throne, he belonged to Tazuga."

A Kaipponese warrior stepped forward with a whip. Another shoved a blade under Usheon's garments and ripped them open so his back was exposed.

Jaime marched forward, but Eridene wrenched him back.

The Jaypan and Glaiddish officials gasped.

Hideous scars malformed Usheon's back from another lifetime: overlapping lash marks, swollen callouses, melted flesh where the horned dragon of the Fire Emblem was branded on with hot metal.

Jaime couldn't explain his sudden fury.

He was about to throw himself between the Kaipponese and Usheon, but the King of Glaidde beat him to it.

"Enough!"

Every word that came out of him was an explosion of thunder.

"This man will be tried fairly, or you will face Glaidde's wrath."

The bald warrior calmly translated: "The Emperor says you are *majiku,* and so are your false court trials. Please keep out of His Imperial Holiness's way or you will see Fire as your Sage-mother did."

Gildas Brennte bellowed from the saddle. Viro Tazuga stayed quiet and withdrawn. For a second, Jaime was certain the elder King would rip the Emperor's throat out.

"Remember, you small-cocked bastard," Gildas roared, "this peace between you and me is temporary."

The bald giant started to draw his *kendao,* but Viro held up a hand and turned his head profile.

"Oh, yes, Gildas, it is. Say, we have time now. Why not finish what we came here for?"

His Moderna, though accented, was crisp as embers. The lords of the Western Kingdoms fell silent. Gildas knitted his scraggly brows.

Jaime held his breath.

What did they come here for?

King Gildas grunted. "Preparations—provisions need to be made. The boys need rest. And a war trial must be assembled before anything else. Then you and I may speak about concessions and the like."

Emperor Viro chuckled lowly. "No games please, Gildas."

"Everything in its proper place and time—"

"*No games.*" Viro's oily black eyes flashed. "Larfour Kingdom is dead; my Kingdom has long surpassed it in supremacy. As for Glaidde—" He smiled sharply. "Not worth discussing." Jaime froze as the Emperor's eyes severed through him. "*This* mere island lags behind thrones of power. Thus, it is my right, by the holy gods, to declare it a province of Kaippon."

"Now hold—"

"Eh? Will you stop me?" Viro's lip curled. "Did I not burn your Sage-mother?"

Several Glaiddish drew their swords, but King Gildas raised a fist. His knights gritted their teeth and stood down.

"Are you calling a duel?"

"Eh?"

Gildas Brennte slammed his palm down. "I will call it then, you dragon-faced son of a bitch."

"Excellent. You will burn, fat one. Shall we name the stakes?"

Jaime felt Eridene's shoulders tighten against his. It was obvious what the Emperor would demand: the Water Kingdom. Her Kingdom.

The torches danced across Viro's angular face. "If I win, the Air Kingdom and the Sageling"—he glanced at Jaime—"are mine."

He staggered.

"He can't do that," Jaime hissed in Eridene's ear. "Jaypes isn't a prize for the West to claim! The people—Cassie and I—"

"Only one boy?" King Gildas said.

"Ottega's spawn is charred offal. I have no use for him."

"Then, if I am victorious, I will place both boys and this Kingdom under the Royal protection of Glaidde."

What's going on?

Why were the Kings involving Jaypes in *their* war?

The color drained from Eridene's face. "Jamian, I think…Viro will take you as his apprentice and train you into a Fire Sage. He'll use you to tip the scales against my Kingdom."

"I would never—"

"He will *force* you to serve him. He will break you in ways you can't imagine—I've seen him do it before. And once he wins the War of the West and conquers Glaidde…"

"Viro's going to destroy the Unity."

Jaime peered up at the circle of sky. The banestorm was now crossing into Central Jaypes. With one furious snap of lightning, rain began to trickle down into the Colosseum.

It's already beginning.

"Eridene, we have to stop them. If we don't—"

But it was too late. The decision was sealed when the Western Kings venomously shook hands.

The Kaipponese dragged the trembling herald back into the stands, snarling at him to announce a duel. The present audience cowered and sat in place as the Western Kaipponese pointed their blades at them.

The Glaiddish commander ordered his men to take Jaime into the infirmary, but he resisted them again.

"They are battling for Jaypes Kingdom," he spit. "*My* Kingdom. I will stay here and watch."

The commander backed off with a stilted bow. Eridene and Toran helped him into the upper stands. Everything below was now occupied with Western officials.

Energy seeped out of his wounds. Every step was excruciating. Eridene's lips pursed with concern. But Jaime took her hand again, gave a quick squeeze.

The fires from his duel with Usheon glowed across the Colosseum. Still, the two Kings took their places on opposite sides of the arena. Viro shed off his full silk regalia, like a dragon shedding its skin, till only a light kimono clothed him. Colosseum staff rushed to change the tapestries to Water and Fire.

The familiarity whirled him into sickness.

How can they repeat what happened? Don't they understand?

Rain poured down from the sky, growing heavier with his every breath. The battle for the Four Kingdoms began.

~⚜~

Unlike his duel with Usheon, no sudden currents emerged from either side. At the Emperor's lead, both of them bowed to each other. Then Viro Tazuga clasped his trim hands together. Gildas Brennte bent his hulking head as if in meditation.

Both of them fell deathly still.

Uneasy anticipation rippled across the Colosseum. But Jaime felt it—a sudden rise in Empyrean energy flooding the space below him. It grew more concentrated until his chest convulsed for air.

Viro was the first to lift his head. A raging serpent of fire lashed across the arena. It was twice larger than anything Usheon had summoned.

Gildas waited.

Jaime wrung the iron railing, drawing the smell of blood.

At the last second, a shimmering wall of water burst in front of Gildas, dissolving the wild flames in a vapor of spray that surged high above the arena. Some of it sprinkled onto Jaime's head.

The realness of that water shook him awake.

A collective gasp erupted from the Colosseum. The officials on the lower levels rose from their seats.

Viro raised his palms again. A thick twister of flame danced around his body, casting his face into light and shadow. His silk trains billowed. Jaime slowly backed away. The Emperor's *avai* energy was the size of a leviathan compared to the grapeseed of his own.

How is that possible?

How could one man house so much energy—

The twister burst into hundreds of smaller shafts of flame. The fireballs drove the King of Glaidde towards the stone wedges. His body flitted into a blur—as fast as he had seen Arrys move in western Jaypes. Why wasn't he fighting back?

Gildas drew near the spot where Usheon's current had struck Jaime. Pivoted around. His body radiated a glow like the seas in the midst of a storm, a raging bright turquoise.

He's biding energy—

Shards of water gathered together to form a gigantic sphere, shielding the Glaiddish King inside. Viro's fire currents battered viciously against its walls. Unable to penetrate. The Emperor's *avai* smoldered larger. With its growth, the fire currents grew thicker, until one finally burst the water sphere open.

But instead of crashing flat against the wedges, it abruptly soared upward in a massive tidal wave. Its shadow fell on the officials. Their tiny shapes screamed, scrambling to higher seating.

Water crashed down on Viro's shaved head with all the force of a collapsing citadel. For a terrible moment, the Fire Emperor's body disappeared inside it.

Eridene's thumb drilled into Jaime's palm.

Is it over? Is Emperor Viro dead?

A hand fell on his shoulder. Jaime blinked hard, trying to see through the blinding rainfall.

Arrys smiled grimly.

Jaime forced a pained smile in return. *You're okay.* The Larfene joined him behind the railing, his sage-green eyes fixed on the duel below.

Toran pointed at the tidal wave. "Hey, look!"

Within the dark waters, a yellow glow blistered from inside. Jaime shielded his eyes.

Suddenly, the wall of water dispersed throughout the Colosseum.

Under the downpour, Viro Tazuga stood upright, drenched, his chest rising and falling heavily. Hate twisted his face into a snarl.

Jaime gasped. All four of them backed away as a monstrous shape rose high into the upper circuits.

The intensity of this new fire current must have equaled a catapult's missile knocking into a curtain wall. Jaime slammed against the stands, gasping in pain. The current's energy seared his *avai*.

Arrys was the only one left standing, his eyes narrowed, his breathing steady.

Cries erupted from the lower stands. The remaining spectators began to flee the Colosseum.

Slowly, the unified current formed a horned dragon of flame. Every sickening pulse of Viro's mammoth *avai* battered Jaime's. As if alive, the current opened its jaws and thrust itself towards Gildas's doll-sized shape. The fire continued to rage against the flat of the ground until the tip of the dragon's tail died away in a violent spark.

The arena went dark.

Jaime struggled to help Eridene up. A cry broke from her throat. He held her for comfort against the burning pain in his leg.

Viro flitted off the wrestling pit, over the artificial river, across the island of wedges, until he was less than ten jumps away from the King of Glaidde.

A smaller current of fire swept over the still darkness, searching for an upright body. It was impossible that Gildas could have survived that last current.

Or so he thought—

A single water current rushed to meet it. Eridene's eyes widened with hope.

Against the dark, a blossom of bright blue materialized. A thick layer of sweat and rain sullied Gildas Brennte's face, his fury spilling into his glowing eyes.

He was alive.

Teeth bared, Viro leapt off his stone wedge to meet him. As the Kings flitted across the heart of the arena, the overpowering energy of their currents put out the last of the torches. The Colosseum grew darker than the skies.

Rain fell harder. The ground quaked under Jaime's feet. Now, the only light came from the glowing bodies of the injured Sages.

"This is murder," Jaime whispered.

Arrys's attention switched to him. He gave a subtle swing of his head.

Follow me.

Jaime blinked in confusion, but he let go of Eridene, limping away into the end of the aisle.

"Prince," Arrys said, "I could not retrieve the medallion. Too many guards."

He swallowed. "That's okay. It doesn't matter now. Nothing can stop this."

Arrys's voice lowered. "I had my suspicions before, but I do not think the Temple treasure gave you power of Air."

"What do you mean?"

A violent tremor passed through the ground again, throwing Jaime onto his knees.

Visions of the past reeled through his mind: the way Commander Julias said Jaime reminded him of someone he knew; the way he saw no resemblance of himself in Usheon's face; how he could only feel Air, but never Fire; how the one time fire appeared on Mount

Alairus, Cassie was present. And Achuros's voice: *When you became my apprentice, you reminded me of Lairdos so much.*

"You are Ascaerii," Arrys said.

He choked. "But—how is that possible? Unless...they had a child they told no one about."

Arrys gazed at him unblinkingly.

"Hold on—Achuros mentioned he used to serve in the Capital. I never thought twice about it, or how he ended up in Arcurea— but what if the Queen asked him to leave because she wanted him to hide me from Usheon?"

That had to be it. It was the only explanation.

Shock overwhelmed him as the burden of Lord Jaypes's prophecy lifted off his shoulders. Usheon Ottega wasn't his father. All this time, the prophecy hadn't been about him at all.

"I'm a Sage of Air!" he cried.

Only Arrys seemed to hear his shout above the roar of currents. But Jaime's joy dissolved as he switched his gaze back to the Kings.

This duel wasn't about the West. It was a battle for the Four Kingdoms, and no matter how it ended, it would swallow up the last free Kingdom into the Western war. The delicate Unity their gods had fought to restore would break forever.

Jaime glanced at the sky. Furious stormwinds ripped apart the New Jaypes banners on the upper circuit. This was *his* Kingdom. Only he could stand up and fight for it.

"'And he said, 'You cannot overcome this storm,'" Arrys quoted.

I swore an oath the day I agreed to train with Achuros.

"Help me get to the roof?"

Arrys nodded. Jaime quietly stepped away from Eridene and Toran. Their backs were turned to him, their faces showing unrestrained fear, illuminated by the alternating glow of ocean blue and magma red.

The steep incline of stairs grappled with his lungs. Several times Jaime stumbled. Arrys didn't let go. Rain pounded against his injured leg. But he held in the screams, gritting his teeth.

One, two, three, four. Breathe, Jaime.

A door opened up into the highest circuit. Jaime gave Arrys a nod and scaled the last steps on his own.

Briefly, he glanced down at the arena. The Kings were mere flares of light from all the way up here. A fall would mean instant death.

The Kingdom's air currents snapped at him, no longer recognizing him as a friend. Jaime peered into the gaping mouth of the sky. His tiny body felt like a bite away from the churning void.

He was staring at the heart of the banestorm.

You cannot overcome this storm, the winds hissed, echoing Arrys. *Cannot overcome. You cannot—*

"I am the storm," Jaime declared.

Carefully, he hoisted himself onto the inner balustrade. The weight of his injured leg almost made him stumble.

His fear vanished.

The air was so pure up here, so clear, like he was breathing in the element of Air itself. Something in his *avai* opened. Air swirled into his lungs, washing them clean of the sickness he carried with Jaypes for fifteen years. Gaps began to appear in the blanket of clouds. For a split second, he swore he saw all four corners of his Kingdom for the first time.

Gusts wiped away the crusts on his eyes.

Here was the island's tallest mountain: the pinnacle of the Jaypan race, the greatest wonder on the island, the midpoint in all the Kingdom of Air.

I made it, Mamá.

A deep ache throbbed in his chest. Jaime closed his eyes,

rehearsing Lairdos Ascaerii's banestorm sequence.

Low rumbles rolled above him. As the rain hammered his hair flat and the gusts tore at his chiton, he willed his focus to sink deep into The Empyrean. He called out to Air's spirit with his *avai*.

An ancient current, nameless, unfocused, forgotten, stirred in the lowest layers of the spirit dimension.

This was the same current he had awakened the night he first touched the medallion.

Something roared inside the crashing layers of clouds. The gusts transformed into a raging hurricane. The tears he held in for years broke from his eyes, vanishing into the rain. Behind the curtain of his eyelids, his *avai* unified with Air's.

After an era of slumber, an ancient current woke. It reached out to him, wrapping itself around him.

Ascaerii, *it said.*

And Jaime understood its untold power, bowing before it. The wild current bowed in return, offering itself to him.

Jaime spoke to it with his *avai*, urging it to calm.

The winds passed harmlessly through his strings of hair. Above him, black clouds clashed against each other, crackling furiously, as the storm bent to his will.

The Colosseum began to rock.

The Western officials on the center stands grabbed hold of any firm object within reach.

Eridene pointed to the uppermost circuit, where a faraway shape stood in the heavens, glowing bright as a morning star.

"Over there! He's over there!"

Hundreds of old air currents gathered from the furthest reaches of Jaypes Kingdom, joining together into the point where Jamian Ascaerii stood, forming a single massive current that surged up into the heart of the storm.

⁓ᴄᴇ⊱✦⊰ᴖ⁓

On the central plains, the mouths of the Jaypans who fled opened in awe as they watched the glowing shape on the balustrade, untouched by the storm.

Some clenched their fists in hope.

Others held each other, brothers-in-arms, crying tears of relief.

⁓ᴄᴇ⊱✦⊰ᴖ⁓

With everyone distracted, Reizo Kita hopped into the arena's edge where the King was still chained. The Chief Strategos unwrapped the chains from the nail.

Usheon nodded in thanks. Both of them switched their gazes to the upper circuit.

The Jaypan King's eyes thinned.

Though he did not show it on his face, from deep within those eyes, a worn smile formed, his first since the declaration of the prophecy.

⁓ᴄᴇ⊱✦⊰ᴖ⁓

Thunder crashed into the center of the Colosseum, splitting apart the belligerent currents of Water and Fire. The Kings of the West fell on their heels, torn out of their trances.

As the great air current cleansed the Kingdom, the rage of Air slowly faded.

Jaime let go of The Empyrean. The white rays glowing from his body remained for a second, before they, too, faded away.

Life suddenly drained out of his *avai*.

His knees folded. A breath escaped his lips, and he fell into the dark arena below.

As Jaime closed his eyes, a blurry water serpent twisted up into the sky towards him.

PART FOUR

KINGDOM OF SONG

CHAPTER FORTY-ONE

Distant cries of eagles, and the whispers of seashores, stirred him. These were noises he had never woken to.

His eyes watered from the touch of air.

Flames kindled in a silver firepit, casting gems across a rug with geometric patterns. It had to be foreign; he'd never seen anything so elaborate. Groggily, Jaime pulled the covers aside. Bandages covered his leg burns. They ached like Empyrean hell.

A blurry shape sat by his bedframe, staring at him. Jaime squinted as his vision refocused.

"*Commander?*" he gasped.

Julias Markus, oiled and scented, was in the white toga of a Senator. Without the ash and blood on his face, he was hardly recognizable.

"Hello, Jamian Ascaerii."

A grin broke through his face. "Where am I?"

"You are in the King's royal chambers in the Palace of Ascaerii."

He collapsed against the bed, sucking in a breath. The air was so sweet and light. Misted with rosewater. No such luxury existed even in Florin Menander's villa. Strongboxes with ornamental hinges populated the room—*this* was larger than his entire home on Mount Alairus. In place of wooden shutters were windowpanes, filled with glass. And in place of oil lamps were three-legged bronze candelabras, shaped like bearded, shaggy-maned elhornes.

How many bushels of barley could I buy with all this?

He goggled the ivory headboard, hand carved with garlands of grape vines, olive trees, and windflowers.

The Commander pointed at the rug. "That is a gift from the first High King of Larfour."

A short breath wheezed out of him. "Does this mean Mamá is alive? And the others on Mount Alairus?"

Julias nodded. "Kassios Ottega helped us win that last battle. That was when we realized the truth about him, and you. I rode to the Capital first. Your mamá insisted on staying behind to help the wounded."

Jaime breathed a sigh of relief.

"Not many first year Sages could have done what you did, Jaime. You are touched by Lord Jaypes."

"Could Lairdos have quelled that storm?"

A pause.

"Yes. I see his blood in you. I always did, but I was afraid to believe."

"What happened to him?" he whispered. "And Mother? Why did they tell no one about me?"

"Your blood papá and mamá loved you very much, Jaime. But someone out there wished to obliterate the Ascaerii. That is why, on the night you were born, my sister fabricated a miscarriage. Before the entire matter of Ottega's invasion, the airpriests were to raise you in the High Temple under Achuros's oversight. They swore to your parents never to reveal who you were. It was the only way to keep you safe."

"From what?"

Julias fixed his eyes on a fresco of a storm brewing over laurel trees.

Jaime's voice fell. "From the same things that made Lairdos walk off the cliffs, right?"

"What—"

"I know about the Darklings. I know everyone thinks they're dead, but they're secretly roaming Jaypes. Maybe even the other Kingdoms. Aren't they?"

Julias's larynx bulged, but nothing came out of his throat.

"Why, Uncle? Why did they kill him?"

"You must promise…" The Commander pinched the leather cuffs on his wrists. "Promise you will never repeat what I am about to tell you."

"I swear on Lord Jaypes."

"One month before your birth, your papá was summoned for an audience with the High King—"

"Of *Larfour?*" Jaime gasped. "But…no one has seen a Larfene for fifteen hundred years."

Except Eridene, Toran, and me.

"The Kings of Air, Water, Fire, and Earth assembled in an ancient city in the Far East. Our Kings received a vision…" Julias looked away at the firepit.

Jaime gripped his arm. "Uncle, I *have* to know."

"The Black Temple showed them how each would die. Unless they forfeited their sovereignty over the Four Kingdoms, the Darklings would extinguish Sage rule."

He couldn't feel the fire's warmth.

It's already happening. The Darklings have been tracking me. They must've thought I was an Ottega, like I did. And now that the whole world knows I'm an Ascaerii…

"But *why?*"

"Without the Sages, stability and order collapse. The institution of our monarchy, and the Four Kingdoms, crumbles. And the delicate Unity falls into back into supernatural disasters—it almost started in Jaypes. You are familiar with the Legend of the Four?"

"Uncle, but why now? Why would anyone want those disasters to come back? It would destroy us *and* them—"

"There are worse evils out there than banestorms and rainfire, Jaime."

"Like *what?*"

Julias rose to his feet. "I've said too much. These are not nightmares I wish to burden you with."

"But—"

A sudden rap on the door made them snap upright.

Whoever was outside didn't wait for an answer. The painted doors burst open, and a dark shape marched inside.

"Great gods, is there a funeral happening in here? And I'd been told the Prince was alive!"

The shape threw open the rich drapery. Daylight set the gypsum walls ablaze. Jaime shielded his eyes.

"*Achuros?*" he shrieked.

He leapt out of bed and threw himself into his mentor's arms, but his leg gave way and he crashed on the rug.

"Get back in bed, boy!" The airpriest bent over to lift him off the mosaic flooring, and puffed out when he realized his apprentice was now too heavy for him. He glanced at Julias for help, and with a sigh, the Commander plucked Jaime up with one arm and set him back on the gilt bedspread.

Achuros set down a chalice of wine. "Ah, man, why must you be so morbid all the time? You're making me want to crawl into a grave when this should be a happy scene."

The Commander grunted.

Before Achuros had a chance to pull up a footstool, Jaime crawled over the mountain of his bed and threw his arms around him. Today, Achuros smelled of airstreams.

His mentor chuckled. "Alright, alright. So I heard a certain Air Prince saved his Kingdom from a tyrant. Three tyrants, actually."

"Achuros, we have to talk about—"

"You will meet the Western Kings later. I heard they were flabbergasted after that show in the Colosseum!"

"Achuros—"

"The people are singing your name in the city streets. Hoopla, hoopla! You've earned your right to rule." The priest nudged Julias. "That boy is *my* apprentice, you know. The boy who defeated a Fire Sage? The one who harnessed thunder? Did you know he is *my* apprentice?" The Commander grumpily withdrew his arm. "Not a Fire Prince at all. The son and heir of Lairdos Ascaerii! Now that is a story we should discuss."

"I already pieced it together," Jaime said. "My mother asked you to take me out of the Capital because—" He met eyes with Julias. "Because of my father's death. His suicide—it frightened her. But something happened. You gave me up."

"Hold on, I did *not* give you up. I was intercepted by—" Achuros paused. "Well, I was intercepted on the thoroughfares. I thought you died in the attack."

You were intercepted by Darklings. And then? Hida found me by accident.

Jaime lowered his voice. "We have to talk about Arcurea. When I left, you were dying…"

The airpriest rubbed his peeling hands together. "The Menanders were defeated."

"And…?"

"They are alive. Damasia kept them under arrest in an attempt to lure you to her. Still in Arcurea, I believe."

He let out a long breath.

"And you? You're alive. How is that possible?"

Achuros looked away, hauling something over his neck in haste. "Oh. It almost slipped my mind. This is yours."

Jaime's eyes shot open.

His stone medallion.

"After the second duel, I took the Relic from Damasia. The Senate believes I threw it into the sea. I trust you understand now the danger of its powers should the wrong hands wield it."

"Doesn't this belong to the Temple?"

"Julias and I agree the airpriests would have wanted you to safeguard it as your father did before you."

Jaime nodded and looped it around his neck. "The Temple—"

"Something the three of us will discuss in due time." Achuros cocked his head. "My ledger. Did you see—"

But Julias cut in obliviously, shuffling around his pocket. "Ah. I had almost forgotten a gift of my own..." It took a second before he fished up a bronze key. Jaime raised his brows.

"What is it for?"

"One of the strongboxes. You will know when you see it." Julias took the wine and guzzled. "Now I must be going, and you also, priest." Achuros glowered. "Before anything, I believe there is a judiciary that awaits to speak with you."

"About what happened in Arcurea?" Jaime interrupted. "I pardon him from all crimes."

"Yes, my Prince. The Archpriestess also gave a confession."

"What confession?"

Achuros spoke up. "I gave her your whereabouts, yes. But it was a trick. When you came to Arcurea, the Relic was within my reach for the first time since Lairdos's suicide. I thought I could lure her in. Kill her finally, with Air. But the timing had to be right. I waited for Sojin to return with more men because, well, I could use the buffer."

"I wish you'd told me sooner."

"As I remember, you did not want to talk about it."

Julias placed a hand on his beside. "Rest assured, Jaime, he will be exonerated."

He climbed out of bed despite Achuros's scowl for him to stay put. "There're people I have to see." When they were in whispering range, Jaime squeezed the old priest's arm. "Good luck with the trial."

"My ledger—did you happen to see it anywhere?"

Jaime hesitated. "No."

Achuros's forehead creased with worry, but he bowed his head. "Never mind. I will see you at dinner tonight, gods willing."

As they went their separate ways, Jaime asked a courtier for directions to Cassie's room. The royal living quarters were on the upper floor, away from the palace's official wing below. Still, these private corridors were crawling with his ministers. When he stood outside the Prince's rooms, the royal physician bowed and left the room.

He froze in place.

Kassios Ottega sprawled like a corpse over his bed. The worst of his burns were wrapped in pads. Everywhere else was wet with blisters.

But his face—

A golden mask covered it, locked into an eerie *U* of a smile. Jaime's fingers hovered over its edges. Just as he was about to lift it to see the face underneath, a croak stopped him.

"Jaime, is that you?"

The words were bumbled and slurred from a tongue that hadn't spoken for several years.

"How do I look?"

Jaime opened his mouth, then closed it. "Good. It's a cool mask."

Cassie sighed. "Everywhere hurts."

"We're half brothers."

"I know."

"What happened?"

"At the Colosseum? The Western officials—"

"I'm not talking about the Colosseum."

"I don't really remember."

"Try to remember."

Cassie's fingers twisted at the bedsheets. "Mamá told me that the night the airpriests showed up at the Capital with the prophecy, Father ordered to have me brought to him. I was only a day old. That was in 2982. August." He shuddered. "Mamá feared he would kill me, so she rode away with me to the northeast. We were fugitives for years. I hated it."

Cassie opened a rip in the sheets.

"On my seventh birthday, I started showing my fire powers. Mamá tried to hide it, but I couldn't control it. Some cuh-cuh-cocksuckers in our village saw the fire currents and reported me to the royal garrison."

"They were afraid," Jaime observed.

"And then..." Cassie's voice cracked. "They realized who Mother and I were." He swallowed. "She hid me in Charis's wagon and told me to never stop running. I—I saw what happened after. Before they ever had a chance to take her, she drew her knife—" Cassie shifted his masked head. "That's why I...well, pre-pre-pre—"

"Pretended?

Cassie forced out the slurred word. "Pretended. No soldier would think a cripple could be the King's son, even if I was of age. You would understand."

"I understand."

"The acting was hard at first, but with everything that happened, it started to become me."

Jaime didn't offer a comment. His younger brother's eyes popped open behind the mask.

More words blurted out.

"I owe it to you for shaking me out of it. That last moment outside Townfold, when I saw you surrendering for the people, that's when I couldn't take it anymore. Jaime"—his throaty voice splintered—"I didn't mean to pose you as Usheon's son. That time with fire, at Hilaris's burning—it was my emotions. Fire tends to appear when I'm emotional."

"But it was convenient, wasn't it?"

Cassie released the bedsheets. "I—I know what I did was wrong. I just wished Father knew I never wanted to overthrow him. I hated the prophecy as much as he did. Maybe more."

Not so long ago, Jaime had once thought the same thing.

He squeezed Cassie's hand. His brother looked up in surprise.

"I know how hard it is to be brave," Jaime said. "I made a lot of mistakes too."

Cassie's voice thinned.

"I don't really have any right asking you this, but…Jaime, I want to make up for what I did. If you give me a chance, I'll prove myself to you and our people. I'll take care of you like you took care of me."

Jaime slowly stood up.

"Cassie…are you asking me if you can be King?"

His hands darted under the bedsheets. "No—I mean, maybe. Yes. Do *you* want to be King? Honestly?"

He drilled his gaze directly onto Cassie, who wouldn't look at him. "Why do you want to be King?"

"I'm sorry. It doesn't matter—"

A knock interrupted them, and an old politician craned his neck inside. "Your Highness." Both of them looked up. The politician dipped his head to Jaime. "A private meeting commences before the Air Throne. Their Holinesses request that you please join them with urgency."

He glanced back at Cassie. "Let's talk later. Brothers?" Jaime held out his hand the way Toran had for him in Arcurea.

After a pause, Cassie took his hand.

Squeezed.

Squeezed so hard, it hurt.

"Brothers," he rasped.

Jaime followed the old man out of the room, his hand aching. The gold mask behind him, smile frozen on his back, suddenly made his flesh tingle.

Why would Cassie ask me to be King if he avoided being Prince for eight years?

His guide, the palace steward, introduced himself as Horos Phillipus. All prim and prude, Horos danced him into a marble foyer held up by flowered columns. Guards dressed in silver capes bowed their heads as he approached. Another one opened the door.

"Please, Your Highness," said Horos.

Jaime's sandals found themselves on a floor of polychrome marble—blues and purples and pinks and colors he didn't even know existed in stone. The builder would've had to mine from all corners of Jaypes for this. *And the cost.* It hurt his head to think. The ceiling was a sky away, coffered with panels of brocaded air currents. False columns held it up, crowned with windflower garlands. All of it converged into the apse above him, draped by a tapestry with the Air Emblem washing over the throne.

His father and mother ruled from here, once. A man and woman who had probably never seen Mount Alairus.

What a strange thought.

"Come forward, Jamian Ascaerii," a stentorian voice said. "Take a seat."

Jaime switched his gaze to the long table set in the middle of the room.

A score of military officials rose to their feet at his entrance. The Kaipponese bowed low. At both ends, the Western Kings stayed sitting, although Emperor Viro looked uncomfortable in his chair.

An empty seat awaited him in the middle.

Jaime passed it.

The room fell dead silent as he limped up the steps, stood before the mighty Throne of Jaypes. He turned around to face them.

"I'll stay standing."

A peddler could drop a brooch and the Kingdom would hear.

The officials clenched their teeth at his brazenness. The Kaipponese, who stayed bowed, looked like they were going to hack him apart.

Where is your return bow? Not even to the Emperor? How offensive!

King Gildas cleared his throat. "We are finishing here, but we agreed you should be informed of the present state of affairs. Come. Listen." There was a drained air about him today, despite his expressive hand gestures. "We found some records of great interest."

"What kind of records?"

"Well, the identities of Usheon's bastards. Only two exist—girls, sightly as mushrooms, if I may say. Or three, if you count that gangling little guppy, Kassios Ottega."

Laughter echoed in the throne room.

Jaime said, "I will treat them with honor. They'll live here, at the palace."

The Glaiddish officials stopped laughing. Gildas Brennte leaned forward, forehead wrinkling in disbelief.

"*Jamian Ascaerii.*"

The tapestry quivered from Gildas's bellow.

"As one Sage to another, I offer you friendly council. Do not let anyone challenge your sovereignty. Remember that you, as us, bear the sanctified House of your god."

"Are you saying I should kill them?"

"Battles are costly to the royal treasury. Remember that for your descendants, and especially for your allies."

Jaime gritted his teeth. "They will live."

The Emperor of Kaippon burst out laughing.

Fire blazed in Jaime's chest, giving him the boldness to meet eyes with Viro Tazuga. A year ago, he wouldn't have dared. But at his open stare, the Kaipponese sat ramrod straight. One leapt to his feet.

"You do not look upon the Emperor, *majiku*," he spat in heavily accented Moderna.

A lurking shadow emerged from the corner—the giant warrior with the malformed scar. He gave a nod. One of his subordinates ran a *kendao* through the offending Kaipponese's midsection.

Jaime gasped.

The Glaiddish jolted upright, their hands on their broadswords. Their faces turned green as the blade slid back out. Blood pooled all over the marbled floor.

"So sorry," the giant warrior murmured.

His anger dissolved into fear. The moles on Emperor Viro's face shifted as he returned a tight smile to Jaime.

These Westerners are crazy. The sooner I get them out, the better.

Jaime shakily turned his gaze to Gildas. "Your Holiness, what will happen to Usheon?"

"Many of his followers will be executed, including Reizo Kita and the Archpriestess. And in two days, so will Usheon."

Panic flared up his body. "But Usheon is a Sage!"

Gildas glanced at Viro. *Care to explain?*

But the Emperor pretended not to see him. The older King sighed.

362

"A Sage who breaks his oath to uphold his element must be punished. Usheon failed two elements and violated a host of divine laws. The consequences are written in the Sacred Codex of our Holy Church. That small-eyed bastard knew the consequences when he crowned himself King, and more—started a war. As the High King is now but legend, that responsibility falls on us."

What about both of you? You let him reign for fifteen years before you decided to do anything.

And suddenly, Jaime understood.

Eridene said she had sent her court messages about the state of Jaypes. She intended the Water Kingdom to help him. But instead, Glaidde saw how vulnerable Jaypes was. And on the day of the prophecy, while Usheon and Jaime were closed in a tight space, the Western Sages jumped in to usurp his Kingdom.

Both of you thought you'd capture me and annex Jaypes for your war. That was the reason for your duel.

But they didn't expect he would be strong enough to stop a banestorm. Jaime held in his fury.

Gildas's water currents may have saved his life in the Colosseum, but both of these Kings were his enemies.

They were not true Sages.

"That is all, Prince Jamian. His Imperial Holiness and I thank you for your service to our gods. As soon as certain matters are addressed, we will depart Jaypes."

The King of Glaidde gave a respectful nod.

Jaime knew how to play this game too.

He dipped in a bow.

As he was making for the doors, the scarred giant ordered everyone's leave. The officials scrambled out behind Jaime without questions. Then Emperor Viro's righthand stepped out of the throne room last, clicking the doors gently behind him.

"These are to remain shut until the conference finishes," he ordered the guards. *His* guards. "Their Holinesses' orders."

The giant's black eyes turned to him.

Move on, boy.

Jaime dashed off with a shiver, but his feet dragged. As long as he was breathing, the Western Kings would try to maneuver him, but he resolved to keep Jaypes neutral from their war. No matter what.

Well, I might as well find Horos.

A storm of things was growing on his mental to-do list.

At the end of the day, after dodging statesmen, military officers, and palace staff all demanding his attention for every crisis in the Kingdom, he happened to pass the throne doors again.

They were still shut.

Jaime stopped, uneasiness creeping up his skin. He approached the Jaypan guards and gave them a firm look. They glanced at each other, but did not stop him. He pressed his head against the doors.

The chatter inside was muffled, but a draft passed under the crack and carried their words to him.

"I *must* know the truth, Viro."

Spoken through the roof of a mouth, husky and urgent— Gildas's voice.

"Years ago, the High King summoned us to council. Remember you?"

No answer.

"Our great Houses renewed our sacred alliance—you as well— when the Black Temple showed us the affairs to come. I said, *remember you?*"

Nothing.

Still, Gildas continued.

"Now Nyzarêtor and Ascaerii are dead, just as they foretold. You are next in line. *You*, Viro! Yet I've heard unnatural reports escaping out of the shrines of Kaippon."

Silence.

"That Jaypan prophecy of rubbish had something to do with the Darklings, didn't it? Usheon was a pawn—"

"Eh, please! This is dangerous talk. I assume your rudeness derives from your barbarian ignorance—"

"But you knew this already. You knew it long ago. Perhaps our war has nothing to do with our Houses. *He* is forcing you to serve, is He not?"

"How do you assault my honor so shamelessly—"

"Viro Tazuga, you little ball of shit. You would betray the Sages and our gods—"

"You *dare* speak to me this way!" The Emperor's voice flared past the doors. Jaime drew his head back. "You most offensive of impotent barbarians, always spreading tales to taint my family name! *Kudeimoshu!* And I shall return the favor. There is no more peace between Tazuga and Brennte. This ceasefire between us is over."

Jaime hid behind the nearest pillar. Not long after, the doors burst open, and a luxurious shape in a stiff-necked overcoat marched away.

His head swam.

The Black Temple? Who's Emperor Viro serving? And the prophecy. They're saying there was never a prophecy at all?

No, that's impossible.

His gut tightened.

The Storm of Jaypes was over, but the Western Kings made it sound like a second storm, a larger storm, was brewing on the horizon. And he wasn't entirely sure this new enemy would be human.

CHAPTER FORTY-TWO

At dawn, his stepfather was going to die.

Jaime tossed and turned. He tried meditating, counting, even sipping on a mug of goat milk, but nothing worked. Those two little girls hugging Usheon kept flashing through his mind.

Finally, Jaime called for a servant to send for Achuros. As Jaime waited, he sat on the edge of his bed and tapped his ankles against the mattress. *One. Two. Three. Four.*

A few minutes later, the door opened with sputtering.

"It's in the middle of the night, boy. Summoning me like a common servant—"

"I'm sorry, Achuros. This palace feels bigger than Arcurea. I didn't know where to find you."

"You better have woken me for good reason."

"Where are they holding Usheon's courtiers? The high-ranking ones."

The airpriest cocked his head. "In the city prisons, of course."

"I want to talk to Reizo."

"What! Are you mad?"

Pushing himself off the bed, Jaime limped into Achuros's face. "If my stepfather is going to die tomorrow, I need to know some things."

The airpriest grabbed his mug and drank, but when he realized it wasn't wine, he scowled.

"Alright, but we will make this quick."

They put on a pair of cloaks and stole out of the palace on horseback. Achuros led him to the west side of the city. Earlier in the day, Jaime nearly fainted when Horos told him a million people lived in the Capital. *Arcurea's* size still overwhelmed him. Now, as they passed towering temples, giant statues, and paved streets of beeches, he could easily see that amount filling this foreign world.

When they reached the entrance of the prisons, the porter above the gate called down.

"Who goes there?"

Achuros lifted his hood so the guards could see his face, and nodded at Jaime to do the same. His mentor asked for directions to Brosidos Naxagoras, the Captain of the Guard. The porter warily signaled for his men to raise the portcullis, and led them into the brooding stone structure.

They stopped outside an office door. Achuros told him, "Wait here."

The door was left open a crack. Jaime peered inside the office.

A large gray-haired man in uniform stood before a desk piled high with warrants. He nodded to Achuros. They exchanged low words. Minutes trickled away. A small pouch of coins was exchanged, and the door opened.

"For your efforts, Captain," said Achuros.

The stark man nodded to Jaime the same way he had to his mentor—briskly, all business—and stomped down the hallway.

What if Gildas or Viro already paid him to guard Usheon? How many of my own Jaypans are under the West's coin?

Jaime shook the thought out uneasily.

"My men will show you the rest of the way." Captain Brosidos left them at the first door. Another guard led them down an ancient staircase that winded down into the dark. The air grew cold and damp. He swallowed a cough.

The staircase opened into a hallway of cells.

"Second to last, on the right," the guard said.

Achuros waited by the guard, every muscle in him strung tight. "Go on, Jaime."

He recognized none of the other prisoners he passed. Jaime stopped before Reizo's cell.

A silhouetted shape paced against the torchlight. *Clink. Clink.* Wrists shackled to long chains drilled into the walls. He was stripped down to a thigh-length wool tunic.

Jaime coughed.

The Strategos wrested for the bars. "*Osei!* Prince! Thank Fire, you—"

"Tell me what happened to my mother."

The relief shattered from Reizo's face.

"Excuse please?"

"I need to know the truth about the Queen. Sarendi Markus. How did she die?"

The Strategos laughed shakily. "It is a long story." He resumed pacing. Jaime pressed himself closer to the bars.

"I have time."

More shuffled pacing.

"*Reizo.*"

The Strategos pulled up short. He cursed under his breath in Kaipponese.

"How about I tell you the truth about what happened to the King in Kaippon. Eh? Before we arrived?"

"Only if it explains what happened to my mother."

His black chains coiled at his feet as he sat down and spread his legs. The night was flickering out. It took all of Jaime's patience not to yell at him.

"My lord was born in southern Kaippon, in an impoverished province ravaged by warlords and bandits. He was an orphan, did you know? The streets scarred his *avai,* but he survived. As Imperial law goes, he was conscripted into the army in his twelfth year.

"As seasons passed, my lord ascended the ranks and gardened prestige—"

"Garnered."

"Please?"

"Never mind. Keep going."

"As I was saying, he gardened many prestige. One day the Emperor bestowed him the titles of daimyo and General. His first campaign was to capture a key Glaiddish port. He succeeded. But in the second half of the second year…"

Reizo lifted his head, his face wrinkled in vague annoyance. "Sorry, why does this matter to you?"

"Just continue."

"One night, we were attacked by the Glaiddish royal marshal. Ah." Reizo's eyes lit up. "The same month Jaypes lost the Air King. Yes. Month of October, 2981. It was early snow, and I was very younger. We were outmaneuvered fivefold. But defeat is no option in the Imperial Army. Every Kaipponese warrior knows he must accept his shame with death.

"And yet, my lord would not abandon us to the Glaiddish." Reizo smiled sadly. "He was no general like we knew. He gave us many moral—"

"Morale?"

"Remind us of our families, and if we had none, of our brotherhood when we most wanted to decapitate."

"Capitulate."

"My lord led us like we were men, not stinking meat. The retreat he ordered saved us all that night."

"And then?"

"Eh, then? It is obvious what happened then." Reizo snorted. "On our arrival to Kasai Soto, the Fire Capital, my lord was dragged into the dungeons below the palace. I hear rumors Tazuga stripped him bare and force him standing for a month." He rubbed his brows. "They pulled his arms out of his sockets and shattered his *kendao* hand. When they done, the Emperor branded him, stripped his titles, and turned him back onto the streets.

"Wherefore, he was never the same again. Perhaps it was anguish, or pain that burden him his entire life, for when it reached peak a few days later, he accidentally discovered Fire. This no good. The Fire Throne already had a male heir. Little Tairo, the Emperor's son.

"The Emperor somehow found out about my lord. In that last hour, my lord looked to the east, remembered no Sage in Jaypes. For vengeance, he plot to survive. To *live*, you see, to prove to Tazuga he was no master of Ottega. My lord had much men who would die for him, so at his command we left. It was a narrow escape, great Lord of Fire—we raised anchor just as the Imperial armies galloped to the docks. When we arrived to Jaypes, we was safe and free at long last."

"But…what about my mother?"

"Your *masan*," Reizo muttered. "Well, His Holiness never forced your *masan* into anything. The poor woman was in such mourning when we arrived at the Capital, she would not leave her chambers for a week."

"He forced her to marry him."

"*Suki*, he did. But he left her be, and never consummated their marriage that night." Jaime blinked. "It was *she* who came to him asking for a child."

Grabbing the bars, Jaime hissed, "You're a liar!"

"Please give me peace, Prince. When you—well, when that other boy, that other Prince—when he was born the next August, His Holiness loved him more than food and air. The prophecy ruined everything. After the Queen fled him, many hope we had for the King's recovery from his past, gone. It was worse than Tazuga's torture. Nothing could mend his heart."

My mother didn't take her life. Usheon murdered her.

And yet, as Jaime stared at the ground, Reizo continued:

Ten years after his coronation, the King stared through the windows of the throne room. Crisp leaves fell from dead garden trees. The sky was dark with clouds. Starlings no longer sang as they did for Lairdos Ascaerii.

No matter how many fires Usheon lit, he was always cold. His coal-black eyes followed the crumpled leaves floating in the dark gusts.

"We should have never left Kaippon. I have become the very man I tried to escape from."

"Eh?" Reizo moved to the window. "Please, your heart is far purer than any Tazuga that has ever lived."

After a long silence, Usheon lifted his head to the sky, where the god of his people dwelled inside storm clouds.

"Was it worth it, Reizo?"

"My King?"

And Usheon whispered a poem in Kaipponese tongue:

"Perfect windflowers

Though plucked in the prime of spring

Wither by autumn."

Quietly, Reizo continued, "He never wanted to hurt you, *Osei*. He search for you because he angry. You were all he have left. For your sake, he have to believe he could undo the prophecy to honor your mother. We, his advisors, told him he had to let you go."

Jaime backed away. "He—that doesn't justify him. Or the Royal Decree. Hundreds of thousands of people died. Because of him."

Reizo beat the air. "The rebel lords exasperated everything. They told lies of your whereabouts and attacked our men when we searched towns. Stinking maggots dividing our Kingdom! Eventually, we have no choice but to use force—"

"Don't blame this war on the Jaypan people. They're the ones who suffered most from your invasion!"

"*Osei*," Reizo sighed. "Usheon is no Viro."

"Usheon is no Lairdos," Jaime shot back.

He turned to leave. The guard unfastened the ring of keys at his waist for the exit door.

Reizo's mouth dropped.

"Ah? Wait! I told you the truth! You cannot leave me here!"

Achuros raised a brow at Jaime, but he covered his face with his hood.

"Lead us out of here," his mentor told the guard. They ascended the staircase and the door locked behind them.

As soon as they were back on the streets, Achuros took them under a bridge. Both of them dismounted. The old man opened his mouth to comfort Jaime, but Jaime interrupted.

"We only have a few hours. I need your help setting Usheon free."

"*What?*"

"I have to do this," he whispered. "My stepfather may have done a lot of terrible things, but killing him isn't right."

"Boy," the priest roared, "are you *mad?*"

"*Shh.*" Jaime winced.

Achuros splashed across the river for the saddle, but Jaime

grabbed the reins and wrested them out of his grip.

"Will you help me or not? You and Uncle Julias are the only people in the Capital I trust—"

"Now then! Leave Julias Markus out of this. Believe me, if *he* finds out, you can be sure he will have both of our heads."

"Does that mean you'll help?"

Achuros paced in circles, hand pressed to his forehead. "Give me a second to think."

Somewhere nearby, a drift of priests sang low hymns. The storm drains gurgled. Seagulls cried over them.

Under his breath, Achuros muttered, "Madness, utter madness…"

He peered over his shoulder. Jaime mustered the most heart-wrenching look he could.

Sighing, Achuros cried, "Alright, alright! Enough of that. I'm only doing this because you are Ascaerii…"

In the darkness, the priest patted his robes, revealing another pouch under his sash. "The Captain of the Guard is under Tazuga's pay. It will take more than a few sorry coins to bribe him, so you best fully compensate him in the morning."

I knew it.

Jaime would certainly compensate him by arresting and replacing him.

They returned to the prisons. Achuros spoke privately again with Captain Brosidos. A bowl of incense burned between them. Jaime watched everything through the light of the door's crack.

The Captain turned his back. Murmured something Jaime could not hear. An uneasy frown appeared on Achuros's face.

Sweat trickled down Jaime's temple.

Jaypes was no match against Kaippon, especially in the ruins of the civil war. If the Captain reported them to the Emperor, the latter could invoke the Sacred Codex and do anything he wanted to Jaime.

As Achuros was slowly showing himself to the door, the Captain said something. The priest stopped, turned around in surprise, and handed over the coins.

Stepping out of his office, Brosidos said to Jaime, "I pray you know what you are doing, Your Highness. Ascaerii I serve, not that imperious fool, Tazuga. But should your own people find out that you were behind this, you will reverse the reputation you have established for yourself."

"I will take responsibility if that happens."

Captain Brosidos escorted them back to the entrance. "Ottega is being held in the lowest layer of these dungeons. I will send a swift to the gate commander to give passage."

Jaime stopped. "There's one thing I need to do first."

He ignored Achuros's scowl and headed down the passageway he exited not an hour before. Without questions, the Captain sent several guards after him.

At the bottom of the staircase, Jaime asked for access to the general cell block. The head guard reluctantly unlocked the door and handed him the keys.

His gait swift, Jaime stopped outside Reizo's cell.

The Strategos's head rose. Alarm cracked across his face as Brosidos's guards gathered at the entrance.

"*Onega ida!*" Reizo backed against the wall. "I pray you, allow me the honor to take my life with my own *kendao*—"

"Shut up," Jaime snapped.

He jammed the keys into the lock. The Kaipponese's black eyes burst open.

"When you see Usheon, tell him you are both…" What was that political word the City-States used? "Ostracized."

"Eh?"

"You are *never* to return to Jaypes."

"Where will we go?"

"I don't care. That's your problem. You have two hours before the search parties of three Kingdoms come after you."

Reizo Kita shuffled out of his cell. He glanced at Jaime like he was about to say something. But then he bowed low, his stocky shape vanishing into the night.

Jaime closed his eyes to hold in his emotion.

Firelight diffused through the bars, striping his face with light and darkness. Part of him wanted to see his stepfather one last time, and as he followed the Brosidos's men out, he made up his mind to.

But at the top of the stairs, guilt sank in.

At the last second, he let Achuros tug him back to the palace. And once he was back in his room, alone, regret weighed his belly down, and the tears he had been hiding escaped his eyes.

EPILOGUE

In the royal peristyle behind the official wing, Jaime inhaled in his deepest breath yet.

Cypress, medlar, and pomegranate trees whispered at the humid breezes caressing their branches. Golden eagles perched on the great statue of Jaypes Ascaerii in the central fountain. Southern heat thickened the air. This small retreat, tucked away by the Skyrros Ocean, was bursting with life. The Kingdom's long fall was coming to an end.

Jaime brushed his sandal against the paved flooring. It glittered from a mosaic of red, brown, and black volcanic glass. His life on Mount Alairus seemed so far away. Even now, that hurt.

He started to read Book Two of *The Legend of the Four* when his eyes caught movement in the distance.

The spitting dragon banners of New Jaypes were being taken down from the battlements. In their place, elhornes leapt into the skies, their great antlers like crowns on their heads.

And in the foreground, a cloaked shape stood between two palm trees, idly watching too.

Jaime dropped the heavy tome. "Arrys!" he cried, dashing across the garden. His leg was getting stronger. This time, he didn't stumble. "How did you get past the gate command—"

The Larfene grinned.

"Oh. Right." Jaime reached for the small hoop in his ear. "Here, this is yours. It's raising a lot of questions—the politicians think I'm starting some new modern age fashion."

Arrys caught his wrist. "Keep it. It will stop my people from cutting you into cubes when you visit Larfour."

The smile faded from their faces as Arrys shuffled into his cloak and pulled out Achuros's ledger.

"I must present this to my High King. Your mentor was a friend of the Darklings—"

"*Darklings!* Achuros?"

His cry erupted across the peristyle like gulls taking flight. A royal guard shifted into view from the west entrance. Another from the north.

"Your Highness?" they called.

Arrys stayed hidden under the umbrage of the palms. Jaime swallowed and called back, "I'm fine!"

His breath heavy, Jaime shifted his attention back to his friend.

"What did it say?"

"This is a book of nightmares."

"Arrys. What does it *say?*"

"Your priest and that Archpriestess helped the Darklings fabricate a prophecy so they could wipe out all Ottega—"

"Why?" he panted. "How does he know her?"

"They once served in the High Temple together, even loved each other. Both believed the modern Sages were corrupted. They wanted to rid Jaypes of your stepfather. Only problem is, he did not know Ascaerii blood still lived. He loved Lairdos a thousand dunes more than he ever loved the Archpriestess. And he loves you. That changed everything."

Jaime turned his back. It felt like he was falling from the

Colosseum's upper rim all over again.

"Achuros is still alive."

Arrys frowned. "You must execute him. Immediately."

"I can't," Jaime whispered.

"Let me slay him then, before he draws hellfire upon you and those you love—"

As Arrys was drawing his sword, Jaime leapt forward and grappled his wrists.

"No!"

Arrys's hot breath fell heavy on his nose. Green light flared across pupils. The Larfene's *avai* energy swelled—a titan wavelength overpowering Jaime's—comparable to the Western Sages.

Fear stabbed Jaime's chest.

I still don't know what he is. No, I do. He's a Darkslayer, friend or not.

But Jaime held his stance. "Achuros is family to me," he whispered. "I don't have a lot left."

"He is one of *them*—"

"Back in Arcurea, he took my side instead of the Archpriestess's. And you said he loved my parents. I'm not an Ottega. He knows that now. I trust him with my life."

The waves of Arrys's feral energy dipped. His eyes became clear of bloodthirst again. Jaime let go of him.

After a pause, he released his hilt. "I cannot protect you from the Far East, Jaime."

"I know. I can protect myself now, Arrys." Deep breath. "If you want justice, let your High King judge him. It's time to see if the Guardian of the Kingdoms is more than just legend."

Arrys smiled grimly. "May it be as you say."

"But do me a favor." The shadows of the canopy shifted over Jaime's face. "Find out what they want, and write to me. I'll kill them before they ever get it."

"Jaime, ever you need a friend you can trust, I will always be here."

"I know," he whispered.

His friend placed a hand on the purple sash over his shoulder. "You did well, Prince of Jaypes. I think we will see each other again soon."

"Do Larfenes have any sayings for parting occasions?"

Arrys smiled and told him, and Jaime repeated: "May the earth pave smooth your road."

"Let the winds lead you, and you shall find your feet, my friend."

Though Jaime's chest throbbed, he watched Arrys push off the tree trunk and disappear into the garden. Not long after, a giant hawk soared over Aeropolis Capital and vanished into the horizon.

⚜

An hour later, trumpets sounded across the city grounds.

Jaime sprinted over marble benches, past lush arbors and rows of great statues until he was at the palace's grand entrance.

Below the columned entrance, a Glaiddish retinue unloaded themselves inside the bailey. His eyes searched. As usual, Eridene and Toran were bickering. He grinned.

Jaime cupped his hands and called out to them.

His friends' swiveled around, dropped everything, zealously sprinted up the steps to get to him. Jaime's cheer vanished from his face.

He held up his hands. "Wait—easy—"

But Toran's big body bowled him over. Jaime cried out from the surge of pain in his leg.

"Hey, Juno! Miss us?"

Eridene caught up in a light puff. She exchanged a peculiar look with Toran, and both of them burst out laughing.

"What?" Jaime demanded. "What's so funny?"

Toran roared wildly. "Your eyebrows are gone! They must've been singed off!"

"*What?*"

He'd been so busy learning how to write letters and entertaining everyone who demanded his attention that he hadn't taken the time to look at a mirror.

"Gods!" Jaime cried. "No one told me! Are they going to grow back?"

That only made his friends laugh harder. Eridene wiped her eyes. "Don't worry, Jamian. They probably—"

"*Won't!*" Toran said.

He slapped Jaime's back hard, knocking the air out of him. "I can't believe you're still alive, man. It's like you just won't go away. You're disappointing a lot of people, you know that?"

Grinning, Jaime tackled *him* to the ground. His best friend exclaimed in surprise, crashing into Eridene. They rolled down the staircase, knocking over crates of gifts. Eridene's angry shouting turned into laughter as she joined in, wrestling with them both.

For the rest of the afternoon, they played and laughed in the royal peristyle until a Glaiddish official called Eridene inside. Toran followed her, and with their horseplay broken, Jaime grudgingly followed Achuros into the Assembly Hall for a meeting of his own.

At eventide, he found Eridene alone on the south portico facing the open ocean. Awnings billowed between the columns to shelter out the heat.

The skies silhouetted Eridene's profile into purple, limning her features with the fire of evening. His breath stole in his throat.

You're a dream come true.

He sat next to her on the bench, handing her a bowl of grapes. Eridene shifted her eyes away from the sea. Cicadas tickled his stomach, worse than they had before his duel with Usheon.

"So." She tugged at the sash on his shoulder, brocaded with the Air Emblem. "What's it like being King?"

"I'm not the King."

"When is your coronation?"

He ducked her eyes and peered at the sky. "You know what I really like about being royalty?"

"What?"

"It's kind of nice getting to shit in a box of gold."

Eridene burst into laughter. Jaime gave a small smile. "Sorry. I shouldn't be so vulgar in front of a lady."

"No, no," she hawked, "you haven't met Glaiddish men."

"So I guess you can return to your Kingdom now."

She wiped her laughter tears, her humor fading. "First thing in the morning. King Gildas doesn't want to waste time or our men on Usheon's escape." She brushed his elbow with hers. "I am so sorry, Jamian. I don't know how such a scandal could have happened."

"Yes, it's too bad." He turned away.

"It *will* be strange to be home after everything that happened."

"I bet your father would love to have you back." He tried to sound happy for her.

"The city's so beautiful. I'll really miss Jaypes." She nibbled a grape, drank in the ocean. "I never thought I'd say that."

He fought the embarrassing urge to clasp her hands. "You can always come back, Eridene. Any time you want. I'll be right here."

A coy smile settled on her lips. "Well, now that you are King—"

"I'm not the King—"

"You can always visit me in Glaidde. Say, perhaps I could even invite you to the Royal Court. I do believe if we had another Sage, we would win the war against Kaippon."

Jaime pushed the grapes away. "You saw what war did to Jaypes."

"I know, but I've also seen what you can do—"

"I'm not involving Jaypes in another war. No matter *what*." He rose to his feet. "And if you knew any better, you'd tell your Kings to stop your war before disasters tear up your Kingdoms—"

She stood too. "I didn't mean to upset you."

He kept his back turned.

"All I'm saying is that your help would mean a lot to Glaidde." Pause. "And me."

Jaime stared up at the awning, fluttering wildly in the seawinds. "Would it really?"

She put a hand on his shoulder. He turned around. She met his eyes calmly. But her fingers were shaking.

Why are they shaking?

Neither of them brought up their kiss in the Colosseum. And now that they were beneath open skylight, suddenly, he was irrationally afraid to do it again. He hadn't been thinking straight that night.

But there *was* a pull between them.

Wasn't there?

It was like she was the arbor, and he was the grapevine, their *avai* begging for a fusion that would rock the world into the biggest shockwave yet. They would be at the center, only they would exist, the eye of a marvelous storm.

Jaime felt every thud of his heart. His ears were hot. His throat stretched thin. He didn't trust himself to talk, so he slowly leaned forward.

If he was misreading everything, this could damage—or even end—their friendship.

Eridene leaned in too.

The morning she left, peace evaded him.

The hollow in Jaime's belly grew. He couldn't explain it—he first felt it during his parting with Arrys, and then again watching his best friends ride out of Aeropolis's gates.

His mission in Jaypes was over, but the winds whispered to him that this was just the beginning. And the second Eridene had mentioned adventures, he knew where his next one would start: finding out the truth about his father's suicide.

Suddenly, he remembered the key Julias gave him two days ago. Jaime reached under his pillow. It had to be for a strongbox in his room.

You will know when you see it, his uncle said.

Jaime began fitting it into every chest he could find. Nothing worked until he found one under the window and pulled it out. It had a small keyhole about the size of the key he held in his hand.

Jaime fitted it in.

It clicked open.

A silver wind chime sat in its polished bronze belly. Etched underneath was a forgotten lullaby.

Below him, the chimes of the city sang in unison, carried by the wind, becoming a melody that was so familiar to him.

And then, he remembered its words:

Thick rains flood over blades of grass
Over the sky, low thunder brews
Birthing life to a dark morass
But let the winds lead you

Perhaps it was his imagination, but the breezes brought in two voices from the past. One was deep and hearty. The other was softer than silk. Both sang to him with the winds.

A storm is beginning to rise
Forever it seems to ensue
Sweet, wipe your tears now, do not cry
Let the winds lead you

Jaime rose to his feet and hung the wind chime over his windowsill. It shimmered and joined together with the greater melody of Aeropolis.

He opened his mouth and sang too.

Quietly at first, but his own voice grew stronger, birthing life into the air currents like his father before him.

Like the night, it will come to pass
And when the dawn returns at last
Hear the whispers in the breeze
Let them lead you, step past the trees...

As the currents caressed his cheeks, a half sphere rose over the Skyrros Ocean, blazing over a new Kingdom.

My child, you are home.

Dear Valued Reader,

Thank you so much for reading through! Like Jaime, I believe you have an inner legend inside you. I hope you find ways to tap into it every day. Don't let traditional education and the world tell you who you can and can't be. RISE and fight for the call in your heart. The world needs YOU.

Above all, I'd love to hear from you! I promise to personally answer every email. Connect with me at any time at jasmine@jasmineyoungauthor.com.

If you'd like exclusive bonuses, free content, illustrated extras, and insider updates on the next *Four Kingdoms: Origins* book, subscribe at www.jasmineyoungauthor.com. You'll receive a special welcome gift for joining the Epic Legends family.

Cheers to becoming the legend of your own story,

Website: www.jasmineyoungauthor.com
Email: jasmine@jasmineyoungauthor.com
Facebook: www.facebook.com/stormfirethenovel

BE A HERO AND LEAVE A REVIEW!

Your feedback is crucial to an author's career. How? Every review makes a big impact in widening my exposure and thus my ability to reach, impact, and inspire more people like you. Also, honest reviews help me grow as a writer. I want to make sure you enjoy the upcoming books I write even more.

So be a hero today and leave me a review. I read all online reviews and am grateful for yours.

JASMINE YOUNG

After Jasmine obtained her MA at Columbia University, her world was upturned. Two semesters of teaching led her to realize the education system wasn't showing young adults how to grow to their highest potential. At twenty-two years old, she decided to venture out on her own hero's journey, beginning with her childhood dream of becoming a published author. Since then, she has been using stories to call young people out onto their own heroes' journeys. Jasmine currently resides in snowy New York (with longing eyes on Florida). Despite the conventional messages we are taught in school to seek security and conform, she believes anyone anywhere has an inner legend waiting to be called!

Made in the USA
Middletown, DE
11 January 2020